BLACKWATER VAL

WILLIAM GORMAN

Crystal Lake Publishing
www.CrystalLakePub.com

Cover Design:
Ben Baldwin—http://www.benbaldwin.co.uk

Interior Layout:
Lori Michelle—www.theauthorsalley.com

Proofread by:
Guy Medley
Jan Strydom
Sue Jackson

for Emily, whenever I may find her

2000—2013

CONTENTS

AUTHOR'S NOTE

Foremost, special thanks must go out to everyone who helped me with this book. To Carmen Velasquez for her backgrounds on witchcraft and on the origins of evil, and the late Dr. Robert Klint for his unique perspectives and all the medical info—you are missed, sir. Thanks also to Paul Dale Anderson, Joe Mynhardt, and C. Hope Clark. And to Suzanne, of course, above all else.

Remember that in your hands you hold a work of fiction. Although some of the cities and regions surrounding 'the Val' are quite real, and while the Black Hawk War did historically take place, the town of Blackwater Valley itself and all its inhabitants exist only in the mind of the author. Any resemblance to actual events or persons—living, dead, or *undead*—is coincidental. Enjoy. Don't be a stranger. And oh, yes, just ignore those frittles when they come.

W.G.

No man shall know my race or name,
Or my past sun-ripe or rotten,
Till I travel the road by which I came,
Forgetting and soon forgotten.

—Robert Ervin Howard, *Surrender*

PROLOGUE

Somewhere in Germany

1945

HE MANIAC, **MARENBACH** thinks within the unyielding darkness, partly in contempt, partly in fear.

Mostly in fear.

He squints in the musty gloom of his secluded shop at the small man before him, at the slicked-down hair and the dead, terribly vacant eyes. A bit of mustache set above a mouth of bad teeth, the nervous tic in one corner of that mouth. At the large German shepherd heeled by the man's side.

At the armed squadron of SS guards gathered in tight behind him.

Marenbach blinks and proceeds *Deutsch zu sprechen:* "When would you wish it done, my leader?"

"As soon as possible," the little man says with vehemence. He also speaks in German, but the Austrian dialect is unmistakable. "The glory is coming to a close. It is almost over, I'm afraid." The eyes seem to sadden.

"May I see it?" Marenbach asks, holding out his

hand. He prays that he doesn't tremble; the dog is watching his every move.

"By all means." The man reaches inside his long leather overcoat, producing a golden ring which he places in Marenbach's palm. "It was my father's," he adds, becoming slightly hoarse.

Marenbach turns the ring over and over, examining it in the dim light. It's pure gold, of that much he is sure. But the stone is a puzzle. An intaglio square of amber brown, yet nearly transparent. A variety of quartz. Carnelian perhaps.

"Minister Goebbels recommended you highly to me, Marenbach," the man hazards. "Can you do it or can't you?" One gloved fist clenches and unclenches in vast impatience.

"Yes, my leader. I can and I will."

"Excellent!" cries the small man, chest heaving, breathing something unpleasant into the other's face. "But remember, it must be irresistible. It must draw the masses, you understand. Above all—it must be everlasting. *Everlasting, yes! The poison must be wiped from the earth forever!*" He jerks convulsively, disheveling a single forelock of oily hair. The eyes dance.

Jesus God. He wants more. Ten million lives, and still he wants more.

"You will, of course, be paid quite generously for your services," the man says now, regaining some composure. "I do know how to take care of my friends." A momentary icy stare emerges. Then a grin, revealing those horrid teeth.

And Johann Lewis Marenbach—alchemist, sorcerer, astute occultist and mage—shudders in revulsion. He has heard much about the *Fuhrer*, the knotted rumors: of him being the second Christ, a lover of animals and children; homosexual mass murderer, one quarter Jewish himself; an inbred sadist, a masochist, a black-hearted abomination.

They, but a few.

Marenbach was not this man's friend, nor did he wish to be. Nor did he believe that he ever would be. Nevertheless, he would do whatever this man wanted, be it invoking an ancient and diabolical curse onto a ring of gold or anything else. He would do it, because if he *didn't* do it . . .

Well, there were some things worse than curses.

This Marenbach knows for a fact. For he has seen. On more than one occasion, in his mind's wandering eye, he has seen these travesties of—

—humanity? They call this humanity? A room-sized gas oven filled with wretched, fleeting souls? A corpse-ridden chamber for the dead and dying? Humanity? *There, huddled in a corner, a tiny girl writhing and convulsing in silent terror, choking and defecating and swallowing her tongue in reaction to the noxious fumes. And there, a gauzy skeleton of a man, naked and blinded, praying and shrieking and clamping his penis safely between his thighs as he curls into a fetal position and smothers. And yet here, a crippled young mother, head shaven and body broken, singing and weeping and exhaling her final breath into the mouth of an infant she cradles and rocks, even as a bitter*

asphyxiating cloud envelops her and her child.
Humanity? They call this—

—humanity. Oh yes, there were some things far worse than curses. Deep in his darkest meditations has he seen it, and upon awakening has witnessed more viable, visible things. Heaping mounds of shoes and boots and slippers and baby booties. Of blond hair and black hair and gray hair. Ashes, bones from the incinerators. All telltale signs that somewhere, despite the pride and the cheers and the electricity, something dreadful was going on.

Somewhere, something.

"I shall leave you to your work then, yes?" the dark little man says sharply, jarring Marenbach from thought. Before he can respond, however, the other snatches up his free hand and shakes it once, hard and quick. "Goodbye, Johann," he tells Marenbach in a serene voice. For a brief schizophrenic instant he actually believes in this man, in his honor and purity. But then his hand is released and the feeling, gone, even as a lone *Schutzstaffel* jackboot holding a Bible snickers at the back of the room.

"Blondi!" cries the *Fuhrer* now, spinning on his heel. The Alsatian moves obediently with him, staying close at his side. Marenbach, fending off a sudden wave of nausea rippling through him, doesn't have a chance to reply or even to salute. The small man halts and turns back, the dog turning with him once more. Something catches Marenbach's eye.

"I have said this before and I shall say it again," the man speaks in the darkness, to no one in particular. "I know how to maintain my grasp upon people, even long after I have gone." He pauses, pondering for a moment. "It will be glorious, will it not?" With that he whirls and disappears into the night, his elite personal guard following and falling in behind him.

Marenbach stands alone and shivers in his musty shop, the last of the sick feeling dropping away from him like a deathbed sheet. He glances down at the ring he holds, but glances up again. Then he frowns, realizing what caught his eye before. It was the dog; the German shepherd had been wearing a *swastika* arm band on its left front leg. A Nazi arm band.

The maniac, Marenbach thinks, and sets about his work, and dies.

PART ONE

HOUSES OF THE HOLY

There were pits where mad things drummed . . .
—Robert E. Howard

CHAPTER ONE

I

ECAUSE OF THE skunk, they were marked
from the beginning. It'd run out into the highway
so suddenly that Richard Franklin had, in turn, run
over *it* before he ever had a chance to brake. Startled,
he jerked his foot off the gas pedal, feeling first the
resistance and next the sickening *give* beneath his
Bridgestone Firestones, and then the smell had hit.
Richard and Katie glanced at each other, noses
wrinkling. Franklin had resumed his speed, trying to
get away from the invisible pungent wave as fast as he
could. But it was already too late.

With nothing else that could be done, really, he
continued to cruise, approaching an overpass and
keying up the power windows on the Chevy Blazer. He
shook his head, teeth clenched grimly at the irony of
it, letting out a disheartened sigh.

"You okay?" he asked his only daughter.

Katie nodded, looking down at her activity
books. "Yes," she said. "What was that, Daddy?" She
pulled a magenta crayon with slow precision from
its box.

"Dead skunk laying in the highway, hon," he lied. "Smells bad, huh?"

"A little."

Richard followed US Route 20 along with the other traffic going west. He noticed it had begun to rain, so he clicked on the wipers. In the overcast distance he saw an exit sign coming up fast:

```
IRENE EXIT           1C
BLACKWATER VAL       ¼ MILE
ROCKFORD             ¾ MILE
```

He changed lanes and watched for the ramps, trying to breathe solely through his mouth, letting the first exit sail by. Some kind of commotion drew his gaze down off the overpass, to the ground beneath them, and to the right. He saw two county sheriff's cruisers and an ambulance, their lights strobing dreamlike. And a television news van with its broadcast antenna extended; from this, a female reporter loped like a hyena, the assistant beside her trying to tweak her hair and makeup on the run, while brandishing an umbrella above them like some kind of Michael Jackson crony. Striped barricades were already in place, flares being thrown down. Below, in the center of all this buzz, was what appeared to be a partial section of the secondary artery that had seemingly caved in, creating a huge sinkhole where the road had been.

Richard strained to see and caught a brief glimpse—*insanely*—of what looked like human bones down inside the collapsed pit, amongst the earth and broken fragments of blacktop, strewn muddied bones and a darkened skull . . . or two . . . *or* . . .

"What in the *f*—?" he couldn't help blurting, catching himself as the unsettling spectacle vanished under the billowy cascade of a blue swimming pool tarp. Then Katie was looking also, to see what was so interesting. Richard tried to distract her, quickly coming to his senses. "Hey, Katie, did you ever finish coloring that picture? The one you were working on?"

"Which picture?"

"You know, the one with the seahorses." He fumbled at her books with his free hand, but she was having none of it. Not a jot.

"Isn't any with seahorses. Who are those people down there, Daddy? What are they doing?"

Beyond the overpass now, Richard saw the second off-ramp coming up ahead. He put on his turn signal and got ready. "I don't know, hon. Are you sure there aren't any seahorses in here? Better look again." He snatched at one of the books, feeling like an utter fool.

Katie was looking around strangely, all around the outside of the vehicle. "Why are people wandering on the road like this? They're going to get hit."

All at once his fingers grasped the Blazer's steering wheel in a death-grip, and he felt something awful and familiar stir and crawl up into his belly. "That's silly, Katie," he laughed, almost choked. "No one's wandering on the road."

Her pearly gaze was focused, quite intent, aimed straight out the drizzled windshield. "Can't you see them?" She started to murmur, reaching absently for her father. "Waving to us . . . giving me frittles. But their eyes—" Then, with quiet understanding, she said: "Oh."

At that, Richard Franklin felt a shiver ice through him. He merged off 20 and took the exit a little too fast, jaw muscles working. The bizarre scene below them came into view again as they descended the spiraling ramp: there and gone, visible and gone once more. "This thing didn't do much good, did it?" He made a last attempt, toying with the Yankee Candle air freshener looped over the rearview mirror, twirling it for her. "I still smell that skunk in here." Finally, mercifully, the sinkhole site and whatever brand of nightmare occurring there disappeared behind them, fading back into the surrounding cornfields as he motored away.

To their left some Holsteins were scattered, even a few American bison calves milling in the lower pastures, rich pastures bordered by rail fences and flanked with nut, maple, and fruit trees just starting to turn. Farther up near a barn some young hands in checked, flannel shirts were bucking bales of hay to feed the ponies in the late-afternoon mist. Katie watched the calves, and Richard wiped the sweat from his brow with his shirtsleeve.

Ten minutes later, when they pulled into the small town of Blackwater Valley in north-central Illinois, every nose that was out of doors knew they were there.

And so, they were marked right from the beginning.

Despite all the curious stares they got as they drove by, though, one small boy with a wind-burned face looked directly at Katie and winked.

"Hey, Katie-Smatie," he teased, still cringing inwardly at the framed image of that live skunk vanishing under the Blazer, at the pit back there and whatever in hell he imagined he'd seen, "looks like you've already got yourself a boyfriend." Katie smiled, blushing a bit, and Richard felt an ache in his heart. He realized he could not remember the last time he'd seen her smile.

Richard pulled into a Sullivan's Foods, situated back and away from the road they were on, and cut the motor. He sat for a moment in the stillness, listening to the engine tick down. He restarted the vehicle and flipped on the AC, set the parking brake, then unbuckled and stepped out into the balmy September air (which didn't help the lingering sickly sweet stench by any means). A few locals gawked in their direction, from cars and from yards, and Richard seemed to feel every eye upon his daughter and him, inspecting these new strangers here. He mopped his face again with rising unease.

That's right. I'm back. Been about eight years or more, but now I'm back. Won't be here long, though, so don't worry. Bear with me.

"What are you looking at, Daddy?" Questions. Kids and their questions. Like Carter and his endless supply of little liver pills, as the old saying went.

"Just thinkin', babe." He peered through his open door into the running SUV. "Do you want anything from the store?"

Katie started to shake her head, but stopped. "Maybe a Creamsicle," she said, expression hopeful.

"Coming up. Wait right here, hon. Keep the doors locked the way I showed you, okay? Windows up and doors locked?"

Katie nodded and repeated the words: "Windows up and doors locked," as he closed his side and went into the market, dropping the locks with the spare remote on his backup keyring.

As he made his way down an aisle he heard a liquid gurgle coming from his stomach, so he gently pressed his belly in with one hand and held it there. His nerves were acting up, getting that good old acid flowing. Soon it would be in his goddamn throat.

The last thing he'd wanted to do was attract attention in his hometown, and he had already failed at that; the worst was yet to come, he feared.

Richard found the dairy section and grabbed a twelve-ounce container of cottage cheese (the only food that seemed to help settle his nervous stomach) and went to the ice cream freezer and took out two Creamsicles, one orange and one raspberry. In the checkout line, he grabbed a pack of Rolaids and took out his wallet. Then he walked back outside and climbed into his odorous Chevrolet Blazer, carrying the items in a plastic bag.

"Here, hon. I got you two of them."

"Thank you," Katie said quietly, taking them both.

He popped the lid off his cottage cheese and looked down at it. What was he going to eat the stuff with, anyway? His fingers? He started to get back out, but recalled he might have some Dairy Queen spoons in the glove compartment. Before he could think it through, Richard had opened it and was staring at a woman's turquoise scarf—his dead wife's winter scarf. His heart lurched and he shot a sideways glance toward Katie beside him, but he was sure she'd already seen. He snatched a red plastic spoon out of the compartment and slammed it shut, diverting his eyes guiltily.

14

Brilliant, just brilliant. Hasn't she been through enough?

There were no excuses. He should have gone through the vehicle for any painful reminders, before setting out upon this sorrowing journey. But he hadn't, and there were no excuses. All the arrangements that had to be made, all the things which had come at him from every possible direction after her hit-and-run death, and still none of it let him off the hook. Not even the reality that he had Michelle's cremains inside a copper urn in one of the suitcases in back, right now, like a fucking Thermos of coffee . . .

"I'm all right, Daddy," Katie said, surprising him. "I know why we're here. I'm all right."

Richard faltered a smile her way, fighting tears that had welled into his eyes. "Oh," he barely breathed, brushing the hair away from her round face and touching her cheek. Then his gaze fell away. "You're more than all right, sweetie. Much more than that. You know?"

After he'd finished his cottage cheese, and Katie likewise her ice creams, they pulled away from the market and headed north on Reed Farm Road, and eventually took Arvam Drive west. When Richard spotted the Nautical Museum, things started looking familiar again. He glanced through the museum's opened doors as they went by, seeing the mammoth rusted anchor suspended inside, a bygone remnant of some venerable but long-forgotten ship. The rain had slackened now, so he clicked off the wipers, turning onto Kennedy School Road and following it another half mile or so. He passed the hulking relic of the old elementary school and saw a church steeple jutting in the distance beyond it. Two more blocks and it was there, the Nain Lutheran Church, standing on the corner of Kennedy School Road and Glassman Avenue, where it'd stood for God (no joke intended) only knew how long. Richard's look softened when he saw it, and things came back to him as if he had opened a dust-covered scrapbook. Sweet, darkish, musty things.

"See that church, Katie-Smatie?" said Richard. "That's the church where Mommy and me were married."

Katie gazed at it, transfixed. "Can we go inside?" she asked.

He started to say something, and then looked at her. "Sure we can. We're in no hurry, are we?"

Katie shook her head, eyes huge and filled with wonder.

Richard pulled around the corner and parked across from the church. The two got out and crossed Glassman Avenue, holding hands; Katie still carried a gummy Creamsicle stick with her. They ascended the tree-shaded steps together to the wooden double doors, and Richard reached to grab one of the silver handles.

The door was locked.

A sign to the left read NAIN TRINITY LUTHERAN, and below that REVEREND JULIAN, PASTOR, and still below that VISITORS WELCOME, but Richard saw nothing telling any days or hours for the services. He tried the other door, shrugging, with the same result. "Sorry, Katie. I guess they're not open today."

Katie frowned, obviously disappointed. "I thought churches were always open," she said. "Like hospitals."

Richard grinned. "Not always, babe." He squeezed his daughter's little hand, reassuring her. "Don't worry. We'll come back some other time, okay? Before we leave for home."

"Yes," Katie sighed. "Some other time."

They walked past the chapel's lightning-struck bur oak and down the steps again, still holding hands; Richard said a quick and silent prayer there, hoping miserably that their skunk had not suffered much in its final moments out on Route 20. Then they got back into their green Blazer and continued along Glassman Avenue as the sun peeked through a clouded late-September sky at them.

2

Behind the locked doors of Nain Trinity Lutheran, a large Indian man with deep-set eyes stood guard in the blackness. He was a descendant of the Sauk tribe of Native North Americans, and he stood with his arms folded across a barrel chest, his back to the doors, his long dark hair pulled into a ponytail that flowed down the back of his immaculate suit. His sculpted face held no discernable emotion.

To one side of the church's pulpit rested a giant, gleaming silver cross in its stone base. On the other side a statue of Jesus Christ towered, robed and bedraggled, arms stretched out pleadingly. Between these two markers lingered the shadowy figure of an old man. This man's gaze lifted from one to the other, and back again, his head tilted at a curious angle, like a dog watching a flickering TV screen or perhaps hearing one of those silent whistles from the old

Johnson Smith catalogs. He closed his eyes in meditation (Messiah or the *crux* from which he sprang? Chicken or the egg?) and rocked gently around on his heels, swaying mutely from side to side. In the church's corners burned sleepy-weepy candles, trying but failing to illuminate the confused darkness.

The scent of menthol and pepperwort mingled in the still air with the wafting aroma of incense.

At that moment Simon Julian, pastor of the Nain Lutheran Church, opened his eyes and turned to face the man standing at the doors. He spoke three hushed words to him.

"They have arrived," were those words.

The Indian gentleman smiled in the flickering gloom.

CHAPTER TWO

I

RICHARD **DECIDED THEY** should probably check into a motel before heading to the house, just in case. No telling what might happen later in the remains of this day, so, 'better safe than sorry' became his instant mantra. He drove back out to the rural fringes of town and got them a double room, at a place called the Nightlight Inn, not far from Illinois 72 and the old Penfield Monument Works—where most of the region's grave markers were still made. Richard carried their luggage in, and sat two leather bags on the beds, opting to leave the third suitcase containing Michelle's ashes and their emergency cell phone outside, in the vehicle. Then, after pondering a moment, he turned a light on and the television on low, and locked the unit up behind them before pulling away from the cheerless L-shaped motel. He couldn't explain why, but Richard felt the need to keep his dead wife's remains nearby for right now. It was just an unseen urge to stay close to her, he guessed, to keep the three of them together as a family for as long as possible, until Michelle's

19

birthday came and brought the inevitable, the unthinkable along with it . . .

September twenty-ninth.

They started back again, past the deserted Monument Works—its chicken-wire fenced yard was dotted with stone tablets, he noticed, some blank, some only half finished, leaning like little soldiers in jumbled rank—only they took a different route this time. Not wanting to traverse the same path twice, Richard circled long way around and stuck to the outskirts, avoiding the obligatory road construction and entering town from the north. He took Shaw Woods Road, winding his way through a deep and heavily forested area named after one of the original village's stalwart founding fathers.

Blackwater Valley was actually part of the Rock River Valley, the so-christened Rock having dug its own mighty course directly through this prairie region, twisting and flowing southwesterly for 150-some miles before emptying into the fabled Mississippi River. The small town lay nestled within a slight lowland depression—as if hiding here in the middle of the heartland amongst the rolling hills and fields of corn—which often kept it slightly cooler, in both winter and in summer, than any of its outlying environs. Farther south were farming hamlets such as Ogletree and Davis Junction; to the north, Rockford with its cookie-cutter suburbs (the largest neighboring city, next to Chicago) and beyond that, the Scottish-founded area of Argyle, Illinois. Eastward you'd find tiny Irene, unless you blinked. While to the west, across the river, more corn-growing burghs like Lightsville and Westfield Corners awaited. Yes, nestled safe and sound, they were. Or so it seemed.

Richard and Katie cleared the expanse of woods abruptly, crossing in and out of the shadow of the ancient and decaying Shaw-Meredith House as they descended toward the heart of town. Richard frowned and turned the radio on, surfed around and tried to get some local news, something about that grisly route collapse maybe. Finding none, he settled for some music instead. On their right lurked Hebrew National Cemetery shrouded behind its trees and high, wrought-iron gates, and down a ways on the left came the Old North Cemetery.

The town itself, population of roughly 7,700, cradled its dead protectively at its center, as did most Midwestern towns. Soon they passed another graveyard on their right, Calvary Catholic Cemetery this time, its mausoleum visible off in the rear. Richard zipped by, keeping a wary lateral eye on his daughter, and thought, *Three boneyards right in a row, sitting almost triangulated to each other. Like they were planned that way.* Indeed, the cemeteries had probably come early on as the rest of the township began to spread out, growing in all directions.

Augustus Shaw's old hilltop Gothic Revival home and the aptly named Shaw Woods surrounding it (where Richard had hunted as a young boy, in a clearing known to locals as Duck Blind Point) covered most of the north end, which they'd just passed through. Back down to the south the Reed Farm and the Monument Works marked that edge of town, near the bypass. Closer in, running crossways, was the Honey Run Road, which would deliver you to the doorstep of Cassie Patrick's Honeycomb Haven—an apiary run by a retired widow, who in her spare time, besides bee-keeping and bottling homegrown honey, made little cross necklaces from horseshoe nails to sell—and then on to the new ethanol plant, out past those abandoned grain silos still owned by Admiral Lawrie. At the northeastern borders was an apple orchard and several acres of land kept by the Blessing family, used for growing Christmas trees and harvest-time pumpkins, while southwest you had the Anasazi Bridge (where poor young Ollie Echols drowned himself in 1977) crossing the meandering Rock River there. Farther along *it* you'd find Jasper Park seated on the river bend, with its sandy baseball diamond and red-brick shelters and its historic old gallows tree, an imposing Eastern cottonwood once used in early pioneer days for both public hangings and midnight lynchings alike.

There were other small businesses, as expected—Lehman's Candle & Quilt Shoppe, the Gospel Book Store, Meg's Café and DeRango's Countryside Meats, Styx & Stonze Botanicals, the Prairie Dairy—sprinkled throughout the gently sloping layers of midtown proper. Plus the usual dregs and derelict dives, out around the railroad tracks, where prostitutes and their pimps still lingered in the deserted freight yard's shadows on most nights.

Town Hall meetings were the last Thursday evening of each month, at the renovated Riding Club horse stables on Platt Street, Richard recalled. Everyone was welcome, the prostitutes included. It was a typical Midwestern scenario: small town that yearned secretly to be a big city, but remained stuck with its feet mired right where it was; ever part of the Corn Belt, ever sitting on the deadly rim of Tornado Alley. Michelle and he had gone to school and grown up here together, fallen in love as mere children, really, then had fled Blackwater Valley as soon as they were able, in order to start their lives anew somewhere else. But that's how it was. You either ended up staying your entire life in a place like this, until they planted you here, or you couldn't get away fast enough. Upper midwest America, absolutely.

And at the center sleeps its dreaming dead in their neat, muted triangle, if they do dream at all. Now who in hell *had said* that? Richard blinked the thought away, changing radio stations.

He found some crackling Led Zeppelin and left it there, drumming his fingers along with the slow, deliberate beat. Looking at the rows of quiet, old-fashioned homes floating by, with not one now but two church spires visible, and with the peak of the condemned bell tower rising above the trees, Richard found himself shivering despite the warmth. Hearing the jazzy-bluesy "Tea for One" moaning out of the speakers was uncomfortably eerie for some reason. Maybe because he'd traveled these same roads in his youth, listening to this same staticky music by day and by night. No other music came close for him and the circle of friends he was a part of back then. The mighty LZ was the be-all and end-all of rock bands. If you didn't like it, hey hey, you could hop on out of the car any time you pleased. Watch your step, ma'am, and thank you for choosing Greyhound—

He smiled, recalling the title of a Zeppelin album Michelle had listened to endlessly, a title she'd used more than once to describe these very same residences of her then-hometown.

"Houses of the Holy," Richard murmured as he drove.

"Is that the name of this song, Daddy?"

He glanced over at his daughter. "No, hon," he said, laughing. "Just thinking again."

"Oh." Then: "Is this song older than me?"

"It sure is. It's way older than you, Katie-Smatie."

"Oh," she acknowledged, and fell silent.

Richard's gaze returned to the dwellings lining both sides of Ralston Avenue, the street they were on now, even as one song ended and another Zep tune kicked in—this time it was "Thank You"; the station was obviously in the middle of a block here—and he couldn't help but think again on Michelle's moniker. There *was* a song by that title also, "House of the Holy", but not on the particular album of that name. It got held over and came two years later, on their next release. But that was Led Zeppelin: they did what they wanted, conformed to nothing and to no one, like the marauding Viking hordes they sang about. No label that was put to them ever stuck. They somehow managed to remain untouchable, above the critics' sniveling reach, beyond the manipulations of the music industry as a whole. A record-company exec's worst nightmare. But oh, the magic and depravity they made for a time.

"Thank You" did its famous organ fade-out to near silence before fading back in and ending full tilt. The third song they rolled out was "The Girl I Love She Got Long Black Wavy Hair", a remastered gem from the group's rare BBC sessions. Wasn't it known as "Willow

Tree" at one time? Yes. He couldn't help smirking, thinking how this always reminded him of "Moby Dick" each time he heard it, with a little "Travelling Riverside Blues" thrown into the mix. Pure fun, this was . . .

Richard looked in the rearview mirror and caught himself grinning, like that dopey kid back somewhere in his boyhood, but when he glanced forward again and spotted the girl on the yellow bike, sailing off a side street and straight into traffic, his hands squeezed so tightly on the steering wheel that some of his knuckles popped.

She was beautiful and leggy and tanned all over like his wife had once been, wearing white shorts and a white halter and tiny headphones over her ears, and for one startled moment the sweat froze in his pores as he involuntarily jabbed at the brake. It was enough to screech the tires, send the Blazer sideways a bit. The girl shot them an annoyed scowl over her shoulder as she flew past, and suddenly Franklin had to fight back the urge to scream at her. Scream at the top of his lungs for her to watch out, because someday she was going to get herself killed doing that shit. Get herself killed leaving the library one moon-splashed summer's eve . . . perhaps . . . yes, run down by some lunatic in a giant dirty old shipwreck of a Pontiac Parisienne, with the words *WASH ME* traced onto its side, who'll keep right on going maybe. Just keep right-the-fuck on going—and who drives a *Pontiac Parisienne* anyway? . . . who in hell even *owns* a behemoth like that anymore?—while she dies there twisted and broken in the road a few minutes later, according to the statement of the librarian. Dies so terribly, voiding her bowels and bladder in her final ruinous throes.

And they'll never catch the bastard. That's the kicker. The night librarian disappears immediately after, and they'll never catch the bastard who did it. Never catch anyone. Oh . . . dear . . . God, why did my Michelle have to die like that? Answer me. The leukemia was already killing her. Wasn't that enough? Richard glared up at the lofty church steeples now, felt that stark bitterness seething within his guts once more. *Why not take this one, too?* he thought contemptuously, from some barren-black place. *Right here in the street? She's not doing anything either, you son of a bitch. Just riding her bike, minding her own business. But that's about your style, isn't it?*

He snapped the radio off in the midst of Robert Plant's banshee-like wail and loosened his grip, unclenching his teeth, hoping Katie hadn't seen him. Fumbling to unwrap his berry flavored Rolaids, he popped one into his mouth and began to chew it. He watched the young girl in his mirrors as she pedaled her yellow ten-speed away, riding with no hands.

"Daddy?" Katie said, making him jump. "Have I ever been here before?"

"You mean to Blackwater Valley? No, babe. You've never even been out of Maine, until now."

"Oh. That's funny . . . " Her gaze sharpened, but went dreamy as her thoughts drifted unspoken. Richard resumed his speed and eyed her for a moment. He sometimes wondered about children— wondered about them the same way he wondered about the nighttime stars and microorganisms in the sea. And each time he wondered, he always ended up shaking his head in a dumbfounded kind of awe.

Not every kid was empathic either.

"True," Richard said out loud as he crunched, then slowly looked in his daughter's direction. She was already staring at him, naturally.

"Still thinking?"

He rolled his eyes comically and she laughed. "Yes, Katie-Smatie. Still thinking. What are *you* doin' over there?"

She shrugged. "Nothing much."

"Hmm."

After a pause: "Daddy?"

"Yep?"

"How long are we going to be here?"

"A couple of days, hon, until the twenty-ninth." Again, the knuckles whitened a touch on the steering wheel. "Until Mommy's birthday."

"Oh. Right." She stared out her window, squinting tiredly in the sunlight, which had come out and stayed.

Richard watched her some more, then glanced at the glove compartment. Taking in a shaky breath, he let it out and turned his eyes to the road. *One moonsplashed summer's eve.* He would do what he'd come here to do, fulfill his wife's last wishes, if he could; her dying earthly requests—first, try to make some kind of lasting peace with Michelle's parents (if at all possible) and second, take his wife's ashen remains from the suitcase behind him, on her birthday, and scatter them at the place of her special choosing. Where they'd first fallen in love so long ago: their own hallowed ground, where the first hand-holding and that tentative, terrifying very first kiss happened. Then he would go. He'd take his six-year-old daughter and head east for Golitha Falls, Maine. Back home to the empty Dutch Colonial with its sad little greenhouse awaiting them there on Charismatic Lane. And he would try to begin anew. Try to pick up everything and continue on without her, finish that damned second novel his agent and publisher were still waiting on, by now *so* overdue. They would try their best, widowed and orphaned, try to go on without her in their lives.

Their angel, their shining morning star.

He drove onward, made a right and a couple of lefts to get around some street repairs being done. Old-timers around town were fond of telling visitors that there were only two real seasons to contend with here in the great state of Illinois, this land of Lincoln: winter and road construction. The old-timers relished in the relating of snippets of wisdom like these. Sometimes to the point of driving a person bats—or rather, once again for illustration, what old-timers preferred calling 'shack-wacky'.

Richard took a quick detour through an alley and swung past a small yard sale wrapping up business for the day, at last turning onto the thoroughfare called Brazier Drive. This was it. He shook his head, not knowing any answers, not knowing what the outcome of this all would be. Only time would tell *that*.

Then he blinked, sitting up wide-eyed in his sticky seat. He stared out the windshield and a smile came grudgingly over his lips.

"Still there," he said. "Check it out, Katelyn Jane Franklin. It's still there."

2

Chip Priewe sat in his police cruiser on a sidestreet next to the Memorial Hall, sipping strong black coffee from a Styrofoam cup he bought at Meg Bilobran's little café, around the corner. He blew on it and sipped, blew and sipped, and observed the dark green Chevrolet Blazer with the man and the small child inside, coming down Ralston Avenue. He watched as they went past Memorial Hall (taking note of the strange vehicle's Maine plates), watched—blowing and sipping—as seventeen-year-old Julissa Quigg, who sang in the church choir, came tear-assing across traffic on her yellow bicycle. The Blazer went into an abrupt skid, its driver overreacting slightly. The girl wasn't actually going *that* fast, didn't really come close to them, but the Blazer with the mean-looking CPS grille guard out front lurched nonetheless, locking its brakes and causing everyone to look in their direction.

On they went a moment later, continuing along Ralston Avenue and out of his sight while the Quigg girl disappeared the other way, most likely headed home for dinner. He watched her go, following her white shorts and long sun-bronzed legs as they pumped.

No harm, no foul. Still, she did have those stupid earphones on, listening to music instead of paying attention to the street sounds around her. He'd have to mention it to her sometime, put the fear of the law into her. Or not. Who knew? *Like to put* some*thing into that one, truth be told.*

Priewe stared at his left hand briefly, at the wedding band on his ring finger. He snorted, squirming uneasily; the thought of his ill-conceived and even more ill-fitting marriage tightened his insides. It'd been one of the worst mistakes of his life, had almost ruined him. No wonder you had people going around in such desperate states. Desperate straits and desperate states, amen to that. Nervous Nellie types, jumping at shadows and turning gray with worry and leaping off bridges and such. Nervous as *cats*. You saw them all the time, shuffling to and fro like they were set for the rubber room or something. Total human wrecks, because of the choices they made.

He glanced at the old Civil War cannon resting in front of Memorial Hall, wondering not for the first time if it was really still loaded, like that retired history-buff Navy prick Jack Lawrie always claimed it was. Wondering how easily, if need be, one's head might fit in front of its gorge, and if that said head might disintegrate wholly from one's shoulders were the huge, dormant Union beast to awaken and recoil one last roaring, deafening time—

Sipping cautiously at the hot coffee, Chief Priewe swallowed and whistled through his teeth. Not a pleasant prospect, no sir, but one to consider nevertheless. *If need ever be.* And what was it with these kids, anyhow? He enjoyed music, too, like anyone else. Well, good music at least. He didn't get all this horseshit, this mindless garbage being passed off today. Who in hell needed illiterate shit blaring into both ears all the time, or a cell phone jammed against their head every waking moment? Only dimwits, he'd concluded, low-bred idiots afraid of having an actual coherent thought come at them. Heaven forbid that should happen. Just another example of the buzzsaw this country was headed for, with today's generation of dopes at the helm. What a fucking future. Human flotsam and jetsam, every one of them . . .

30

Some static traffic issued forth from the car's police radio and Priewe leaned forward, listening. He tuned up the volume, but nothing else came. *Piss shit.* He'd been monitoring what was going on just east of town—something big, by the sound of it—for the last hour or so. It had started with a call between a couple of Ogle County boys fielding reports about a section of the roadway that had fallen in, out beyond the interchange. No injuries or anything, nothing unusual to speak of. After a time a shout had gone out for the Rockford cops to the north, could they please come down, because it appeared they had themselves a possible 'situation'. Odd. Several minutes later an order was given by some unknown voice for an ambulance and for the county coroner, if she was available, and to keep unwanted gapers away from the sinkhole vicinity. Crime scene procedure, he couldn't help thinking. Odder yet. The radio traffic intensified for a bit, culminating with an ambiguous request for a tarp or canvas of some kind—maybe a swimming pool cover would do. Priewe had chimed in, curiosity getting the better of him, saying he could snag something quick and be out that way in ten to fifteen minutes tops. But he'd been sharply rebuked by that unknown voice, informing him that his assistance was not needed, and how everyone should stick to their own jurisdictions for now. He had radioed an affirmative 10-4 back, and then had listened to the stinging, intentional silence which followed.

So, here he sat, uninvited to the dance, while something big went on out there—really big and decidedly odd, he gathered—even as extra uniforms from Rockford made their way south to take part. Here

Chip Priewe sat, blowing and sipping on his coffee, *not needed*. Well, they could take that jurisdiction and stick it in their ass. He knew who they were, these Rockford men given the green light over him. He used to do a lot of security work in that town, years ago, so he knew them all right. Knew the ones on the take from the squeaky cleans, knew the juicers from the wife beaters, the fine upstanding family men from the closet pedophiles. They were the same ones who, back then, had pegged him and his kind as ham-and-eggers, or nickel-and-dime rent-a-cops. That was before he landed this gig, though. He was a full-fledged Chief of Police now, Constable of his own jurisdiction. So fuck them all, flatfoot cunts that they were, for leaving him out of their loop. Trying to hold him back, always keeping him down.

Like the cunt waiting for him at home did.

He took another swallow, jaws clenched tightly. Worst mistake of his life, without a doubt. He wondered where his deputy chief was during all of this, why *that* inky black bastard hadn't checked in. Or the other fuckwits for that matter. Well, he would ride them good enough later on, let them know who called the shots out here. Dish them all the grief and the boondocks dirt-water rounds they could handle, because in the end it only came down to one thing. The age-old, everlasting Golden Rule: shit rolls downhill. No matter which way you plugged it, shit *always* rolls downhill. That was the reason you had people going around in such desperate states these days, afraid of any and every little thing which might happen; afraid most of all, he truly believed, of their own undoing. Nervous Nellie types—

Like the driver of that Chevy Blazer, for instance. Jumping at shadows. *And what did they have to be so nervous about, anyway? A man and a little girl like that. In a small town like this?* Made you stop and wonder, yes.

Snorting again, Chief Priewe thought he would have to keep an eye on them for sure, these strangers in his town. For the time being, though, he merely sat, and blew and sipped, listening to the police radio and trying not to think of what waited for him back home.

3

Meanwhile, something stirred inside the condemned bell tower, which stood sentinel over town, haunting its gloom there. It moved slowly at first—this *flesh* thing—shambling, quiet as a nun. Its left side wasted and gone limp, the thing dragged itself to the rotted stairs and began inching up them, knowing where all the breaches and weak spots lay, mewling as it maneuvered, barely audible; a whispering of dust motes in its empty, soundless lair.

The old rope still dangled from somewhere above, hanging in moldered ruin, witness to all these many cascading decades. Pigeons fluttered in sudden alarm. When at last it reached the top, it pulled itself with one good appendage onto the squared walkway and began rounding the great and rusted iron bell, searching out the belfry openings in this hushed, secret still. *North, east, south, west. Ahh.* Shafts of setting sunlight streamed in, creating an orange glow like diffused hell licking in at the weather-blasted peak of the tower. *Ahhh.* The thing looked across scant fields, high above the tallest of trees, trying to blink the brightness away, shielding eyes that peered like blood blisters from the hoods of pale flesh in its face. It squinted painfully and spied the boxlike Memorial Hall in the ruddy distance, an idle police car beside it. And something else, someone in overalls (*Syd Cholke?*) way up on a ladder, trimming tree branches back from the power lines above Brazier Drive.

But when it saw the tall man standing and holding hands with a small child, down near the deserted Lawrie Theater, this being froze and began to tremble. It stared and it stared, until the blisters which were its eyes seemed about to burst. Then it fell back into the cloak of its crawling darkness and shuddered, howling out piteously from a rictal, tongueless gape of mouth.

The mourning doves and remaining pigeons took wing in their bright terror.

4

The building stood just as it had the last time Richard saw it, more than eight years before. Vacant and deteriorating: a relic the good citizens of Blackwater Valley simply refused to tear down. It was done in what might be called a Byzantine style, with longish breast walls and topped by an Oriental-like dome on its roof. The place had once been known as the Midday Theatre, because of the daytime matinees screened here in its early years.

He vaguely recollected that a handful of workers lost their lives when the dome collapsed during the initial construction in the 1920s. But from the mid '70s on, it would be called the Lawrie Theater, named after the former Navy admiral who purchased it and ran nightly movies there with his wife Lorraine.

In 1986, the year Chernobyl melted down into a dead zone and the shuttle Challenger disintegrated in the frosty skies over Florida's celebrated stretch of Space Coast, the building closed its doors for good as giant, multi-screened monster showplaces began to blight the landscape. Most small theaters could not compete, and ultimately went the way of the drive-ins and mom-and-pop grocery stores. At least he assumed Lawrie still owned it, anyway—Jackson Lawrie owned property and structures all over town, including the Nautical Museum and the old bell tower. Most of the properties sat unoccupied, like this one.

He noticed some scattered plastic letters that had been left behind on the rigid canopy over the theater doors, letters which might have once spelled out movie titles such as *Peggy Sue Got Married* or *Stand by Me*, but now resembled only an errant jumble, like alphabet soup up on the marquee billboard. On the elongated side wall of the theater was a mural, faded and peeling badly, but intact just the same. The mural Michelle and he had painted.

They parked and got out, Richard leading his daughter by the hand. In truth, he had forgotten all about this painting until a few seconds ago. Now his gaze swept over it with fondness, taking in every detail again, every little nuance. There was a lush pine forest, its needled spires reaching for the heavens, and a castle sitting on a mirror-glass lake while the dark Mountain of Power loomed gargantuan in the background. An empty skiff floated ominously alone, moored, abandoned among some water-draped rocks.

And his favorite: a large ruffled owl in a greatly gnarled black maple (part of its beak and one big unblinking eye chipped away and missing), and the mandatory shining knight upon a white steed, all poised beneath a cloud-riddled chalky blue sky. Plus two signatures in acrylic gold and the tiny '88 scrawled in the lower left corner, obscured by ivy which crept along the crumbling foundation.

It struck him suddenly that the hands of his deceased wife had helped create this—had stroked and daubed and had coaxed it into being, with brush and sponge and exterior semi-gloss—once upon a long time ago. He reached out to touch it but hesitated, unsure, not knowing what ruminations he might stir and bring to life here.

They had both finished college by then and were home planning their futures together. It'd been Michelle's idea, and naturally, he had gone along with it. The theater was already vacated and Lawrie, whom Richard had done scores of odd jobs for while growing up, had no immediate plans for the structure and said he didn't mind. Coupled with the fact that George Deadmond, Michelle's father, had a whole garage full of leftover paint cans he'd probably never find a use for. So, two lovestruck kids (Richard had been 24 and Michelle only 22) spent most of that sweet summer making promises in the daytime, making love at night, and leaving behind their own visions of grandeur on the side wall of the empty Lawrie Theater.

Something caught his eye, and he glanced up. A wooden plaque was affixed at the top center of the mural above the sunrayed cloudburst. He chuckled aloud when he read the words engraved into it: HERE

BE DRAGONS. The sign had been the finishing touch, a private joke between Michelle and him, because dragons there were. Some of course were visible, like the one preening near the lakeshore or the one rearing up before the knight's lowered lance, but others they had hidden in the background, painted and blended them devilishly in where you had to look hard to find them. Like the one squatting fat and obscene and leering out from the forest wall, or the one crouched beneath the castle's drawbridge. Or the one slavering and lurking in the mouth of a shadowed gorge in the vast mountain, surrounded by kindling-stacked bones of the dead and the recently devoured. Yes, here *be* dragons.

"Know who painted that picture, hon?" said Richard finally, gesturing to the mural.

Katie shook her head. "Uh-uh. Who?"

"Your Mommy and I did. See our names at the bottom?" He moved closer and pulled at the clinging ivy, glancing back at Katie. She was nodding, her eyes big and sparkly. "Before I was born, right?" she asked.

"Yep, sweetie. Before

(*squash, anybody?*)

you were born—" He blinked stupidly, his words wavering before trailing off, and he stood immediate and straight. What the hell? His mouth was dry; he licked his lips. Noticed his heart had revved up, just a beat or two. Katie was frowning at the mural, her brow creased in thought, and Richard felt that tug at his guts again. No, oh no. Don't do this . . .

But all she said was: "Daddy, why is her name changed?"

Richard caught his breath. "That was Mommy's

maiden name, Katelyn. Before we got married. Michelle Deadmond. Then she took my last name, and she was Michelle Franklin." He beeped her little nose playfully. "Same as your last name. Katie-Smatie Franklin. Got it?"

She giggled, the sharp edges leaving her beautiful round face. "Got it."

Richard looked up at the painting, his own frown deepening now as he felt the breeze touch his skin. It gave him a warm feeling gazing at its distant hills and fields like this, bringing back vibrant remembrances of days which had passed by much too quickly. But there was something else just under the surface, something bad, like the lingering traces of a forgotten nightmare, hanging on to you the way cobwebs did after you've blundered into them. Like a stain beneath the pleasant memory, one he couldn't quite place. Couldn't put his finger on. But he felt it clear as day, and it

(*get your nice, ripe squash here!*)

chilled his bones. He moved instinctively back a bit, vaguely aware of some harsh distant sound, a sudden rush of birds in flight somewhere. He was startled when a gruff voice came from above.

"Heads up!"

Richard caught sight of a stout workman in the trees, dressed in big overalls with an orange-and-yellow reflective vest over them, standing on a ladder pruning back branches. A twig fell to the sidewalk and he moved his daughter away. He stared up again, and realized with some embarrassment the person on the ladder he'd figured for a man was in reality a woman, her breasts large and heavy and her close-cropped hair tucked under the NASCAR cap she wore. Katie looked, too, and the worker squinted down through thick safety glasses.

"Need some help, son?"

"What?" *Son?*

"You look like you're lost," said the woman, smiling back at them with tanned features. She wielded a long pole saw in both hands, leaning out to smartly take down another branch.

"No," he told her, "just browsing, is all."

"Ah. Sure is a hot one though. Too hot." She paused. "Like that motor oil commercial on TV back in the old days. You know? 'It's hot. It's *too* hot. There's going to be an accident.' Remember that one?" She barked laughter, throaty and deep like a lifelong smoker would laugh.

"Seventy-two," murmured Katie absently, gazing at the mural.

The female tree trimmer glanced down. "How's that, sweets?"

Richard cleared his voice and spoke up. "She says it's seventy-two degrees out."

"Oh dearie, it must be warmer than that. And with this humidity—"

"Eighty-eight," Katie declared, and Richard felt his face flush. Hoo, boy. How should he explain this? He looked up at the woman, shading his eyes. "Humidity is eighty-eight percent, I guess."

"How in the world does she know that? The radio?"

Shuffling his feet, he said, "I don't know how she knows it, but she does." He glanced lovingly at his daughter, then looked skyward. "Can't explain it. Sorry."

"Huh." The worker seemed speechless at this, reduced to grunts. She adjusted the cap on her head and reached out to trim away a good-sized tree limb. That accomplished, she leaned over and said, "Browsing. You looking to buy?"

"Oh, no. Just taking a peek at my handiwork here. I painted this thing, years and years ago."

"Is that right? You really painted it?" She raised the glasses to her forehead, peering down with that big smile again, one eyebrow cocked quizzically. "You from the Val?"

"I used to be," Richard said. "But no, not anymore."

"Uh-huh." The woman nodded. "Once you're from the Val, son, you're always from the Val. Didn't you know that?"

"I'll keep it in mind. Thanks."

"Mm, you do that. I'm Sydney, by the way. Holler if you need anything." She lowered the safety glasses onto her nose. "Nice to meet you two."

"Likewise," he told her, his voice rising. "This is Katelyn. I'm on the wall there, left-hand corner." He gestured toward the spot, looking up and tipping her a wink. "Under the ivy." He couldn't be sure, but he thought she might've winked back before returning to her work. Richard started to lead Katie away but paused a moment longer, staring at the crumbling mural again. The warm feeling was gone, fragmented, replaced instead by a persistent gnawing at the back of his brain—like the clicking of a beetle trapped behind a section of paneling. He frowned hard, trying to make some sort of connection out of his broken thoughts. He could not, however, and yet he shivered just the same as if

(*the bastard grinned at me*)

an unseen icy hand had brushed the small of his back.

Christ, what in hell is it? What's wrong?

"Come on, hon," he said to Katie, walking back to the Blazer with her. They got in and drove slowly down to the end of the block, parking across the street from the peach American Foursquare home with the neat brown trim and the copper, crescent man-in-the-moon weathervane mounted atop its roof pinnacle. Richard shut the engine off and sat a while, thinking. Or trying not to think. One of the two. There were remnants assailing him now, snatches of his own warring memories, some filling him with joy, some only with hurt and self-pity. Some with fear. He didn't care anymore. He'd driven the past three days to get here and he was tired and he didn't care. At some length, he turned to face his daughter.

"This is it, I guess," Richard said quietly. "Ready?"

"Yes," she said, but she neither looked or sounded very sure.

"It'll be okay. Hop out your side, sweetie. Let's go in."

As Katie was rounding the front of the vehicle, Richard got out and dropped the locks with a click, checking each door handle. He beeped the SUV's alarm system, activating it. Richard met her halfway and took her by the hand, pausing to scan the windows of the house.

"Love you, Katie-Smatie," he let her know.

"I love you, Daddy."

As they crossed Brazier Drive, a small boy brandishing a super-blaster water pistol chased a small girl down the sidewalk. "If you do, I'll tell!" the girl screamed as she ran. "I'll tell! *I'LL TELL!*" A curbside mailbox bearing the street numbers 1422 stood out front with a newspaper folded into the lower holding compartment, so Richard slid it out. It was an evening edition of *The Rock River Guardian.* He smiled faintly, and tucked it under one arm as he continued walking. Far off somewhere floated the dreamy sound of a Fleetwood Mac song. Somewhere closer, someone out-of-doors popped a beer can tab as the Chicago White Sox crackled on a radio in the background. Nearer still, a large dog barked once, sharp and lone and distinct.

Houses of the Holy, Richard thought as they walked up to the hushed Deadmond home.

CHAPTER THREE

I

REVEREND SIMON JULIAN strode methodically about the inner sanctuary of his church, extinguishing the candles. He didn't touch them, heavens no, but blew their wicks from a safe distance into smoldering cinder with pursed, wrinkled lips. Some might have found it strange, this, how Julian chose to surround himself with the very things most portentous to him—silver and fire—well, some of his kind would find it strange, assured. Those of his own unique ilk. But the temerity of it never failed to amuse him, even though he did keep his distance.

The man named William Salt, still guarding the doors, watched him as he made his way around the perimeter to the four corner alcove tables, each coated in brick-dust residue. He murmured something as he did this, something so soft that the Indian could not make it out, even with *his* well-honed ears. Salt did hear the last part of it, however, the Reverend's final utterances.

"Relinquish," whispered Simon Julian, standing now before the last tapered candle. Instead of bending and blowing it out, he blew quietly this time into his own closed fist and, from a good three to four feet back, opened his hand toward the candlestick with a flourish, as if releasing dandelion wishes upon the wind. Or a thrown, post-coital kiss. *"Relinquish,"* he repeated, his voice a raspy hiss. The candle flame wavered and abruptly winked out more than a yard away.

Something trembled in the black church then, seemed to sigh almost, and a cold draft made its way through the darkness, scrabbling up the brickwork and over pews, twisting and convulsing up the aisle toward the doors. William Salt felt it pass but did not move; he remained stock-still with his arms crossed before him. Outside, the great lightning-struck oak rustled uneasily. An airborne crow, caught in the unnatural current, flopped and cawed until it was finally able to fly clear, glossy feathers ruffled but otherwise intact—this same crow would later peck out the eyes of its own young and leave the nest a scene of blood, torn black tufts, and carnage before soaring off in pursuit of interests unknown.

Across town a young couple sitting on their front porch felt a chill and shivered, the eerie sensation vexing their good spirits and reducing them to ash in one fell swoop. The recently wed couple, with the name Putnam on their welcome mat, had been relaxing and drinking sweet tea outside for a while. They had also, quite coincidentally, witnessed the arrival of a dark green Chevrolet Blazer into their Blackwater Valley midst not long before. Now though, feeling this sudden unseen cold, something sputtered out and died inside them like . . . well, like the snuffing of a flame.

44

The two stood up and went into their cozy bungalow, came out again a minute later with an infant; their fourteen-week-old son blinked repeatedly in the angled sunlight, just wakened from his late nap. They fussed over him, carrying the bundle with care up the paved driveway to the open garage. They went in, and together they climbed inside their Ford Focus and shut the doors, the wife on the passenger side holding the tiny baby still wrapped in its blue blanket, her husband behind the wheel. The man started the car and they both let their windows down. After a bit the woman began to rock, cradling her son, her gaze fixed straight ahead. Soon she began to sob, her mouth working wretchedly, tears spilling down her cheeks. The husband shushed her, stroked her hair. He turned on some music to help comfort her and left the radio on low. The remote control was not working, so he had to get back out of the car and drag down the stubborn garage door. Then the man returned to the running vehicle to sit with his wife and newly born child in the choking, amassing fumes. To sit and to wait for some awful, unspoken covenant, as yet unfulfilled.

No one noticed them at all.

Behind the bolted, storm-beaten doors of the Nain Lutheran Church, Reverend Julian tilted his head back and applied some eyedrops into his rheumy eyes. He squeezed them shut, grimacing in the murk. He looked up and winked mockingly at the Christ statue, whose sorrowful face seemed to sadden even more in the shadows. Julian smoothed his loose, wispy strands of snow-white hair into place and switched on the old church's electric lights without warning. His Native American associate didn't flinch, did not even blink.

Wiping his eyes with a handkerchief, the Reverend turned to look upon the man at the doors. "I'm disappointed, *Prarsheen*," he said. "I thought that you, above all, would've known they had arrived."

"I knew," the huge Indian replied, his voice like the stone grate of a mausoleum's crypt.

Simon Julian raised an eyebrow. "Oh?"

Tapping the side of his nose with the stub of one severed forefinger, William Salt said: "They smelled like skunk."

"Ah, yes. Of course." The Reverend nodded, and the two smiled dutifully at one another. Pocketing his eyedrops and handkerchief, he turned back toward the church pulpit with a covetous, enduring light coming to life somewhere in him, somewhere within his ancientness. He rubbed his palms together. "Well, time to get cracking, yes?"

2

Waiting for someone to answer the door after he'd knocked, Richard didn't think he would be able to make it. He ran a hand through his prematurely thinning hair, eyes shifting all around and eventually finding the outdoor thermometer gauge, which hovered at the 72-degree mark, no less. And as his stomach did a lazy, nauseous somersault that threatened to send his cottage cheese out two possible exits at once, a dozen thoughts whizzed through his weary mind.

What am I doing here? I must be insane. What am I going to say to them? Jesus, what can I say? 'I'm sorry.'? God almighty, this is bad. Real bad. I must really be losing it, that's the only explanation. Why did we even come here? I know what—go back to the motel. Right now. Go to the motel. We don't have to see them. They'll never even know we were—

"Daddy, you're hurting me."

"Sorry, babe," Richard apologized, relaxing his grip on Katie's tiny hand. He swallowed, felt his heart thudding hard, and for a second he considered it. Seriously considered turning and fleeing. Before he had a chance to make good on that alluring (if somewhat cowardly) alternative, something happened. He glanced up Brazier Drive, and saw their mural on the side wall of the Lawrie Theater in the distance. Then it hit him like an invisible punch to his lungs. His vision swam and his knees nearly buckled, causing him to turn and set himself right down on the stoop, light-headed.

"Hoo, sit for a minute with me, Katie-Smatie," he told his daughter, trying not to raise any alarm, and she sat beside him on the porch steps. No one was coming to the door, but then Richard hadn't knocked with any real conviction, either. Just gave the screen door a light, half-hearted rapping. But looking from this viewpoint now, here upon the Deadmonds' front porch, he saw a different panorama suddenly. Like squinting through a prism, back into another distorted place and time. With this newfound sight something had come at him from the past and had almost taken the legs out from under him—a missing piece of the puzzle, recalled and placed back where it belonged. He remembered, oh yes.

It had been a week or so after the mural was started. They'd only done the background stuff, the

47

forest and the mountain, and were just beginning in on the clouds. Richard did most of the main cloudburst himself, with rays of colored sunshine slashing and slanting through it from behind, while Michelle created bits of cotton fluff adrift in the blue. It was about that time a stranger had begun coming around.

He came just before dark, every night, and would stand and stare at their wall for increasingly longer and longer stretches. Neither of them knew his name, but Michelle had heard the man was disabled, or had some kind of congenital disease which affected his mental state. Something of that nature. Whatever the case, they'd sat together in the shadows of Michelle's front porch—*this* very porch—and had watched him as each night he approached, studied what new images they'd added that day, and then went on his way. After a while Richard started calling him Sallow Man, and anyone that ever saw him would've understood why. He was tall and thin, could not have weighed much over one hundred and forty-five pounds, in fact. His clothes were too big for him, shirt and trousers bagging up and hanging off his frame like burlap sacks. He also wore a bucket hat upon his head without fail, not unlike the Scarecrow's hat in *The Wizard of Oz*. But odder yet was his skin tone, what they could see of it. He appeared pale, almost bloodless in his face and hands. 'Pasty-faced' was how they had described him to Michelle's mother, Glee, after catching their first glimpse of his ghostly visage in the darkness up the street.

Suspicious of this creepy, unknown night-caller, but fearful of telling him to get lost in an up-close confrontation, the two of them had decided to try and discourage his nocturnal visits. One evening, they strung fishing line to keep this Sallow Man out of the theater's side lot, but, overprotective of their unfinished baby, they had gotten carried away. Gathering all of the empty soda cans and beer bottles they could find, Richard and Michelle had attached them and strung them together, crisscrossing the lines and running them in and out, around the nearby trees and telephone pole, creating what turned out to be an intricate maze of fishline. Then they had quickly left the darkening area and retreated to Michelle's porch, as a brief summer shower commenced, and they had waited.

They did not have to wait long.

As dusk and the rain fell simultaneously, the two young lovers huddled in the shadows with Mr. Deadmond's binoculars, keeping close watch. Soon, pretty much on schedule, the Sallow Man had showed. In the last twilight glow of day they saw him start into the vacant lot, approaching their painting. Michelle gawked through her father's binoculars, while Richard had to squint to see. They watched the tall, gaunt raggedy man as he walked toward the wall and right into the outermost circle of invisible shin-high string. Noise came as he spun and began to entangle himself; empty cans clattered, and Richard was sure he heard some of the bottles breaking. It was then that he realized the whole thing had been a grave mistake. Because instead of moving away, which had been the original intent, the Sallow Man staggered farther into the lot, twisting and turning, his broomstick legs becoming hopelessly tangled in the spiderweb of fishing line. More soda cans rattled and clanged, and the tinkle of shattering glass came again—though Michelle later swore up and down it had only been the sound of the rain. They saw him spin and whirl, prancing hideously in his confusion and panic. Next, he fell, sprawling right in the midst of the knotted line, and the bottles and cans.

Then came the wail.

The pallid giant laid on his back and screamed, and Richard bit down on his own tongue so hard it bled. The Sallow Man wailed, a long miserable cry of fear and anger, maybe pain, which seemed to go on and on, shredding off dismally at the end. What happened after that had shocked Richard even more.

Michelle Deadmond, love of his life, had never exactly been rocket scientist material. This he always knew, as he'd known the same of himself. She was no slouch, either. Sometimes though, caught up in the heat of the moment, she could do and say some goofy things. Like the time back home in Maine, when the clothes dryer had blown a belt and started smoking down in their cellar. Richard would never forget how Michelle, when the attending firemen rushed in and asked her where the basement was, had clutched on to little baby Katelyn and replied in wild-eyed hysteria, "It's downstairs!" Richard had still been on the kitchen floor laughing twenty minutes later, after the small fire was out and the engines had left. Laughing so hard with a mixture of hilarity and relief, while his wife stewed and glowered angrily at him from their sunny breakfast nook, that he could barely breathe.

But this . . . this was something different, and it was Michelle who laughed. Wasn't it, Richie boy?

You got that right, Richard thought, gazing up the

block at the mural and no longer seeing it. It was Michelle, caught up in the moment, who had laughed.

The night-trolling Sallow Man had toppled over and fallen, perhaps into a pile of broken green Heineken bottles and shards, and lay shrieking in the rain. Richard had involuntarily almost bitten off his own tongue. And Michelle, binoculars still in hand, threw her head back and laughed in the darkness, high and loud. Brayed like a loon in a cage, and he'd jumped, blood already gathering in the corners of his mouth. He snatched the binoculars away from her, clamping one hand over her mouth, but not in time. When Richard peered through the lenses toward the deserted Lawrie Theater he came close to pissing his pants.

Richard saw the Sallow Man sitting upright, and looking in their direction. He had heard Michelle's laughter, there was no doubt of that; Brazier Drive was completely silent except for the patter of falling raindrops, and Michelle's inopportune schoolgirl peal had stood out like a gun report in a canyon. He'd heard them, all right, and now he was trying to spot them. Richard noticed something else.

In his fall, Sallow Man had lost his bucket hat. And in the dim light from a nearby streetlamp, gaping through Mr. Deadmond's opera glasses (as the old man referred to them), Richard got a good long look at him. *Too* long, he would later muse on many an occasion to come, in midnight retrospect. The pale man's head was huge, too large for his thin body, like his clothing. It was nearly twice the size a normal human head should be—incredibly—and had no visible hair on it at all. It glistened in the rain, looking

51

like an enormous, bleached honeydew melon that was close to exploding.

Squash, anybody? Richard had thought crazily at the time. *Get your nice, ripe squash here! Look, no seeds!*

Buried deep within that ghastly misshapen skull burned two eyes, searching, blazing out from beneath white fleshy hoods, with no eyebrows or facial hair whatsoever that might have served to break up the unadorned monotony of it. Richard clenched his teeth and grimaced. This was not *The Wizard of Oz*, oh no, he remembered thinking. Dear God, this was *The Hills Have Eyes* going on here, or maybe something worse. Then, as a sudden cold began to bloom in his testicles and rise, he saw the felled ghost-white figure lift one bony, livid hand . . . raise it and . . .

He pointed right at them, pointed at them and grinned.

"Get in the house," Richard had whispered, but Michelle only grunted in refusal and tried to get the binoculars back for another gander. The Sallow Man had gotten off the ground, clumsily but swiftly, and had begun to untangle himself.

"Get in the fucking house," Richard had croaked this time, his mouth dry as boneyard dirt. He hauled her to her feet and had pushed in through the front door of her house in a panicky sort of terror, almost knocking them both down. But he paused long enough to bring the binoculars to his eyes one final time. Behind the screen, Richard searched and focused until he spotted their Sallow Man again. He saw him coming down Brazier Drive through the rain, lumbering towards the quiet Deadmond home with clattering cans and pieces of broken bottle still dragging behind him, coming on those horrible broomstick legs and with his billowing sack clothes and his monstrous swollen head. Coming for *them*—

Richard wiped his face with his shirtsleeve, reaching absently for Katie. They had been crouching right here in the summer darkness, with the porch light off, nearly an entire block away. He could not have possibly seen them. But when he came running, the two of them locked themselves up inside the house and had doused every lamp, not daring to venture outdoors again until the following afternoon. Hell, they didn't even go near the mural for almost a week, until they thought it safe, although they never saw the Sallow Man again. That wasn't the point.

There was no way he could have seen them, absolutely no way. But he had. He'd pointed.

. . . And he grinned. The bastard grinned at me.

"Christ," muttered Richard, his skin prickling into gooseflesh, or what Katie sometimes called the 'frittles'. "This is ridiculous." He glanced at his daughter, who was looking him over. "Sorry, hon," he said. "Want to try this again?" Katie nodded, and they both stood up and turned around. Enough of this shit already, he decided, thrusting the nightmarish vestige from his mind. Time to shake it off, leave it in the dust. Cut it the fuck loose, Richie boy, because you've got more important things on your plate. He smiled dimly at his only daughter and steadied himself, raising a fist to knock hard on the screen door before him. Yet even so, he could not prevent his gaze from being drawn one last time up the block, to the long mural fading beneath the trees, and to the stout, sturdy worker still on her ladder there. Nor could he block the female tree trimmer's joking words, which all at once came washing over him in a mad, final rush:

It's hot, it's *too* hot. There's going to be an accident . . .

There already was an accident, lady, his own thoughts echoed, *in a peaceful little town back in New England. Someone ran my wife down in the road. Ran her down one night while she was riding her mountain bike home from the neighborhood library and left her to die, the same way I left that skunk to die out on US 20 today. So how about it, Sydney? I have to deal with this horror show about to begin for real here. You said to holler if we needed anything— how about a little help with* that? *Where is your big, sweet promise-filled ass now, new friend?*

Gritting his teeth, he popped another Rolaids tablet and knocked harder. The sound of movement came to him this time, a shuffling from the inner hallway. The front door opened.

CHAPTER FOUR

I

HELLO, RICH," said Franklin's father-in-law from behind the screen.

"Hi, George." Richard shifted on the porch, wishing dearly to God that he was someplace else, anyplace—even a few houses over, where he'd heard the White Sox game on the radio, would be better than this. *Break out another cold brew, buddy!* he felt like yelling. *I'll be right there! Who's up? What's the score?*

Then Deadmond pushed open the screen door and stepped out, extending one liver-spotted hand to him. Richard knew he had to be in his sixties, but the man looked a great deal older than that now. His face seemed haggard and worn, the eyes red and sunken behind his bifocals. He looked almost wizened beyond recognition, as if he'd aged fifteen years since the last time Richard had seen him, a month ago at Michelle's funeral.

He's going to die pretty soon, Richard thought morbidly. On the heels of that, immediately: *Jesus! What a thing to think!*

"How are you?" Richard said, letting go of Katie to grasp his father-in-law's hand.

"I've been better, son," confessed Deadmond. "You?"

"Tired is a good word, I suppose. I . . . I don't really know what to say to you, George." Richard faltered for words, clearing his voice and needing to cough. It felt as if an uncut diamond was lodged in his throat that wouldn't go down, and it wasn't the Rolaids. "I'm so . . . I can't even . . . "

The two clutched each other for a moment and a sense of such profound guilt descended upon Richard Allan Franklin, reducing his soul to the size of a single grain of sand, that he gasped for air.

The old man spoke quietly. "It's all right, Rich. I know how hard this is. Everything's all right."

Richard stepped back, avoiding his gaze. A shudder ran through him, seeking to bring his deflated spirit back to some sort of life. He looked up with difficulty. "George, this is Katelyn," he began, sounding awkward. "Katie, hon, this is your grandpa. Remember?"

Oh, what a mess. This is Katelyn, and this is your grandpa, and this is the last chance you got to run, pal. So run. Run all the way to Comiskey if you have to. Wonder who's on the mound today? I wonder—

These thoughts were all cut short when he saw his father-in-law's eyes. George Deadmond knelt down somewhat stiffly and looked at his only granddaughter for just the second time in both of their lives, and something sparked in his aged, dimming eyes. Something undeniable.

It was eternal affection. No two ways about it.

"Why, sure she remembers me," George beamed, his face aglow. "Don't you, sweetheart? Hey there, Katie Jane."

"Hello."

"My, if you're not the prettiest little sweetheart I've ever seen, I don't know who is," the old man said. "You know what? I think we could all use something nice and cold to drink, how about it. Would you like that, honey Kate?"

"Yes," Katie answered, smiling as best as she could.

George straightened, and something dangled loose out of his shirt collar—a long brass key on a cord around his neck. "Well, then," he said, tucking the key back, "let's go inside."

That was how Katie Franklin met her grandfather again.

2

The house was just as Richard remembered, only it seemed a lot smaller now. He knew how dumb and cliché that sounded, but it was true. A sweet, flowery aroma hung in the cool entranceway, one vaguely familiar to him. The first thing he saw as they passed into the living room was Michelle's framed high school picture sitting on top of the big console television set, and beside it a handcrafted photo box with words around its edging: *If you live to be a hundred, I want to live to be a hundred minus one day so I would never have to live without you.* The quote was attributed to Winnie the Pooh, and the center of the box frame held one of Michelle's baby pictures.

The TV was the Deadmonds' reliable old Curtis Mathis, surely so out-dated that it couldn't possibly even work anymore. He stared at it, a hint of a smile touching his lips ("I object to all this sex on the television," Michelle used to joke in her best British, Monty Python voice. "I mean, I keep falling off!"), and he felt that rough diamond trying to rise again.

George's recliner rested right where he would always remember it being, with a small Oriental design rug on the floor, in front of it. Several plants hung suspended from the ceiling in knotted wool slings, but none of them could be giving off the scent he smelled; they were mostly Wandering Jews, he noted, with a spider plant or two mixed into the fray.

On the wall above the television was a chipped plaque (Michelle made it fly across the room at him once, in a fit of heated anger) which read I ASKED JESUS HOW MUCH HE LOVED ME. HE SPREAD HIS ARMS WIDE AND SAID "THIS MUCH.", AND HE DIED. Off to the left behind the recliner was an overflowing bookcase, and in a corner to the right of the swinging kitchen door sat an Italian moon phase grandfather clock, the steady cadence of its polished brass pendulum the only sound to be heard above the gentle whir of the central air. The odd, yet comfortable combination of all these things made Richard's heart ache. He glanced at Katie and saw her looking at her mother's senior class photograph, and he tried to imagine how much her little heart must be aching, too.

Taking the folded newspaper out from under his arm, he handed it to George. "Found this in your mailbox. *The Guardian* still puts out an evening edition, I see."

"Always has." Deadmond paused. "Oh, that's right. You used to work there, didn't you?"

"Feature writer and some copy stuff—Local Vibes section." He rolled his eyes for effect.

"Right, right. I'd forgotten. Well, you always did have a flare for the words, son. Will lemonade do okay for everyone?"

Richard and Katie nodded, and Deadmond disappeared into the kitchen. After a minute or so of rattling around, he came back with tall glasses of pink lemonade on a small tray. "How bad of a drive was it, Richard?" he asked, setting the tray down on the end table next to his chair. "Did it take you long?"

"Three days," Richard said, still somewhat nervy. "But we stopped a lot, you know?" His insides were coiled up, waiting. Expecting something.

"Mm, I surely do." He carefully handed them their drinks. "Rich? Please, you and Katie sit down. Go on, anywhere you like."

They sat together on the floral-print sofa by the front picture window. The same sofa upon which Michelle and Richard used to make love. Why the Deadmonds kept it around this long, he hadn't a clue. Now though, father and daughter settled side-by-side, without wife or mother, widowed and orphaned in the end. They found one another's eyes briefly and smiled. Richard stared at her a moment longer, his gaze traveling up to Katie's moppy hair. It was a darkish, curly chestnut brown, like her mother's; she surely hadn't gotten it from him. Katie had inherited Michelle's eyes also, her irises the palest pearl-gray color he'd ever seen. But where had Michelle gotten them? Because neither George or Glee—

Richard started at the thought, nearly dropping his drink. Glee. That's why he was uneasy, apprehensive. Sure. Glee fucking Deadmond.

George sat down in his recliner and cleared his throat. "What do you think of this heat of ours?"

"It's a treat," said Richard. "Flurries are already flying in Maine."

"That right? Well, it'll be happening here eventually. Bad storms out west, I guess, heading this way. Big cold front. Warm air won't be around for long, I'm afraid."

"Really? I didn't hear."

"Not to worry," the old man went on. "Won't hit for a while. Yepper, some bad storms rolling in."

"Huh." Richard felt a foolish grin (*yepper; he still says yepper*) coming and he caught himself, straightening his crooked face. Wiping at his unshaven neck, he could feel the sweat roll down inside his shirt. He was still perspiring heavily, even in the cooled house. It was almost claustrophobic. All in tingling anticipation of Her Royal Highness, queen Glee . . .

Deadmond was out of his chair, tinkering at the bookcase with his back to them. He cleared his throat again. "Rich, did you get everything taken ca—" His sentence broke off midway, and he turned quick to look upon Katie. His eyes were strikingly red, and his lip trembled. "I just meant . . . we'll probably . . . " He looked away, toward his books. "Oh, forgive me," he murmured.

Richard set down his glass and got up, went and stood next to him. Putting a hand on the old man's shoulder, he struggled for his own words. "She's in the car, George," he said finally, softly. So terribly. "It's all been handled. She's home now." He felt him tense, felt the muscles go rigid beneath his grip. Then those shoulders sagged as if strength had abandoned him all at once. Deadmond turned to his son-in-law, face darkened, his eyes teary. He sniffed and adjusted his bifocals, mouthing the words again: Forgive me.

"Nothing to forgive," Richard said.

Katie meanwhile—who'd felt her father jerk a moment ago beside her, but had pretended she had not—glanced up at the whispering pair and asked George, "Could I use your bathroom, please?"

"Why, sure, little honey Kate. Come with me and I'll show you where it is, okay?" The old man took her by the hand, but hesitated. "Is that all right with you, son?" he said. Stung by the question, Richard nodded and watched them walk down the hall past the coat rack and up the Cornish staircase there at the end, leaving him by himself to listen to the rhythmic tick of the longcase grandfather. It was nearly 5:30 PM according to the clock, and would soon be a new moon by the look of it.

He perused the books in the case, briefly scanning their titles. There were some dusty World War II tomes below, most likely George's, and several of Glee's books on cooking and gardens—and where *was* she, anyhow? He saw volumes about ancient Egypt and the pharaohs, the construction of the pyramids and such, while the upper shelves were filled with political books, everything from Pat Buchanan to Arianna Huffington, William F. Buckley Jr. to Gore Vidal. One title caught Richard off guard and made him laugh aloud: *On Politics and the Art of Acting*, by the playwright Arthur Miller.

Richard peeked out the picture window and checked on the Blazer. He milled around the quiet living room, examining various items; knickknacks and whatnots, collected prudently and placed about with loving care over the decades. Miniature china dogs, a snowglobe of the Valley of the Kings. He saw gold trophies from Michelle's basketball tournaments and from her many outdoor varsity track and field meets, and lots of Waterford crystal pieces—some clear, some tinged in a rainforest-green hue—even a set of tumblers from the 1962 Seattle World's Fair.

The dichotomy of the room struck him: here it was, the year 2000, our long-awaited Millennium arrived, and yet here were so many old and outdated objects mixed in with the new.

He made his way to where a framed newsprint page hung upon the wall, over a desktop computer hutch. He squinted at its headlines, hearing the faint creak of movement on the floorboards above him. It was a sheet daily from Springfield, Illinois, a capital paper called *The State Journal-Register*. The article told of none other than one Mrs. Glee Deadmond, celebrated Blackwater Valley denizen and school board superintendent, her growing groundswell of support and her highly anticipated campaign push toward the Illinois General Assembly—

"Holy shit," Richard breathed. She was running for state representative now? The Illinois *Senate*? He'd never heard any of this before. But then he and Michelle's parents weren't exactly on chummy terms either—ever since he'd 'lured' their baby girl away to live a life certainly most unbecoming in southern Maine, of all places. Nobody forced Michelle to come with him. She decided that for herself, once he'd landed himself a decent New York literary agent and had decided to head for the East Coast to try and make a professional go at this writing thing. She'd even entertained ideas of becoming an author herself; she loved writing children's stories for Katie, didn't she? Even worked on the illustrations with her.

It was Michelle's own choice, when all was said and done. Ultimately she had wanted to get away as much as he. And they blamed him for what had happened, he knew they did.

He knew. Because he blamed himself for it, as well.

***

Katie sat in the silent bathroom, trying to go, in the same room where her mother had sat and gone when she herself was a little girl. She could smell the fragrant aroma of flowers even up here. She could feel the essence of her dead mother close to her, could almost sense the soft touch of her fingers caressing her hair. Katie closed her eyes and concentrated on the lingering scent. She closed her eyes tight, because others were here with her, as well.

They'd begun to gather, as they always did upon finding her, a host of stained, saddened figures, crowding in as close as they dared. Though their numbers were vast she was aware, thankfully, of only the closest, those who huddled in nearer than the rest, like so many gauzy moths to a flame.

She saw men and women here, young and old mingled alike—no discrimination among these torn wraiths and whatever had befallen them—dressed in strange, bygone clothing she'd never seen outside vintage pictures or old movies.

They had no solidity, moving more like vapor trying to congeal in the air. She saw a dripping teenage boy with what surely must've been a broken neck approach between their smoky limbs, his head lolling down in front of one shoulder at a horrible angle. The boy carried a cat in his arms, but there were gaping holes in his wretched form, holes she could see right through. None of the figures spoke, only watched her with empty, ruined sockets.

Katie caught the stink of sickness, of feverish flesh that hung about them, and damp earth. The ripe stench filled her nostrils, threatening to smother out her mother's sweet fragrance. So she closed her eyes and began to rock, fending off the frittles and fighting to hold on, to keep the flowery aroma alive in her mind.

She imagined herself in her own bathroom back home, hundreds of miles away from here. She could hear birds cheeping outside the window, could even see the wooden sign hanging on the back of their bathroom door. She focused hard and was able to read the words painted on it as if they were hovering before her:

Mom's Reminders

Brush your teeth . . .
wash your face,
Don't leave your clothes
all over the place.
Hang up your towel
and washcloth, too,
And please remember . . .
I love you!

Katie heard humming in the room somewhere, and

then she heard the echo of her mother's voice repeating something she'd told her many, many times at moments like this. *You don't have to be afraid of them, Katie-Smatie. They've only lost their way, is all. Don't be scared.* She felt a warm hand slipping itself into hers. *Can you remember that, when they come? My brave Katie milady . . . ?*

She smiled and opened her eyes. They were still there, of course, the stained and wretched ones, and two others had joined them. These new arrivals seemed different somehow, *fresh,* and wore clothes that were at least more familiar to her. It was a man and a woman holding a tiny bundle, and the odor of exhaust fumes rolled off them in dizzying waves as they drifted nearer. The sodden boy with the lollygag head stroked his calico cat, and she felt their innumerable gazes resting upon her, forsaken, bereft of life, all seeking the same thing.

Her smile faltered a bit, quivering, trying to collapse in on itself. She held it there on her round face, though, smiling and rocking as she tried to go, being as much of a *brave Katie milady* as she could now for her mother. She smiled and she rocked, trying to go and trying desperately not to cry, and concentrating on her faraway mother's faraway words.

They've only lost their way.

3

Richard took a sip of his pinkish drink and set the glass down, thinking he might have to use the bathroom himself soon; the acidic lemonade wasn't helping matters. He sighed and wandered through the front foyer area with its dark, heavy draperies on the walls, pausing to toy at the keys of Deadmond's hand-carved antique Kimball piano which squatted there. An envelope was taped to its side, and he noticed a small handwritten *C* upon it.

He could almost picture Michelle, seated on the wobbly bench, struggling to play the theme from *The Exorcist*, instead of practicing her classical music lessons like she was supposed to. On the other side of the foyer was the door to George's study, slightly ajar. Richard poked his head in and looked around. He pushed the door wide and stared in disbelief.

If the rest of the Deadmond home was nothing but neat and prim, this room was utter chaos by comparison. The large study had been choked off with cardboard boxes, their bulk crammed against the walls and flowing outwardly into the center of the cherry flooring. Even a long leather sofa was littered with them. Mahogany tables and two desks, a big one and a mid-sized one, were heaping with piles of paperwork, old mail, and newspapers.

A tall floor lamp, with its shade missing, illuminated the mess, and a 12-inch LCD screen TV was on and sitting muted atop the cluttered smaller desk. On one wall hung a giant world map, while a display case adorned the wall opposite, containing an autographed Sammy Sosa All-Star baseball bat. He grinned at this—poor Georgie and his Chicago Cubs, keeping the faith for his beloved team all these long, interminably endless years.

There were bookcases in here, too, and Richard was surprised to see his own first novel, *Malignant Regions*, mixed in with the other texts. The book was a highly fictionalized account of his wife's battle with leukemia, and although the critics had been kind to him, sales never really launched into the stratosphere as he'd hoped. It wasn't the debut piece he intended, but he had felt compelled to write it at the time because of Michelle's dire condition. Still, he did snag a two-book deal from it; now he could return to those original ideas he'd scrapped earlier on and work at what he wanted. He wondered which one of the Deadmonds had acquired it, and what they thought of his prose. Richard could only imagine, and none of what he imagined was good. After all, the young woman in the story ended up living through her ordeal, didn't she? So much for fairytale bullshit endings.

Richard spotted something above the big desk and moved in for a look, pushing a scuffed leather armchair off to one side. It was an old fireman's helmet propped on a hook—half melted and twisted terribly, the metal eagle's head and the number 20 on its crown so fused and burnt black they were barely recognizable—a relic of George Deadmond's firefighter days and the inferno that almost blotted him from the earth. As Richard recalled, the old man went on battling blazes for many years, even after that close call had occurred. George was a fireman at his core, Richard surmised, just like his dad before him, who laid now under an imported stone of Dutch, pelican-gray granite, sleeping with the other dreaming dead somewhere out in Calvary Cemetery's manicured grounds.

The smell of flowers permeated this room also, though no plants could be seen. No candles or air fresheners, not a single Glade plug-in. He turned and considered the hodgepodge, taking in the entire depth and disarrayed scope of it. Then Richard froze. On the small television screen he saw the flickering images of that road collapse outside of town. The sinkhole site where he could've sworn—

"Rich?" It was George, peering around the door at him, and Richard sucked his breath in. "We're downstairs again. Katie Jane's in the living room." Deadmond glanced curiously about the study, looking embarrassed. "Thought you'd want to know. Is there something you needed, son?"

Richard felt the embarrassment also, and his ears reddened. "Sorry, didn't mean to come in here but . . . on the TV . . . " He pointed, and the old man stared. "I wanted to see this for a second. Do you mind?"

"Oh, no. Sure. Go ahead. I was watching this, as a matter of fact, when you knocked at the front door." Deadmond had begun to search for the remote, appeared confused, lifting his bifocals to the top of his balding head. Richard glanced around and found it first, handing it to him.

"Really? We passed it, George."

"What?"

Richard nodded. "Katie and I, we drove right by this thing on our way into town today. Near the bypass. I saw something strange out there, George. It looked . . . " He hesitated, his brow creasing. "Hold on." He ducked back through the foyer and across to the living room, peeking in at his daughter. "Hey, how you doing, babe? Everything okay?"

Katie was seated on the floral sofa once more, holding her glass of pink lemonade. "Yes." She rocked slightly, he noticed. "Can I have my coloring book and crayons, Daddy?" she said. "The special book?"

"Uh, sure. I'll go out and get them for you in a minute, okay Katie-Smatie?"

"Yes, all right."

Richard blew her a kiss. "Be right there. Promise." He walked back into George's study. The television sound was on now, a woman reporter speaking. He could see that blue swimming pool tarp as it billowed and flapped behind her, wanting to tear loose of its moorings and ascend upon the wind. "What is it, an old graveyard they uncovered or something?"

"Hmm? Oh, I think not. Why do you say that?"

Richard watched the screen closely as he spoke. "I'm pretty sure I saw human remains down in that hole, George. In fact I'm positive. There were a lot of bones, even some skulls." He chewed at the tender inside lining of his cheek.

"Did Katie see it, too?"

"No. I tried to keep her occupied, keep her looking away."

"Good, good." The old man nodded. "Well, this reporter here seems to think that, what you just said. That it might be a disused cemetery of some kind that got plowed under and asphaulted over. Indian burial ground, perhaps. Or maybe that's what she's hearing at the scene, I don't know. She's not from around here by the looks of her, and neither are most of the policemen you see in the background. Out-of-towners. But no, I don't think that's what they've found at all."

Richard stared at him. "What else could it be?"

"Do you remember what the name of this town used to be, son? Back when it was founded?"

"Before it was Blackwater Valley? Hang on, I should know this." He strained his brain a moment. "Wasn't it called Shaw Valley? Yeah. After Augustus Shaw, one of the first settlers. Built his big creepy house in the woods overlooking town, right? The name got changed later on, though, at some point."

"That's right. Now, do you know why it was renamed Blackwater Valley?"

"Uh, I don't think so." Richard felt as though he'd learned all of this at one time. "I assumed it was because the town's on the river, or from it being part of the Rock River Valley. Something along those lines." He suddenly felt foolish.

Deadmond took the eyeglasses from his head and began cleaning them with his shirttail. "Well, the original village of Shaw Valley was platted in 1829, and thrived almost immediately. But in 1832, the year of the so-called Black Hawk War, malaria struck the township's settlers. Devastated them. A bad strain, too: raging fever, blood in their urine, massive destruction of the red blood cells. Malaria was also known as 'blackwater fever' in those days. The old-timers didn't know what was happening to them, I think. They got sick and started dying off, didn't know how to stop it. They thought they were cursed."

"Cursed? From malaria?"

"The war against the Sauk Indians had turned into nothing but a massacre, and they knew it. Most of them knew, so they reckoned they'd been cursed. People were dropping like flies, and it spread fast— men, women, the children. They probably panicked. It's said that Augustus Shaw's brains cooked inside his skull from fever, up at that house of his. He survived it, but most of his family didn't. All accounts, he was never the same after that. By 1835 more than half of the village was gone. The area was already being referred to as Blackwater Valley throughout the region, and the name eventually stuck, to everyone's chagrin."

"So the town was named after the disease that decimated it," Richard echoed. He remembered this story now, remembered it from his school days here. Then something dawned on him. "Wait a sec . . . didn't Michelle do a paper once on Chief Black Hawk or something? Sure! In high school, wasn't it?"

"You got it. I helped her with it, too." Deadmond tried to smile, but couldn't quite manage. "Chelle and I, yes," he murmured, the broken thought trailing off as he caught himself, cleared his throat and continued. "Anyone who was sick, or even suspected of being sick, they were rounded up here in the Val. Pious old Augustus Shaw himself led the charge on that, I guess, during the frenzy. Though I've read he was probably certifiable by then, a genuine raving lunatic. People were rounded up just the same. They didn't know what was happening to them, see?" The old man sniffed, placed his bifocals on his face. "At the height of it, they started throwing bodies into mass graves, and not all of them were dead yet either. A lot of people were buried still alive, Rich."

He stared at his son-in-law, eyes rimmed in red, looking again as if he'd aged a decade over the telling of this tale. After a few moments he glanced back to the television screen.

"No, that's not a cemetery they found out there," said George Deadmond with quiet certainty. "It's a *plague pit*, son. I'd bet anything on it. And there's lots more of them around here, you know? Has to be. Yepper, this whole damned town is built right on top of them."

"THEY POISON THE HEART"

by Michelle Brooke Deadmond

(an excerpt)

This is how it was, the mud and the rivers running red with the blood of the innocents, their many death screams filling the air. This is what it had come to, but it all needn't have been.

In 1832, after being cheated repeatedly on promised land deals and erroneous settlements, Black Sparrow Hawk led the remainder of his people—by now starving and sick, at least half of them women and children—out of Iowa and crossed the Mississippi River one last time back into the Illinois prairie lands. Lands which had been taken unjustly, the land of his ancestors. Together, these dying bedraggled few would be hunted relentlessly and yet would continue to elude capture for several months, until meeting their tragic end. Before that, came the

~~ Prelude ~~

The scandalous treaty in question was struck in the year 1804 and dictated that the Sauk American Indian tribe vacate their land when eventually it sold, which it did a quarter of a century later in 1829. One of the stipulations concerning their move was that the tribe be given enough maize to get them through that first winter, but the government did not honor its promises; the Indians were forced to comply, to leave their Illinois side and be pushed westward across the river into those unorganized territories known today as Iowa, having little say against the overwhelming military might shown. But an old Sauk warrior called Ma-ka-tai-me-she-kia-kiak (translated as "Be a large black hawk") disputed the validity of the original treaty, saying the full tribal councils had not been consulted in 1804, would in fact have never given their authorization for such a ridiculously one-sided deal. A decorated veteran of the War of 1812, in which he fought alongside the British in their campaigns against the invading white Americans, Black Hawk as he was simply known was not a hereditary tribal leader but rather an appointed war chief. Angered by the loss of his birthplace, met with famine and the hostile Sioux to the west and believing the entire land-ceding treaty was fraudulent to begin with, the aging Indian warrior captained a band of around 1,200 followers back over to the east side of the Mississippi River in the spring of 1831—to reclaim their native heritage.

What they found was the Illinois heartland in ruins, former fields of corn trampled by cattle, the plains fenced off by settlers. All was lost, everything they'd ever known, the sacred places wherein their hearts still resided. Gone.

This untimely invasion caused a panic among the squatters there, and the Indians were driven back across the river's currents without real incident and with very little bloodshed to speak of. Within four short months, however, the Sauk band and their families were back, in desperate hopes of reoccupying their old lands. They were said to have killed a few dozen Menominee Indians this time, their sworn hereditary enemy, and panic-stricken white settlers began imploring the government for help. Again, the dogged band was persuaded west without much bloodshed. But in April of 1832, faced with an aching starvation in their bellies and led by 65-year-old Chief Black Hawk, the Sauk Indians crossed the Mississippi once more and moved into their ancient tribal territories along the Rock River. The Governor of Illinois saw these entries into the state as a military invasion—even though it was widely noted that no American Indian tribe in history had ever gone on the warpath taking their women, children, and elders along with them.

The band of Sauk, now down to well under a thousand, made camp overnight at what is present-day Blackwater Valley. Their mood was upbeat and content as they talked long into the night and shared tales of former glory around the fires. At sunrise they struck out north and headed upriver, following the gentle promise of the haunted, shimmering Rock. Unbeknownst to them, their days were irrevocably numbered by this point, for an order of 'extermination' had already been sent from the Governor's office to the Secretary of War . . .

CHAPTER FIVE

I

NOT WANTING TO leave his daughter alone for too long, Richard headed down the hall. How in hell had he forgotten the history and facts about his own hometown like that? Jesus, he used to know them . . . was *supposed* to know them. And Michelle's high school term paper—how had *that* slipped his 'writerly mind'? It was almost as if a pall covered him, shrouding over his memories once he had left this place, and now that he was back the shroud was falling away . . . the pall lifting.

He supposed it was true then, Thomas Wolfe's immortal words, published posthumously of course: You really couldn't go home again, not without displacement like this, without that feeling of having lost something, something which can never be fully retrieved.

In actuality it was not all that surprising. He supposed he'd always wished to forget this place, and now he had. Literally. Selective bits, at least.

Richard brought in Katie's pastel crayons and her special activity book, the one she and her mother had worked on together during Michelle's illness, and sat watching with George as she spread her things out neatly and began coloring on the living room floor.

The old man could not hide the pleasure he now felt, the simple delight at being able to observe her this way. "What are your plans tonight, Rich? Have you two eaten yet?" His eyes didn't leave Katelyn as she scribbled, nor did the smile ever leave his face.

"We'll probably just grab something somewhere," said Richard. "I never figured . . . well, we didn't want to get in the way." The rapt gaze was broken and he looked up; the old man's disappointment was apparent when he did. "Didn't want to put anybody out." It was a lame-ass excuse, Richard knew, but he wanted to get clear of here before it got dark, before she—

Richard sighed, rubbing at one temple. He felt a headache coming on, and there was no need for it. No need for ducking and running like this. Trying to avoid what was to come. He was a grown man, for God's sake. A *widower*. "Why, what'd you have in mind?" he said.

George thought on it: "Oh, I was going to suggest Dom's or CeeCee's, is all. Pretty decent Italian food. The Piccadilly Restaurant is only right down the hill here. Or there's always my freezer in the basement, full of beef burger and steaks, and the backyard grill."

Katie sat up, mildly interested. "Cheeseburgers?"

Richard and George both laughed, and Katie grinned at having done something entertaining. She belly flopped back down and resumed her coloring. "Can we do it tomorrow maybe?" Richard said. "Got a motel room for us earlier, here in town. All our stuff is already there." He massaged his temple, trying to break up the oncoming throb. The oncoming Bitch—

oh yeah, it was coming all right, and she was gonna be a Bitch. He could already tell. "Plus I've got this headache, from the drive."

George nodded, sensing his son-in-law's discomfort. "Sure, Rich. That would be fine." He shifted his feet, stared down at them. "Give me time to get everything ready, anyway."

"I see you have a celebrity in your midst," said Richard, trying to get off this subject and quick.

"Hmm?"

Richard gestured toward the framed article on the wall. "Glee's a superintendent now, and running for Senate? When did all this come about?"

"Oh." The old man chuckled, whisking invisible lint from the thighs of his pants. "*That.* All happened out of the blue, that. Funny, actually. She was on the school board one minute—you knew that, right?—then the next they're selecting her to fill the district superintendent position. Hired her over a couple other hopefuls; locals, I guess, trying to move up. Anyhow, earlier this year she gets interested in taking the Senate run. Attended a few 'Meet the Candidate' deals first, and all of the people seemed to love her, support her ideas and everything. And *bango*, that was it. Funny." Another chuckle. "She has her own show now."

"What?" *Own show?*

"On television. It's a weekly broadcast shot right inside the church. Small local show, no sets. But there she is, coming right into people's living rooms and bedrooms every week. It's really remarkable." George sounded proud, but the very notion made Richard cringe. Christ . . .

"Wow, that really is." *Church?* "Remarkable, I

78

mean." Oh brother, had he suffered a stroke or something? Such banter issuing forth . . . college educated and all. He needed a fix for the headache, he realized. It was already accelerating, getting worse. A tumor perhaps? Ah yes, wouldn't that be perfect.

"I can get you something, son. Tylenol, or we have Advil?"

Throwing bricks into the Grand Canyon, he couldn't help thinking with a trace of humor. The moon phase grandfather clock was striking six, and Richard took this as his cue to stand up. "That's okay, don't worry about it," he said with a dismissive wave. "We're both pretty beat, so we should probably—"

Just then came a noise, a single loud sound from outside the house towards the back somewhere, muffled, and now it was George's turn to come to his feet. "Oh my gosh," he exclaimed, jumping up. "I completely forgot!" With that the old man was off and running, through the swinging door leading to the kitchen; Richard caught a glimpse of the bird's-eye maple cabinets on the other side as the door swung back and forth in his wake.

And there went my chance, he thought as he watched him go.

2

Ms. Cassie Patrick had never remarried after her husband's death, had never felt the need to.

Her bees were her life. No room for anything else, she supposed. Her husband Lawrence had left her disillusioned and twenty-five thousand dollars in debt when he shuffled off this mortal existence, and who in heck needed any more of *that*? No. The honeybees would do nicely, thank you. Bees didn't send you tumbling headlong into bankruptcy court.

Cassie stood in her sloping yard, looking off to the west, her hair covered with a brightly colored bandana. Her worker bees weren't back yet; the hives were virtually empty. Soon it would be getting dark. She rounded one corner and walked alongside the length of her home, surveying the upright, rectangular boxes on wooden legs, there in a row. No drones were zipping about, no steady buzz greeted her. Where could they be this late? Yes, it was warm for this time of year, but still—

She'd been able to keep the house (quite lucky for her) in the bankruptcy deal, keep her business running out of here and keep her head above water permanently after that—she had retired from the hospital as soon as she was able in order to concentrate full-time on her bees and her honey-harvesting operation. Cassie liked it here, and people genuinely liked her, too. The Blackwater Valley town council, upon learning of her plight, had even gone about legally changing the name of this dirt road she lived on to the Honey Run Road, to help out her cause and send new business her way. So, this place had become her refuge, a port in the storm of her widowhood. She felt blessed indeed, at times.

Yet the bees were her biggest delight. She hadn't purchased them, but rather had acquired them in exchange for barter goods; it was long held around these parts that purchased bees would never prosper, and therefore neither would *she* prosper or her

Honeycomb Haven. Old superstitions died hard out here in the sticks.

But prosper she did, and the good luck was due to the honeybees, she believed.

When one of her younger sisters got married, Cassie Patrick placed a piece of wedding cake outside each of the rectangular box-hives for them to enjoy. So the prosperity would continue unbroken, and so that her sister's marriage would in turn prosper also.

Sales of her pure bottled honey went through the roof. Likewise, Cassie's homemade cross necklaces and keychains that she fashioned out of Capewell horseshoe nails and twisted copper wire soon became the must-have keepsakes of the region, popular with the blue-collar set, patriotic veterans, and Christian crusaders of every shape and ilk.

She was aided by the revelation that locally grown honey was being touted as an allergen-resistance builder and for its many healing properties—on and on the good luck went, it seemed.

When she mourned her own husband's death (miserable, unreliable S.O.B. that he was), the bees had mourned along with her. She had draped all the wooden hives with black crepe for veils, lifting these only after Good-Time Larry's burial to share sweets with them, and other foods brought to the funeral feast. Such were the ways of rural folk.

Now, though, something was amiss. The workers should've been back from their pollination and nectar gathering, but weren't. There was hardly any activity at all around the movable frame hives, in fact, no sign of drones or anything else in flight. This wasn't right. Summer was over. It was creeping inevitably on toward autumn: soon she would have to start treating the hives with powdered sugar, getting them ready for winter. The bees' excursions should be dwindling, and they should be keeping closer to home, not venturing farther away.

She wondered briefly if it had anything to do with the new ethanol plant out on Honey Run, that monstrosity which everyone living around here had fought so hard against. Or if not, what else might've occurred. Something to do with the queens? Had the broods swarmed, taken enough honey surpluses for their exodus and then skipped out on her, to start anew and build their golden colonies someplace else? This time of the season, so late in the year? Cassie bit at her lower lip. She continued to stand in her yard and look to the orange-and-red streaked horizon, like a worried mother waiting for her errant children to return home.

3

He liked the way she screamed, he had to admit—it gave him pleasure. He liked the feel of driving himself into her, the tightness as he worked his flesh into hers from behind, even after all these years. Enjoyed the sound his hips made grinding and slapping against her firm ass this way, the way she screamed out his name like he was physically hurting her.

Yes, Jack Lawrie liked pouring the coals to his wife Lorraine.

That's what they used to call it when he was still in the Navy: you poured the coals into the engine of a locomotive or a fine steamship back in the storied glory days, to get it to respond how you wanted, to ensure peak speed and performance. And so, too, you poured the coals to a fine woman when you were fucking her, for those very same reasons. The retired admiral held the perfectly shaped hips before him and pumped away, pushing his wife from her doggie-style position until she was facedown on the bed, pinning her flat among the tangle of covers and keeping her there as he continued to rock and grunt and to drip sweat all over her back.

Ohh, my sweet Rainey's back . . .

She had tattoos—Celtic knot bands around her right bicep and right ankle, and an image of rosary beads which lazily encircled her neck and draped serpentine down her spine—and *holy* Melba toast, how sexy he found them. Lawrie traced his fingertip along the pattern, keeping the rhythm of his thrusts smooth and hard and steady, traced the scrolling thorny rose vines which entwined the rosary beads themselves, on down to the ornate, double-barred Caravaca cross, tattooed right at the small of her back. He felt himself grow larger and he trembled, the familiar tingle in his sagging scrotum rising up into his abdomen; Lorraine's muffled screams became one long satisfied moan as she felt the pulsing of his cock quicken. "Jesus *fuck* . . . " she cried out, then whispered something inaudible.

She was fifty-nine years old, and still in magnificent shape for that age. From behind (his favorite way of taking her, no great surprise) she could've passed easily for a woman half that. He loved the blond streaks running through her dark hair, the beauty mark at one corner of her mouth. Loved her taut dark skin, too—the way those inked black and gray tattoos resembled shiny living shadows rippling upon that velvet skin. Lawrie reached and pulled her hair absently, listening to the squeal as she responded. He knew his wife bore the cross as a proud sign of her Latina heritage, and she also had a dragonfly (of all loopy things) tattooed on her left tit just above the nipple, but what was it with the Irish design knots? *Where the hell did* that *come from?* he wondered.

The sun's dying rays were streaming in through the bedroom window, and a breeze stirred the curtains. Lawrie took hold of both her arms now, raised up and wrenched them back roughly. He pumped as hard as he was able, hammering his engorged flesh home, wheezing obscene words into her hair. Time to finish this. She was screaming again, the way he liked. He watched her head turn slowly, heard the scream become quite prevalent with this rotating motion: the neighbors must really be enjoying it, he thought, shuddering in his own personal ecstasy, his eyes locked on that glistening tattoo and the droplets of their intermingled sweat rolling straight down the cleft of her ass—

"Oh my God, it's *huge!*" Lorraine gasped, straining to look back at him over her shoulder, and that was it.

He was on the edge of ejaculating, teetering there, helpless, then it was gone. *Lost it.* Jesus *fuck*, is right. How many others had she said that very same thing to? he'd wondered abruptly, for a split second. How many different men, over the long and rocky course of their marriage? And that's all she wrote. He was done, put a fork in him, as sure as if a shit-crippling leg cramp had struck him boltlike from above.

Rainey had her appetites, yes, she always had.

Lawrie was only a handful of years older than her, and God knew *he* wasn't able to fulfill them, but all of the men she'd paraded in and out of this luxurious bedroom, in and out of cheap motel rooms, just plain *in and out*, endlessly, and him the whole time never speaking a word . . .

Because he loved his wife so goddamned much. Loved that shaved paradise between her legs.

"Jack? Sweetie?" she was saying to him. "What's wrong?" She reached a hand back, patted his thigh gently. "It's all right, babe. It doesn't—" He flung the hand away and rolled off her, swearing under his breath. Lorraine sighed, tossing back her mussed hair. She found her black high heels where she'd kicked them off beside the bed, slipped them back on, and slunk naked and oh so slyly away from him. Knowing that he watched, she ran the fingers of one hand up the back of her leg as she moved, teasing them over the moist crack above and up to the tattooed cross in the slickened small of her back. Glancing at him, she continued walking coy and catlike and disappeared inside the master bath, closing the door behind her with a seductive, tinkling little laugh.

Christ on a quarterdeck, thought Lawrie, winded, slumping on the edge of the bed. Incredible. Pouring the coals to his wife's scrumptious ass one minute, but *good*, and then this humiliation the next. He couldn't believe it. Holding his shock white-haired head in both hands, he stared at the floor. She had just returned from her sister's place in Peoria, and he'd practically been on her when she came through the front door, undressing her and manhandling her the way she liked—and now thinking on it, how many cocks did she guide into her from behind while away on that weeklong visit, as she had just done with him? Precisely how huge were *they*?

The phone on the nightstand began to ring, in the middle of his quiet master bedroom here in the middle of his elegant, 4,000-square-foot English Tudor-style house at 711 Lantern Court. He listened to the ringing and he listened to the water running in the bathroom, and finally Lawrie stretched reluctantly and picked up the receiver. He said hello and listened for a time to what was being told to him, his brow creasing into a curious frown. At some length he said goodbye and replaced the receiver, then sat gazing out the curtained window. He lay back against the pillows and clasped his hands behind his head, naked except for a tarnished wedding ring, his erection long gone. Inhaling and exhaling, controlling his breathing, he could hear the water inside the master bath and beneath that, the lilting sound of his wife humming wordlessly.

Admiral Jackson Lawrie stared in silence at the closed bathroom door and thought: *My sweet Rainey's back.*

4

For a moment Richard thought he was dreaming. He heard the back door slam, heard a wild scrabbling noise across the kitchen tiles and then the swinging door before him crashed open—and in came an old friend.

The German shepherd bounded into the room and stopped dead as his heart leapt in surprise. At first the aging dog had no recollection whatsoever in its eyes, hesitated with a strange look and with the rumblings of a growl beginning somewhere deep in its throat. Rich glanced quickly to Katie, who had sat up straight, and he felt a cold hand reaching for him in that second. But he needn't have worried, because he saw recognition flood into the dog's intelligent face as if a dam had burst.

"Blondie!" he couldn't help exclaiming, in a voice higher than usual. The large shepherd raced excitedly to him, her ears flat and tail swooshing, her entire hind end wagging and whipping, and Richard dropped to the floor in his own excitement to greet her. He tousled her and stroked her and tried hugging her, but it was impossible the way she danced around him in circles. She was older and much slower now, her muzzle peppered with silver hair and her eyes grown cloudy and dim, but she brought with her into the room that same joy he'd always remembered.

Michelle had named her after the Debbie Harry '70s band, and he knew she had to be about ten years old. They'd decided to leave the dog behind when they moved from here, mostly because of Michelle's guilt over their departure—another footnote that had slipped him until just now.

George Deadmond walked into the living room, breathing hard. "I almost forgot her out there," he said, "until I heard a bark. Can you believe that?" He shook his head, and Richard thought: *Join the club, pops. Yepper* . . .

Katie was on her feet and drawing near, unable to keep her young eyes from waxing like two full moons. "Whose is it, Daddy? Can I pet him?" Yes, two pearly summer moons, beaming above an upturned crescent moon of a grin . . . moon faced, she was.

"It's a she, hon," Richard said. "This is Blondie, and Blondie is a she." He still couldn't believe that the German shepherd remembered him after nearly eight whole years. "Sure, come and pet her." Katie ran her fingers through the animal's fur, stroking, caressing her black-and-tan coat. Her eyes seemed to grow even bigger, if that were possible. Richard felt the pulsing in his skull ease a bit, the ache growing a tad duller, drawing itself down—but then such was the power of canines.

"Blondie," repeated Katie, her voice a whisper. The dog panted and lay on her side to be indulged some more. "Blondie is a *she.*" Soon her silvered belly was exposed so the young girl could stroke there as well. Richard slid out of their way, stood up and moved to where George was lingering with his hands in his pockets.

"How has she been?"

"Hmm? Oh, she's okay. Not brilliant, but okay." Deadmond nodded. "Got some arthritis, you know. And her hips are going. But whose isn't, right?"

"Right." Richard stifled an urge to laugh. But it wasn't really funny—the deterioration and pain of old age was waiting for each of us; he'd felt the stiffness himself just a moment ago, while getting up off the floor. Our pets arrived there faster than we did, unfortunately. So he chose not to laugh. He instead felt a touch of pity as he watched the shepherd, and he swallowed back a rising regret. It would've been nice to have her in Maine with them, nice for Michelle to have had her, once she became ill. But who could've foreseen such things . . . who could have predicted a sorrowful outcome such as this? Not in a million years would he ever have imagined anything as terrible as this.

George sat back down, and Richard followed suit and did the same. "I can't tell you what a comfort it's been, having her here these last few years," said the old man, as if picking up on his son-in-law's thoughts. "She's been a blessing to us. Glee used to say so, used to say as much, all the time."

In lieu of the daughter I took, Richard's mind sprang up. *That's what you mean, right?* He closed his eyes, letting the implications of it sink in. *That is why she left her here, exactly why—knowing things then only she could know.*

When he opened them again he saw Katelyn standing side-by-side with the animal, one tiny hand on Blondie's back. The dog glanced down the long hallway toward the staircase and let out a low whimper. "It's okay," Katie bent and told her. "Come on, girl." The shepherd padded over to Richard and nuzzled his arm, tail wagging, pushing her head deep under that arm. He played with her whiskers the way he used to, tickling her face, and she appeared to draw her lips back into a smile. Katie rejoined him on the sofa as Blondie sneezed tremendously. Katie laughed out loud, clapping both hands to her cheeks.

"Oh no!" said Richard, leaning forward to rub the dog's muzzle all over, trying to negate the tickle. "I'm sorry, pup. Come here." Her tail swooshed and she pranced, pawing at him, and Richard could not help but grin. The dog's happiness was contagious. Soon though, she was staring cautiously down the corridor again. She blinked once, twice.

Katie held one finger in a *shhh* signal. "Okay, pretty girl," she repeated, and this time Richard stared at his daughter. Blondie took this as her cue to hop up onto the sofa, right between them. She curled in a slow circle and plopped down with a grunt, her head on Rich's lap, who looked to Deadmond quickly.

"It's all right," came George's response. "She's got run of the place, pretty much. Always has. House isn't really a home without a big dog in it, right? I like to think so anyway." He took a long drink. "Remember the blizzard when she got into those damned coleus plants in here, had that horrible reaction to them? And you rushed her to the emergency vet clinic? You saved her life that winter night."

Richard nodded, scratching the ruff around the dog's neck, while Katie patted her crooked hind leg gently. He did actually; funny how he could remember *that*. George finished his lemonade and set the glass down, clearing his throat.

"Tom Truitt's out again," said Deadmond. He paused. "Released him early, I guess. Did you know?"

"I did. He contacted me awhile ago, well, tried to at least. I kept missing his calls. But yeah, I heard." Missed his calls. Truth was he let the answering machine get every one of those messages, then never called him back. Richard had been occupied with caring for Michelle, and wasn't about to be deterred from that for anything. Even though Tommy Truitt and he had been the best of friends, once upon a distant time.

"That so?" George said. "Huh. Got himself a job doing construction, remodeling houses around town. Some landscaping. He's living down at the end of

Telegraph Road now, near the old abandoned Sunset Drive-In." Another pause. "You two used to be pretty close, didn't you, Rich?" When his son-in-law nodded, he asked him earnestly: "What happened?"

Richard sighed. "Oh, you know. Just things. We drifted our own ways. He went his, I went mine." There was sadness in his voice, and Deadmond cleared his throat again. Richard sat up straight. "Life happened, I guess you'd say."

"Yes. Yes, it has a way of doing that sometimes."

But Richard did not feel like getting into this, didn't really want to rehash how Tommy and he'd done nothing but drink and party their youth away, or how Richard had grown out of the behavior while Thomas had continued in it, spiraling ever downward until eventually he wound up in prison. For what was it again—burglary and drug dealing? Selling speed? Yeah, that was it. Rich used to write Tommy often back in those days, and send along copies of every article and short story he managed to get published, in order to keep him going behind those bars. Keep the contact going. Especially after Tom's young fiancée died while he was still on the inside that first time, serving his initial sentence. *What was her name now? Oh, good grief.*

Instead he asked Deadmond about the Illinois Senate, about the whole campaign bid again. The old man told him it was actually the upper chamber of the Illinois General Assembly—who knew?—and how the election wouldn't be held until 2002. Even so, he went on about how busy Glee had been keeping herself, serving on the Children's & Senior Services Advisory Council, and on various other healthcare and education boards, touting any humanitarian cause she could find along the way in the interim—

Hawaiian girl, wasn't she? Of course. Tommy's beautiful, mocha-skinned fiancée from Hawaii. Yes. And her name . . .

—how she'd filed all the necessary papers, really had her ducks in a row this time, had gathered more than enough signatures and had submitted her certified petition to the Secretary of State. With that, *viola*, she was officially in the running. Simple, really.

. . . was it Kalani? Kaleho? No, Kyoko, that was it! Her name was Kyoko.

Richard remembered now, because her name had been in all the papers Thanksgiving of that year. *"Terrible business with that Kyoko girl,"* the neighbors had whispered to one another in their hushed tones, in driveways and behind hedgerows and across slat fences that miserable, rain-drenched November. *"Have you heard the latest? Just terrible. So young, so pretty."* Because her nude body had been found in a field, raped and beaten to death, at Ogletree where she was staying with her recently divorced mother, lying face-up amongst bits of cornstalk debris with the freezing rain filling her open mouth and vagina and eyes. *"Have you heard? It was revenge of some kind, all because she got mixed in with that drug-dealing, jailhouse trash she was engaged to. Terrible business. And so, so very young."*

It had been hinted at, yes, that her connection to Thomas Truitt had cost the girl her life, that she'd been killed by someone with a grudge to bear, some associate of Tommy's in one of his many nefarious dealings. Nothing had ever been proven, however.

Truitt was never the same man again, once he got out of the slammer. He withdrew from everyone, Rich included, and became a virtual ghost after that, haunting the Val's streets.

The names of two men eventually came up as 'persons of interest' in Kyoko's murder investigation, but it all led nowhere in the end. Richard lost track of him after the move to Maine, and never really made an honest effort to reconnect. Much later he learned that Tommy had gone back inside a second time, this time, for some foolish penny ante parole violation or other. Too penny ante to even recall, he supposed now, since he could not remember what it'd been. Something quite curious had occurred, though.

Those two suspects interrogated in the Hawaiian girl's death—gang banger wannabes the both, with rap sheets as long as one's arm—turned up dead themselves in that same sleepy community of Ogletree, their bodies (or what was left of them) segmented and strewn in butcher-shop-floor fashion all up and down some railroad tracks, severed limbs and spilled organs flung, heads decapitated as they lay next to each other pointed in different directions across the ties.

A local school bus driver, "Big" Minnie Dean, discovered them at dawn along her route, where supposedly the pair had wandered out onto the tracks in the middle of the night, laid down together, and then had either fallen asleep or passed out right there until a train ambled by and took care of the rest, leaving the stink of scorched iron and rending in its wake. *Both of them.* Yes, curious indeed.

Now Tommy Truitt was out again. Hmm. Maybe Richard would amble by his place tomorrow or the day after and ask him about it, ask him what he'd been wondering for some time, what everyone in this vicinity was, in fact, probably wondering—*How's it hanging, Tom? Oh yeah, hey, by the way, did you have your fiancée's killers sliced and diced while you were on the inside? How'd you arrange it? How in the* fuck *did you pull that one off, Tommy?* Yes, maybe he'd just amble on by, like that train had—

Or not.

Deadmond asked him if he was still writing, adding how much he'd enjoyed his first book. Richard considered asking how Glee had liked it, but thought better of it ultimately.

Blondie stretched with a groan and thunked one heavy forepaw across his leg, and all at once her ears twitched hard and her head jerked around on his lap. Then she was down from between them and at attention on the carpet, gazing strangely. Only this time Richard could've sworn he'd heard something, too: the echo of a sobbing voice, barely audible, wafting along the hall toward them from somewhere beyond the coat rack—a soft, weeping child's sigh that almost sounded like something else for a moment.

George was still talking; Katie sat staring straight ahead. The German shepherd and he exchanged nervous looks, and Blondie backed away over to where George sat, even as Richard felt his scalp begin to prickle. Because the phantom sob just then had sounded like words of some kind, God help him, and the words seemed to have said something very clearly.

5

Alice Granberg closed up the Styx & Stonze Botanicals shop for her boss and headed home for the evening. It'd been a slow day indeed, hardly any business to speak of. Mrs. Van Meers, the owner, had pulled out shortly after noon herself, leaving Alice to handle things alone. This serious lack of customers just lately had, in reality, been going on for some time now. As she began walking, Alice glanced up from the sidewalk and laughed at what she saw—WE HAVE GAZING BALLS!—the sign in the shop window which never failed to make her smile.

Alice made her way through town on foot, the same way she came, oversized sunglasses perched on the brim of the floppy sun hat she wore to work that morning. She was a delicate, willowy young person, with collarbones that jutted like ivory carvings against her porcelain-white cliffside of chest. Bright auburn hair fell in a silky cascade over her freckle-flecked shoulders.

She hugged herself as she walked, as the deepening dusk turned cooler around her; she probably should've brought a wrap instead of the stupid summer hat. When she arrived home, with teeth chattering, some ten minutes later, at the Regan Street apartment, Alice's lesbian lover Syd Cholke was there to greet her apprehensively at the door. Sydney kissed her cold lips, led her inside and closed the door. Then she had no choice but to inform her of the bad news, starting off with the old standby *I don't know how to tell you this, but* line, that Alice's pair of peach-faced lovebirds had gone berserk and tried to escape, shortly after Syd had gotten home. Both of them had flung themselves repeatedly in a wild, screeching frenzy against their wire cage bars, for no apparent reason. She couldn't get them to stop. The male bird had perished outright, the female succumbing and dying breathless a bit later from its self-inflicted wounds. Sydney went on to tell how she hadn't wanted to bother Alice at work and ruin the latter part of her day, since nothing more could've been done. How instead she'd sat in the kitchen and smoked cigarette after cigarette in sick dread of this conversation they were having.

Alice listened, and became colder, until the sensation seemed to permeate her very bones and her teeth clattered uncontrollably. When she started to blubber, her sturdy lover picked up an *Addams Family* collectible glass from an end table coaster and threw water in her face, knocking the floppy hat and sunglasses off her head. Syd consoled and held her until the shaking stopped, kissing her deeply and massaging one small sprout of a breast until she had her jag under control.

All at once Syd realized she could use this, use Alice's loss to her own advantage, get her to try things she normally might never consider in this dazed, vulnerable state. The special bureau drawer, filled with sex toys and lubes, awaited in their bedroom, didn't it? Maybe, figured Syd, petite little Alice might just go for the strap-on tonight—not a standard size model but the *big* boy—a favorite of Syd's to use on her tiny younger partners, especially after oral when they were good and primed and ready for it. If they could take it, that is. The one so big it came with its own zip code, the one her beautiful young redhead here had always been reluctant to try.

Alice stood rooted to the spot and shivered, her

lower jaw quivering, teeth still wanting to chatter. She stared past her lover to the living room window as if something were outside in the streets, saw an automobile of some kind traveling past the apartment then. Suddenly she felt a subtle twinge in her belly, and placed her hand over it as she sensed the truth: something *was* out there in the gathering gloom, beyond the curtained window. Through her fragile and oddly detached mind she felt a tongue probing her mouth and felt her left breast being manipulated, could feel strong fingers toying with it and pinching at the nipple. She felt her face patted dry and her gaze was drawn forcibly away from the window, to look instead upon her older lover's burning glare, even as the pinches became painful, more urgent. She felt herself being shuffled around and led again, and she allowed herself to be led—

For now.

Sydney guided her into the bedroom, tugging Alice's clothing off as they went, wetting her thick lips. She knew the damn lovebirds' mess would have to be dealt with at some point. In their desperation for flight they'd literally bashed their own brains right in, defecating on themselves and each other in their madness, but Syd certainly hadn't wanted to tell Alice about any of *that*. The canary cage with the awful glut of shit and bloodletting sat outside on their back steps for the time being, a Marilyn Monroe beach towel draped over it. Syd knew it would all have to be cleaned up, but later . . . or better yet tomorrow, she thought hungrily. After the amazing night of lovemaking which lay ahead of them.

6

Julian locked the rear door and lingered out back of his church with Salt awhile. Pausing to put his spectacles on his face, he read from a piece of paper, handing it over to the Indian gentleman for a moment before taking the instructions back again. They shared a few words together, then each of them climbed into their own vehicles and left in separate directions; the elder man in his crystal white Lexus sedan and William Salt in a begrimed and bedeviled Land Rover Discovery.

The Native American followed orders fairly well most times, all the better for the good Reverend. Because if there was one thing Simon Julian despised it was getting *hands on*, with anything.

Except where it counted, of course, where it mattered most—the reason for The Fall in the first place, he supposed.

Reverend Julian motored through the Val in style, surveying the quiet, darkening streets and the various homes now coming to life from behind his ultraviolet-tinted windows. Such a shame to see them brought low. See it all returned to dust, the kingdom of his flock. But, *We are but ash, every one of us . . .* was it not so? Yes. That's the way it had always been, every place he'd ever gone on his wide travels. Corrupt as many as possible, leave ample seed behind, and move on. This was the way. They'd each been given the grace of free will, hadn't they? *Always.* Back to before the ancient times when he roamed the world as a magician, and back even before that, to another age, when he was still called *Del'ardo—*

98

He cruised along Regan Street on his way home, past the ornamented Cholke apartment, the one with chrysanthemums growing in red clay pots and a harvest wreath on the door and moonflower blossoms opening on the trellis out front. Yes. Where it mattered most, he thought, smiling. Julian frowned and stared at the lighted windows. He circled around the block, past the apartment again, slowly this time, tipping a wink in that direction.

. . . *Soon now, soon.*

The Reverend swung onto Shaw Woods Road, following it through the heavy forest of birch trees and oaks on both sides, wending his way up a narrow dirt lane which became more and more encroached by straggling brambles the farther he ascended. He glanced to the west through grasping, arthritic tree limbs, to the coppery-bloody tint visible in the ashen sky. Only then did *it* slide into view, at the top of the rise, the relic known as Shaw-Meredith House. The enormous Gothic Revival dwelling stood just as it had for more than a century and a half, its massive hulk squatting in the dense foliage, keeping itself hidden except for the protruding peak of its highest turret. Town children liked to claim these woods were haunted, and perhaps they were right.

Moss grew over the house, over its pillared portico and the twin set of stone lions out front. Twisting creeper looked as though they were attempting to devour the manse along with the remains of any fountains and crumbling statues yet standing sentinel in the huge, overgrown yard. Even the calcified hitching post and its iron ring had been swallowed up by unchecked growth. Brambles had spread everywhere, festooned over the yawning archways, branches reaching out inquisitively as if trying to push in through the thick walls.

The house was woeful and an eyesore, being consumed from within as well as without, but still, it bore the remote marks of grand antiquity in its giant frame and foundations, deep inside its moldering bones somewhere. It was an echo from another time, and for that reason alone the township of Blackwater Valley would never bulldoze it down.

It waited for the Reverend, the *Orchestrator*— deserted and mute and harboring its secrets there, leering out at him with a kind of primitive, terrible purpose.

Well, not *deserted* exactly.

Pulling up into the circular drive and stopping, Simon Julian turned the car off and closed his pale eyes, looking pleased. He listened to the cooling *tick* of the engine, and to the desperate solitude. Somewhere off in the misty woods an owl hooted and flapped its wings in quick abdication of its throne. His smile widened. Soon, all was silent beneath that descending canopy of hushed, twilit calm.

¶

"Why Richard, hello," said Glee Deadmond, her purse over one arm like Jackie Kennedy in an old *Life* magazine photograph. Richard's mouth fell open as if to speak but he closed it quickly, fearing he might stutter.

They had been sitting and talking: George mentioned where Tommy Truitt's current construction site was, in case he was interested. He also informed him of the recent passing of an unfortunate, ailment-plagued lady named Mrs. Wintermute who was just laid to rest over the weekend, a retired teacher of Michelle and Rich's. Franklin knew her, he'd confided, recalling vaguely how the woman used to help him during the book fairs in elementary school, when he could never seem to make up his mind and choose from the array of books available.

Richard commented on the flowery scent hanging in the house, only to have Deadmond skirt the issue. He excused himself to feed the dog, but Blondie only picked at the nuggets he put down for her.

When he sank back into his recliner again, talk was turned to the Reverend Julian at Nain Lutheran Church, the church from which Glee's weekly TV segment was broadcast live. And how (speaking of the old Shaw place, as they did earlier) the reclusive cleric had taken up residence in the dilapidated Shaw-Meredith House now, of all blasted spots.

Richard couldn't place the name with a face, but he did remember some of the stories surrounding the ominous home. Memory was such a funny thing, wasn't it?

George thought Julian had always been pretty much a piss ant, little more than a turnkey, really. How in hell he'd gotten to be head of the church George would never know. Even so, he was the one who did the services for poor Mrs. Wintermute, by golly.

Richard asked whatever happened to the pastor who'd married Michelle and himself. He was shocked to learn of *that* man's embarrassing retreat from town, several years ago, with an elder pregnant wife in tow. "*Holy* . . . um, mackerel," Rich muttered cagily in front of his daughter. "Weren't they in their sixties or something?"

Shaking his head at this, Richard stood up and stretched, needing to use the restroom, but the thought of going down the hall gave him pause. Down that long hall and into those shadows beyond the coat rack where he and Blondie had . . . where he'd heard a childlike voice whispering and immediately dismissed it as—

There she had been in the doorway, Glee Deadmond in the flesh. Richard practically ran smack into her. "Hi, Glee," he managed at last, floundering, caught with his guard down, having no graspable idea what to say. "George is, er, right here."

For fuck's sake.

Thankfully George *was* there, right behind him. "We were just talking about The Glee Club program, dear," said the old man, "and how much Richard and little honey Kate would like to see it sometime. We've been having a nice visit. Come in and join us won't you, Glee?"

Glee Deadmond moved straight into the living room, breezing past her son-in-law as though he were something transparent. She shot him a glance going by. "We're doing a show tomorrow at the church, if you're interested," she said in passing. "Well, I'm very glad to see you both made it safely. I was starting to think we wouldn't be seeing you, started to get worried. I am glad you're here." She took a seat next to Katie, and before Richard could bridge the situation in any way Glee was already making conversation with his daughter. "And how are you, little bit? Good, I hope. I'm your grandmother, you know . . . I do hope you remember me. Are you hungry, Katelyn? Have you eaten today?"

"Yes."

"What did you have specifically?"

"Creamsicles. Two of them."

"Two—?" She turned to stare. "Richard, I don't really think Creamsicles are the healthiest thing for my long-lost granddaughter to be consuming between meals, do you?" A look of distress crossed her face. "My word, it wasn't *instead* of a meal, I do hope! Tell me it wasn't, Richard."

He felt a tremor of annoyance. *But it's the 'Quiescently Frozen Confection', Glee,* a voice gargled inside him, wanting to gush forth. *Try one sometime and mind your own business, you stone-faced bitch, you.* George had fallen back into his chair, seemed to be deflating before Richard's eyes. Glee placed her purse down beside the sofa, waiting for an answer.

"We had lunch before we got into town," Richard said. "We were heading out to dinner right now, actually, but George was being such a gracious host we sort of lost track of the time." He decided to shift gears. "He's been telling us about your senate campaign, Glee. Congratulations on that, by the way."

She appeared bemused, scoffing, primping at her pinned-up downtown hairdo; the mound of dark hair piled on top of her head seemed immense. "Oh, nonsense. The whole thing is becoming quite tedious if you want to know the truth. But thank you anyway, Richard. And you're not leaving so soon, are you? Why, I've just gotten in the door. Now back to these

Creamsicles—Katie probably shouldn't be having those too often. I mean, we don't want her getting pudgy for her age, do we? She could probably stand to cut back on sweets."

Richard bristled.

"Besides, my Michelle Brooke would want what's best for her," she added.

The tension had come alive in the room, amassing fully and instantly after so many years, as if it had never left, merely seeped into the walls and waited here in anticipation of this moment. The pulsating throb was back in full force now, targeting the back of his head this time. Richard gritted his teeth against the pain. It might well be a migraine, the way the blood vessels felt like they were constricting at the base of his neck and skull, the way it pounded with every beat of his heart. Who in fuck could tell?

Glee was fussing over Katelyn, but she swiveled and spoke again, doing some gear-switching herself. "Has there been any progress in Maine, Richard? Any luck with the authorities there?" She flicked a sideways look at her granddaughter next to her. "You know whereof I speak."

Richard could have laughed almost. Oh, you're good. Goddamn. Coming right in and taking over, shifting gears like I could never hope to. Senate, hell—go for Everest why don't you? Go for Pennsylvania fucking Avenue, and send us a postcard when you make it. Because you just might . . .

"This dog hasn't been a nuisance, has she? I do hope not." Glee snapped her fingers and Blondie flinched, hunkering down next to George's recliner; the old man let one arm dangle over and stroked her fur.

"She's been fine," Richard snapped, a little too sharp. He squeezed his eyes shut and rubbed at the back of his neck, trying to stop the ache there. "Um, nothing new in Maine. They're still looking."

Glee rose from the sofa, nodding, patting Katie on the head as she did. Moving toward the door, she smartly retraced her steps the way she'd come in. All of a sudden Richard jumped when he felt her hands on him from behind, felt her icy fingers right through the fabric of his shirt, her lush perfume filling his nostrils. His eyes flew wide and he tightened. Glee began to rub at the muscles, massaging his shoulders and the base of his neck. "These knotted-up cords won't do," she said. "My . . . so tense, Richard." Her hands continued to work, loosening the muscles, and he began to feel the tension break a bit—the sensation was awkward and uncomfortable. Katie was watching him from where she sat, he'd noticed.

"Should I help you, Daddy?" the girl chimed in. "Should I make the headache go away?"

Richard gave her a look, an indiscernible tilt of the head, raising a forefinger like his daughter had done with the German shepherd: *Shhh*. But only raising it chest-high. Glee whispered to him now, speaking softly into his ear. "Where is she, Richard? Have you— is my Brookie here?" Her voice quavered, wanting to crack. Like the one down the hallway had done a short while ago, trembling along the walls and willing itself to be heard.

Seee . . . how I've waited for you, he was now certain the boy's voice had sobbed quietly, as if expelled upon a hushed, subtle breath. Like something that had once been alive but which was not any longer, strangely familiar somehow, something without substance or shape. *Seee . . .*

He faced Glee, thought he saw tears, her emerald eyes wet behind the crystal-clear rimless lenses. "Yes," he heard himself say, "yes, she's here."

The woman placed one hand on his arm. Richard glanced down to where she touched him and there it was: the man's gold ring with the amber-brown square setting that he always remembered her wearing, but could never figure out why. Her gaze dropped, and she walked toward the sofa, turned back again, unpinning her hair and giving it a wearisome shake. "If it's not too much to ask, George and I would like to spend some time with her. To have her here with us for a while." Glee met his stare. "Is that all right, Richard? Would it be possible?"

"With me?" Katie said, and Glee couldn't help but smile.

"With you, too, little bit. Richard Allan?" Glee's eyes seemed to twinkle behind her designer glasses. He took in the image of his mother-in-law, standing in her heels and silk blouse, and her matching jacket and skirt, with glittering diamond earrings visible through the hair she'd unpinned.

Her hair. He finally noticed it, the brown and silver-streaked hair washing down her back, washing down and down. Jesus, how long had she been growing it this way? It fell well past her slender waist and didn't stop until, amazingly, the ends of it reached the back of her thighs. *Wow,* thought Richard, not believing how striking she looked with it let free. "All right, Glee. That'd be fine."

"Thank you. Now, when can you be over in the

morning? I'll clear my day, of course, and I hardly ever sleep anymore anyway. Can you come early? By sunrise perhaps?"

He coughed into his fist. "Well, that might not work for us." *Is she joking?*

"Splendid. I want to spend as much time as I can with my faraway family. The whole day if possible! Oh, you understand. I do hope so, Richard. You two are all I have left."

George said, "We can have that cookout, son. Take in the show at the church maybe." He gave Richard a desperate look.

"Sure. Sure, we'll be here early. I can't promise sunrise, though. We're pretty worn out."

Glee took Katie in her arms, hugged her granddaughter to her. Then she hugged him as well, and Richard found his mouth open again. When she pulled away he saw it, a single teardrop glistening in the outer corner of her eye. *I'll be damned*, he thought, feeling his head pulse and his throat tighten, thinking he'd never see the day . . .

"Bless you, my little bit," she told Katelyn.

Not long after they were saying goodnight to each other; Richard made sure Katie gathered up her things, reminding her not to forget the special coloring book. He promised they'd return tomorrow while his only daughter dawdled about, one arm filled with her belongings and the other playing with Blondie. As they exited the house, however, Katie seemed upset. When questioned, she fretted as if she'd done something wrong.

Richard comforted her, assuring her she had not. "Everything's peachy, hon," he insisted, "just fuzzy-peachy. So don't worry." Katie giggled at the phrase, as she did almost every time.

Glee saw them out, clicking on the light so they wouldn't trip in the darkness. The air had turned damp, and the encroaching shadows chilly after the warmth of day. A gigantic black moth flitted around the burning porch light.

"See you dark and early!" Glee called after them with a pleasant wave.

They both waved back. Glee Deadmond glanced perplexed for a moment at the peculiar black moth before closing her front door and shutting the light off several seconds later.

Seee . . .

Richard snorted. "Right. Fat chance of that happening." He shivered, listening to Katie's giggles rise to a screeching pitch as they hurried through the dusky gloom, toward the Blazer.

8

William Salt kneeled in the dirt of Old North Cemetery, holding a stoneware plate in both hands overhead, as the evening fog crept stealthily into the sunken depressions around him. On the plate were a few ears of corn, some pumpkin seeds and various nuts, a sweet potato, and a fresh channel catfish pulled from the Rock River by him the previous day. He kept the food offering aloft, thrust up toward the sliver of night-sun, which had shown itself in the starry sky. Finally he lowered it, placing the stoneware plate on the ancestral grave mounds before him. Reaching into the grass he took hold of the small Sauk war hatchet, hefted it with his four-fingered hand, liking the feel of the hickory haft wrapped in buckskin leather. Standing straight, the man spread his arms wide and chanted low, the pair of tethered, blood-speckled hawk feathers dangling loosely below the razored blade of the tomahawk.

When he'd finished his nocturne, Salt wheeled and made his way out of the dark cemetery. Leaving food was no different than how the whites left flowers behind for their deceased, but if he were to be spotted here he would be deemed crazy for sure. He wasn't crazy. He was just biding his time. His Sauk ancestors buried back there, the ones with honorable spirit warrior names like Deercreek, and Two Knives, and Red Sky Gall (he would not disgrace them by using their Christian-given names, even though it was a Christian graveyard they had been planted in), well, it was too late for them. But Salt waited and bided his time. Or rather, *Prarsheen* waited. That's what the old medicine man called him, his ghost-pale Reverend. He told him it meant *He Who Lies in Wait*, and that's exactly what he was now.

The large Indian stumbled over something, kicked a dead raccoon out of his path and then continued skulking through the markers and shadows. That was the second dead raccoon he'd run afoul of tonight. Plus he noticed a lot of birds were beginning to drop from above, turning up in the oddest places around Blackwater, with their wings twisted and pointing to the sky. All quite strange, frankly. The ancient Romans had watched the skies and the birds, Salt knew, believing they could interpret signs of things to come from their migrations. Then again, they'd rummaged about the innards of sacrificed animals, too, trying to read them like Gypsy tea leaves. Well, that Holy Empire had fallen, hadn't it? Like this one would topple some day if he had his way.

That's what the old man had promised him, that the land which was once theirs would be returned to the surviving remnants of his people, one day. Returned to its past glory, as it was, before the devils had come. No more handouts. No more government subsidizing or standing in line for the white man's smirks and charity.

He believed in Simon Julian, had seen the Ghost Reverend perform miracles of a sort, things his Native American eyes could not refute nor his proud heart ever comprehend. The stuff of visions, they had been. Julian had even given him the sacred Sauk hatchet.

Salt had distant relatives who lived up in Wisconsin, and he heard that several bands of his Indian people also remained to the west—3,500 or so Sauk that had intermarried with the Fox tribes and dwelled together near a place called Tama, Iowa. So there *were* descendants left, ones who could stand and take back their heritage alongside him, claim it for their own, their fates guided by the great and ever-present Spirit of the *One*. All he had to do was remain steadfast, remain vigilant in his belief. Let the old man direct him, and keep doing the tasks he asked.

Like the ones yet to come.

This was the bargain struck, for his unquestioning obedience. Soon, all would be amber waves and purple mountain majesties again. For the true of heart among them, that is. The *true* American natives.

And all the Ghost Reverend had asked of him as

down payment—a kind of promissory note—was William Salt's own, self-severed forefinger.

CHAPTER SIX

I

THEY HAD CHEESE ButterBurgers and crinkle-cut fries at a Culver's, not far from their motel. Richard grabbed an Imitrex and two Excedrin from the suitcase in the backseat, swallowing the tablets down with gulps of Cherry Pepsi from the soda refill fountain inside.

The harsh restaurant lighting hurt his eyes, made his head pulsate, but finally the ache did begin to ease. They ate pretty much in silence in their booth. When Katie would glance up at him, Richard made sure to be grinning widely at her—she grinned back and laughed each time before returning to her food. That's all she really needed from him, a little reassurance every so often.

When they got to the Nightlight Inn he parked as close to their door as possible. The spaces nearest were mostly taken, and Richard had to settle for one several slots over. He carried the last suitcase containing their cellular phone and Michelle's urn into the motel room, mentally noting that the SUV still smelled as skunky as ever. Once inside, Richard remarked how stuffy the closed-up room had gotten since this afternoon, to which Katie replied something about it being seventy-eight degrees, offhandedly, and yet quite sure of herself in that unnerving way she had. The television set and light were on, and their leather bags were as he'd left them. He turned on the air-conditioner unit to see if he could cool the place down a bit before settling in.

Richard made sure the motel room door was securely deadbolted and chained and saw to it that Katie brushed her teeth, then he snuggled his daughter into bed and read to her from *Stellaluna*, stroking her hair until she drifted off to sleep.

He kissed her forehead and watched the 10:00 PM news, before clicking the TV off and laying the remote on top of it. Kicking off his shoes, he went to the window and gazed through the vertical blinds into the lacey darkness, into that September night.

His headache was mostly gone. The Imitrex had worked, or the Excedrin, or the combination of both; only a slight tug at the back of his scalp remained.

Jesus, were those bats? he wondered at once.

Dipping and flitting under the sodium lights, out where their Blazer sat in the shadowed parking lot. Or had it been the children's book he'd just read to Katelyn, fruit bats and owls, and cleverly named birds, affecting his imagination? He continued to stare for a time, alone, to stare out and listen to his own heartbeat . . . and to remember.

But lately, remembering wasn't all it'd been cracked up to be.

Forgetting, he thought dismally. *There's something to pray for.*

113

2

Deep in his grieving heart, Richard Franklin knew he would never be able to forget his wife's funeral. Nor the cremation which had followed. It had been an overcast day in southern Maine. The dreary, slate-gray August sky had threatened to send raindrops down upon everything, though it never did—already there was a hint of chill in the air, sign of what was to come.

They'd all gathered at the Nefstead Mortuary & Crematory for the service that afternoon, Nefstead's being one of only two mortuaries in their small community. The other, Chisholm's Funeral Home, had met with a disastrous scandal some time back and had since lost its honorable reputation in the town, not to mention its financial standing.

The reported story went that old Mr. Irwin Chisholm, getting on in years and needing some extra help with the family trade, had employed his 33-year-old nephew, Arthur, to assist him down at the parlor. The charming and talented Art, whose nickname was Chewy, was to be Win Chisholm's saving grace. The rumor around Golitha Falls, however, was that Arthur Chisholm, not being the most stable of persons to begin with, should've listed 'closet necrophiliac' as a qualifying interest on the résumé. In landing the job at his uncle's mortuary he hit the proverbial jackpot, as it were. Talk got around swiftly and the gossip mill began its grind; suspicions soon arose, and were at last confirmed late one winter evening by a hired security guard making his rounds. The guard, a former police detective, supposedly happened upon Win's careless nephew in the embalming room close to midnight, down inside the basement of the rambling funeral home.

(Arthur Chisholm was doing his thing, quite oblivious, going strong on the recently autopsied corpse of a teenage female suicide when he was discovered. According to the tale, which had been elevated to the legendary ranks of *epic* storytelling by now, the horrified ex-detective had drawn his weapon in the shadows, put the squared barrel of his Taurus .380 semi-auto to Chewy Chisholm's rhythmically bobbing head and had spoken the words: "Come, and I'll blow your pigfucking brains out." Yes, the most legendary of ranks. Richard often imagined what might've happened afterward if the tabloids had ever gotten wind of the entire unsavory affair, the truth of it all. He used to picture the headlines, conjuring up various tasteless captions in that writerly mind of his, like: *Jizzum's Funeral House of Horror* and *Chewy Got His Gun*, even the truly hideous *Working Stiffs*, glaring out from drug store window displays and in coffee shops throughout town. Not pretty.)

Needless to repeat, everyone had gathered at Nefstead's for the service.

The Deadmonds flew in from Illinois, and their presence only served to make an unbearable ordeal even worse. Michelle was their daughter, for God's sake, and of course they would be there, but that didn't make it any better. Not for any of them.

And because of the falling out in Blackwater Valley, and the subsequent ill will which followed for so many years after, Richard had to introduce George and Glee

115

to a granddaughter neither one of them had ever met before. That was bad.

Michelle had an open-casket visitation; his wife's face hadn't been damaged much in the accident. She'd looked beautiful, everything considered. While her poor frame had been destroyed, her face was still exquisite. A slight bluish pallor of her skin remained, though, which they couldn't cover entirely. The leukemia had done that. No autopsy had been performed, but her long and lanky runway model's body was ruined, had to be reconfigured before being fitted for size to the rented casket. People used to remark often on how very tall she was: Richard stood almost 5' foot 11", but Michelle topped him coming in at over 6' 2". No wonder she'd won so many high school basketball trophies.

Richard and Katie stayed nearest to the coffin, Katie clutching a lady's-slipper orchid from their greenhouse in one tiny fist. At the end of it, Katie placed the single orchid between her mother's breasts and softly whispered to her, "Goodbye." Richard Franklin had wished himself dead at that moment—but then, who would look after *her*?

Friends and relatives came and went, and Katie sat with her newly found grandparents. Everyone cried except for Richard. He was in too deep a shock to cry yet. All he'd been able to do was look from Katie's living face to his wife's lifeless one, from Michelle back again to Katie, thinking over and over: *She could've stopped it. She could've stopped the cancer . . .*

It didn't matter anymore. Because even if Katelyn could have stopped the leukemia, there was no way in hell anyone could've ever stopped that Pontiac. Which meant Michelle would be just as dead, either way. It did not matter, he kept telling himself. So why drive yourself crazy? What difference did it make?

Yet it did, it made a lot of difference. Always would.

Katie had wanted to try, desperately so, but Richard and Michelle had both refused her. They forbid it. It was too dangerous . . . *much* too dangerous. After all, headaches and sore throats were one thing, but *leukemia*. Suppose that after she halted its progression and took it from her, suppose she couldn't get rid of it? What then? If it remained inside her and began to spread, began to grow as it had within Michelle—what then?

No, it was unspeakable. Unthinkable.

But little Joey Spencer, Richie, a voice had echoed in his already numb mind at the mortuary. *Don't forget Joey Spencer's appendix last year.*

Richard hadn't forgotten.

After services were over, Richard informed the Deadmonds that he and Katie would be in Illinois as soon as they could, when everything was taken care of, to make sure Michelle's final wishes were honored. Katie was still on summer vacation. She hadn't actually started her first grade classes yet, but a lot of rigmarole had to be put to rights first (there turned out to be an excessive amount of red tape to go through before the school even pulled their hooks out and excused her), plus many other arrangements to be made.

Richard chose to stay with the body of his deceased wife as long as he could that day. He sent Katie off with his father, an attorney who'd traveled in from Minnesota where he lived; Richard's mother had passed on some time ago, before Katie had even been born. The Deadmonds were the last to leave, besides him, and Richard bristled at the idea of letting his daughter go anywhere with them at this point. He couldn't explain it, but an irrational premonition of sorts had abruptly, instinctively arisen in him. A premonition warning him that if he allowed Katelyn to disappear for even a moment with these two grief-stricken grandparents from the Prairie State, he might never see his daughter again.

Once he was alone, he pulled a chair over and sat beside Michelle. He still could not cry, although he badly wanted to. Instead, he had sat and gazed at her sweet loveliness. Then he noticed something he hadn't before—Michelle's hair was growing.

It was nutty, *fruitcake* nutty, but her hair continued to grow. Her fingernails, too.

He knew what the 'experts' said on such matters: that it was impossible, that what you were seeing was wishful thinking, dead flesh merely receding and making the nails appear to grow. Press-ons, perhaps, or the salon magic of the funeral home's stylists. But the so-called experts were wrong. Richard remembered how his wife's hair had looked, knew exactly how long it'd been. How long it was before the accident and how long after. Jesus, he knew how it had looked before this goddamned service had begun, and it was different now, more vibrant. He caressed it, unbelieving. It wasn't a wig either, but her actual hair. Michelle's curly chestnut-brown mane was still growing, continuing to thrive several days after her death, flourishing just as lustrously now as it ever had while she was alive. If not more.

Richard had shaken his head, sitting in stunned

silence, not understanding anything anymore. He put his hand over his wife's cold hand. No, not cold, but certainly not warm. It felt more like a mannequin's hand, really, a hand with parchment paper stretched tightly over it. Richard had turned the hand and examined her fingernails, found them to be in the same condition as her hair, utterly exquisite and healthy. He straightened Katie's pink orchid and abruptly caught his breath. Because there were stains on her dark blouse, opaque, creamy . . . two stains bleeding strangely through as if she—

Richard had almost gasped. He'd seen this before, seen it after Katie had been born. *Michelle's breasts were leaking, swollen and ripe with life somehow, leaking milk days after her death.* What in God's name? It couldn't be.

This was just an empty husk before him, a shell of something that was no more. Still, she looked as though she might wake up at any moment, yawn and stretch. He had continued to hold her hand in a kind of awe and reverence, half expecting to see her eyelids flutter. He even said something to her once. She did not reply, of course. But he'd been more reluctant than ever to leave her, leave her to the cremationist and the incinerators while she seemed to have growth and metabolism. How could he let them take her? How could he abandon her like that . . . and for *what*? An appointment with a fucking blast furnace?

But it was what she had wanted.

He grasped her wrist and thought about everything. The way his wife had looked while pregnant with Katie, how she'd glowed. He thought about the wretched, cowardly disease that had attacked her later on, stealing the living essence right out of her. Now here she lay in a box for show, and life was running back into her. Fucking hell.

He thought about the way his daughter's pale pearly eyes changed their hue eerily with her moods—irises lightening when she was happy and clouding over dark when she was mad or sad—as her mother's once had.

And he thought about the murderer who'd been behind the wheel of that car. That dirty, killer car with the words *WASH ME* smudged into one of its sides. That's what the night librarian had said, wasn't it? Oh, and that the paint color had been sage, he believed. Sure, and what happened to *that* fat fuck anyway? An enormous man named Nate Bitters: rotund, flamboyant, versed in several world languages as head of the library's Collections Department, and sole witness to the hit-and-run that took his wife's life.

Mr. Nate Bitters, an odd duck he was, or so they liked to whisper around town. Odder yet since his disappearance. One minute he's giving a quick, jittery account of what he saw to the authorities, and the following day—*abracadabra*—he's gone. Smoke in the wind. No messages, no traces, nothing. Gone, like an obese Harry Houdini. What in *the* hell?

He'd realized then that all there was in life was heartbreak. From the warm, safe cradle to the cold-as-ice grave. Pain and misery and heartbreak, with some fleeting good times sprinkled in. Things seldom worked out any differently, Richard knew, except in a few rare cases.

Like the strange and miraculous case of Joey Spencer, for instance.

BLACKWATER VAL

Joseph Spencer was one luckless child. In his brief ten years he had already been through a kid's own private version of hell: bronchitis which developed into double pneumonia, a bout with rheumatic fever, the lengthy divorce of his parents and even being hit by a bus once and knocked clean off his banana-seat Schwinn. He'd survived all of these, and had actually come out none the worse for wear. But when his inflamed, abnormally oversized appendix had burst on the playground, that fall day of Katelyn Jane Franklin's inaugural year of school, he'd gotten lucky. Pure and simple.

Because Katie had been close by, and she . . . well, she was just Katie-Smatie.

When it happened, panic had seized the teachers present. The children remained unperturbed, concerned with things other than the seriousness at hand, but little Katie had realized the danger. She had quickly comprehended the fear on her elders' ghost-white faces. She'd reacted in the only way she had known how.

One moment everyone was at play, (the small school's kindergarten through sixth grade classes all allowed on the playground together for recess), talking and shouting, romping about in the dead, skittering leaves of an elm tree that rose from a circle of grass at the playground's center. A group of pupils was singing, led by their substitute first grade teacher in the verse of an old harvesttime melody:

"Hallowe 'ee 'een
The witch is riding high . . .
Have you se 'ee 'een

121

Her shadow in the sky?
But beware,
Don't you dare . . . "

All at once something was wrong, the playing stopped but the shouting continued, rising in alarm and pitch. One of the children was down—not one of Katie's kindergarten roommates, but an older boy from one of the higher grades on the school's second floor—down and shaking, clutching at his right side. Then he became still. The phys-ed teacher shrieked for help, her voice cracking.

Assistance didn't come, just more cries. Katie barely heard these shouts. By contrast, she registered only the affliction before her as she made her way to the stricken boy. She took the motionless, vacant-eyed Joey Spencer, who had teased her once or twice already since school began and even kicked her in the shin on one occasion, in her frail tiny arms and located the malignancy. She ignored the sickly sweet stink of vomit, which had issued forth from the feverish boy and assaulted the crisp October air, her left hand coming to rest over the area of his veiled appendix rupture.

Next, she had somehow absorbed it. *Transposed* it, perhaps? Drawing it from his inner workings and taking it inside her own diminutive self. Then, after bickering with it as a mother might argue with a disruptive child, Katie Franklin had canceled it out. She stretched her other hand, reaching for the elm's trunk, and laid that hand upon the tree's massive base while humming the way Michelle and she often did.

Katie found herself being pulled away, and

suddenly Joey Spencer was rushed to one of the teacher's automobiles, limbs dangling, and was driven out of sight. They took him to the closest hospital, Meadows Memorial, where a dour-looking medical technician retrieved him from the emergency room and attended to his condition.

Meanwhile, Katie was told by her elders that she shouldn't have gotten in the way like that, she could have cost Joseph his health, maybe even his life. She was scolded and good, more out of fright than corrective discipline, but she had merely grinned at them all. Grinned and held up her small hands, fingers splayed, squinting one eye shut against the bright autumn sunlight the way children do, telling them it was okay, the poison 'suspendix' was gone. He was going to be fine—fuzzy-peachy, as her father was fond of saying. She even suggested they let him come back and play, that he shouldn't be sent away just for being sick.

And over at the Meadows, amid the daily hustle and bustle of sick people either getting sicker or getting well, or simply dying, examinations showed nothing at all wrong with Joey Spencer. Blood work and scans revealed to everybody—the boy's parents included, who had forgotten their past differences and had raced to the hospital together—that ten-year-old Joseph Spencer, who'd never had an appendectomy in his life, no longer possessed an appendix either.

As if it had never been there to begin with.

While the genius ER gods pondered the significance of all this, Richard and his wife already knew what had happened. Had been waiting for something like it. They weren't perplexed as were the others, because it had happened before—with admittedly less impact, true.

Like mother, like daughter, wasn't that how the saying went?

(Richard had gone to the playground once after the incident, gone to see the elm tree and the fissure where Katie had touched it and discharged that negative energy. A gap was opened there, had ruptured the tree's trunk but not killed it, creating an ugly, jagged knothole where kids might someday hide toys or trinkets, like Boo Radley and the scamps in *Mockingbird* had done.)

Inside the funeral parlor he continued to watch his wife's motionless form like someone in a trance, reliving these moments and memories beside her casket, all the while clasping onto her. He even recalled the time with the hypnotist, when they had sought out a psychotherapist in hopes that a session or two might be able to clear up some things.

They'd met with him together, Michelle and Richard. Kate had been left out of it for the time being. She didn't need that kind of scrutiny at such a tender age. Besides, Michelle was the main attraction here; she had been born into this world with the gift first, later passing it on to her daughter. Only twenty times stronger . . . second generation phenomenon and all that. Why bring Katie in until some preliminaries could be done? Wasn't the less said about the entire situation the better?

It made sense, in that fruitcake nutty sort of a way. So the two of them had gone, and Richard had stayed in the room with his wife during the hypnosis. Michelle, her mind and body weakening by now, had requested it.

His beloved had had a sudden paranoiac notion of the doctor putting her under and then privately doing bizarre and perverse things to her, and worse yet, making her do bizarre and perverse things back, in the ultimate new twist on the old "now flap your arms up and down and cluck like a chicken" routine. Richard informed her that her therapist was not Vincent Price or Bela Lugosi, just a simple hypnotherapy counselor from Toronto, Canada.

Dr. Martin Ponds was the name on his office door, and though he appeared a smidge out of the ordinary at first (his resemblance to actor Michael Sarrazin was uncanny, right down to the tranquilizer-glazed puppy dog eyes), Richard assured his wife that the doctor was in all probability a solid professional. He had a Doctor of Clinical Hypnotherapy degree on his wall, although he was quick to point out the ornately framed diploma was currently an 'unrecognized' degree by any accredited Mental Health bodies in the United States.

"Really big in the UK and India though," the doctor had said with a wink and a grin. "Monstrous big. But so is the idea that cows can house our reincarnated souls. Go figure, eh?" He broke into laughter at this, while Richard and Michelle had chuckled politely and traded uneasy glances between themselves.

The Reincarnation of Peter Ponds, Richard had thought foolishly as he sat there, harking back to the Michael Sarrazin movie of the 1970s when he was a kid, trying desperately to avoid the man's bloodshot gaze. Because if he looked at him, was forced to look into those glassy fried-egg eyes of his too long, Richard felt he might very well begin giggling and not be able to stop.

Peter Proud smiled, and their visit had proceeded.

They chatted for a bit, and the Franklins told him what the problem was and what they hoped to achieve by this session. Lied through their teeth, actually, telling of Michelle's sleep loss these last several months due to nightmares. Michelle told him how the dreams were keeping her up—haunted dreams of strange and unnatural places, of people she did not recognize . . . to the best of her knowledge anyway. The good doctor had leaned forward with interest, listening, nibbling at the bait which had been dangled so delicately before him.

Fishy fishy in the brook. Fishy fishy bite my hook . . .

Richard had chewed the soft inside lining of his cheek, fighting back the titters, all the while thinking: *My God, I'm going crackers.*

They went on to explain how they had heard today's hypnotherapy might be just the thing, might help assess the situation. Maybe even cure it altogether.

Dr. Ponds informed them they'd heard correctly, and that they had come to the right place in their discomfort. He conveyed how the procedure known as regressive hypnosis would more than likely uncover the mental obstacles frustrating Michelle's slumber.

Richard and Michelle had glanced at one another, and then nodded at the doctor. Expert hypnotic regression—jackpot. If anything it might give some brand of insight into Michelle's intrinsic inner workings, those deep-seated recesses which no one, herself included, had ever dared explore before. Maybe they could learn something about her paranormal 'gift'.

He would be taking her down to the Theta level brain state, the doctor explained before beginning: a detached realm of knowing where he would attempt to tap in and communicate directly with her subconscious. Once there, the session could take on a life of its own, Ponds warned.

But all Michelle had done while under was mutter things about falling, endlessly falling. Gibberish about having a twisted spine, and her flesh and bones melting; a body ravaged by fire, leathery, with black fibers running riot throughout it. She had actually used those words: *BLACK . . . FIBERS . . . RUNNING . . . RIOT*, speaking in a flat, monotone voice that was more than a bit spooky. Something *TATTERED* and *ANCIENT*, which felt *CORRUPTED* and *DISEASE RIDDEN* to her.

The doctor, interpreting all this to mean Michelle herself, had quietly asked Richard if she had been sick recently and was stunned to hear of her leukemia diagnosis, information that should've been given to him beforehand, he was prompt to point out. Yet it was the voice she'd used that unnerved him most.

When she resisted coming out of it, Richard had panicked. Everything was fine, assured the doctor. Nothing to fret about. She was in a deep, timeless place—a place from which she didn't want to return immediately.

"Just a mind floating in a void," he whispered, and Richard felt his scalp crawl. Nonetheless, there *was* something else they could try, while he still had her under. Dr. Ponds suggested that as an alternative treatment, his particular field of speciality might be of some use. It didn't happen often, but there had been a few instances, he recalled. A few cases of spontaneous remission. Enough so that it was worth a shot, anyway.

"The body has the amazing ability to heal itself hidden somewhere within, Mr. Franklin," he had said low, while Michelle murmured on in someone else's deadpan voice. "If the mind can be put into the right state. Maybe not to cure itself completely, but to begin enacting repairs. Slow the advancement of the attacking disease perhaps and lessen its devastation. As I said, though, it's an outside shot at best."

Michelle's particular brand of cancer offered less than a 30% chance of survival, yet here was this man with his diploma on the wall throwing them a lifeline, claiming that his wife's subconscious might actually be instructed to generate new cells inside her failing body—

WINGS, Michelle had uttered a few feet away, causing both he and Ponds to start. *FLARING. BURNING.* Then, after a lengthy silence: *BEHOLD . . . OUR . . . FLESH.* Again, Richard had chewed at the inner lining of his cheek, feeling Katie's frittles spring up all along his creeping skin when his wife spoke. *FOULED*, she said with an almost guttural growl and Richard had shuddered, giving the doctor the green light, telling him to go ahead.

Ponds vowed in a thin, whispery voice to try his best. He added solemnly that sometimes the hypnosis therapy, at the very least, had helped other patients in cases like this live out their lives in comfort and in less pain.

He used a simple, post-hypnotic suggestion, instructing Michelle Franklin that her body would start to heal, start repairing itself from the inside out.

128

Ponds told her whenever she experienced distress, felt any kind of fatigue or pain that she would merely close her left hand into a fist and once she did, everything would grow calm and become right as summer rain for her. Fear and anxiety and malaise would evaporate, and the symptoms associated with her illness would pass into nothingness as her body grew stronger and healthy and filled with life again.

For months thereafter Richard would watch her do this unconsciously, as she chose to forego the nauseating chemo treatments for natural biologics instead, opening and closing her left hand into a fist. Watched her do it more and more often as the craven, insidious cancer ever progressed, spreading from her bloodstream into the organs of her body, not even aware she was doing it, never letting on to his sick wife what had transpired between the psychotherapist and himself that day in his office, praying and hoping beyond all hope that somehow it would work and she'd get well.

The funeral director had interrupted then, disturbing him from these recollections. She was to be taken from him. Taken away to the adjoining abbey where the crematory was housed. A sense of desperation had seized him at that moment—he wrested with his own grasping hands, trying to hold them in place as the man in the dark suit told him they were closing soon, that he was sorry but they couldn't wait any longer. Richard had nodded and stared at the floor, one hand throttling the other because there was nobody else to be throttled in this. No one deserving, at any rate.

No one within reach.

129

Richard had learned a long time ago about cremation. He knew the ashes given to families weren't really ashes at all but pulverized bone chips and burned fragments run through a cremulator, leaving them a fine, sandlike texture. Michelle's casket with the detachable bed liner would be rolled discreetly out of sight, and its removable fiberboard box lifted from the interior so that the casket's outer shell could be reused again. Next they'd take her from the chapel to the crematorium to be placed straight into the incinerator, body and liner bed and all, where she would roll upon a motorized trolley into consuming flames in excess of 1,500 degrees Fahrenheit.

When asked beforehand, Richard had stated he most definitely did *not* wish to view 'the charge', that part where the removable liner trundles down and disappears inside the cremator, and who in frozen hell would ever want to witness something like that anyhow? Christ, he still remembered the story his grandfather Walter had told him when he was a kid, about the time his coworkers and he had once observed a cremation taking place back in the olden days, from the very crematoria rooftop where Walter and crew were laying hot tar with scoop shovels.

Of what they saw the industrial coal-burning furnace do that day, down through the opened exhaust system.

Supposedly, they'd all stopped their labors to watch a cadaver being cremated, which they could see quite plainly via the roof's air ducts, their turbine vent caps having been removed to be cleaned by the men. When the dear departed's receptacle was placed inside the chamber and locked off below them, and the burners all were fired up, the curious roofers—hand to God now, he'd sworn—had seen the dead gentleman's body as it first jerked and convulsed and then sat bolt upright amid the blast furnace flames, thrusting up and out of its box, a hideous shriek tearing and trying to come alive somewhere within it, like a person trying desperately yet unable to scream themselves awake from a nightmare.

He told of how they'd jumped, goggle-eyed, blanching from their vantage point above with hands clasped over mouths in horror, and a black man name of Alton Finch had puked a deep rich purple (from the two pieces of blueberry pie he'd eaten at lunchtime that day) right down the front of his gray flannel work pants and all over his own shoes . . . but how Fred Satterlee, the rooftop foreman, had merely leaned over to Richard's grandfather on his tar-caked shovel and said: "Just the muscles is all, Wally, contracting and roasting. Like a chicken pot pie in your wife's stove with a bit of meaty vocal cord still warbling inside it!" Walter had almost thrown up himself then, and ditto Richard upon recalling the goddamned story at the time. As far as he knew, neither of them had ever touched another pot pie as long as they both lived.

Richard had recalled something else sitting there as they carted his Michelle Brooke away, another nugget of wisdom his grandfather had passed on to him. That no matter how thoroughly they cleaned those retort sections of a crematorium, a tiny residual amount of bodily remains was always left inside the blast chamber itself, and that this residue ended up mixing with subsequent cremations, on and so forth, and into the future, so that a little of each person being incinerated blended into the next and on into the next, their essences mingling and combining.

It was then, only after they had taken his dead wife from him and after recounting this story—imagining Michelle's flourishing hair and beautiful, milky sweet breasts being vaporized and oxidized, her remains intermingling with all those unfortunates, reduced to ashy bits right *now* and intermingling with all those before and the many which were to follow—only then did he break down and was able to weep, toppling from the slight wooden chair he had slumped in and collapsing on the chapel floor in great wracking, soul-ripping sobs . . .

3

A bat hit the window suddenly, thumped hard against it, startling him from thought. He flinched backward, thinking *Woo!* even as another swooped close and nearly did the same thing. Leathery wings flapped—and why would they do that? Wasn't their biosonar supposed to prevent that sort of thing? Echolocation, or whatever it was called. One landed shrieking on the outer sill and Richard recoiled, reeling back and almost falling.

He turned off the light, figuring it must be drawing them. Then he closed the blinds, but not before hesitating a moment, thinking he'd seen something . . . a shape outside, standing in the blotchy darkness across the road, in the thickening fog that had begun to gather. Back amongst the leaning tablets over at Penfield Monument Works—

Was someone watching him this whole time, while he had been standing in the brightly lit window?

Richard looked again, peering through the glass but seeing nothing. The shadowed form was no longer there. He shut the blinds, pulling the heavy drapes and moving away. Shaking his head, he realized how very tired he was.

He retrieved the cell phone from his suitcase, checked it for any messages and, finding none, placed it on the wall charger for the night. Richard used the bathroom and left the light on over the sink, keeping the door open partway. He climbed into the bed across from Katie and closed his eyes, arm across his forehead, turning the wedding band he still wore around and around with his thumb. Soon he was snoring gently in the dark.

During his slumber, he dreamt awful dreams of the things which might have been, unfulfilled hopes and wants, disquieting things he'd be unable to remember upon waking.

He dreamed about the Sallow Man pointing at him through the falling rain.

But what he didn't know—could not possibly have known—what Richard never saw that terrible funereal day in August was the way the air had shimmered as gauzy smoke rose from the crematory's stacks: the eerie green-and-white-and-violet lightshow taking place high above Nefstead Funeral Home. An *aurora* of pulsing waves and bright refracted colors swirling, rising up from the incinerator's brick chimneys to illuminate the darkening Maine sky. Or how that unearthly glow from the charged particles remained visible long into the night.

CHAPTER SEVEN

I

WHILE RICHARD STIRRED in his sleep, caught up within the folds of some nightmare, others were awake this night. People bustled about Aubel Farms, where the working barns were well lit, a soft glow coming from the cast-iron wall sconces inside. Two of the Aubel family's prize cows had decided to give birth at this late hour, and everyone involved was concerned due to the recent losses among the livestock.

The midnight laborers went about their tasks with frowns of worry knitting their brows, hoping for the best. One of these farmhands, though, a haggard man in his fifties known as Ditch Richards, stood outside in the field now looking up at the sky. He went out to smoke a cigarette in private, away from the barns and the others. He began to wonder if it'd be like the last time; he prayed that it wasn't. Dreaded it actually, dreaded having to burn any more dead-born calves. He stayed outside in the cool evening air and smoked for as long as he could, his eyes rimmed in red and his hand trembling as he pulled out a pint bottle of Old Grand-Dad bourbon and drank from it shakily.

Someone called his name—Cal Aubel, the middle of the owner's three sons—so he slipped the whiskey bottle back into his pocket, trying to quell his jittery nerves while moving back inside the barns for the next round.

Elsewhere, Jack Lawrie was up and sitting in his magnificent cherry wood library on Lantern Court, sipping a vintage port in his favorite Tuscan leather armchair and pondering the current circumstances.

He thought about all the ill omens of late; about his sweet, hot-blooded Rainey, and the same dilemma being married to her always presented. He thought about the troubling phone call he had received earlier from one of his oldest confidants. Also about that mass grave out there and the bones laid bare in it, this latest plague pit uncovered (or shrieking pit, as he'd heard them called while stationed overseas in Europe) and the odd condition the remains had been found in, with jagged brick shards jammed into some of their mouths and the skulls wrapped in head-shrouds, as if to keep them from awakening and feeding on anything. *Holy* blood pudding.

Oh yes, and the news that Rich Franklin was back in town with his daughter. Jack sat and pondered on it, and began to wonder what exactly he was going to do regarding the hypothesis he came up with.

And as George Deadmond stood and listened to the whispering in his fragrant home, Chip Priewe listened to the wheezy gasps and erratic breathing inside his own, and imagined just how he would kill the sleeping cunt in the bed next to him.

2

Somewhere within the char-black recesses of Shaw-Meredith House, Simon Julian lay stock-still in dormancy, lying face-up with his eyes wide open in the liquid blackness.

The structure seemed to breathe in and out around him with a horrid, hushed resolve. Inside the dark its walls appeared sound, the window shutters closed, its roof unbroken . . . but the house itself was anything but sound. It was an enigma with its massive walls of thick squared blocks, and its nine-foot-high, roughly hewn doors hanging on pivots, same as the shutters did. Cavernous rooms with ceilings nearly twenty feet high in the air, twice as high as a normal house. All features which led the occasional curious passerby to conclude the place must have been built by giants. Or built *for* giants, perhaps.

Shadows swirled over Julian, crawling, straining to reach out like living, aware of things in the gloom. A brown recluse spider moved furtively across the Reverend's unstirring face. Even in his state of suspension, his right arm tightened around the ornately-carved rectangular box it guarded so closely.

He continued to stare, a thin layer of dust beginning to form on his corneas. Then the old man blinked and his covetous thoughts crept to the little girl again. The spider curled up and frothed its fangs, went scurrying on through the tarry black.

While elsewhere still a young man named Aaban Darwish, whose first name meant literally 'angel of iron'—back in his sun-scorched, sand-choked homeland six thousand miles away—slept the peaceful sleep of the truly righteous. He smiled as he drowsed, safe within the confines of his host's elegant abode.

Oh, how he liked the way that sounded: *angel of iron.*

CHAPTER EIGHT

I

T WAS THE SMALL, black hours and the streets of the Val lay deserted, except for a stray traveler or two: Lucy Dixon on her way home, coming off the late-night nurse's shift and zipping along now while visions of her pillow-top mattress danced in her head. Phil Jenrette, the local high school football coach, cruising toward the old freight yards across town, while his wife and children slept, in search of a prostitute by the railroad tracks—and either a young girl or young boy would do at this bleak hour, since Mr. Jenrette wasn't too choosy in that way. And the kid whose name nobody could ever remember, heading out in his broken-down cargo van, choking and stalling and sputtering all over the sleeping village to deliver his morning edition stacks of *The Rock River Guardian* safely to their drop-off destinations.

Each of them drove past the permanently darkened Lawrie Theater at some point or other on their witching-hour excursions, and yet none of them looked up. Not one took notice of the black plastic letters which had been rearranged on the marquee to form a warning—

TKE HUR AND LE VE NOW

—misspelled hurriedly amid the jumbled letters and old matinee show times on the canopy billboard over the abandoned theater's doors.

2

Somewhere in the chill night along a lonely stretch of Interstate 80 in northeastern Ohio, state police were making a traffic stop. A trooper on highway patrol witnessed someone throwing blows inside a rolling vehicle, watching as it swerved in and out of the lines. He moved into place behind them and radioed the location and description: a red Ford F-150 pickup truck—the good-ol'-hillbilly-boy's transportation of choice around these parts, another trooper joked, radioing he'd be there momentarily to back him up— then he hit his lights. The red pickup continued to weave for an extra quarter of a mile before edging over and pulling off the turnpike onto an exit called Salt Springs Road. The state trooper sat in his cruiser with its red-and-blues flashing and his spotlight trained on the halted vehicle, running the Ohio plates, waiting for his backup to arrive. He could see three individuals inside, but it was the male driver who'd been hurling those punches.

They were sitting at some burg's city limits; a sign up beyond the idling truck read: McDONALD ~ OHIO'S FINEST VILLAGE. Just another small town, like so many others out here, where most homeowners were still required to carry mine subsidence insurance due to so many of the houses having been built atop old mine shafts—coal mines, and salt mines.

Two additional cruisers slid up, one in front as blocker and one to the rear. The first trooper radioed these new arrivals the stop was for an illegal lane change. Failure to signal, and a lot of weaving. He also broadcast no wants or warrants, but that the driver had definitely been smacking the hell out of someone. The three of them exited their vehicles in sync and approached the Ford from different angles, shining their Maglite tacticals through the windows, their free hands resting on their holstered service weapons.

Male in the driver's seat, woman in the passenger, a young boy in the back of the extended cab.

They ordered the engine shut off and asked the driver what the problem was tonight, catching a whiff of alcohol. The worn-looking brunette gal in the passenger seat was trying to hide her face, obviously battered, left eye and cheek already swelling while blood dripped from her broken lips. The driver was ordered out, and the initial trooper on the scene gave him all of two seconds to comply before flinging the truck door wide and dragging him clear. This one was tattooed and big, sluglike—Jabba the fucking Hutt wearing a sweat-soaked tent for a T-shirt—but the officer extracted him from the Ford's cab with practiced ease. He tried to voice his protest, mealy-mouthed from booze, slurring something which sounded like it'd come through a mouthful of horseshit. The state trooper held him up, noting the mesh ball cap and the mustache and goatee; standard hillbilly fare, he thought, and whirled the driver around to slam him face-first into his truck. For good measure, he shot Mealy-Mouth a hard forearm to the back of his skull, knocking the Marshall Amps cap from his shaved, medicine-ball sized head.

For the woman. No charge.

While the second officer assisted in cuffing the suspect, the third, seeing the situation was in hand, wandered toward his cruiser. The less he saw of this the better. So he made his way up to the McDonald, OH., sign to dally there, tinkering with his flashlight. Across the isolated exit road was another sign, a wooden one on posts in need of repainting that declared GOD BLESS AMERICA. An electric flood lamp had been stuck into the ground below it, aimed up to illuminate it and the two American flags on either side. Behind the sign was a ravine. The third trooper strolled across for a look. He nudged the brim of his campaign hat back, to peer over the edge and down the embankment, and . . . and was that something down in the dar—?

He jerked around toward the red pickup, following the scream.

They had handcuffs on the driver, had him jammed against the truck's side with legs spread, while the kid wailed at the sight. The two officers glanced in at the sobbing brunette, saw the terror-stricken look on the young boy's face—frightened not of what was happening right now, they realized, but of what was surely to come to him and his bloodied mother after this was over. The second trooper got the gal and her kid out of the vehicle, held them in his arms and talked to them both. This left the first trooper alone with Mealy-Mouth, gave him opportunity (if not actual cause) to raise the man's cuffed arms high behind him with his left and then to put the stick in with his right. And put that bitch in he did, slamming his pistol-grip baton flat and hard and forearmed into the drunken driver's kidneys, for *extra* good measure. The wife beater gasped and went down with a grunt of pain, and then pissed himself in writhing spasms at the trooper's feet.

The third trooper watched a bit longer before turning away to peer again over the edge, into the ditch off the side of the road. A ditch which could have been a former salt bed itself decades ago, where halite, or rock salt mineral, might've once been found and mined out by the truckload. He squinted in the dark, inching closer to the edge so he could shine his Maglite down. Then he froze.

The rear section of an automobile was visible in his flashlight beam. Half submerged, protruding partway from the rainwater and thick mud at the bottom of the fifteen foot ravine. He hollered for the others, telling them excitedly of his find, and soon the Salt Springs Road exit just off the Ohio Turnpike was crawling with law enforcement officers who'd appeared out of the woodwork, along with a tow truck and driver summoned to the scene. After a struggle the wreck was hooked up, and the city tow driver fought his way out of the muck and mire to begin winching it up from the marshy, water-filled ditch.

It was huge, as long as a boat—a sage, 19-and-81 four door Pontiac sedan, it turned out; license plates gone, vehicle stickers all scraped off—and it took a hell of a long time to haul it up to the road. The GOD BLESS AMERICA sign was knocked askew during this, one of the display flags ending up on the ground. A young uniformed officer righted it again, carefully brushing Old Glory clean; he looked ready to salute.

When the automobile finally made it to road level and was secured, and nothing or no one could be scoped inside, the three initial troopers brought a locksmith kit to pick open the Parisienne's trunk. At last, the lock cylinder popped and the lid was flung wide for their efforts, the state troopers—their mealy-mouthed, wife-beating prisoner long forgotten in the backseat of a highway cruiser—winced at what they saw.

Crammed into the closed darkness, tucked neatly away in the reeking cavernous trunk before them was what remained of Mr. Nate Bitters, former night librarian, decomposing at an amazingly accelerated rate within this warm, upholstered sarcophagus of his. He appeared to have been hacked to death with what might've well been a small ax or hatchet type weapon, the scalp missing from his bludgeoned, penetrated skull.

PART TWO

THE GLEE CLUB

He comes—fog dim—the ghost that will not die,
And with accusing finger points at me.
                                    —Robert E. Howard

CHAPTER NINE

I

THE GREASE-YELLOWED WALL clock above the griddle read 11:20 AM when Officers Clemency and Crider walked into the café for their order. Meg Bilobran saw them enter and retrieved their sandwiches from behind the counter, a Reuben and a turkey club on sourdough, and then met them at the cash register. With a weary smile, she handed the paper bag to the uniformed black man, the deputy chief.

"Here ya go, fellas, all ready. How are things, Palm?"

"Oh, same old same old. Can't complain. Mm-hmm. You look tired, Meg."

"Morris, my cook, and Jilly Sweet both called off, so I'm runnin' the gauntlet by myself today. Running being the key word. Nothing sweet about it, either. Ha. So how are you, Bobby? How's that pregnant wife of yours holdin' up?"

The younger and newer of the two officers grinned. "She's holding fine, Mrs. Bilobran. We're just waiting and hanging on."

"How many times I told you, babes? Call me Meg. Anything else for ya?"

Palm Clemency ordered a couple of large coffees, while Bobby Crider examined the slowly revolving desserts in Meg's carousel pie case with keen interest. "See anything you like?" she asked, coming back with the coffees, and the young man laughed.

"I see a lot that I like. But I'd better not, Mrs. Bil— uh, Meg."

Clemency tossed a ten and two fives beside the register and told the woman to keep it. She smiled that weary smile again, ringing up their order.

"Thank ya kindly."

Reaching below, she quickly lifted forth a bulky Canon 35MM camera on a tangled neck strap and without aiming clicked off several rapid-fire shots of them both before replacing it again. The deputy chief scratched his chin.

"Still banking on that big art gallery exhibit someday, Meg?"

"Never know. Get me outta here for a while at least, it would. Sorry for hitting and running, but I'm short-handed and playing catch-up. Take care, guys."

With that she was gone, back behind the counter to the grease pit of a cooking area. The two police officers strolled out of the small diner, nodding cordially at the other customers seated at their booths. After they'd left, the once-pretty woman wearing the hairnet turned to place a slab of bacon down with a satisfying sizzle and crack open an egg on the hot griddle. Next, she found herself gazing down. For the egg she had just emptied was made up of all white, contained no yolk inside it at all. Nothing but the egg white.

Meg Bilobran crossed herself without thinking

about it, without even knowing why. And on she went with the rest of her short-handed, playing catch-up day.

***

Richard sat with Katelyn on a picnic table in Jasper Park, watching the sparkling Rock River flow by in the autumn sun. Listening to the trees. Earlier that morning they'd partaken of the Nightlight Inn's continental breakfast—Katie had cold cereal, spooning the toasted oat pieces out of her Lucky Charms and saving the soggy marshmallow bits and sweetened milk for last, while her father grabbed a half-stale Danish, wishing it was a sausage Egg McMuffin instead.

Richard decided he'd swing out and see his friend today, maybe let Katie Jane spend some time with her grandparents and Blondie. First though, he had to get the Blazer through a carwash. It was *imperative,* as his New York agent was fond of repeating to him over the telephone. Then he'd try to catch up with Tommy Truitt at the construction site George had told him about.

It would be awkward seeing him after so many years, but he wouldn't mention anything touchy. Nothing about what a bitch prison must've been. And certainly nothing about all that gruesome business, or what an *ultra* bitch it must've been for poor Minnie Dean that day, the school bus driver who happened upon the god-awful spectacle all over those railroad tracks—

No. Best not to even bring it up . . . like Big Minnie must've surely brought up *her* sausage Egg McMuffins that morning.

149

Stop, Richard thought. *What are you, like eleven or something?*

Katie was staring dreamily at the water. Stroking her hair, he asked: "Pretty isn't it, hon?"

"Yes," she said. "This was where you met Mommy?"

"Well actually, no, I first met her in grade school. Saw her in the halls a lot. But this is where I first held her hand, and this is where I got up the courage to kiss her for the first time." He took his daughter's tiny hand in emphasis and kissed her on the top of her head. She broke out in a smile of contentment and blushed, blinking in the daylight, still sleepy-eyed.

"Kissing Mommy," she murmured, conjuring up some pleasant memory in her mind. "Yes."

Richard walked her back to the SUV, past the centuries-old cottonwood tree; Katie watched it curiously as they crossed its gnarling shadow.

Before long they had pulled out of the park.

The two saw a variety of faces on their drive through town, even spied the lady they'd met yesterday, the woman high up, trimming branches back. Richard waved to her but she seemed preoccupied, and failed to raise her hand this time. Last night's fog had burned away in the morning sun, leaving only thin wisps of mist clinging to the cornfields and curled in low-lying areas. They were supposed to be at the Deadmonds' place by now, but there was no way Richard was rising so early and heading out like Glee had wanted them to. Besides, the Chevy they rode in still stank sickly sweet and rancid sour to all high heaven.

The Queen would just have to wait. They'd be there soon enough.

2

"Lynyrd Skynyrd? *Lynyrd Skynyrd?* Are you fucking kidding me?"

Richard heard this from where he leaned against the freshly scented, sparkling-clean Blazer, and he recognized Tom Truitt's voice immediately. His palms went clammy and he faced Katie, who sat in the passenger seat, keeping his back toward the young man and the older one passing by.

"Listen," said Tommy, stopping at some bushes near the curb, "you know how living in a trailer is the redneck, white-trash version of the American Dream? Owning your own home and all that? Well, that's what Lynyrd Skynyrd is to classic rock and roll."

"Nah, you're wrong," the younger man argued. "I think Skynyrd has to be one of the best of all time."

"Wow. If you think that, then *wow* . . . you're a bigger idiot than your physical volume would indicate, my friend."

"Huh?"

"It's shit, dude. Southern-fried shit. In cold weather, you can see the steam rising up off it. *Shit.*"

A smile tugged at Richard's lips, and Katie said: "Is that your friend, Daddy? The one you're looking for?"

"Yes, Katie-Smatie, that's him."

His daughter giggled. "You look like you're hiding. Aren't you saying hello?"

Richard grinned at her, dropping his voice. "When they're done talking, hon," he stage-whispered. "Wouldn't want to interrupt, that would be rude. How're you doing in there?"

"I'm fine."

He reached in and notched up the radio volume, which he'd left on for her. Just then the young man behind him spoke. "What about Ozzy?" Richard rolled his eyes, knowing what was coming.

He heard: "Let me tell you about that, too, kid. I saw Ozzy Osbourne twice, once with Sabbath and once without them. This was back in his supposed 'heyday', don't forget. Both times somebody invited me along, so I got to go for free basically. And both times I *still* demanded my money back. A fucking cadaver would've put on a better show."

The young man scoffed at this. "Pretty bold coming from a guy with a naked, dickless angel on his T-shirt."

Richard adjusted the passenger door mirror to get a gander at what was behind him. Sure enough, Thomas Truitt had on a ragged old Zeppelin *Swan Song* shirt to go with his dirty jeans. His shaggy blond hair was still shoulder length, but Rich noted plenty of grays in the mix. He was wearing Gargoyles shades and tan leather work boots, and the two stood near a rust-eaten Dodge truck and a Kawasaki motorcycle sitting in back of the Blazer on the street.

"For your information it is not a dickless angel," said Tommy carefully. "It's the sun god Apollo. And I wouldn't talk if I were you, man: I've seen you wearing a Poison T-shirt."

"So?"

Tommy whistled. "Kid, in my day the only people who listened to Poison were teenyboppers and cream puffs. That's it."

"Hmph!"

"Sorry, but it's all shit. Once again, *shit*."

"And this isn't?" said the kid, gesturing to the winged silkscreen logo on Truitt's shirt.

Tommy pulled the T-shirt away from his sinewy torso for effect, a smirk on his face. "Greatest rock band ever assembled."

Richard was grinning also; he looked at the ground so Katelyn wouldn't question him. The whole exchange had the feel of fun to it, but still he was glad he'd kept the radio up for her. The younger man jabbed a finger. "Greatest? You gotta be joking."

"Hey, you don't believe me? Don't take my word for it—get yourself a copy of *The Song Remains the Same* concert flick and watch the live guitar solo during "Stairway", kid. Forget Hendrix and his distortion gimmicks, and piss on all this 'watch how fast I can play' bullshit . . . you've never seen *any*one make an electric guitar sing like that and you never will again. Ever. Jimmy Page parted the fucking heavens and played directly to God on that Madison Square Garden solo, and you'll never see anybody like him again in your lifetime."

"You're an elitist fuck, you know that?"

"Yep." They smiled at each other with shit-eating grins. "What's your point?"

The young crew worker shook his head and changed the subject. "Man, I'd've bet that drywall ceiling board would have stayed up with those nails. I'd've sworn it."

Tommy shrugged. "We MacGyvered her. She'll hold until we get the right screws up in there." He glanced at his wristwatch. "You bring back lunch and I'll make the hardware store run. See you in fifteen. We good?"

153

"On it." The kid climbed onto his motorcycle and kick-started it to life, lurching off with a squeal and a nod. Tommy turned toward his truck, and that was when Richard inhaled, winked at Katie and stepped away from the Blazer.

"Double T," he said simply, head tilted at an angle.

Thomas Truitt glanced at him and then did a double-take, lifting the mirrored Gargoyles to his crown, eyes widened in surprise. Both arms dropped to his sides and stayed there. "Well, fuck me," he finally breathed.

"Maybe later, after dinner and a show," Rich offered. "I see you're still schooling the youth around here on the finer points of superior music."

"Someone has to." Tommy cracked a smile, and they looked at each other for a freeze-frame moment. Truitt started forward. "Little Richie Franklin, goddamn. It's been a while. How the hell are you, man?"

"Well—" began Richard, extending his hand, but Tommy had already grabbed him up in a bear hug which quite possibly might've compressed a few ribs. "—all right, I guess." He gasped for air, a laugh escaping him. When at last he was put down he shook his friend's hand. "What's new, Tom?"

"Shit, not a whole lot. Nothing new ever happens here."

Richard noticed the cross necklace he wore, which appeared to be made of nails twisted together. "That's pretty cool," he said, tapping it with his fingertip, resisting the urge to flick Truitt's nose when he glanced down.

"Yeah, isn't it? My Aunt Cassie made this, out of

154

her horseshoe nails." Tommy studied him. "How'd you know where to find me? Or did you?"

"George Deadmond mentioned you were working on a house over this way. So I just, you know, sort of wandered by."

"Your father-in-law, sure. Wow." His face became somber. "Um, I read about your wife in the newspapers. Hometown girl and all. Michelle, right? I was sorry to hear that, man. Really."

Richard glanced away with a pained look. "Thanks. Hey, I'd like you to meet my daughter. She's right here." He beckoned toward the Chevy. "Katie? This is my friend Tommy. And this is Katie, my baby girl."

"Hello there, Katie," said Truitt, peeking into the vehicle.

Katie smiled, happy to be part of her father's reunion. "Hello."

"Huh, wow. She's a beaut, Richie." He regarded him with mock scorn. "So, where is it you're living again? Vermont? Rhode Island?"

"Maine. We live in Maine now."

"Right. I'll be." Silence. "Maple syrup and Stephen King—you mean *that* Maine?"

Richard grinned. "That would be the one. Don't forget the lobsters, though."

"Course not." Another pause, then: "Ever seen him?"

"What?"

"Stephen King—ever seen him? Spotted him standing in line at the post office, or in Long John Silver's or anywhere? You know."

"Not yet," Richard chuckled. "I hear he's starting to winter in warmer climes. Can't do the snow and cold anymore. Or doesn't want to, I suppose. Bones took a real pounding after that accident."

"Right. Unbelievable, wasn't that?" Tommy bowed his head. "Ahh, well . . . how the mighty hath fallen."

"Jury's still out on that one. Say listen, Tom, you got anything going on later? I just meant if you didn't, we could get together maybe."

"What's up?"

"Oh, nothing. Nothing. I'm dropping Katie off at her grandparents so she can spend some time with them, is all. Thought if you weren't busy we could catch up or something, hang out for a while. We're here for a few days before we have to turn around and pull out again. But if you've got things going on, hey, don't even worry about it. I'm not trying to impose or anything."

Scrutinizing his watch, Tommy said, "Can you be back here around three? We should have this ceiling job up and all painted by then."

"Sure." Richard felt relieved. "Absolutely. I'll meet you here."

Truitt nodded, and turned to observe a police car as it slunk by, its driver staring at the both of them for a long time before it rolled on. Tom whistled through his teeth, mumbling low. "That's right, Prick-we. Keep gawking. Maybe you'll break your neck."

"Who? Who's that?"

Tommy grunted, drifting away from the green SUV and from Katie's ears. "Chief of Police. You remember old Prick-we, don't you? Biggest prick in northern Illinois." He saw Richard's expression and realized that he didn't. "Priewe. Worked security at the hospital up in Rockford, back when we were kid orderlies there."

Suddenly the light dawned. "Mr. Priewe, right! Used to strut around the halls like John Wayne. Hospital rent-a-cop, always talking shit? We called him Prick-we instead of his real name."

"*Chip*," said Tommy with disdain, as if a bad taste had crept into his mouth. The face he made reminded Richard of youthful days gone by. "Colossal prick," Truitt finished.

"And *he's* police chief? Holy God damn, I thought you said nothing new ever happens here."

"Well, almost nothing." Tommy locked gazes with him, clearing his throat. "Hey, I've gotta hit the hardware store so's I can get back. But it was great seeing you, Rich. You too, Katie." He waved to her.

Richard could not wipe the smile off his face, nor did he wish to. "Great seeing you, man. I'm glad I caught you."

"Here at three? You won't forget?"

Richard tapped his temple. "It's up here."

Truitt laughed. "One thirty-six, right?"

"What?"

"Your IQ . . . it was always one thirty-six, wasn't it?"

Well, how in the fuck— "Yeah, that's right. How the hell can you remember that?"

Tommy only grinned. "All up here," he said, tapping his own temple as he climbed into his blue-over-silver Dodge Ram. "I'll see ya, dude." He started up the truck and was gone.

"See you," murmured Richard, watching him go. He blinked, his smile changing to a frown. But yes, sure he still remembered things like that. He'd never left here, after all, as Richard had, except for his stints at Marion State Penitentiary. Yes. So of course, he had hung on to his memories even more desperately than ever, in a godforsaken place like that.

Richard continued to look on until the blue truck had vanished from sight.

CHAPTER TEN

I

IT *REALLY WAS FUNNY,* Alice thought as she sat listening to Mrs. Van Meers's resonant Corinthian bells chiming in the light wind. Priceless. The look on Syd's face last night, that dripping look of shock and bewilderment.

Funny, how things turned out.

In truth, Alice Granberg wasn't actually a homosexual. She'd only gone along with things, certain things, for as long as it was convenient. After all, she'd had no place to stay, no one to turn to. Sydney had taken her in after Alice's shithead excuse for a boyfriend had found someone new and kicked her without ceremony to the curb. But Syd Cholke had gotten something out of the deal, too. You better believe it. For as long as it was convenient . . . nothing more.

No, Alice preferred to think of herself as an 'Anne Heche style' lesbian. Alice suspected there were probably a lot of girls out there like Miss Heche and herself, young ladies who for whatever reason—be it getting burned by abusive shithead boyfriends, or be it angst-laden rebellion, or just being the typical *hey, stop what you're doing and pay attention to me* types—decided to try the same sex on for size. She had plenty of friends back in college who'd experimented with gender switching as a fad, because it was the 'in thing' to do at the time. Anything to be an outlaw, to not go along with the pack, but they weren't real lesbians either, only masqueraders; straight, then gay, then bi, and then straight again. Girls that for a while, though, under various circumstances, ended up sleeping with the real thing: androgynous women who looked and acted more like men than anything else.

The way Syd Cholke did, for instance. Syd was plenty gay, all right, butch as they came. Still, you'd never catch her marching in Gay Pride parades or wearing a T-shirt which proclaimed *Lesbo and Loving it!*, or flaunting in any way. That wasn't what Sydney was about. She only wanted to live her life and be happy, no matter who knew or didn't know. She didn't want attention, was never into broadcasting her orientation like some were. She just wanted to get lucky and find herself someone to call her own and grow old with. Jeez, she still slept with her childhood baby pillow, if you could believe it—and Syd's own loony-job of a mother was the one who had to re-cover the pitiful thing with new material for her daughter every year. Now wasn't that the sweetest thing ever? Either that, or it surely was the creepiest. And yet—

Last night she had gone too far, beyond the pale, and suddenly it was no longer convenient.

Alice had allowed herself to be undressed and led to their bed. She let Sydney go down on her as usual, lapping at her and gulping softly beneath the sheets. Alice closed her eyes like always, in the semidarkness was able to imagine her ex-boyfriend doing this to her, until she came hard and long, giving her female lover what she desired. She'd allowed Sydney's fingers inside her, probing, stretching and opening her. She had even allowed the warming lubricant to be spread over her thighs and inside her tingling slit and ass.

But when the enormous strap-on had been brought out, when Sydney harnessed it on and oiled it and tried forcing that thing, that curved monstrosity between her legs, Alice had soundly rebuffed her advances.

As Syd became more persistent, Alice had pushed her away not once but twice, finally reaching up quite by accident into the headboard above her and dousing her lover in the face with a *Munsters* collectible glass of water she'd found there (only fair, since she'd done it to Alice first . . . *tit* for *tat* . . . and besides, everyone knew *The Munsters* kicked *The Addams Family's* ass), to make her cease.

"Mffffffttt!" Sydney had spluttered, taken totally by surprise. "You little *bitch!*" She scooted forward on the bed, grappling with her, trying again to force the lubricated strap-on inside. Alice had pulled one leg back and lashed out fiercely with it, kicking Syd in her mountainous tit and knocking her right off their bed with a crash.

That's for pinching mine and hurting it, bitch, streaked the thought across Alice's mind. *Tit for tat . . .*

She laughed aloud on the screened-in porch, clamping a hand over her mouth so no one would hear. Yes, Sydney Cholke was about as butch as they came, but the sight of her floundering around on the bedroom floor, trying to get her footing, that was too much. It'd been truly comical the way she had rocked back on both heels, fuming, drenched and beet-red in the face, sputtering and trembling in anger with the ridiculous bowed dong strapped to her and with that dyke 'do of hers sticking up. It took all of Alice's will to remain straight-faced.

Instead, Alice said: "Don't come near me again, Syd. I mean it. *You keep the fuck away.*" With just enough menace in her voice, and one hand resting on her naked tummy, that Sydney shrank back from her in the shadows, retreating into the bathroom.

Alice Granberg would allow nothing to endanger the child she could already feel growing inside her womb. Nothing in heaven or on this earth.

She avoided Sydney the rest of the night after the incident, dozing lightly on the sofa, listening for sounds in the apartment they shared. In the morning she'd played possum while Syd got up, lying there and pretending to be asleep until she was sure her lesbian girlfriend had left for work, off to trim her damn trees again. Then Alice had packed up her things and had gone for good, examining the lovebirds out back before leaving the keys to Sydney's apartment in the empty *Addams Family* glass on its coaster for her to find. One final *fuck you* for the road, Anne Heche style.

Now here she was, staying with her boss Lillian Van Meers until she could figure out what to do. It wasn't so bad, and at least she could get a ride with her each day to the Styx & Stonze Botanicals shop. Mrs. Van Meers had insisted on her staying, once Alice explained what her roommate had tried to do to her, and her unborn baby, last night. The old lady said she could stay for as long as she needed, and told her to take the day off. She'd handle things on her own down at the store today. Alice made a mental note that she'd have to start getting ready soon, get ready and head on over for The Glee Club showing at the church tonight. It was, after all, the biggest thing going in this boring little place. Right now, though, Alice relaxed on Mrs. Van Meers's porch swing and closed her eyes, listening to the Corinthian bell wind chimes and their divine resonance as it carried on the sun-warmed September breeze.

Funny, she thought as she stroked her belly gently with her fingertips, *how things turned out.*

2

At the center of town slept the dreaming dead in their neat, muted triangle, indifferent to the concerns of the world. No one living traversed any of the three graveyard's peaceful grounds at this moment, which was strange in such nice weather. All of a sudden a small cry squeaked out, and a barn swallow fell stone-dead from the sky, landing among the chiseled tombstones of Hebrew National Cemetery. It came to rest toward the back near the wrought-iron fence, in the tranquil section of graves situated apart from the others on a slight rise. High above, the derelict Shaw-Meredith House loomed in its woods. The tiny bird's outstretched wings retracted slowly, drew in, twitched, even though it was lifeless . . . had exhaled its final breath.

The dead stirred unquietly within their earthen berths beneath the ground.

CHAPTER ELEVEN

I

DEPUTY CHIEF CLEMENCY** and Bobby Crider ate their lunches on the bench in front of the Public Safety Building. Crider took a bite of turkey club, watching as someone mowed the Post Office's narrow strip of lawn across Elm Street, mulching leaves as they went. A squad car glided to the curb, blocking his view, and Chief Priewe got out.

"How we doing, boys?"

"Chief," said Clemency. The younger officer could only nod, his mouth filled with sourdough bread. "You aren't eating? Meg's being generous today: my Reuben really got loaded up on the corned beef and Swiss here."

"I'll grab something later. Listen, I want—"

Priewe stepped back from the sidewalk, just missing Karl Kissick as he sailed by on a skateboard, student book bag slung over him like a full parachute pack, clicking away heedlessly at his Game Boy. The kid glanced up for a second before returning his attention to the handheld game as he rolled past.

"Hey, stay off the walks!" Priewe barked. "Goddamn kid. Those Kissicks really are shit-for-brains, the lot of them."

ЯLREŘWA TER Unl

Crider had finally swallowed clear. "Aw, he isn't bad."

"No, Bob? Let's see, the parents had two sons and they named them both the same damned thing. There's Carl with a C, and there's Karl with a K. How brilliant was that? Took some real gray matter, that one did. I have a feeling the Kissick babies were likely dropped on their heads more times than anyone in town cares to admit. So, how far can the kids be behind their own idiot parents in the shit-for-brains department, Bobby? Tell me."

Crider exchanged looks with Palm Clemency, shrugged. Priewe glared about and spotted two teenage black girls—the Billups twins, Charese and . . . offhand he could not remember the other one— chattering on their cell phones as they cut over and headed for the Arby's, on lunch break from the high school. The police chief stared a long time, observing the twin girls' smooth brown legs as they walked by, their ashy-colored knees. Reesie's more than the other girl's, for some reason. He wetted his dry lips and watched her through narrowed eyes. "It's the dumbing down effect," Priewe said. "Yep."

"What is, Chief?"

Priewe turned. "Theory going around says the more high-tech America gets the dumber we become, depending on what the technology is used for. You know, sort of like 'you are what you eat'?" He gestured toward the black girls crossing Elm, phones pressed to their heads as they prattled. "There's your technology for the new Millennium, boys. Right there. Electronic gadgets and gizmos. All designed to make losers feel like winners, make the nobodies feel like somebodies.

165

Stupid mindless shit. And the best part is the dumber everyone gets, the more acceptable it all becomes, until these dumb-asses become the norm."

Bobby Crider started to speak but Clemency bumped him in the shoulder. *For Chrissakes, just leave it be.*

Priewe regarded his two officers again, cocking an eyebrow. "Remember all those Y2K morons, at the beginning of the year? Fucking hilarious." His gaze went distant, faraway yet not seeing. He let out a tired sigh. "Well, people like to feel important, I guess. Even when nothing could be further from the truth. No wonder they sell so many of those damn things, cellular phones and video games and such, all the nobodies in the world, wanting to feel like somebody. Meanwhile the dumbing down continues. People are so . . . so *disposable* these days, aren't they?" The chief smiled sadly, shaking his head.

He focused, recalling why he'd stopped here.

He told them both to keep their eyes on a vehicle with out-of-state plates, dark green Chevrolet Blazer out of Maine, bad-ass chrome grille guard on her, a man and a snip of a little girl inside. Priewe's deputy chief cut him off, informing him of the visitors' identities, how it was just Richard Franklin and his daughter back in town after the tragic hit-and-run death of Michelle: George and Glee Deadmond's girl that he married from long ago.

Priewe nodded. "Right. I did read about that. Any reason they'd be hanging around that jailbird Thomas Truitt, you can think of?"

"Well," said Clemency, finished with his Reuben and wiping his hands on a paper napkin, "Truitt and he go back a ways. So yeah, he'd probably get together with him again. Why?"

Priewe pulled out a spiral notepad, ignoring the question. "You got a middle name on this guy? Anything about his background?"

"He's a writer, I know that much. Had his first book published and everything. Middle name Allan—two A's, two L's, just like Edgar."

"How's that?"

"Mr. Poe, I mean. Nevermore?"

The police chief looked at him dully. "How is it *you* know all this?"

Clemency couldn't help grinning. "I went to school with him twenty years ago, that's how. Richie and Tom Truitt both. Mm-hmm. We were going to be poets back then, the three of us."

"Poets," Priewe repeated. "Uh-huh. Naturally." He flipped his notepad shut, putting it, and the pen away. "And aren't you the smug one with the jokes there, considering that middle name you have? Why in the world any mother would name her son Palm Sunday, well, it's beyond me. Just saying."

The chief bade them farewell, sauntering up the steps of the Public Safety Building. He turned back, reminding them not to forget to swing past the Island today, to run at least a few patrols out that way from now on—some of those boondocks dirt-water rounds he was fond of doling to the subordinates, just to remind them of their place. That done, Chip Priewe disappeared through the building's doors with a smile spreading across his face.

Prick, Bobby Crider thought as he chewed the last of his turkey club.

2

Richard met up with Tommy at three o'clock and followed his weatherworn Dodge Ram out to Telegraph Road, thrumming his fingers on the steering wheel as he drove the rural route. He'd left Katie with the Deadmonds after spending a few hours there himself, but he was beginning to have second thoughts. He was probably just being overprotective, but the whole idea of separating from Katie, for any period, gnawed at him.

He hadn't been away from her for more than a few minutes at a time since the funeral, like yesterday when he ran into the market—and what in blazes had he been thinking, doing that? Was he punchy from being on the road so long, leaving her out in the SUV by herself? Granted, this was a small town where most everyone left their doors unlocked at night, Richard's hometown even. Still, it made him feel edgy. And guilty.

Not just being separated from *her*, but from them both.

Richard had brought Michelle's ashes to the house, setting the container down with care on their coffee table as promised. They visited pleasantly, no one mentioning the macabre centerpiece or even glancing its way. Then, while he'd sat scratching behind Blondie's pointed ears, Glee Deadmond had risen from her chair and picked up the copper urn, moving like someone in a dream. She placed it on top of the Curtis Mathis console television (which was switched on and still working, astoundingly, tuned to a local PBS station) between Michelle's baby picture and her framed high school portrait. After that, Glee sat gazing at her dead daughter's urn with an incredible sadness radiating from her, until Richard had to look away.

He informed his in-laws he'd be gone for a bit, that he ran into Thomas Truitt earlier, and wanted to drop in on him this afternoon for a quick reminisce. He detected a slight grin on George's lips, but Glee merely grimaced. Richard added he'd be back to eat dinner and to see the church production after—and what time was it again? Yes, 6:00 PM. Back in plenty of time. He asked Katie, once more, if it was all right with her, if she didn't mind staying with her grandparents and Blondie for a few hours; again, she told him it was all right. That she'd be fine.

Before departing, Richard gave in and excused himself to use the Deadmonds' facilities. He walked down the hallway, past the coat rack, and listened as he went. He climbed the Cornish staircase to the upper floor. Once there, he thought he did hear something. An odd noise of some kind, clicking somewhere. A *click*, followed by the echo of a *clack*. He moved along the dimly lit corridor, past the main bedroom and Michelle's former bedroom, ducking into the restroom on his left. When he'd emptied his bladder, Richard flushed the toilet, washed and dried his hands, and stepped out into the hall to make his way back downstairs.

He paused at Michelle's bedroom door, lingered, wanting to see what it looked like inside now. Placing a hand on the doorknob, he became aware of his heartbeat in his ears. He tensed, listening over his shoulder as the sound of the toilet tank filling down

169

the corridor trickled off at last. There it was again, faint. *Click.* Quiet once more, only his heart thumping, then—*click. Clack-click.*

A child laughed, distinct and close by.

Richard's breath stopped. He whirled and froze stock-still in the empty corridor, his head cocked to the side. Was that Katie? He felt himself trembling. No, it had come from the room across from Michelle's, from what used to be Glee's old sewing room. He crept until he stood in front of it, placed one hand on the smooth, cold knob, and withdrew it again.

Click.

He pushed the door open and looked inside. Boxes were visible against the walls, bolts of fabric and canvas rolls leaning near the squatted, drop-clothed silhouette of the sewing machine. His eyes fell upon the card table standing in the center of the tight room, a checkerboard on it with red and black pieces in place, as if abandoned mid-game. The jumped pieces were stacked to one side in little piles. There was another small envelope here, like the one on the foyer piano, taped to the table's edge: *My C* had been scrawled across this one. Richard's brow furrowed, and he took a hesitant step forward.

Hello? he wished he had the nerve to say.

An eerie whisper seemed to come from somewhere within the cool shadows of that room. A cold prickle ran up his spine and down both arms, and Richard closed the door swiftly and started downstairs. About halfway there another shiver caught up to him on the narrow staircase, like something reaching to touch his back. The hairs at the nape of his neck went up, gooseflesh rising all over him.

He never looked behind him to see.

Richard made sure that Katie had her activity books and crayons, including the special book. He gave her a piece of paper with his cell phone number written on it, made her read it aloud to him before tucking it into her pocket. He told her to call him for anything, anything at all, and her Daddy would come like lightning and get her. For any reason. He whispered to her before leaving, near the moon phase clock, suggesting that she keep an eye on Mommy's jar for him. When Katie asked why, he repeated to keep an eye on it, carefully, but without letting on to anyone. He winked, kissing her forehead and promising to call and check in on her. Richard paused and stared at the cremation urn on top of the TV console, thinking, *I'm doing it, Michelle, I'm doing what you wanted,* before slipping through the front door and away from them all.

Now here he sat, steering his way out to Telegraph Road, feeling guilty for leaving his only daughter in the very prim, suddenly very strange Deadmond house.

3

As Aaban Darwish approached the church grounds he showed little to no emotion, remaining fairly composed, even though an electric rush of anticipation surged through him.

He made his way up the sidewalk with hands stuffed into his jacket pockets as he walked, past the oak tree, and cut into the side parking lot where already people had begun to collect. The pastor was there, talking with congregation members. The huge

Indian man was there also, cooking meat on a charcoal grill in his immaculate suit. It was the church's picnic gathering, the one they threw together each week before the big spectacle inside, as long as clement weather held out for the year. Simon Julian spotted him and raised one hand in a wave.

"Hey, Reverend Julian," said Aaban when he was within earshot. He almost pulled his own hand from his pocket, but thought better.

"Greetings, my boy." Julian moved away from the guests, coming over to stand beside the olive-skinned young man. "And how goes things in your world?"

"Oh, they're going, you know. Between homework, classes up at the college and my job here . . . well, there just aren't enough hours in the day."

"*Ach,*" the Reverend kidded him, "it's good for you, Abby. Idle hands and all that." He laughed an old man's laugh. "So, how are you getting on at the Lawrie's? From what I've heard it would be easy to lose oneself in that spacious place."

Aaban forced a smile. "It's not bad, sir. Besides, I hear you could get lost pretty easily in that big house of yours, too." *Name's Aaban . . . not Abby.*

Julian regarded him with surprise. "Indeed. You *could* lose yourself therein, my boy. Quite so. Have you ever been?"

"Pardon?"

"Ever been inside it?"

"Oh. No, never had the pleasure. Not yet." Aware of the doddering pastor watching him, Darwish scanned the other gatherers, taking in some of their familiar faces. His gaze came to rest on William Salt's grill.

Julian saw him looking at it through half-closed eyes, saw an expression of visceral disapproval creep into his youngish, swarthy face but pretended not to see.

"You must visit some time. Wondrous old house. *Wondrous.*" The old man smoothed back thin strands of white hair and gestured toward the picnic table, to the brats and buns and grilled ears of corn there, the potato chips and soda cans. "We have Midwestern delicacies, my boy. Help yourself."

"That's all right, Reverend. I'm good."

"Are you sure?" Simon Julian snatched a pork tenderloin and a sandwich bun from the tabletop array, wrapping them into a napkin and offering it up to him. "Looks yummy." He observed Aaban's dark eyes, the way they locked onto the foodstuff, unblinking. The Reverend thrust it closer, had to repress a smile when Aaban leaned back in loathe from it.

"I don't consume . . . meat," said the young man, jaw tightened. "It's unwholesome. Shortens the lifespan, you know?"

"Ah, yes. Of course. Well—" He set the swaddled sandwich down on a stack of paper plates, stepping away from the picnic table. "—you'd best be getting inside, I suppose. Give everything the once-over, my boy, as only you can." He started to turn but noticed the other still staring, eyes crawling over the tabletop spread, flicking to Salt and his barbecue grill and back again. "Aaban? You should be getting inside now, don't you think?"

The younger man blinked. "Um, yeah. I probably better, huh?"

"Make sure all the carpets are vacuumed and the oratory floor is swept out, would you? Oh yes, and please light the candles for me. And some incense. I'll need you to stay around after and help tidy up as usual, if that's all right?"

"Sure thing. You bet."

"Well, back to schmoozing," Julian said out of the corner of his deeply wrinkled mouth, a sly look clinging about his crow's-feet crinkled face. "This artsy-craftsy crowd here, they always come fashionably early. See you inside."

The Reverend made his way to the picnic area again, while Aaban headed for the rear church door. The young man swung around and watched as the old man mingled, avoiding handshakes and chatting with Mr. Lehman, owner of the small Candle & Quilt Shoppe in town. He saw Simon Julian stop to retrieve the grilled tenderloin sandwich from the table, raise it as if for show and then bite into it, chewing heartily and nodding toward him.

Shouldn't eat that, thought Aaban Darwish, smiling back, withdrawing a hand to open the rear door. *You might die from it one of these days.* He vanished inside Nain Lutheran Church. His other hand stayed shoved deep into the pocket of the black denim jacket he wore.

CHAPTER TWELVE

I

TOMMY TRUITT'S RAMSHACKLE little house had no front porch steps. They had disintegrated into nothingness over the years. This is what Richard noticed first about the place, and the way the whole structure leaned. Just a pinch to one side.

"Didn't know I'd be renting a lean-to," joked Tom as he showed him around, "when I read the ad in the paper. Woops . . . renting with option to buy, make that." Truitt hopped up onto the porch with the ease of someone who'd done it countless times, offering a hand back to Richard and helping hoist him up over the space where the stairs should have been. "I'll get to that one of these days."

Richard nodded. His friend lived alone out here, so the house was sparsely furnished: an opened sofa bed in the living room surrounded by various used, thrift-store items, obligatory big-screen TV on a stand against the wall, some rickety chairs circling an old cottage drop-leaf table in the kitchen.

A tattered color photograph of Kyoko was attached to the fridge door with a *Hellraiser* Pinhead magnet.

Richard spotted it and looked away, saying

nothing. There were no other homes nearby. Truitt's place virtually dead-ended here, with rippling tall fields all around it, and the deteriorating Sunset Drive-In sitting in the middle of one across Telegraph Road.

They sat on the uneven porch, legs dangling where the steps used to be, drinking a couple of Michelob beers Tommy had brought out.

Richard gazed over the wild flora of the field—the goldenrod and meadow foxtail, the purple-stemmed rises of cat's tail—and was reminded of Michelle's tiny greenhouse in Maine, and the exotic flowers she once grew. Her *Monstera deliciosa*, or fruit salad plant, the lady's-slipper orchids and walking irises, and her personal favorite, the night-blooming cereus she raised—nurturing and coaxing the gangly-looking plant along painstakingly, year round, just to see it open its big snowy petals for one solitary night before closing itself at dawn again for another full calendar cycle.

"Hope you don't have allergies," Richard said, watching the sea of reed stalks and grasses ebb and flow with the breeze. In the distance he could make out a corner of the gabled roof of Shaw-Meredith House, and the square-hatted turret tower, barely visible off in the high woods toward town.

"Nope. Not since I was a kid."

"Good deal."

Tommy said, "If I could ever scrape the money together I wouldn't mind buying and reopening the drive-in someday. You know, restore her, bring her back and then run the place from right here. Walk across the field to work every day." He laughed. "Sit here and watch my movies playing after dark. Take the winters off."

"Huh." *Her* . . .

The Sunset brooded, rotting and forgotten (save for one, thought Richard) in its field. Weeds sprouted up where cars used to park, its darkened screen sagging and slashed with angled holes. The land where it—*she* sat was perfect actually, well-drained, and sloping gently down and away out there, far from any city lights or traffic, like an outdoor theater was supposed to be. Rich could almost close his eyes and imagine the crunch of gravel under his tires, the smell of popcorn and hot dogs floating from lighted concession stands, imagine the crackle of speakers and the huge canvas screen flickering while a sky filled with stars shimmered overhead.

"Hell, I even heard about a drive-in, *fly-in* movie theater," said Tommy. "After World War Two, it was. Some guy opens up this drive-in, only it has room for cars *and* for small planes on the grounds. Cars down front, then the planes would land and fan out in the rear. When the picture's over, someone uses a Jeep and tows the planes out so they can take off again. No shit. Whole thing was just one giant airfield." He snorted. "Now if some retired pilot can come up with that, I ought'ta be able to bring cute girls and greasy food and midnight showings back to the Sunset Drive-In. You'd think."

"Huh," Richard repeated.

"That's the dream anyway," said Truitt. "Fucking crazy, right?"

Richard was shaking his head. "No. No, it isn't, Tom. It's a damn fine dream, matter of fact." He spoke softly, with sincerity.

Tommy smiled, taking a drink from his hourglass-shaped brown bottle. "So, how long you guys here for? When do you have to leave?"

He told him about the ashes and about his wife's dying wish; what he must do with them on her birthday, now that she was gone. "September twenty-ninth," he emphasized. "Day after tomorrow."

"Feast of the Archangels," Tommy said, nodding. "Christ's birth date, to boot."

Richard hesitated, his beer wavering at his lips. He lowered the Michelob. "Come again?"

"That date," he said with a sideways glance, "Michelle's birthday. She shares it with someone famous! It was also the birthday of Jesus Christ, they're thinking maybe."

"I don't get it—what's the punch line? Who is 'they'?"

Tommy rolled his eyes and began to explain. "There are certain biblical scholars—"

"Uh oh."

Clearing his throat, Tom continued. "—certain highly regarded biblical scholars who claim that by using key dates of events and milestones in the New Testament, they can decipher that Jesus wasn't actually born on Christmas Day. Instead, according to the original Greek manuscripts, they believe he was *conceived* on that date: December twenty-fifth. And that he was born nine months later, on September twenty-ninth."

Richard gaped. "Are you . . . ?"

"Another thing: the Holy Bible says the shepherds were all watching their flocks by night, the night of the birth, but that doesn't happen in the cold winter months around Bethlehem. Not in December, at least."

Richard stared at him, incredulous.

"What?" said Truitt, taking a swig of beer. "Anyway, they claim they can prove it." Feeling his friend's eyes on him, Tommy held his Michelob up. "Judge gave me a lot of reading time, ya know. Hear, hear."

"Wow, I guess so." At the mentioning of his prison sentence, an awkward silence followed. Uncertain, Richard finally said, "New one on me. Well, who's to say? You're more up on it than I am, man. Never heard of anything like that before. Only preacher I ever paid any attention to was Dr. Joel Nederhood, the guy who used to be on television."

Tommy was grinning. "*The Back to God Hour*, that was his radio show . . . and *Faith 20*, on WGN-TV out of Chicago. I remember him. Good guy—not a phony bone in his body."

"Holy *jeez*. Some wicked memory there, Tom."

"Yep." Truitt kicked his feet lazily back and forth off the stairless porch, like a kid swinging his legs off a pier. "Speaking of television, have you seen any of these new shows popping up? Reality TV they're calling this shit. Unbelievable, dude."

Richard told him no, he hadn't, had no intentions to for that matter: "I learned everything I ever needed to know about life from watching *M*A*S*H* and *All in the Family* on Saturday nights when I was growing up."

"I heard that."

They bantered comfortably then, about this and that, about Rich's chance glimpsing of the sinkhole pit yesterday and the newest gossip around town, sipping beers in the hazy-lazy sun. Richard noticed some large fluffy clouds moving in, drifting across that angled sun every so often. It remained a beautiful day, though.

They talked about the freelance work Tommy was doing as a remodeler, and what he comically referred to as a bid assessor. And Richard's writing and his book's publication, how Truitt had indeed read it, had the paperback in the house in fact. Richard ended up signing it for him, before their afternoon together was done.

Tom asked him about life in Maine, and learned how most of the native Mainers were wary of him, considered Richard just another intruder from 'out Chicago way'. No welcome mats to be found, not really. They stayed on the subject of Chicago; the slow disappearance of its icons and all the changes the city had gone through over the years, how the old Chicago they once knew was being chipped away bit by bit. Tommy mentioned that their one-time school buddy Palm Clemency was the deputy chief now, second in command only to Chip Prick-we himself. Palm Clemency, the only black kid they ever knew who was into Robert E. Howard and classic rock like they'd been. They talked Lovecraft and Poe, of course, their favorites, and discussed the merits of all the Howard movie adaptations made of late—most of them just garbage, except for John Milius's operatic version of *Conan* maybe, the best attempt put forth so far. Finally, Rich sucked it up and cleared his throat.

"Listen," he began, "I'm just gonna come out with this and say it, alright? I'm sorry I never got back to you when you called and left those messages. After we moved east. I had a lot going on at the time, a lot going on with Michelle. It's no excuse—I could've easily picked up the phone. But I was doing my best for her, trying to keep her healthy, and alive. Trying to make it week to week. Anyway, I'm sorry."

"Yeah . . . and how'd that pan out for ya?" Truitt murmured under his breath, too low for Richard to hear.

"What's that, Tom?"

"Ah hell, don't worry about it," said Tommy, louder. "We're all pretty much helpless, man, in the long run."

"Hmm? Helpless?"

"Helpless in our lives, with everything in our lives. We can't keep 'em safe, Richie boy. Can't keep anyone safe. It's all an illusion."

Richard fidgeted, his mouth tight. He knew he spoke of Kyoko, and Michelle, too. But he couldn't help thinking of Katie suddenly, so very small and fragile. Precious Katie-Smatie, his sensitive girl, so tuned in to things she shouldn't be, things that no living soul should . . .

"Did I tell you about the ghosts?" said Tom out of the blue, causing Richard to start.

"Uh, no, don't believe so." *Dear God.*

Tommy made a sweeping gesture toward the forbidding Shaw mansion. "Ghosts are at it up there. Lights burning at night, movement in the windows. We . . . have . . . ghosts, I believe."

Richard laughed nervously. "Yeah, that would be the pastor. George Deadmond told me: Simon Julian lives there, pastor from the church. It's him you're probably seeing at night."

Truitt had his crooked grin on. "I knew that. I just wanted to"—*change the subject*—"see if you knew it.

So, exactly who is this guy anyway? I've heard around town he performs miracles."

Richard told him about the Reverend, all he knew of him, at least. About his mother-in-law, Glee, her connections to Nain Lutheran and her political aspirations, and the televised program scheduled to take place this evening.

"What I want to know is, why in the fuck would anyone from a church want to live in that place?" said Tommy, to which Richard could only shrug. "You remember the stories, right? The things that happened there?"

"I remember the stuff about old man Shaw, sure. George and I were talking yesterday about the pandemic, and the plague pits all over town. Crazy fuck lost his marbles in that house."

Tommy drank. "More to it, though, more that happened later on. Don't you remember what they used to say about Grace Meredith? The one who lived there, long after the Shaws were all dead and buried?"

"I think so . . . it sounds familiar. Prominent family, right? Because the Meredith name got added into the town records. Long as I can remember, it's always been called Shaw-Meredith House."

"Yep."

"Wait. Is she the one who killed herself?"

"That she is. Husband up and leaves her, takes their nine children with him and vanishes. *Nine children*, can you dig it? Leaves her saddled with a mentally disabled sister, that's what I've heard—just the two of them, living alone in that big rambling bitch of a place. This was like 1930 or something. So anyway,

182

Gracie Meredith decides to end it all. But, do you know how she did it?"

Richard shook his head and Tommy leaned in close, talking low as flighty grasshoppers arced through the fields. "She sits down at her kitchen table one morning, neat as you please, and she starts eating match heads. Breaking the heads off wooden matches and eating them, one after another. All they had in the house—maybe a thousand, maybe more. Who knows? Enough to show up in an autopsy . . . but not enough to've killed her, they said. All day long, popping them in and down the hatch. All through the night. So then, when she finally realizes the sulfur from these match heads isn't working, just making her sick to her stomach, Grace Meredith goes under the kitchen sink and finds a box of rat poison. Something called Rough on Rats, real vicious shit. She sits down again and begins spooning the powder into her coffee and drinking it. Even poisons the retarded sister, Rachel. Puts it in her Cream of Wheat or whatever and feeds it to her. Sits back down and merrily on she goes, mixing it with her morning Joe, forcing herself to ingest it until she's done herself in."

He finished his beer and tossed it into the blue recycling bin just off the porch; its crash was explosive in the remote quiet. Once the echo had faded, Tommy went on in his hushed tone.

"Can you imagine the patience that took? The sheer fucking *will*—swallowing those broken-off match heads one at a time, choking down cup after cup of arsenic-spiked coffee. I mean, at some point the cramps and vomiting must've hit her. It must have, right? Shitting all over herself, hallucinating maybe.

You can only guess at what went on up there, Rich, the things that must've gone through Grace Meredith's mind at the end. Seriously, what has to happen to make a person do something like that? To get them to a place that dark in their life? I've been to prison, man, and I'd never try anything that bad."

Richard watched the ancestral house closely as Truitt spoke, what was visible of it. Tommy's voice was whisper thin, as if wary the structure might overhear what they were talking about somehow. "Suicide by consumption, it was ruled: that's what they used to call it in those days. Well, murder-suicide, technically. And that Rough on Rats shit? She probably only paid a few cents for a big box of it at the local hardware store."

It was a secret thing, this, what they were sharing between them.

"I remember the undertaker," Richard said, "the guy who bought the place when we were in junior high, I think. Do you? He lived there with his wife a few years, until she got drunk one night and fell down the main staircase inside. Broke her back and her neck, I heard. I saw the big ambulance when it took her body away . . . I was riding my bike through the woods, and I saw the ambulance. Then a week or two later they found the undertaker out in those same woods, hanging in the trees by a rope. Do you remember that? It was near the clearing where we used to hunt, not far from the house I grew up in. Out around Duck Blind Point."

"Know what I think?" said Tom, and Rich shook his head. "I think we need some more beers. Sit tight." He jumped up and disappeared inside his home, the dust-filled screen door slamming comfortingly shut in his wake. Richard polished off the rest of his Michelob and tossed the bottle into Tommy's bin, gazing at the lofty, protruding turret of Shaw-Meredith House in the distance. He felt a chill on his skin and blinked several times, wondering what Katelyn was doing at that moment. So he pulled out his cell phone to call and check on her quick, and just to hear her voice.

2

Within the chapel's sedate darkness, a butane utility lighter flared harshly as Aaban walked around and lit the corner candles and the incense. When he got to the pulpit, he took his time lighting each pillar in the candelabra upon the raised lectern, staring into the flames. Fire made him think of retribution, and that in turn made him think of eternity. He glanced down at Reverend Julian's open leather-bound Bible, at its strange words. The pages appeared to be so old they might crumble at the slightest touch; Aaban had to resist the urge to feel of their antiquity beneath his fingertips. Smoky light was filtering in through the stained glass. He faced the pews and looked out across the vaulted chamber. Then he closed his eyes in the flickering shadows and began clicking the utility lighter on and off in his hand. On and off . . . on and
(*fire comes, and retribution*)
then off, listening
(*and eternity comes with it*)
to the echo in the silence. He continued to work the switch rhythmically, eyes closed, began to feel an erection grow inside his black denim jeans. Feel it grow, and distend, and bloat—

He heard a noise and opened his eyes. It was a distant sound, a door closing perhaps, someone moving elsewhere in the church, getting nearer. Aaban walked down the center aisle between the giant silver cross and the Jesus statue and exited the chapel quietly, heading for his locker.

He clicked the butane lighter on and off as he moved, thinking about fire and about retribution, and eternity, too, and about young supple virgins waiting somewhere in the hereafter for him.

3

The bees were in the trees . . .

Cassie could see them from her house, in the bushes and locust trees where they had swarmed, down the slope which led to the small pond at the bottom of her backyard. They conspired there, the low buzzing sound of their carryings-on lifting on the breeze and rising up to where she stood. Cassie humphed.

Well, I'll be a motherfather, she thought angrily, and started down the hill in a huff. Cassie glimpsed the plastic bottle filled with liquid smoke (a much safer alternative for quelling and immobilizing honeybees actually than the harmful, old-fashioned smokers once used) hanging on one of the upright box-hives. She considered taking it for the briefest of moments but continued on without it. "Shoot," she muttered to herself, "shoot, *shoot!*" When she reached the bottom of her yard she watched them and tried to make sense of it, tried to figure what precisely was going on here, and why. She squinted into the sunlight, waving a hand about her scrunched-up face.

The first sting took her by surprise, for she'd never been stung before, not by any of them, in all these years. Cassie felt it on her upper lip, felt the burning sensation as it immediately began to redden and swell. Then another, a sharp pain in her forehead just above the eyebrow. She yelped and bent over, facing the ground, swatting at her head. "Cotton-pickin' chicken pluckers," she grumbled, not wanting to swear or be unladylike. Not yet. Even though it burned, was starting to itch. "Shoot, guys!" The buzz among the locusts' yellow-gold leaflets droned and grew higher. She could hear it hovering above her, the noise becoming agitated. The next instant they were around her face, drawn by pheromones, sensing and reacting to the attack. As the bees came teeming out of the trees and bushes like a cloud, began to sting their keeper on her bare legs and arms and her face, Cassandra Patrick's grumbles became cries of pain, those cries changing over into wild shouts of panic and fright.

"Shoot! *Shit! HOLY SHIT! YOU ROTTEN LITTLE MOTHERFUCKERS, YOU!*"

She spun and she screamed, flailing like a whirling dervish in the grass. Cassie let out one long wail which finished as a strangled sob, then her pinched-shut eyes flashed open and she ran, ran for dear life and dived headfirst into the nearby pond. The bees followed, swarming out across the cool greenish water, striking at her once the splash had settled. Even after she was still and her thrashing had ceased the bees continued to sting her and die, going after Cassie's unmoving helpless form, darting at the back of her bandana-adorned head. Later, when her unconscious, floating body rolled lazily over in the pond and she at last began to breathe again, they returned to attacking her exposed face and mouth.

Their uneven buzzing rose in pitch until it became maddening.

CHAPTER THIRTEEN

I

JULIAN EXCUSED HIMSELF and was at last able to slip away inside his church. He needed solitude, just a brief respite from their tedium and banalities before the commencement at hand: the setting in motion of it all—faith against doubt, and everything that would follow. Besides, William Salt would occupy them, keep them assuaged with food and drink until he returned.

He made his way slowly, achingly, feeling the corrosions of his own body, the shrinking of his bones. Each day he applied the pepperwort and menthol for their deep heating attributes, but they did little good. This vessel was at its end, was breaking down and deteriorating with every step he took—twice already had the heart stopped beating, once upon the operating table during a routine knee replacement procedure and once while shoveling snow from the front walkway of Nain Trinity Lutheran. Twice he had waited patiently, hidden within, prepared to abscond and move on to another if necessary, and twice the heart had been resuscitated, the workings brought back into continuance. It was merely a waiting game now, he knew. What better time to leave it all and begin again, eh? Another millennium gone. The timing of it seemed perfect . . .

The Reverend pulled out his eyedrops and paused, tilting his head back; just another of the many failings this current host experienced. These eyes were old and rheumy, and stayed so dry most of the time that the drops were a necessity. He wiped the excess with his handkerchief as he continued along, entering the chapel room and closing its doors. He remained facing the double doors a moment, head cocked to one side. The candles were already lit, that much he could tell, their dim glow casting shadows which wavered over the brick. But there was another smell besides incense here, something else in his inner sanctuary. At his back. A smile touched Julian's lips, realization coming to him even before the voice did.

" *'And the Lord said, Simon, Simon,'* " it quoted in the dark, " *'behold, Satan hath desired to have you, that he may sift you as wheat.'* "

"Ah . . . Luke," said the Reverend, still facing the doors, "one of my favorite Gospels. Then again, there aren't that many of them. To what do I owe this pleasure, Jack Lawrie?"

Silence. "I think you might know."

Julian turned around and looked upon the man with the shock-white, crew cut hair who stood at his pulpit, thumbing through his Bible's pages. "Know? I'm sure that I don't. You read German, Mr. Lawrie? How quaint." He smirked. "Do be careful with that. It's very, very old."

Lawrie perused another page or two, and closed the leather-bound book. "Yes, I can tell," he said.

"Good to see you, Reverend. Been to Germany have you?"

"I've been many places, Jack." Simon Julian wondered how he'd gotten in here, how neither Salt or himself had noticed him enter. "Services won't be starting for a while yet. Aaban is here somewhere, tinkering with his maintenance equipment. Perhaps you'd like for me to—oh, and how is your exchange-student arrangement working out, by the way? Tell me, are there any benefits to be collected for doing that sort of thing, Mr. Lawrie? Government recompense? Please, do tell."

"I'm not here to talk about the boy," the retired admiral said, stepping down from the candlelit lectern. "I have a few questions for *you*, though, if you wouldn't mind humoring an old Navy shark."

"Well, by all means, question away!" He clapped his hands together, and waited for the reverberation to fade. "With the help of the Almighty I will try and answer to your satisfaction." His mouth curled around that last part, the word *Almighty* in particular.

Jack cleared his throat. "Thanks. I just wondered what you thought of all the strange happenings around town—as a religious leader of the community, I mean. Were you aware?"

"I was not, but now I'm intrigued. Go on."

"There've been some unexplained incidents: wildlife die-offs, birds mostly. Several unnatural births have occurred among the livestock at some of the local farms around here . . . crops turning bad, animals acting crazy, things of that sort." He paused, then resumed. "You've heard about the Putnam family? They were found dead in their garage this morning from carbon monoxide poisoning. All three of them."

"Ah, yes. So I was informed. Very tragic." The Reverend lowered his head as in sadness, but his eyes shone brightly. "We're doing a little something for them later on, during tonight's service."

"Little something?"

Julian smiled to himself in the gloom, and looked up. "Just a dedication to the family. A few prayers of absolution, you know." He stared at the other. "What was his name again?"

"Henry," said Lawrie. His voice quavered.

"Henry, yes. Henry Putnam." He glanced upward and winked at the Christ statue, neat and quick. "Tragic indeed."

Lawrie cleared his throat once more. "It certainly is." *Was that a tic, or did that son of a bitch just wink at me?* "Did you know them?"

"Only from worship. Only . . . in passing." The smile had to be suppressed, to keep it from reigniting back into life.

"Is there something funny about this?" said Jack, louder, and Julian went rigid in the candlelight. His eyes narrowed and his mouth went tight, and when he answered, the words floated like icy wraiths turned loose inside the quiet, high-vaulted chamber.

"Not in the slightest. Please, do get on with it, Admiral. There are preparations yet to be made. A camera crew is arriving."

"You don't find these things odd, Reverend? Any of what I've mentioned?"

"Unfortunately, no. Creatures die *en masse* all the time in nature, and no one ever explains it. Everything living has to perish, Mr. Lawrie. Sometimes the chosen method is suicide, yes. Death comes to us all. It's simply the way things are."

"That's it? No ponderings, no divine theories according to Scripture? Chalking it up to God and those mysterious ways of His, at least? Anything?"

Simon Julian stiffened again, and this time something stirred uneasily in the chapel with them. "Don't use that word in here," he said flatly. A low rumbling sound, which seemed to come from everywhere and nowhere at once, accompanied his voice as background. "Don't."

"Beg your pardon?" said Lawrie, perplexed. "What word?"

The Reverend smoothed back his few remaining wispy strands of hair, taking in a deep breath and letting it out; it was becoming apparent this conversation was not going to end well. "Was there anything else? Sure I can't fetch your student boarder for you? Wouldn't take long to find him."

Lawrie ignored this. "Something bizarre is going on, and I think you may know more than you're sharing. Did you get that Bible in Germany, Reverend? Is your family from there?"

"No, actually. My bloodline is Nordic, I believe, Mr. Lawrie. The Julian name was pronounced with a *Y* back then, of course . . . no *J* sound at all to be found."

"*Yool*-ian," muttered Lawrie, trying it out. "Tell me then, Reverend *Yool*-ian, what do you make of these plague pits of ours? Another one just opened up out near the city limits. That makes half a dozen so far, and counting."

193

Julian tut-tutted him, the guise of an old man returning.

"Know anything about them?"

"*I?* You can't be serious." He looked away. "I mean, really . . . "

"The Third Reich was well acquainted with pits and corpses, as I understand it," Jack said.

The Reverend froze, swung toward him. Lawrie couldn't tell if he was grinning or grimacing, until he detected the sarcasm in the man's voice.

"Is that what you think? *That's* what this is about? You believe you have a war criminal here in your hidden-away valley? A *Nazi*?" His laughter boomed, filling the sooty-dark chapel and seeming to shake its very foundations.

"I have an old friend from my military days," said Jack, crossing his arms, "and this friend thinks they might know you somehow. Thinks they've seen your image before, in an old German photograph album from a long, long time ago. Some of us fought over there, Reverend. Not me personally, but if there's one thing Germany has taught us over the years it's that we should keep a close eye on her. The events of 1870, and 1914, and 1939 have proven that, I believe." He paused. "Anything to say? To confess?"

"Oh my, but you are clueless, Jack, aren't you. You genuinely have no idea what is in your midst. You never have, have you? No. For if you did, you wouldn't have the courage to even stand before me with such trivialities. Such *nonsense*. Senseless, is what you are. Begone from my church, please."

"Not until I get an answer. Tell me about the pits."

Julian sighed, turning to trace upon the brickwork.

"How utterly ridiculous. Those plague pits were here long before I ever came to this place. You know that very well, Jack. I didn't dig them, and I most certainly did not fill them." An eerie calm seemed to descend, and all at once the old man came to a decision. "I merely *prefer* them, is all."

Lawrie looked bewildered. "You *what*?"

"I savor them, the misery they hold. I relish the torment and the suffering that was once wrought here. It's comforting to me. It . . . it's what I do. What I came for."

"My God, are . . . "

"I told you not to use that word," Julian warned him, his back still turned, a sharp, savage edge on his voice. "Not here. Not again. Don't you *dare*."

"The word 'God'? Why in—?"

"He abandoned us!" hissed the Reverend, wheeling upon the other; Jack felt his first real hint of fear, and he stepped backward. "Cast us *out* . . . and for what? Our lust? Our *degradations*? *To forsake us so?*"

"Forsake? What does that mean?" Jack trembled slightly. "Do . . . do you mean the way Jesus was forsaken?"

Simon hesitated, regaining his composure. A grin broke out, began to spread blackly. "Oh, no," he said, almost cooed. "No no, my ill-informed friend. Contrary to what you've heard, your savior's dying words were not, 'Why hast thou forsaken me?'—*oh, no*." A ravenous light seemed to come alive in him, making the old man appear straighter, much taller than he had been mere seconds ago, as he strode about the shadowed chamber. "Rather, they were this: 'Now I am sinking, and darkness covers my face.' Yees . . . that's what dribbled from his lips up there." The smile widened, twisting horribly and drawing back, and the light coming from within him sparked and caught fire in his gleaming pupils as he looked up to the silver cross. "I know. I was *there*, Jack Lawrie. With the mourners that day, there among the weeping, and the glassy-eyed zealots, outside the North Wall of the city. The place they called Skull Hill. What do you think of that?"

Holy quiche Lorraine, was all Jack could think right then, and how maybe he shouldn't have come here today. How much he wished he was still at home, nestled between his wife's semen-sticky thighs. "Uh, I'm not sure. What the hell are you saying, Reverend?"

"It actually looked like a human skull, did you know?" He wandered the perimeter, moving closer as he spoke, drifting in and out of presence as his words became far-off, distant sounding. "So many buried there, beyond the Damascus Gate. Muslim. Christian. Jew. Executed, all thrown together in unifying quietus. So many. Of course, nothing could top the Black Death for carrion comfort now. Talk about your plague pits. The Reich? *Ach* . . . damned Germans liked to mix the ashes of all those incinerated bodies with manure, and use it to grow their crops. But the Black Death—*there* was a celebration. Grand times . . . never ending." He'd stopped in front of the oratory, the inner light, that spark of illumination zipping and tracing patterns across his ancient flesh, creating a map of fiery lines which spread and began to crack, threatening to split open the façade he wore. "Grand times," he said again, lost in some vast profane emptiness.

"What the hell are you saying?" Jack repeated,

completely flummoxed, and Julian turned a slow, vacant stare upon him.

"Ah, still here?" he murmured. Jack's blood chilled in the shadows. "I thought perhaps you had left. Tell me, Admiral Jack," he went on, "have you any idea how many men have copulated with your wife? Do you ever think about it, about the sheer volume involved?"

Lawrie made a clicking sound in his throat. "You . . . "

"Oh no, not *I*. Her womb is barren and dead, as well you know. I prefer something riper. More *fertile*. But there are others, alas, who care little of such things. Yes . . . many, many others."

"You son of a bitch," Lawrie said, shaking. He was met by the Reverend's laughter. *"Damn you!"* The admiral suddenly exploded into movement, snatching up the lighted candelabra from the pulpit and hurling it at the old man. Julian sidestepped, moving fast for a person of such advanced age, and the candles and heavy metal base sailed past him. The Reverend watched it all crash and scatter into the darkened oratory niche, the spilled candlewax already hardening on the floor before the wicks had even blinked out. When he turned back, Lawrie stood a few steps farther up the center aisle, toward the exit.

Julian spoke curtly. "No . . . damn you, sir. I *am* damned. Have you never noticed the sheltering tree out there, blasted by bolt lightning so many innumerable times since I've come to this misfit church? And you're no better off. Your species has damned itself thrice over, for its actions and its reprehensibility. So damn *you*, Mr. Lawrie. Get out of my sight."

The admiral's feet had started to move, inching up

the carpet. "All right. Maybe the proper authorities would do better—"

"You have no sense, do you, Jack? You truly are *senseless.*" The Reverend placed his fingertips to his own lips and kissed them. "Senseless, I say," he rasped, blowing the kiss at Lawrie who felt something approach, something wretched and contorting and suddenly he couldn't help but shudder all over. *"Languish,"* he heard Julian command in the dark, and then he felt whatever it was circle him, quivering, thrusting its way into his mind and through every pore until his vision swam. One moment Simon Julian was there and the next he wasn't, everything swirling into blur, and Lawrie instead saw, in his place, something grotesque and burnt and enormous. He saw it unfolding and rising for the arched ceiling, its face a holocaust of ravaged features and open wounds, its gaze like lava and that hideous, craggy mouth pulling back, widening impossibly until . . . until a chasm seemed to yawn monstrous and bottomless-black in its unrecognizable face . . .

Lawrie cried out and staggered, clapping his hands viciously over his eyes.

"Go home," said Julian from where he stood, "and think about those hundreds of men rutting your wife over the years. That sow of a wife—every man's leavings." His smile was dissolving, becoming sad almost. "Go home and die now, Jack."

Jackson Lawrie hugged himself and fled, bounding up the aisle and tumbling out the silver-handled side doors of the chapel, those unbolted exit doors he'd entered through, falling, getting up and choking, staggering away past the lightning-gashed bur oak.

Reverend Julian, meanwhile, smoothed his hair back and breathed deeply, trying to hold on, hold the façade together a bit longer. He licked his old lips with all of his tongues, catching and swallowing down the final spark still zipping about his seamed, weathered face. With eyes alight he exhaled, striding toward the inner doors that led to the halls of his church.

Just a while longer—

2

The beasts knew what was coming, and they knew it first, before anything else living did, as always. More in tune with their habitat around them, more precognitive to even the slightest of changes, they became strangely aware one day and behaved according to nature's law. The exodus had already begun, wildlife hurrying to avoid the conflict they sensed.

To ensure their continued survival.

Some made it away, others perished. Bats and birds took to the air, while woodland rats flowed down into sewers, turning razored fangs upon one another when hindered. Panicked knots of toads drowned in streams, fish darted off and swam for quicker, safer tributaries. Snakes wriggled their way to the surface, the local fields coming alive with their slithering bodies; farmers believed this to be a sign, a dire portent on their own calling as tillers of the soil. But the serpents were just trying to escape like everything else, escape the vibrations that drove them to a frenzy.

Many animals died outright, their deaths inexplicable in appearance. Birdlife suffered the most casualties, it seemed, simply due to them being *winged* spirits of the air, which didn't seem fair at all, not really. Domesticates had been acting queerly since before this: house pets went stir crazy. Cows began giving sour milk, hens refused to lay and became fatally egg bound.

 . . . Everything culminating at Reed Farm, with the birth of an atrocity, on the far-southern edges of town. And with a miracle born to the owners of the Blessing Acres orchard, to the north and east.

The creatures of the valley retreated, their senses keen, fleeing some impending darkness, something unseen upon the horizon. Even insects took to crazy, running (and flying, in some cases) amok.

Except for the black moths, that is, which had begun to gather eerily now like great, powder-winged messengers bearing news.

***

Aaban Darwish stood at his locker and gazed into it, caressing what he held within. He cupped the grenade in both hands as most would a newborn chick, delicately, and with eyes full of wonder. It was of Russian design, an RGD-5 fragmentation grenade he'd taken from Admiral Lawrie's collection case. The admiral had shown him his private cache of weapons many times, removing them and describing each before putting them back safely under lock and key and bulletproof glass. But Aaban had discovered the key once, while his mainstay was busy with that slut wife of his—and did she ever keep him busy. The whore routinely made passes at *him* even: the official live-in, cultural exchange student of the house. Flirting with him and trying to coax young Aaban into the master bedroom when no one else was around. Disgusting hag.

He'd learned all about the hand grenade by listening to Lawrie's repeated war stories, how it contained some 350 separate fragments, hot shrapnel which would whirl and slice and cause horrific flesh and eye wounds, dealing catastrophic death within a full three meters of its detonation, maybe more. How once the pin was pulled and an audible "pop" was heard—signaling that the inner fuse had ignited—a person would have just 3.2 seconds before it exploded, bringing consuming fire and retribution to all. And of course, most importantly: how the grenade was not a replica but *live*, one that Jackson Lawrie shouldn't even be in possession of to begin with, legally speaking.

"Not a word, son," the admiral would say low-voiced to him at night, locking up the glass case in his book-lined, cherry wood library. "Our little secret."

Now here it was, inside the sanctum of Nain Trinity Lutheran Church. After finding the key's hiding place, Aaban had waited for his chance and today he had retrieved it, liberating the Russian grenade from its case once the admiral had left the house on Lantern Court. Then, he again had to run the gauntlet of Lorraine Lawrie's sexual advances, the gropings and rubbings and pleadings, even the sight of her masturbating herself before him, just to get out the door. To make it here so he could bring a little death to the nonbelievers of Blackwater Valley—at a time and place where he knew it would do the most harm, during the busy weekly service.

Aaban only hoped the old tattooed whore made it

here as well, to preen as usual in her most revealing of frippery, and be among the congregation this evening.

The olive-skinned young man sensed a transformation coming in the newly arrived Millennium, felt it in the air, in the demeanor and the rumblings from his homeland. He sensed the world was on the precipice of some huge and terrible change, and that nothing would ever be the same again thereafter. So, he'd decided he would take immense pleasure by getting in on it, by striking at the heart of these people—the duped and the defiled—thereby achieving immortality for himself, and all the gifts offered in the beyond.

Yet, he had taken precautions. In the slim chance Aaban wasn't killed outright by the blast, he'd come prepared, heeding the age-old myths of his people. In the inner pocket of his denim jacket were a few dozen nails, long funny-looking spikes he had grabbed from a bin the last time the Lawries and he visited that Honeycomb Haven woman, the crazy widow who talked to her bees. Darwish had snatched up a handful and asked her how much, fully intending to pay for them, but the woman who always wore the bright bandanas told him no charge, that she had plenty. She insisted they would bring blessings and good fortune to him. He truly hoped so. For if Aaban *did* find himself still alive when all this was said and done, he must be sure to drive the spikes into the church floor, into the pooling blood of the dead and the infidel damned. Drag himself if he had to and use the hammer pommel of the knife in his belt to pound them in. To keep the *Ifrits* down—the spirit demons which rose like smoke from the spilled blood of murder victims—

to keep them from rising up and seeking revenge against their killer . . .

Him.

His father used to tell him this, before dying in a personal war story of his own, how it was believed that the nails held these demons in place, prevented their deadly formation out of the cooling blood of the unrighteous. Only if he was quick enough, though, fleet of mind and of foot. So, Aaban would drive the nails in with the butt-end hammer of his survival knife, and he would plunge the knife's serrated blade straight back into his own celestial-soaring heart.

Then, all would be well, and well again.

Aaban had telephoned his mother, Islamorada, to hear her voice one last time. He had assured her everything was fine here with his new sponsor family in this new land, telling her not to worry, that he loved her very much and that both she and father would be so proud if—

A crash came from elsewhere in the church and Aaban jumped, wrapping the hand grenade inside a stack of cotton wiping cloths. He heard something else, like a stifled sob carrying down the hall to where he stood. Scowling, he placed the folded cleaning rags carefully on his locker shelf and closed the door, spinning the combination lock and hastening to investigate.

***

—yes, just a while longer. And off he would be with his prize.

But that display back there, and the tedious addlebrain who had instigated it. Extraordinary. What did that fool Lawrie expect . . . to find him drinking

203

Riesling and listening to Wagner in his chapel, dressed in the skins of children? Then, asking for confessions that way. Well, he got one all right. So someone had seen a photograph and recognized Julian after all this time. Of course he was there, the ridiculous fool. He had been everywhere on this planet, surely, at one point or another. Had seen every war, every great and awesome spectacle, from the raising of the Pyramids to the razing of the Eternal City, the medieval fruits of the Black Death to the not-so-Holy Crusades; bloody Golgotha right on up through the Holocaust. He had seen it all, and he would see more.

Before the end came. As it always did.

Indeed, just as that so-described Holocaust had come to an end. He'd been there for it, true. As witness, standing and laughing at the back of the shaman's musty shop while the deal for the golden ring was made, snickering at the pretentiousness of it, the sheer folly.

The absurdity, thought Julian now as he stalked his church halls.

He couldn't help but laugh, after all. The ring with the amber-brown stone was just a trinket, a mere bauble in the whole grand scheme. But then little Mad Adolph himself was only a court jester: village idiot; a lowly foot soldier, at best. Who else but a madman would do the things he had? Surrounding himself with holy relics and Christian mysticism, amassing the priceless antiquities he did—more wealth than one could ever use—things such as the Crown Jewels of Charlemagne and the venerated Spear of Destiny, the actual lance-point said to have pierced Christ's side while upon that *crux* of his. Plundering the unplumbed mysteries of The Amber Room. Collectively just a schizophrenic mishmash of obsessions, really. Testimony to one lunatic's delusion, with Julian there as witness. Yes, the sights he'd seen, the abandon and the marvels he'd been privy to. Including the very *pinnacle*, back even before the origins of space and time:

The heavens. The pure firmament, and the wondrous grace of all heavens above.

And he had been cast down along with the others. Exiled, the bolt thrown on the gates. Set afire and cast out to fall and to fall, until he was certain they could fall no longer, and then to fall farther still, screaming within a crushing vacuum of silence where no ear could hear. Crawling . . . blind and forsaken, imprisoned . . . chained deep down in a black abyss, their once-divine flesh riven from bone and only charred shreds remaining. Condemned, *graceless*, fettered in utter darkness among choking sulfurous fumes, never to shine, or to see light again. Yet always remembering what was lost, always looking skyward . . .

Even so, their spirit vestiges were allowed to traverse the earth, to tempt and corrupt. Inhabit human form, and to roam and rut and beget, leaving spawn in their wake, the virgin mantle of this orbiting globe spread out before them. Because, of course, the 'creations' had been given free will.

Julian smiled. Memorable times he'd spent, in the guises of a master bladesmith, a king's cartographer, *cavaliere servente* and wandering portrait painter, and a dark, dark magician during the darker-still Middle Ages. Using human vessels around him like so many stepping stones down throughout the centuries, vacating the scarred ruins when it suited him. Or when death loomed inevitable and close by in the night. Staying awhile here before moving on, lingering there for a respite of anguish and the odd, succulent taste of womanly flesh now and again before parting in feigned sorrow. Scattering, crisscrossing the land, never once in all that time catching glimpse of any of his own kind, alas.

Right up to the moment where he ripped his way into this surrogate body of the German military chaplain named Julian Bardulf Simon, who, ironically enough, was in charge of ministering to reek-infested, mass murderer jackboots for a living. He stayed awhile, stayed for the fun, turning the man inside out because he could, turning his first name and last around when it was time to go.

The gold ring *was* an amusing trinket, so he had claimed it for his own, taken it and the Bible and made himself scarce before the bombs had begun raining down in earnest. Would ironies never cease? Poor Mad Adolph condemned the occult, but turned back to it in his wretched, final days. Nazi messiah, indeed. The failed novelist Goebbels alone was advising him by that time because his chicken farmer friend Heinrich Himmler—another self-purported 'immortal' who believed himself an ancient, Germanic emperor incarnate—had already been branded a traitor by then. Little Adolph even chose the date of April 30th, *Walpurgis Night*, to commit suicide. The *nacht* when witches and shades were reputed to walk the earth, trying no doubt to offer himself and his lackeys up to those dark forces which surely must control men's destinies. Yes, things only a madman would do. That was how he perished: a twitching, mumbling village idiot, with two ruptured eardrums and uncontrollable tremors as he pressed the gun muzzle to his head.

It was a wonder Mad Adolph hit the target at all— his own spasming brain.

Now the girl would be Julian's newest bauble. Ah, such a treasure trove was she, such powers for one so young. The mother had to be gotten rid of, and that pained him; it was unavoidable. For given time, the little one might have healed her, made her mother well again . . . and then what? They may never have returned to this place, otherwise. Right here. Where the Reverend wanted them, where they belonged. *Yes.*

But he needed to prepare. That dullard Lawrie, disturbing his peace of mind, asking for confessions back ther—

Julian rounded a corner and ran directly into Aaban Darwish coming the other way. The old man went down, sprawling to the floor, and immediately Aaban had grabbed him by the arms.

"Reverend! Here, let . . . "

He flinched back in something like horror, a wail in his throat, but the younger man was already pulling him to his feet, steadying him. Julian shrugged off the touch, gaping in surprise, and a queer look washed eerily over his features. He blinked it away, mouth still hanging open. "Thank you, Abby," he said, shaken.

"Please don't call me that," Darwish retorted, raising his chin. "My name is Aaban, Reverend. It means 'angel of iron', and I'm very proud of it."

The old man's eyes were clearing. He hesitated, then reached for the swarthy-complexioned man, seeking the contact now which he so loathed. The gnarled hand wavered, unsure, moving to grip Darwish by his shoulder. "Of course, Aaban. To each his own. No offense"

(*fire comes, and retribution*)

"intended. Please forgive me, *Aaban*."

The young man started to say something, but Julian released his shoulder and turned from him, a strained smile plucking at his lips.

"I had a bit of an accident in the chapel," said Simon after a moment, closing his rheumy old eyes. "Dropped some candles in the oratory—clumsy me! Could you get the wax up before services? And relight them for me please? There's a lad."

Darwish headed that way, then halted, looking back. "Are you injured, sir?"

"Oh, never mind me. I'm fine. Thank you, Aaban."

The young man nodded and disappeared around the corner.

. . . *Never you mind, my chicken farmer friend,* thought Julian blackly. *Angel of iron, indeed.*

CHAPTER FOURTEEN

I

ROBERT PLANT," began Richard, tilting his Michelob. His friend leaned, clinking his bottle to Franklin's. "Planty," Tom Truitt said and they took respective drinks.

Katie was fine. When he called the house, George had put her on and she was doing fine. She told him of her day so far, how Granna had fixed her hair, doing it up with clips and a polka-dot bow, and of the games they'd played and the cartoons they had watched. She told of the food they were having: the grilled chicken George was fixing, and macaroni salad, and the tray of assorted vegetables and dip.

A menu devised by Glee, no doubt.

He talked a bit longer with her—at one point she held the receiver to Blondie's ear so he could say hello to her, too—and, once Richard's mind had been put at ease, he told Katie he'd be there soon. By the time he had hung up, sliding the cell phone back into his pocket, Tommy was outside again with two more Michs. Richard mentioned catching that string of Zeppelin tracks on the ride in yesterday and Tommy told him it was an out-of-town station for sure, working their way from A to Z, and how Rich must've hit the dial right in the middle of the T's.

The Double T's, Richard had joked, but Truitt only lamented how none of the local radio stations played anything good anymore, just soulless Top Forty garbage which he refused to listen to.

"You see where they got together for the Rock and Roll Hall of Fame induction?" Richard asked.

Tommy nodded. "Yeah. But it was . . . oh, I don't know. I'm glad they made it and all, but I'd rather remember them the way they were."

"Like Chicago in '77," Rich said, and Tommy's grin bloomed.

They shot the shit about 1977, the year their friend Oliver died in the river, the year they saw them play at the old Chicago Stadium (one of those icons that wasn't there anymore—the Madhouse on Madison). They talked of how Page had demonized his guitar despite the ravages of heroin abuse so evident in him that April night, and how a strutting Robert Plant had retrieved some long-stemmed roses tossed up onstage by an admiring older female fan and proceeded to stuff them down the front of his impossibly skin-tight jeans, thorns and all. How Michelle would've creamed her own jeans had she been in attendance. Kyoko, too.

It was there it had commenced, Richard making the first toast.

"Jimmy Page," Tommy fired back now, holding out his beer. "Pagey," said Richard, and again they swilled.

After a pause Richard raised his Michelob. "Jonesy."

"Pfft," Truitt snorted. "Fuck Jonesy."

"What?" Richard looked mortified. "Oh no. No, no no. You don't get to say that."

"Too late. Already said it."

"Hold on. John Paul Jones was the only one of them classically trained, only one who played multiple instruments. Shit, I think he was the only one who could *read* music to begin with! The man composed, he arranged . . . the professional glue that held the band together. So therefore"—Richard lifted his beer—"to Jonesy."

"Oh, for fuck's sake," Tommy sighed. "Jonesy."

Richard laughed and they drank. Truitt became somber.

"John Henry Bonham," he said. Bottles were raised.

"Bonzo," Richard said.

"The *Beast.*"

They both took swigs, then Richard added: "Kind of a bastard, wasn't he?"

"When he was wasted, yeah," Tom conceded reluctantly. "But he was the greatest goddamn rock drummer of all time."

"No argument." Rich wiped his forehead. "Hoo, I keep toasting like this and *I'll* be wasted."

"I'll get ya home in time for school, don't worry."

Richard laughed. "Yepper. If I knew the way, I'd take you home. Who was it said that?"

"Don't know, don't care," Tommy said, standing up and chucking their empties overboard. "Just thought of something. Wait here." He ducked back inside, emerging a few seconds later with another pair of brews and something else: a small shrink-wrapped pack of some kind. He tossed it to Rich, who nearly howled in delight.

"Vern's String Cheese Whips . . . no frickin' way! Are you kidding me?"

"Dig in, man."

Richard tucked his beer between his legs, pulling out his keys and using the big Chevrolet key to puncture the plastic wrap. He tore into it, grinning, at last pulling a single pencil-thin length of mozzarella cheese from the package. He held it up like a twisted rope of spaghetti, marveling and still murmuring, "No frickin' way," under his breath. "I haven't tasted these in ten years or more." He put his head back and dangled it loop by loop into his open mouth, and began to chew.

"Well?"

All Richard could do was moan. "Pure heaven, dude," he said when able. "Salty, too." He smacked his lips, offering the ten-ounce pack across to Truitt.

"Nothing like the Whips," Tommy said, helping himself.

Richard looked at the label. "Chilton, Wisconsin. Huh. Long way's away."

"Yeah. But they're worth the parole violation, right? Like I said, nothing like the Whips."

Richard couldn't tell if he was joking or not, so he shrugged and lifted his Michelob to drink.

After awhile, Tommy said: "Jasper Park, that's where you're doing it?"

"What?"

"You'll scatter Michelle's ashes at Jasper Park, you said."

"Oh. Yes. That's what she wanted. It was in her will."

Truitt nodded. "Did I ever tell you about the time I went sleepwalking there?"

"Well, Tom, most likely you did, but I can't remember shit anymore, so . . . "

"In my teens, still living at home. Never sleepwalked in my life until then. Never have since, far as I know. Just woke up there one night in my pajama bottoms and nothing else, covered with fucking mosquito bites. I had to hike it all the way back home in the dark, barefoot, and when I got there I was locked out of the damn house. Ended up crawling through our tiny bathroom window to get inside. Fell and smacked my head on the tub, to boot. But I don't remember walking to Jasper Park, don't know how I got there at all. Don't remember anything, except for the drums."

"Drums? What drums?"

Tommy paused. "I heard drums beating somewhere, or dreamed it maybe, and I followed them. Like tom-toms . . . the sound Indian tom-toms would make. That's all I remember. I woke up in the park in the dead of night, not far from the old gallows tree. You know?"

"Wow. That's pretty close to the water. You could've drowned, like Ollie Echols did."

Tommy's shoulders rose and fell. "Yeah, that's what my mom always said. She beat the crap out of me, as I recall."

They both snickered, grew quiet.

"Hey, do you remember Beulah the Witch?" asked Richard abruptly, and Truitt almost dropped his beer. He pinned it against his hip before it hit the porch, easing the bottle down and wiping his palms on his dirty jeans.

"Woops. Sure I do. That wasn't her name though, right? Just what us kids called her."

"No one ever knew her real name, did they?"

Tommy looked away, out towards the tattered canvas movie screen. "Don't think so. Someone came up with that, and it just stuck. From an old puppet show, wasn't it? Witch Beulah? In the '40s or '50s, I think."

"We thought she was an actual witch," Richard said, not knowing the answer. "I mean we were only kids, but we all really believed it back then. Urban legends, huh?" He laughed, munching his cheese. "My mother used to tell me to stay away from out there and leave her alone. Said she was just some old retired schoolteacher living by herself on that country lane, and to keep clear. Leave her in peace, she'd say."

"We used to drive out to get drunk on her property and make it with the girlies," remarked Tommy. "Kill the headlights and get them scared, get into their panties. But there were others who . . . well, they went out there looking for trouble. Some of the kids used to throw stuff at her house, empty bottles and shit. One idiot lit a broomstick up and tossed it into her yard once. Goddamn grass caught on fire and everything. Fucking jackass." He shook his head.

Richard took a deep swig. "I remember the stories, the folklore. They used to say watch out or Witch Beulah would come and get you, come to your bedside at nightfall and slash your throat. She wore a string of bloody Adam's apples around her neck, taken from all her victims. That was one of the folk tales."

"Oh yeah," Truitt cringed, "I remember that one. My old man used it on me. How she'd come and cut out my Adam's apple with a big carving knife if I didn't behave. And how he'd hold the door open for her so

214

she could do it, too." He raised his Michelob to his twisted mouth. "Another jackass."

"It always bothered me, you know? The fuckers who went out there and did damage. That was bullshit. She never did anything to anyone. Just wanted to be left alone, and she couldn't even get that in her old age."

"Yep."

"And then she died."

"And then she died," Truitt repeated, gazing into the fields. Gazing past them.

Richard shaded his eyes, trying to figure out what they were looking at. He waited a few seconds before speaking: "We went back there once, Michelle and I did. After the old woman passed."

Tommy glanced at him, eyebrows raised. "What for?"

"It was snowing—the winter after she died, when they had her house condemned and torn down. We wanted to snoop around, see what it looked like out there. We felt guilty I suppose." Rich smiled weakly. "So we drove out in my parents' car . . . or maybe it was her parents' car. Hell, I don't know. Michelle brought a bouquet of flowers with, and she laid it in the snowy field where the old lady's house used to stand."

"Huh. I'll be."

"Yeah. It was getting late, so we decided to start back. As we were pulling away Michelle saw something."

Tommy kept a lateral eye on his friend. "What was that?" he asked.

"I don't know. She thought it was a person. Someone in the woods at the back of the field, she said, a shape moving near the dried-up creek bed that ran behind her property. Remember? I looked, but I didn't see anything. Just figured she must've imagined it."

"Right." Truitt drank up, finishing his beer. "Probably." He was about to toss the empty and make some quip when Richard's voice came again, barely audible this time.

"I think my daughter's psychic, Tom," he whispered.

Tommy Truitt placed the Michelob bottle down instead, turning to face him. "Can you repeat that, Richie?"

"My little Katie is psychic," said Richard again. "Or empathic, or *some*thing. She sees things that aren't there. People who are dead." He looked at Tommy, his expression unreadable. "I'm afraid of her sometimes." Then he glanced away, with effort.

Truitt sat quietly. "You're being serious?"

"Yes."

"You mean the real thing . . . not like TV clairvoyants, or these parasite 'spirit communicators' you see all around. You mean an actual, honest-to-God psychic, right?"

"Yes."

"Because, ya know, I don't doubt they're out there. I just pretty much reckoned they were few and far between, Rich. That they'd keep quiet about it. Kinda like Army posers. I know certain vets who love to run their mouths about the action they saw, all the enemy soldiers they smoked—but they never did shit. It's all bullshit, just bragging themselves up, see? The veterans who really saw and did stuff, the genuine articles, they're the ones who *don't* talk." He scratched his head. "I always figured if there were authentic psychic people in the world, they'd be like that. Not the phony-ass mediums you see doing cold readings and taking money from bereaved housewives, but the quiet ones you never hear about, who never say a word."

"I suppose so. Yes."

"And what is it with these Civil War reenactment assholes?" Tom went on, thrown for a loop and not sure where to go next. "Every spring this idiot cousin of mine, Mikey, calls up and tries getting me to join his group of Civil War reenactors. First-class clowns, these guys are: talking and playacting like they're a real militia, like Confederate colonels or something on their make-believe battlefields. Most of these pussies couldn't hack a single day in the actual military, either. All they do is play dress-up and camp out with their barroom buddies. What the fuck is *that* all about anyway? I mean, how much of a fucking loser do you have to be?"

"Don't know," Richard admitted, passing him the Vern's.

"Christ, and we euthanize cats and dogs in this country. Unbelievable."

Richard grinned, staring down at his knees. "Not good to hold back, man. Just let it out. Let me know how you really feel."

"Sorry," Tommy said, clearing his throat. "So, go ahead. Tell me about Katie."

Richard told him, the words pouring forth. Everything, starting with Michelle and her gift, how she could heal minor afflictions and make objects fly about when she lost her temper. How sometimes she knew who was going to be on the telephone before it

217

rang. Then about Katelyn, their baby girl, who began chasing lights from the time she was in a playpen, lights only she could see. Of the countless imaginary playmates she had while growing up—the Invisibles—and how strange animals would come right up to her, unafraid, anytime and anywhere. Katelyn, whose eyes changed color and who could tell the temperature indoors or outdoors by the mere feel of it on her skin. Who could heal *major* afflictions and stop all the clocks in the house and who used to lie in the grass in Maine and break up the rain clouds overhead with her thoughts.

Katelyn, who saw specters of the dead around her at any given moment.

Truitt said nothing, just listened.

"Not everyone who dies comes back," explained Richard. "Only certain ones. She seems to know what they're thinking, know what they know. Like they're connected or something, and they've always been here, that's what Michelle used to say. Always have been, always will be."

"Has . . . does she see her mother?"

"No. She's never mentioned anything like that."

"How old is she again?"

"Six, almost seven. But if she touches you while—" Rich hesitated, drawing a careful breath. "If Katie touches you, she can let you see what she sees." He looked at his friend, his eyes becoming hot. "That's when I'm afraid. Afraid she'll touch *me*, and that I'll *see*." The words came out in a rasp, and he covered his face with his hands.

Tommy reached awkwardly, then stopped. "You okay?"

218

"Yes," Richard said, dropping his hands. "I'm just tired. She's my only daughter, all I have left in the world. All I have of Michelle. And here I'm scared of her . . . and that makes me ashamed, and so goddamned tired."

"Hey, you got nothing to be ashamed about. You've been through a hell of a shock with everything. You're probably still in shock."

"I know, but—"

"But nothing. You're taking care of your little girl the best you can, Rich, and you've got nothing to be ashamed about."

Richard glanced out into the fields. "I've never told anyone any of this. You must think I'm out of my mind, man."

"Nope. You didn't think my idea about reopening the drive-in was crazy. So, I don't think you're crazy either."

"Huh." Richard smiled faintly, shook his head. "Listen, when we get settled in back home, and this second book is under my belt and things are all squared away, I wouldn't mind getting in on the ground floor maybe. You know?" He nodded toward the movie screen. "She sounds like a good investment to me. I'd like to be part of it."

Tommy laughed. "Well, *now* I think you might be a little nuts. But I'm not gonna argue."

They sat together a while longer, legs dangling off the stairless porch, gazing across at the Sunset Drive-In rotting in its lonesome field—forgotten, it seemed, save for two now.

"THEY POISON THE HEART"

by Michelle Brooke Deadmond

(an excerpt)

Those that bled out and died quickly were among the lucky, they who never knew what hit them. All up and down the Mississippi near the mouth of Bad Axe River their frantic drums sounded. No one came, though, no allies rose to the call—promises of British assistance were not kept. Even when a second white flag of surrender was hoisted in desperation, the slaughter continued unabated, insatiably. Thus had begun the

~~ *Fugue* ~~

History tells us there were numerous other skirmishes leading up to this, before the end came for them at the Battle of Bad Axe that summer. In May of 1832, appointed war chief Black Hawk and his dwindling band of followers scored a surprise victory over drunken, attacking, and then abruptly fleeing soldiers at Old Man's Creek, in what would shamefully come to be known later as Stillman's Run.

This spark ignited the fire, and the Black Hawk War was on.

It's said that a green, 23-year-old captain named Abraham Lincoln happened upon the battlefield site the morning after with his company of volunteers, and assisted in burying the dead.

Other tribes joined in the ensuing conflicts, carrying out acts of violence for their own personal reasons amid the chaos. Black Hawk's people, now reduced to 700 or less, pushed their way up the Rock River with the mounted Illinois militiamen swarming after them. Their trail was an easy one to follow—the wasted corpses of the fallen had begun to mark their wake, buzzards circling the skies overhead.

Those lagging behind that didn't die of thirst or starvation were executed where they were found.

In July, somewhere along the riverbank encampments, Black Sparrow Hawk learned his hopes of reoccupying their former Sauk prairie lands would receive no support from the Winnebago or Potawatomi, nor from the British army in Canada, as had erroneously been promised to them. Disheartened, the tribe kept going north in a forced, fighting retreat all the way into Wisconsin.

It was here Black Hawk's group crossed into 'the trembling lands', a region of trackless, marshy swamps and bogs. On the pursuit went, the Sauk men, women, and children struggling through stagnant waist-deep water with militia patrols close behind. They guarded their rear protectively as they fell back, moving ever northward, eating roots and tree bark to stay alive, so exhausted from hunger they could put up little resistance by this point. Yet they turned once more near Wisconsin Heights, turned to make their weary stand there. Outnumbered four to one, the Indians opened fire on the advancing soldiers, keeping them at bay while *inflicting heavy casualties. When their musket volleys ceased, the bloodthirsty militia charged the high ground with bayonets fixed but came up empty—Chief Black Hawk and his people had vanished in the falling darkness.*

The next day the band entered the confluence of the Bad Axe and Mississippi rivers hoping to return to Iowa, making for the islands and shoals it offered, not knowing an armed steamboat was already anchored and waiting beyond.

Their time was almost up.

Diminished to fewer than 500—with the old and sick dropping all around—Black Hawk's starved, sleep-deprived followers ran straight into a hail of cannon shot from the gunboat. Braves were dispatched immediately to draw fire away from the main body of women and children. They waved a white flag overhead, but the soldiers who had been chasing the scattered band for months rebuffed their offer of truce and pinned them down in a deadly crossfire. Menominee warriors and vengeful Sioux joined in the attack, the Sauk's sworn enemies. Again someone attempted to surrender under a white flag; again, it was ignored. And as a thick, August morning mist swirled about them, all ranks were closed.

Bedlam reigned, screams of terror filling the river valley, and the annihilation began.

Canister blasts ripped the air while musket fire poured down the bluffs from Illinois and Wisconsin brigades alike. The Sauk Indians were trapped, hemmed in by the ambush—no quarter, no mercy to be found within the horror unfolding. Peppered by cannon shot and by the heavy gunfire thrown at them, young braves and old invalids began falling dead at Black Hawk's feet. Survivors fled for their lives, many taking to the water in desperation. The steamboat turned its guns upon these swimmers, murdering untold numbers of squaws and children, crushing some of them beneath its paddle wheel as they drowned. The Sauk women begged with what little English they knew, scouts futilely sounding their drums. But the shooting continued on, the massacre spreading to both sides of the fog-enshrouded Mississippi, uniformed troops killing anyone running for cover or trying to cross the great river to safety.

A baby set floating on a raft made of bark was bayoneted—another infant shot point-blank inside his mother's papoose. "Kill the nits and you'll have no lice!" one of the soldiers could be heard shouting as he fired, reloaded, and fired again.

Those that didn't die outright were swiftly hunted down and either executed or taken prisoner. A few miserable remnants of the broken band were able to drift away unnoticed, escaping to the west. Meanwhile, soldiers busied themselves scalping the dead, or cutting long swathes of flesh from the bodies to use as razor strops. Half-naked corpses littered the banks, and floated along downstream, tingeing the waters a murky blood red.

Barely 120 Sauk Indians remained alive and in chains. Their comrades were all gone, whole families slaughtered while trying to flee the massacre at Bad Axe. In the aftermath of this ugliness, cholera and malaria would soon begin to sweep throughout the valley and grimly take hold, killing its feverish victims with throes of vomiting and terrible dehydration. Bodies were buried hastily—the river took the rest.

Chief Black Hawk however was nowhere to be found among the captured or the dead . . .

CHAPTER FIFTEEN

I

WHAT'S THE STORY, boys?" said Chief Priewe. "Everything all right?"

"Everything's great," Tommy answered, emptying his bin into the recycling dumpster. "No stories here. Might want to try the library there, Chip."

Priewe went a light shade of red, standing next to his cruiser. Rich and Tom had decided to run the bottles and cans down to the drop-off lot, near the exit road across from Aubel Farms. They took Richard's Blazer, and no sooner than they'd pulled into the lot—wouldn't you know it—reliable old Chief of Police Prick-we had steered right in behind them and gotten out, adjusting his mirrored sunglasses. Just like a bad penny, Tommy had time to think.

"That your bin, Tom?"

Truitt shook the items out and dropped the blue plastic bin to the ground, slamming the dumpster lid closed. "No," he said, irritated, "my friend came all the way from Maine so he could dump his recyclables—you got us." He laughed. "Whose do you *think* it is?"

"Easy, Thomas. Don't get excited." Priewe was grinning, the redness fading from his face. Richard

225

forced down a twinge of apprehension which had risen in him and stepped forward, picking up the bin and putting it into his backseat. He moved up beside Tommy.

"Is there a problem, Officer?"

"See that, Tom? Courtesy. You could take a lesson from your friend." Priewe sized Richard up, noting the wedding band he still wore. "No, no problems. You're the author, right? Sorry for your recent loss," he said, surprising him. Truitt could only roll his eyes.

"Thanks," said Rich, eyebrows lifted. "You've read my book?"

"I know about it. Haven't read it yet, but I respect anybody who can leave their mark that way. Most people end up totally forgotten after they're gone and the world goes right on without them, without missing a beat, unless they've left something behind. Like they never even existed." The chief glanced at Tommy (whose eyeballs were in danger of permanently lodging up inside his skull) and then back. "So, you here writing another one?"

"Well—"

Truitt shifted. "Wait a minute, it's none of your business what he's doing here. We're not breaking any laws."

"Nobody said you were. What's eating at you, Tom?"

"Nothing's eating at me," he said, thinking: *Except your sister, you self-important nutsack.* He grinned at this, and Priewe returned the favor as a second squad car came pulling into the drop-off lot and tooted its horn. They saw (with some relief) that it was Palm Clemency, and he had someone else sitting in the

226

cruiser with him. Priewe turned away, grin cemented in place, and walked back to the other vehicle. After conversing with them, the chief returned to his car and stood by the open door, glancing up.

"Well, honest work awaits. Be seeing you, Thomas. And you there—" He nodded at Franklin. "—be careful of the company you keep." The grin was frozen, his mirrored teardrops staring vacantly out.

Richard forced a smile of his own, feeling a tug in his guts. "Oh, I like my company just fine, I suppose."

One corner of Chief Priewe's mouth twitched, but the grin never broke. He nodded their way. "You enjoy the rest of your day now, boys," he said, climbing back into his police cruiser.

"Will do, there, Chip," Tommy called after him, and Richard's hand itched to grab him by the arm.

When Priewe was gone, they made their way over to the other car and visited Palm Clemency for a bit.

Palm shook Rich's hand, introducing Bobby Crider and conveying condolences about his wife. They gabbed about past times and their town here on the river, about one another's children—Katie was spoken fondly of, and Palm told them about his own daughter, Cimmeria, and his young son who dreamed of being president of the United States someday; they all laughed politely.

As he departed, Clemency told them to best keep clear of Chief Priewe if possible, that he could be an all-purpose prick at times. Then the second police cruiser swung around and drove off with a honk. Rich and Tommy got back inside the idling Blazer and closed its doors, sitting for a moment.

Finally Richard looked at him, his face mock-aghast with bafflement. "The *fuck* was that back there? What are you trying to do, get me in trouble?"

"You *are* trouble. By the way, your SUV reeks, man."

"No, no no. Wrong. It just went through the carwash. And you're the one who's trouble, dude."

"Shit," Tommy laughed, "I'm not trouble. I just trip over trouble. Every time I'm being good, trouble comes along and sticks its foot out and stumbles me up."

"Yeah. Right." Richard pulled out of the lot and started back. After a minute of silence, he said: "I don't know. I kinda liked him." They both lost it then, shooting each other glares and laughing raucously the rest of the way.

Richard dropped Tommy off at his house and used the bathroom quick, applying toothpaste to one fingertip and improvising with this to try and eliminate any alcohol breath before leaving. Such things seldom worked, though. Rich told Truitt he was welcome to come along to the church but he declined, saying he needed a shower badly, and something to eat. Richard bid him *adios*, and said he'd see him again before pulling out day after next.

As he drove away he raised a hand to Tommy in his rearview mirror—at first he thought he was waving back, the signed paperback grasped in one fist, but then he realized his friend appeared to be batting at something as he ducked inside his screen door.

Swatting away big butterflies, it looked like.

2

The ponytailed greeter at the doors kept eyeing their

vehicle, Richard had noticed, and he wondered what the attraction was. *Never seen a Chevy before? Take a picture, why don't you.*

The iron church bells were ringing, while people filed inside in clusters. But the well-dressed American Indian, shaking hands with patrons as they entered, had his eyes locked squarely on Rich's SUV from the moment they'd swung into the lot and parked beside the Channel 35 production truck. Richard stood with Katie and Glee now, and he was *still* staring at it.

They drifted closer to the entranceway. Glee was chitchatting with churchgoers, smiling away as she introduced her granddaughter. Just before they reached the chapel doors, an old, old man dressed in crimson vestments appeared from within; surely this must be pastor Julian. Richard heard him say, "Prarsheen", and saw him whisper something to the large Indian with the ponytail. The old man's attention caught on Richard and he smiled dimly, his gaze flicking to Katie for one passing instant. Then, they had both disappeared into the building, the Reverend going first and the greeter following with a frown of concern, and time enough to spare a final glance back. At last, Glee and the Franklins went inside.

Richard sat in back with Katie and told her about the church they were in, this small-town church where her mother and he had been married. Glee excused herself and headed down to the front pews. George had decided not to come at the last minute, claiming he didn't feel well, but promised to watch the broadcast on TV. In truth, he'd seemed preoccupied even during dinner.

When Richard arrived they ate their grilled chicken

and macaroni salad outside in the backyard. Later, Katelyn and Blondie had retreated to play by a red cedar canopy swing near the little garden at the farthest rear corner, while the grownups sat and talked. Glee caught him off guard and asked if they would be their guests this evening and to please stay the night. Richard, feeling put on the spot, had said yes.

After a few minutes, Richard overheard Katie speaking. He looked and saw his daughter lying on her back in the grass, Blondie stretched beside her. Whether she was talking to the dog or not he couldn't tell.

But he watched as the empty, two-person canopy swing rocked eerily back and forth, steady and gentle, like the pendulum of that Italian grandfather clock inside the Deadmond home. He watched it, unable to look away. Then, glancing skyward and seeing no signs of any 'cloud busting' which might be going on above, Richard had nervously called his muttering daughter away from there. Made her come and sit by him while he told her how cute her hair looked, done up this way.

In the house once more, he noticed Michelle's ashes in the same place on the television set. Richard touched the urn lightly, resisting the urge to lift it and feel its weight. That's when George had bailed, saying he was fatigued, had an upset stomach, and how they should just go ahead without him.

3

William Salt didn't like the Chevrolet Blazer, not at all, did not care for the grille guard attached to its front. The way it gleamed menacingly as if grinning at him.

No, like it was sneering. This bothered him. There was something troubling about it. The chrome-plated steel grille reminded him of a row of gleaming silver teeth, like those of a great and savage beast. William Salt knew all too well about beasts.

The ones at Marion State Penitentiary came to mind, for instance, the ones he served his time with for an aggravated mayhem charge. The southern Illinois prison was itself bad enough, built in 1963 to handle the overflow of inmates from Alcatraz, which closed down that same year—it boasted tiny six by eight cells, concrete slabs with pads on top to sleep on, and twenty-three hour a day solitary confinement. Even so, the beasts within its walls were worse still.

Animals of every type resided there. He saw them, knew the depravities they were capable of behind those bars, and he watched what they did to each other. The assaults and brutal rapes. Yes, he had learned quickly.

Most vicious were the guards, though, more savage than many of the violent criminals housed at the supermax facility. They had the control, the *real* power: their psychological attacks would come first, breaking an inmate down, then random beatings with weapons called rib-spreaders began. Riot sticks equipped with a steel ball on the end. If anybody complained, he got worked over again in the infirmary. Sometimes the rib-spreader would be used to teach a lesson of silence, the prisoner held facedown as the device was inserted with enthused vigor.

Sometimes, surviving the internal damages resulting from this wasn't an option.

Salt survived it. Even when the bloody, shit-slathered club was wrenched from him and used to knock his teeth down his throat, so that he had to be fitted with prison dentures afterward. He survived their 'cock fights' as well, where inmates were pitted against each other while guards placed bets and looked on, the loser ultimately getting sodomized by the winner, and ofttimes by the guards.

Once, a father who'd traveled many miles to see his son on visiting day actually suffered a heart attack and died right there when the young man was brought out. When the father saw the crippling abuse and malnutrition his son had been subjected to.

Retaliation came in 1983 in the form of sudden, brute murder, and two prison guards were stabbed to death by inmates in separate ambushes. After that, Marion went into permanent lockdown, coincidentally, around the same time a young Thomas Truitt was being convicted and sentenced to the first of his two stretches there. Truitt came to learn of those beasts himself, learn up close just what brand of animal stalked the prison's blocks. Nightmares still gripped him because of it, ones from which he awakened shivering and sweat-soaked to this day. But whereas Tom Truitt dreaded those inner demons that chased him in dreams, Salt grew to embrace the nightmares, to draw upon them when needed. He embraced his past instead of running from it, often priming the depths of his own soul in order to enact his hatred outwardly.

As he would do upon the father of the small girl when this was over, for coming here in that thing, for bringing the dead machine which grinned so blankly at him like a huge, metallic—

Then the Ghost Reverend was whispering something into his ear. He frowned, wondering if he'd heard right. He ducked back inside the church, concern biting his features.

Salt threw a final glance over his shoulder as he went, his eyes drawn again to the Blazer's silver grille guard. No, he didn't like the looks of it at all, the way it sneered and gleamed there in the parking lot.

Like the teeth of a great and savage . . . and vengefully hungry beast.

CHAPTER SIXTEEN

I

MAIN TRINITY LUTHERAN'S chapel was filled and Glee Deadmond had them in the palm of her hand. Studio lights on tripods illuminated her, while a camera operator kept her in frame, directed by a second man in a white short-sleeve shirt and tie. There was a hanging backdrop of crushed muslin with the words THE GLEE CLUB—WE ARE UNANIMOUS IN THIS! emblazoned in gold, and Glee wore a wireless mic clipped to her lapel so she could move about unencumbered before it.

To one side of this was the brightly lit oratory, the church's choir at attention within. They had opened services with a hymn: "All the Earth Will Sing for Joy", and Richard recognized the leggy young girl with the yellow ten-speed from yesterday as one of the satin-robed singers.

Glee spoke with a natural ease, addressing the congregation as if accustomed to doing so her entire life. She had started off haltingly, gaining steam as she engaged them on the necessity of healthcare for seniors, and local job growth—things on a lot of minds these days. She began railing boldly against dependence on foreign oil, and illegal immigration, and same-sex marriages. Fearless, she was, in her candor.

Richard squirmed and scanned the room, looking at some of the faces. They seemed captivated, and he observed how a few of them leaned in close, mimicking Glee and the manner in which she swayed fluidly when driving home a point. He spotted that girl again, the one who'd sailed out into traffic, noticing for the first time the slight tummy bulge beneath her robe: what Michelle used to whimsically refer to as *bump action*.

"This is worse than the strip joint," someone said half-jokingly behind him, very low, and Richard turned to see Tom Truitt crouching down in back with a pair of chinos and a polo shirt on. "No seats, bro."

"Hey," said Rich in a church-mouse voice, surprised, "you came."

"Yeah. Decided to see what all the fuss is about." He grinned his crooked grin, chipped front tooth showing, which didn't diminish his rugged good looks in the least.

Richard started to rise. "Why don't you take my—"

"No, sit with your daughter," insisted Tommy, winking at Kate and staying put directly behind them and the last pew. "I'm good."

After a short intermission Glee continued with her rant, talking about the evils of abortion rights and drugs, and of sex education. Someone handed her a white Bible and she held it aloft as she padded back and forth in front of the oratory alcove, lashing out at the disgrace of teen masturbation being taught right in the public schools: "*Yours* and *my* school system!" she exclaimed with a mulish toss of the head, emphasizing her outrage. Richard folded his arms and shifted uncomfortably—the rhetoric had turned disturbing, and all at once he wished he could cover Katie's ears.

Truitt leaned over the pew and whispered to him: "I stand corrected. This is *better* than the strip joint."

His mother-in-law called for a stop to it here and now, deeming these things a poison, and calling for anyone who spread such poison among their children to be held accountable, for some heads to *roll*. Her eyes flashed, glittering like crystal behind her rimless lenses. Someone in the crowd shouted amen and Glee bared her teeth. Then she dropped the Big One, announcing that maybe a good housecleaning was in order, perhaps the firing of the entire Blackwater Valley school staff if necessary, all 239 district teachers, counselors and principals. And how, as acting board superintendent, the United States Secretary of Education might just back her decision to the hilt on this one.

"We must root out these deeply entrenched threats, remove them and all other pollutants from our classrooms. *To keep our future safe!*" In her animation her pinned-up hair came undone and tumbled loose, surrounding her in a nimbus of wavy silver-and-brownish silk as she moved.

After all, they didn't want lowered standards here like other states had allowed, she said, adding heatedly that marching every below-par, failing schoolteacher straight out into the cornfields with their own shovels and bags of lye might just be too good for the likes of them—and what did that *mean*? wondered Richard. But only briefly.

The assemblage sat riveted, hanging on her every syllable, many of them edging forward in their seats.

In closing, Glee spoke on the subject of unification, and consolidating all available resources to keep this the most powerful nation in the world. Her words swelled to the back of the chapel room, mesmerizing her audience, transporting them. She seemed almost electrified up there. At one point Richard caught himself swaying with the others and stopped.

She reminded everyone not to forget their cash or credit card donations, payable to either the church or to her senate campaign. Or both.

It was over. The Glee Club choir concluded with "Alleluia, Praise His Name", Glee herself joining in and fronting the group as they sang them off the air, each young girl in practiced harmony behind her. Richard cleared his throat and patted Katie's hand, nodding at her. She smiled dimly, and he managed a smile back.

When they had finished, the camera and lighting rigs were turned off and the two men broke everything down and hauled it out to the station truck. That was it for the televised bit, it seemed. Glee had taken her seat once again in the front pew, the white Bible on her lap.

"The *hell* was that?" Tommy breathed to himself, shaking his head. Richard wasn't sure, so he said nothing. Glee certainly had a way about her, he had to admit. She was amazing. Especially with her long hair cascading down over her shoulders like—

"Daddy?" said Katie. "What's teen masturbation?"

Richard nearly choked. "Well, um . . . it's something teenagers do, hon." He sensed her watching him, and glanced up at the ceiling arches in embarrassment. "Sometimes. But . . . um, you don't have to worry about any of that. You won't be a teen for quite a while, Katie-Smatie." *Holy brown-ass cow.*

Truitt spoke quietly into Rich's right ear, the side farthest from Katie. "They need a sermon on teen pregnancy."

Richard nodded. Yes, there was more than a little bump action to be found here, true. And whereas he recognized none of the girls, Tommy did, and even knew some of their names. There was Natalie Ward and Julissa Quigg in the choir, and Sandy Pomeroy from the Prairie Dairy ice cream stand. He recognized Charese Billups, too, one of Charlie's twin daughters, and the waitress Jilly Sweet from the café. Officer Crider's well-rounded young wife, and Alice Granberg, who worked at that funky Wiccan shop downtown—their bellies ranging in amplitude from swollen and full ripe to barely discernable.

Christ, even the stodgy church organist Mrs. Bluedorn appeared to be expecting.

Richard saw the ponytailed man peering in now, his considerable bulk filling the doorway. As his jacket fell open he noticed the small ceremonial tomahawk tucked through his polished dress belt. The American Indian threw a quick, unkind glance around before vanishing again. Richard scanned the chapel room, spotting Lorraine Lawrie to one side in a skimpy, low-cut dress. She saw him at the exact same time and waved in his direction, winking seductively. He froze and dipped in his seat, wanting to sink all the way down and disappear. But he couldn't do that, no, didn't dare.

"Rainey's looking good enough to eat," Tom had leaned forward and commented, just loud enough for

Richard to hear. "Woops, looks like somebody remembers you, Richie boy."

Richard sucked air through his teeth. "I thought she was Catholic. What's she doing here?"

Truitt grunted. "All Lutherans were Catholic at one time, weren't they? Until they broke free." He moved closer: "She hits every local church like this, showing off that tight-ass bod of hers. How *did* she taste, by the way?" Richard gave him a startled look.

"How would I know?"

Tommy refused to let it go. "Please," he said thinly, "everyone knows you nailed Lorraine back then. Even the admiral knew it, man."

"What?" said Richard, mortified.

"Oh, ye-e-es. Sleepy-town life, can you dig it?"

Wishing for another subject, anything, Richard watched as a pretty woman in a wheelchair was brought in by her handlers—a physically disabled young blonde, both of her legs amputated. She cradled what appeared to be a plush-toy panda on her lap in twisted hands. They trundled her down the aisle, locking her wheelchair into place next to a pew, and then left her there.

"Yes siree, sleepy-town life," Tommy persisted, crouching behind them.

2

Aaban Darwish wetted his lips and worked at the combination to his locker. He hesitated, listening to the choir music crescendo and then end. He blew on his fingers and spun the lock's dial. This was it . . . almost time. He lost his place and began again, jerking the metal door open at last. Drawing a steady breath he reached in slowly, reverently.

Not there.

He felt his stomach tighten, the long inhalation stopping cold. Aaban swallowed and groped around, pulling out the cotton wiping cloths where he had concealed it. There was nothing, no hand grenade folded inside the stack. In a flustered panic he dropped to his knees, searching the bottom of his locker.

Nothing. No grenade. Not anywhere.

Darwish snapped straight, eyes darting, his face filling with alarm. He never saw the darkness as it formed out of the shadows behind him, did not see the figure taking shape there, approaching with disciplined restraint, barrel-chested and with arms like steel bands. When one massive limb slipped around his neck, curling and locking in a neat chokehold, he screamed out. But nothing issued forth. All sound and oxygen had been effectively cut off.

The young olive-skinned man began to twist and thrash wildly, a rasp-dry rattle in his throat. He tore at the arm clutching him, kicked in wide-eyed desperation at the open locker. Then, he felt himself lifted off the floor and shaken in midair. He tried clawing for the survival knife in his belt. Someone shook him again, harder, plucking the weapon easily away. The chokehold was cinched up and everything grew dim, and finally Aaban knew. Knew there would be no fire or retribution this day, no supple virgins opening themselves like pink, dew-moistened rose petals for him. Had he been able to sob, he would have done so.

The darkness, adorned in its immaculate suit, took him down.

CHAPTER SEVENTEEN

I

THEY WHEELED THE dead baby out at exactly 6:41 PM; Richard knew this because he was glancing at his watch when he heard the sound of the serving cart, and looked up.

Wheeled him out on a metal serving cart, he would later think, appalled. *My sweet God . . .*

Before this happened the Reverend had stood silent for a time, eyes closed in meditation, his palms pressed together, fingers pointing like little church steeples. The rest of the assemblage shuffled their feet and fidgeted impatiently, some of them coughing into fists. When he opened his eyes and began to speak, Richard jumped.

"Welcome, everyone. We've all been acquainted—at one time or another—with the expression 'culling the herd', have we not?" A few nods came, some muttered affirmations. "But what does this mean, precisely: an eradication of the sick? Does it mean reducing the parasitic overpopulation? Getting rid of those too frail and weak among us, perhaps, as your forebears once did right here in Blackwater Valley?

"What think you, dear ladies and gents?" Julian said. "Anyone? Our illustrious youth?"

The old man walked about, reflecting, awaiting an answer he knew wouldn't come. He faced the pews in his ankle-length crimson raiment.

"Ecclesiastes tells us, 'Remember him, before the silver cord is loosed and the clay pot doth break . . . for the dust returns to the ground as it was, and the spirit returns to the creator who gave it.' " One bony finger jutted toward the vault of the chapel ceiling, and Simon Julian stared out. "Good stuff, yes?" There were scattered chuckles. Richard caught himself smiling, his arms still crossed. He detected a hint of accent but wasn't sure what it was.

"It is believed," he went on, "that the soul—your soul, friends—is connected to the body by a thin, invisible line. And when these clay pots of ours 'break', or give out . . . " The old man thumped his torso with both fists. " . . . when our springs and summers have flown, and when the bleak winter of our life grows colder and these clay pots doth *break*—" He struck himself sharply a second time, and the hollow echo of it and of his voice hung frozen in the air a moment. "—once that invisible silver cord is severed, we cannot get back. Ever. The separation of spirit from flesh becomes final. In a word: we die."

The Reverend paced the floor, casting his solemn glance here and there into the audience. "The body becomes no more than carcass, dust—" His eyes flitted about, scanning over them, and then he brought his gaze back again to light upon Richard as he finished:

"—ashes."

Richard's heart skipped, but the pastor was already off and moving.

"For we are but dust, every one of us, and to dust we shall return. But is it so?" He paused in mid-stride, slowly pivoting to face them. "Is this always . . . so? Good people, I say to you now let us remember. Let us remember *him*."

And as if on cue, out came a distinguished bearded man in a neatly tailored double-breasted suit, pushing that metal cart over which a sheet had been draped.

"Medical examiner," Truitt murmured, to no one in particular.

He wheeled it up, halting in front of the church lectern where Reverend Julian awaited within the flicker of the guttered candles. "Thank you, Dr. Mint," said the old man, and the medical examiner evaporated into the shadows to stand. Richard spotted the stethoscope slung around his neck and he frowned.

"This, my friends," began Julian, yanking the sheet away with a flourish uncovering what lay beneath it, "is Henry Putnam."

The motionless corpse of an infant was there, no more than two or three months old, dressed in a zip-up footed sleeper, and the church's congregation gasped in unison even as Richard Franklin started in his seat. A woman cried out piteously somewhere down front, the lament muffling itself and dying on her lips almost at once. *Should've gone back to the motel,* Richard thought. He looked to Katie, who was also frowning.

"*What* in the mother*fuck*?" he heard Tommy breathe hoarsely, and shifted to trade dumbstruck glances with him.

WILLIAM GORMAN

Julian cleared his throat. "Perhaps you've heard of him, and the tragic events which occurred yesterday in our community. If not, well, suffice it to say that Brad and Shirley Putnam took their own lives sometime yesterday afternoon, and the life of their little Henry. Such a waste. But . . . we'll not let this child of light leave us just yet, I think. *No.* I do think not." The Reverend circled the metal cart, and Richard became aware of his daughter watching this all very closely. Too closely. He also became aware that he should do something, like take Katie out of here, for instance, but he remained glued to where he was, his gaze fixed, unable to move or even blink. He thought he heard Tom saying his name, but he couldn't tear his eyes from the serving cart and what lay so still upon it.

"Henry's parents were diseased and weak, yes," Julian told them, "and it was, perhaps, their time to move on, but not this child." He stopped behind the cart and stood unmoving, wrapped in wisps of incense. "*Not . . . this . . . child.* He is ours, this alabaster vessel, this *broken clay pot*, and I believe he has great works to accomplish on this earth. I have faith in it. Therefore, we shall not let him go without a fight. Let us pray, good people. Pray with me." Then, palms heavenward: *"Grace alone."*

The Reverend passed a hand over the dead child, mere inches above, without actually touching it (because Simon Julian despised getting hands on), motioning from foot to head. He did it again, in the opposite direction this time, and suddenly it . . . *he* . . .

A tremor shuddered through the infant's body on the cart, foot to head and back along its entire length.

Someone's scream ripped open the silence inside

244

Nain Church, and the shockwave was like a thunderclap hitting. Everyone jumped. Richard's breath caught in his throat. He stood up, reaching for Katelyn, watching in disbelief as the baby boy rolled his head from side to side and uttered a hitching, quavery wail. Another shudder coursed through him, his little arms and legs shivering now, and a murmur hummed audibly over the pews. Tommy was speaking again, insistent, but Richard could only fall back into his seat, mouth and eyes wide.

Then tiny, lifeless Henry Putnam began to cry and shriek upon the metal serving cart.

***

Miles away, at Aubel Farms in the valley below, as Ditch Richards leaned on his pitchfork just before sunset, lost in dark ruminations, the single dead-born calf from the pair birthed the night before suddenly came alive in the bonfire before him.

He was thinking about farm cows and when they abort, how the sorry remains were usually buried in landfills or incinerated outright, and how here he was, lucky him, stuck in the middle of the burning process. Ditch thought about recent events down at Jim Reed's place, a remote farmhouse on a far-southern lane where he had worked in the past, and what he'd heard. About a creature born there with horrific birth defects—a horse, brought forth with seven legs and with eight hooves . . . the eighth being on the *side of its neck* . . . and what must the odds be for a seven-legged foal to be birthed alive like that? Had to be something like four or five million chances to one.

He heard the pitiful Reed Farm animal had lived a full twenty minutes before—

That's when he saw a sickening convulsion ripple through the dead calf's burning body. He saw its limp, crooked neck straighten, watched the wretched pink-skulled thing struggling to stand up in the fire—stiff-legged, like a hideous puppet on strings—rising and trying to lurch off into the field, its limbs all herky-jerky and with no motor control to carry it. The pitchfork dropped from his grasp as he stared through licking flames into its dull, unseeing eyes. Ditch heard its agonized lows: lifeless one minute and living the next, it struck him . . . yet somehow not alive.

Richards screamed.

He fell over backwards, scrambling away from the bonfire, and got up screaming. Tearing his gaze from the awful sight, he ran for the barn, came racing back out an instant later like a man ablaze himself, carrying Cal Aubel's trusty Weatherby .30-06 rifle with him. He ratcheted the bolt lever and stumbled to one knee, taking aim, his teeth clamped. Another scream bubbled inside him, trying to overflow; the sound he made was not unlike a hot tea kettle close to the boil. Then he fired.

The first bullet caught the calf in the side. It bucked and reeled but stayed on its feet somehow, bounding sideways on those hideous twitchy legs.

Again he jerked the rifle bolt and aimed, arms shaking. His second shot missed altogether, but the third went through the animal's skull and snapped its neck around, breaking it. Richards was already working the lever, frantic, when the stillborn calf kicked and staggered and at last pitched headlong to the ground, fire catching within its wrinkly folds and taking hold again. Finally it lay still, its tongue flopping out of its mouth, and began to burn anew.

Ditch Richards expelled the raspy scream he held, sobbed it out miserably. Falling to both knees, he leaned on the old Weatherby and wept, an arm across his scalding hot eyes. Steadying himself with the rifle, still whimpering, he dug one hand into his pocket and fumbled for the bourbon bottle. Ditch withdrew it, dropped it and groped shakily for it.

He screamed out again when the bolt action 30-06 he was leaning on discharged a final time and blew his right ear clean off the side of his head.

Near the center of town at that moment, while Sydney Cholke sat on her back steps after work, close to tears herself, clutching the extra set of apartment keys and chain-smoking, mourning the loss of her willowy auburn-haired Alice . . . her heart's delight . . . the two peach-faced lovebirds, dead inside their wire cage, reanimated abruptly and both began floundering beside her on the porch.

Sydney leapt straight up, aghast, tearing the Marilyn Monroe beach towel away from the canary cage with a desperate cry. The blood-flecked birds screeched and flopped, wings beating wildly, their breasts heaving. She gaped walleyed at them through a blizzard of feathers, the lit cigarette tumbling from her lips. Syd made a retching sound and her foot bumped the cage, sending it end over end down the back stairs and into the yard, where the little wire door came unlatched, and off flew the two hysterical lovebirds, up and away and into the trees above.

Out at Calvary Catholic Cemetery, the unfortunate, recently interred elementary schoolteacher, known to her pupils only as Mrs. Wintermute, came back to dreadful life with a start—opening her plastic-capped eyes and gulping for air, thinking surely she must be dreaming. She began to shriek for help, bursting the funeral parlor sutures which had been threaded through her gums to keep her mouth closed, not realizing she was trapped in her own coffin down deep inside a freshly dug grave. Not even knowing she had *died*. She gibbered and she shrieked, pounding with her fists, until at last her voice became a shrill whine and she began gurgling in terror, her vocal cords turning to shreds. Still, on she pounded and screamed within the pressing black, that earthy-stenchy blackness surrounding her.

Her twilight pleas fell upon no ears except her own.

***

Richard sat rigid in his seat, hand clapped over his mouth. The congregation hung suspended with him, trying to process what they were seeing. He glanced around at some of their faces: he saw everything from elation to dismay, shock and mania to utter revulsion, some of these raw emotions mingled together. Like him, they were trying to decide whether this was a miraculous thing occurring here, or something else entirely.

"Minty, if you would?" said Julian, gesturing, and the medical examiner stepped forth.

Minty? Richard's brain echoed through a numbing fog. *Minty? Where the hell am I right now . . . where's that TV camera?*

The man with the distinguished beard hooked the stethoscope into his ears and bent over the bawling infant, placing the chestpiece to him. He moved it and listened, moved it again, then straightened and nodded to the Reverend, who nodded back. Dr. Mint faded into his gloom.

Simon Julian looked out over the thunderstruck assemblage. "O Death, where is thy sting?" he said, face filled with leering triumph. *"He is risen."*

A roar went up, the crowd erupting in shouts of jubilation. The baby was growing stronger with every second that passed, its lungs expanding. The Reverend took a small vial from his crimson-red vestments and appeared to anoint the infant's head, motioning to the medical examiner when he was done. The doctor took up the screaming child and handed him off to a woman who had materialized—one of Henry Putnam's next of kin, Richard assumed, the woman that had cried out so terribly at his unveiling moments before. Her babblings rose in pitch as she was ushered away.

Julian faced his flock. "Do you see?" he snarled, silencing them. "Now do you see, the damage your so-called peers can *do*?" He smiled ruefully, perspiration beading on his forehead. "They tried to snuff out a shining life here, declaring our Henry Putnam dead. Someone needs to be held *accountable*. They wrote that child off, resigned to letting him slip away before his destiny could be fulfilled. But sometimes we find in death . . . there is life.

"They have lied to you and to me. They have always lied. I say *no more!*" His arms were thrust before him, spread wide as if parting an ocean. "Tonight, we took it back . . . right here . . . *we* have the higher path. We took it and we shall do so again, herein ever after, from this moment forth. Yea, hear me before it's too late!" The Reverend lunged back toward his pulpit, grasping for his open Bible—

It wasn't there. His hand clawed only the bare lectern top.

Simon frowned and immediately lunged forward again, keeping the momentum going, not wanting to break the spell. He snatched Glee's white Bible from her and left her sitting empty-handed and in disbelief. The pastor held the book up for all to see, shook it at them, his eyes alight.

"This," he said. "*This* is the catalyst. The ones who hide behind it, who twist the words between these covers for their own end. They who would lie to us, and corrupt the earth with their lies." A pause here, a sigh of regret as his arms dropped to his sides. "It's time to cull the herd, friends," he demanded. "Time to rid it of the refuse, and to thin your community of its tainted and soul-sickening numbers. The ones holding you back, keeping you from your glorious rewards.

"I say we must target them before they have a chance to target us. Root them out from where they dwell, for they cannot be trusted. Look around you— open your *eyes*. They are the ones who worship among you, the ones who teach your children. They are your neighbors, your co-workers, and yes, members of your own family. They come with smiles and with promises but they lie. Watch them carefully, and vigilantly. Watch the person sitting next to you at this very moment." Everything had fallen silent now. No one breathed. "Make them answer to the higher path. It is this church's mission to do so, to set a course and follow it through to the conclusion, whatever that might be. Remember, each one of you: veering from our set course in any way is blasphemy in itself. Don't ever forget.

"And this?" The Reverend held up Glee's Bible . . . and where could the other have gone?

Julian gritted his teeth, feeling the disoriented stares upon him. In one smooth motion he ripped the good book he held in half and let its embossed white covers and the torn, gilt-edge pages tumble, and scatter across the floor. He listened to their panicked groans.

"Grace alone," he said, and then he strode out of his chapel room without another word.

Richard was reaching for Katie, finally, but she was no longer in the seat beside him. He stood upright, looking around. Tom Truitt was gone as well. He saw Glee standing down front amid the throng—some of them milled in closer around the metal serving cart, straining to touch it or the fallen shroud sheet. Others had dropped to their knees in prayer, the pages of Glee Deadmond's ruined Bible spilling through their fingers. Most of the congregation just sat in stupor, slack-jawed, stunned looks of bewilderment hanging about them like tattered tinsel halos.

Hurrying out to the aisle, he began making for the doors. He caught sight of his mother-in-law again and she appeared unsettled, her brow creased sharply, hair adrift behind her as she tried to get clear . . .

Richard's heart seized inside his chest, the nape of his neck prickling. He felt the blood congeal in his veins.

Behind Glee, half-hidden within the jostling crowd, stood the Sallow Man quite plainly, his face a waxen mask. The bucket hat was gone and there was a trench coat thrown over his skeletal frame, but it was him. His grayish-yellowy gaze had found Richard.

He sucked his breath in, icy fingers at his spine, caressing all up its length to the back of his skull.

251

"No . . . " Richard heard himself mutter in a croaky voice.

The thin, gaunt nightmare—*his* nightmare from younger times—stared balefully at him. One side of his face drooped. Then the Sallow Man raised a withered arm to point and he opened his mouth, trying grimly to form words. His dark cavity of a mouth worked, missing its tongue, Richard saw, and the flesh crawled over his bones. He looked around him for anyone and then glanced back only to find the chalk-white face gone. Vanished into the throng, nowhere to be seen. Or had it been there at all? Was it in his *mind*?

Richard continued his sprint for the exit, trembling. He felt dizzy, sick almost, but he had time to do a surprised double-take as he pushed out the side doors.

The wheelchair-bound honey-blond woman left sitting in the aisle by herself looked as if she had some *bump action* of her own going on, burgeoning roundly beneath the stuffed panda she cradled in her legless lap.

Tommy was waiting outside in the Illinois dusk, holding Katelyn by her hand in the parking lot. Overhead the sodium lights were starting to brighten against the oncoming night sky. Richard exhaled in relief, wiping a shaky hand across the back of his neck.

"Thought we'd wait out here," said Truitt with an apprehensive look, "in the fresh air."

Richard nearly asked if he'd seen him, if Tom had seen the strange pale man lurking inside, but decided not to. He fumbled for his keys, still trembly, keeping an eye on the church doors.

Tommy watched him. "You all right? You—" His

words broke off. *You look like you just saw a fucking ghost.*

"Let's get out of here," Richard said. "I've had enough religion for one day."

2

Birds were everywhere, their carcasses littering the grounds. Dead birds. Fallen to earth, like so many lumps of coal in the encroaching dark.

The parishioners had departed from the Nain Trinity Lutheran Church; no one was left. William Salt was locking up when he heard the strange noises and looked outside. That's when he saw them, dropping into the dusky parking lot and across the grass, bouncing off his and Reverend Julian's windshields.

Curling to a crisp on the still-smoldering barbecue grill.

And seeing the birds, so many of them, Salt felt the first slivers of fear tingle icily through him.

He closed the doors again and locked them, moving away to find the old man. No one was in the chapel, or the hallways. Then he remembered, and quietly descended the stairs.

Salt crept along a stained wall in the basement corridor, making his way through damp, spidery-cobwebby gloom. Dripping pipes ran lengthwise above him. Ahead, a storeroom door was ajar. He stopped before it and listened. There were noises, *sucking* sounds. Or gagging sounds? He couldn't be sure. He pushed the door inward slightly and peered inside, a sharp stink assailing him.

The refrigeration unit stood open partway, its bulb

casting a dribble of wan light which bled into the semidarkness. In that dingy light, the Native American man made out Aaban Darwish's twisted form lying motionless, pants around his ankles, tied to a toppled chair where Salt himself had secured him—per the Reverend's instructions. He saw slabs of uncooked meat strewn about the dirty floor, the boneless tenderloin cuts Salt had purchased from Countryside Meats for today's picnic, and something else, movement close by.

"What is it?" came Simon Julian's voice blindly from the shadows.

Salt froze, letting out his breath. "Outside. There's . . . there are birds. You should see."

"Not now. Leave, please."

Something chittered in a corner, rustling; the freezer door swung farther open. He caught glimpse of the carnage in the room.

The unmoving body's spine had been snapped, vertebrae clearly crushed, hip bones wrenched and displaced. The ankles were still lashed to the chair legs and his arms tied behind him, but the young man's corpse appeared misshapen somehow, neck puffed like an inner tube, torso distended, trailing slithery intestines.

There were horseshoe nails scattered everywhere.

Salt saw a look of terror on the lifeless face, its bulging eyes, mouth agape.

Darwish's open mouth . . . it yawned grotesquely wide. Salt soon noted the reason why: his jaw had been broken and forced down, ripped almost away, creating a gorge where the young man's lower face used to be.

"I said leave," the voice issued thickly, as if from

the bottom of a well. "This is private, and needn't be observed."

Movement again. Scuttling along the baseboards. Salt became aware of something big just out of range of the light, some hunching, unthought-of thing too immense to even be a person. For one mad moment *it* appeared to him through the blotchy dark— charred appendages flexing and then refolding, chains upon its contorted anatomy, weighing it down. He saw it bent over the mutilated body, probing inquisitively. One deformed claw reached and placed another piece of raw meat into the dead mouth, jamming it in.

The gagging noises began anew.

Salt tried to drag his stare from the sight: Darwish's corpse curled on its side there, close to bursting, his unhinged jaw and the rent orifice being filled. He locked on the boy's death mask for a second, on the hemorrhaged eyes thrust right out of his skull.

A rat scurried past the dead veiny face, pulling its mangled self along with the trap that had killed it.

The Julian-Thing looked back, turning ghastly features at him, a monstrosity showing through its burnt-black ravages.

Salt closed the door.

Ignoring the wet suck sounds, he moved away down the shadowy corridor. He climbed the steps and waited in the hall, wondering what had become of the hand grenade he'd taken from Aaban Darwish's locker, where exactly Julian might've put it. And how in hell the Reverend had discovered the young maintenance man's deceit in the first place.

He listened to a telephone ringing in the church

office, stood with crossed arms until eventually the ringing stopped.

Julian came up from the damp basement looking visibly a shambles, crimson robes in disarray. The old man smoothed his wisps of hair into place and walked toward the restrooms, but when he felt the Indian's deep-set eyes following him Julian swung around.

"What *now*?" his voice carried down the hallway. "Snakes flapping overhead? Milkmaids perched in the trees, giving birth to feathered brats? *What?*" The Reverend exhaled. "Not you, too. Whatever it is, deal with it please. I do not care to know, *Prarsheen*. Unless the nighttime stars vanish from the sky, unless hail and fire and blood come raining down, I don't care." The pastor moved unsteadily to the restrooms, but hesitated. "And get rid of what's downstairs," he said, "so that I may never lay gaze or thought upon it again." He continued on, disappearing behind the men's room door.

The office telephone began a second cycle of rings, and William Salt went to work.

***

Inside the restroom, Simon stared into one of the mirrors. Has it come to *this*? he asked himself wearily, studying his reflection. Celestial messenger, earthbound Host and burning herald—*Orchestrator* of powers and principalities such as he, reduced to this? Rummaging like swine, foraging through human guts and shit? His mouth curled in disgust at what he saw. The nostrils flared.

When he had touched Darwish earlier he'd instantly known all, had realized the boy's betrayal, seen his treacherous plot, and because of it he had lost

256

control. Had gotten *hands on* for the first time in a long while.

Reverend Julian brushed the mirror's surface with his fingertips, watching the glass darken and cloud before him, blistering to black. Once his image was obliterated there, he moved to one of the stalls and stood with rheumy eyes closed.

Oh yes, there would be fire and retribution. *Indeed.* And much more. But only when *he* was ready, when *he* saw fit. Not some trifling, wet-behind-the-ears whelp. Some malignant little cur, perpetually off the leash.

He fumbled beneath his vestments and unzipped himself, began urinating into his own cupped hands now, washing them and his bare arms with the reeking flow of warmth. The old man shuddered at having been brought so low, at losing control that way. He remained at the porcelain urinal with eyes shut, feeling hot piss splatter and course over the flesh of his wringing hands, cleansing himself of the filth of Aaban Darwish's life and death. Yes, the first time in a great long while.

At last done, Julian exited the church men's room, leaving twin trails of droplets behind on either side of him. *Reduced to this,* he thought in anger.

Disease-ridden urine trickled off his long fingers as he walked.

CHAPTER EIGHTEEN

I

ELL?" ASKED RICHARD from where he crouched in Deadmond's front yard.

"Don't know," said Tommy honestly. "Never seen anything like that in my life, man. Maybe I need to hit church more often."

Richard had resigned to staying the night at George and Glee's, so here they were. Otherwise, Katie and he would be out at the motel now, for sure. "Something wasn't right about it. Not right." He chewed the tender inside lining of his cheek, staring at a gruesome Latex lawn zombie which sprouted from the neighbor's darkened yard across the street.

"Nope," Tommy agreed, hands stuffed into his pants pockets against the chill.

They had been outside the Deadmond home for half-an-hour or so, hashing over what had happened, the resurrection they'd witnessed. Richard couldn't shake the feeling it was no miracle, but instead, that— like the rubber zombie rising up across the street—what they had seen in the church was more than just unnatural. *Unclean,* was a word that leapt to mind. And then spotting the Sallow Man like that, on

258

top of it? Too fucking bizarre to even contemplate, to even have been real.

Still, it was funny, how the thin giant's head didn't seem nearly as large and monstrous tonight as it had when they were younger.

There were other Halloween decorations on display along Brazier Drive, amid these sleeping Houses of the Holy. Richard noticed some window-cling mummies, and a bedsheet ghost in the trees. An autumn-harvest scarecrow with a pair of dullish orange pumpkins (whose fleshy insides must be turning to stringy, seeded mush with the warm September days) sat on the porch stoop next door.

"Um, about Lorraine Lawrie—" Richard began.

Tommy waved him off. "Hey, none of my business. Just jerking ya around, you know?"

"I know. But . . . how did he find out?"

"Admiral Jack? He just knew." Tom shrugged. "He wasn't stupid, Rich. Everyone knew."

"Christ." Richard felt ill. "Why didn't he say anything? He never let on . . . my God."

"Rainey's affairs were no secret. You weren't the first, dude, and you sure as hell weren't the last. Jack liked you too much. Always went around talking like you were the son he never had or something, even after you left. Even after he knew."

"Ah, *God*. No." His head hung down. *Shit*. Richard had slept with Jackson Lawrie's lusty wife Lorraine only twice, back in 1987 when she was forty-six years old and Richard just twenty-three, while Michelle had still been away at college and before they'd ever married. Rainey was sultry and simmering, twice his age, the consummate older attractive woman, and she had aroused youthful cravings in him beyond any nip of willpower he might've had to resist. It was the wildest sex he had ever taken part in. He suddenly wondered who else had known—Glee? George?

"Shit," Richard said aloud. He glanced up the block at the theater, at his mural under the dark overhang of trees. Before this evening's developments at The Glee Club extravaganza (whether real or hallucinated) he had actually been entertaining the idea of picking out some paint and doing a few touchup repairs on the mural, even letting his daughter help him. But not any longer. No, certainly not now.

Richard straightened from his squat, feeling his knees creak. "Oh, man." He saw the canopy marquee in the shadowed distance and stared until a car coming down Brazier Drive drew his attention away. The vehicle rolled past, trailing Pink Floyd and marihuana smoke behind it. A minute later a police patrol cruiser drove by. It slowed to a crawl, creeping past the Deadmond home, then continued on after the first car. They could not tell who was behind the wheel.

"Huh," said Tommy, watching it go. He looked toward the house and noticed the German shepherd's pointy-eared silhouette in one of the windows. "Does the pooch stay indoors?"

"Mostly. Except when they let her out back, I think. Why?"

"Good. That dickface Priewe issued a public mandate once stating that he could round up any domesticated animal he caught running loose and have it put to sleep on the spot if he wanted. A few dogs were actually destroyed, I guess, before the town council muzzled his ass and his bullshit mandate."

"You're kidding." Richard shook his head, hearing the crescent man-in-the-moon weathervane squeak on the roof above them. "Fucker."

Tommy told Richard he'd meet up with him sometime tomorrow. He got Franklin's cell number and walked to his truck with a farewell salute. "Double T," Rich murmured, returning the gesture. While the Ram's engine was revving, Richard spared another look toward the abandoned theater and its obscure marquee billboard.

Here be dragons, the thought came on him out of the blue, and he blinked.

***

Inside her lighted living room, Glee sat working at the computer station. Katie wandered over and stood by her, Blondie attached to the girl's hip. Glee became aware of them: "Yes, Katelyn?"

"Mommy always called me her Katie-Smatie," she said matter-of-factly. "Daddy, too."

"Katie-Smatie," echoed Glee, only half listening. "Precious."

Katie dawdled, and asked her grandmother how that baby could have been dead tonight and then not dead. After a long pause, all Glee could say were things like, "I don't know, little bit," or "it was the work of the Lord above". Frowning, Katie interrupted a moment later as Glee clacked away at the keyboard.

"There's something you're supposed to read."

"Hmm? Read?"

"In the bookcase, Granna." Katie crossed the room and removed something from the shelf, came back and set it on the corner of Glee's desk hutch. It was a small, thin volume of some sort, with a worn brown cover and gold lettering along the spine. "Supposed to read it," said Katie again, unsure of herself. Or rather, unsure how to proceed. "Chapter seven," she went on furtively, "uh, page twenty-nine. Paragraph four . . . and five." The girl fell silent, her pearly grays changing over to sea-green. "And six."

Glee relinquished another *hmm*, focused on the bright monitor before her.

"It's important," Katie added, tapping the book. "This, I mean."

"I'll read to you later, dear, okay? Your grandmother has to get this done first. That's my little . . . er, my Katie-Smatie."

Katelyn sighed, moving away from the computer hutch. George came in from the kitchen and asked her to come upstairs and brush her teeth for bedtime. He led his granddaughter by the hand along the hallway and up the narrow staircase, the German shepherd padding after them. When Glee found herself alone, she stood from her chair and walked to the front door. She opened it and stepped outside.

Richard was there on the porch, watching the Dodge pickup pull from the curb in front of the house. He turned to her and started to say something, a half-smile forming, but Glee found her voice first.

"Don't you ever let my granddaughter disappear with that convict piece of shit again," she hissed venomously, nodding toward the street. "*Not ever*. Do you understand me? Do you? Give me some kind of indication that you understand. Give it *now*, you fuck-sorry excuse for a—"

He drew back, recoiling from her flying spittle and ferocity, caught off guard by it, and then she stopped.

Glee trembled, her lips a tight white line. She whirled and strode back inside, looking at Michelle's urn and the pictures atop the television before marching into the kitchen.

***

Richard stood in the cool night air, hearing Tom's truck drive away. He was vaguely aware of several dark moths beating their wings about the light fixture; his mouth still hung wide in shock, so he snapped it shut before one of the great fluttering insects flew straight down his throat.

George and Katie came downstairs as Richard walked into the foyer, closing the front door behind him. Glee could be heard banging around loudly in the kitchen, her voice rising to a shout: "Oh, for the holy love of—can somebody tell me why this damn basement is locked *again*?" George's hand drifted up without the old man even realizing it, checking the corded brass skeleton key inside his sweater shirt. Richard caught the motion.

"I brought the laundry up, dear," George ventured, calling to his wife. "It's right here, dried and folded." A wicker basket of clean clothes sat beside George's chair, where Blondie stood. The swinging kitchen door pushed inward and Glee came through, giving her husband a dour look. She went to her computer and logged off, shutting it down. Then she kissed Katie and told her goodnight. She paused in the hallway and regarded George once more.

"Can you bring them up when you come?" she said, waving a curt hand at the clothes. Her head craned backward. "Goodnight, Richard," she added, throwing another jolt into him.

263

"'Night," Richard managed.

Glee moved down the hall and up the Cornish staircase. Katie lingered by the desk hutch awhile, looking at the small book which remained there. She opened it finally, and tucked something inside the pages.

Richard came to the center of the living room. "Feeling better, George?"

"Hmm? Oh . . . yes. Yes, just a little indigestion I guess. Thanks for asking. Well, goodnight. G'night, honey Kate. You two know where everything is—pillows and blankets are on the sofa. Sleep tight all." Before Rich could say anything else, George had retrieved his wicker basket and disappeared along the darkened hallway. Soon he heard the floorboards creaking overhead.

Richard got Katelyn bedded down on the loveseat, covering her with a fleece blanket. He peered out the picture window at the Blazer, mentioning to her how some of the neighbors had put up their Halloween decorations already. From the loveseat, where she lay bundled, Katie asked him what she should be for Halloween this year. He moved to a different window, one with an electric welcome light burning softly in it.

"You can go as anything you want, hon."

When he peeked through the blinds, he discovered a white envelope taped to the inside of the windowpane. Like the others.

His eyes grew wide as he lifted and turned it gently over in the dimness.

There was a tiny *My C* written on its front side, almost too minuscule to read, like on the one attached to the card table upstairs. Curious, he wanted to open it right there and see, wanted to see what this was all about.

Richard turned it back to the glass instead, smoothing out the tape and pressing it secure again in the electric candlestick's glow. "Love you, Katie-Smatie," he said.

"I love you, Daddy." He heard her yawning and he grinned, fighting the urge to yawn himself. Richard tried spying up the block toward the Lawrie Theater, but could see nothing beyond the window glare. A mental image of the Sallow Man crossed his mind, and he shivered. Their reclusive, long-lost Sallow Man—older now, attempting to speak without a tongue in that droopy, lopsided head of his.

A patrol car crept by slowly out in the street, and Richard withdrew from the blinds with a frown.

. . . *Here be dragons.*

Finding Katie asleep, he figured it safe to use the bathroom. He made sure every door was locked first before ascending the narrow stairs to the upper floor. When Richard got near the bathroom he saw a light coming from within, its door open slightly. Through this he saw Glee inside, pulling a fresh nightgown on over her head. For a split second he glimpsed her nakedness and went flush with face-tingling embarrassment, his breath catching.

Glee Deadmond's left breast was gone. Sliced neatly away, nothing but ugly scar tissue where—

The light went off and out of the bathroom she came. Richard flattened himself against the wall, not moving, hearing the thrum of blood in his ears. Glee halted in the darkness, her hair and gown swirling around her. She looked down the shadowy hall a moment, then continued along the carpet runner, going into Michelle's old bedroom and closing the door. He heard a latch click, a lock being set against the rest of the household—her husband included, he had to assume.

Richard remained still for several minutes, listening. Finally he tiptoed forward and used the bathroom, hastening back downstairs when done.

He stretched out on the sofa, drawing an afghan throw over him and bunching some pillows up beneath his head. *Breast cancer?* he wondered, thinking about what he'd seen, and wondering why Glee had gone into Michelle's room to sleep alone. Wondering what the fuck her problem was. Richard turned off the end table lamp and closed his eyes.

The American Foursquare was quiet, and sweetly scented. There was a wind in the tree branches outside. He heard something and he tensed: a crunching sound, and realized it was Blondie eating her dry nuggets in the dark somewhere. By the florescent light humming above the kitchen sink he watched the German shepherd disappear through the swinging door, then nudge her way back in, bringing another mouthful of kibble from her kitchen bowl into the living room, to devour it there on the rug.

Not wanting to eat alone in the kitchen, wanting to be near people.

Richard smiled, savoring the comforting sound of the dog's late-night feast. He tilted his head and listened to her crunch, his eyes becoming heavy-lidded, thought about all the good memories he'd had with Michelle in this place. Then:

"Who's there?" asked a tiny frightened voice. *"Who is it? Is somebody there?"*

Richard came off the sofa, leaping upright. He sat rigid with the throw twisted around his legs, pulse quickening, and his arm started to inch toward the lamp in the near-blackness.

A cat *mewed* and a phantom boy sobbed close by. Richard froze. Seconds ticked away as he bit at his lip, and finally the night voice quavered to life. *"Let me in—oh please, let me come in . . . "*

It sounded heartbroken, terrified, and Richard couldn't help but shudder. He continued reaching, and suddenly he felt a wet, cold hand grasp his bare forearm in the dark. He very nearly screamed, diving for the end table, almost knocking the lamp over in his lunge to switch it on. The bright light blinded him.

Nothing was there. The home was silent except for the motion of the old clock's pendulum. Even Blondie had hightailed it from the room, leaving dry kibble scattered by the kitchen door.

Katie was fast asleep on the loveseat beneath her blanket.

When his heart had stopped *thud-thudding* and he could at last swallow again, Richard clicked the lamp's three-way bulb to its dimmest setting and left it there, settling hesitantly under the afghan. He lay motionless, gripping his arm where it still tingled, feeling the fine hairs bristle over him.

"Fuck you, frittles," he whispered.

Eventually he got off the sofa and picked up the nuggets, dropping them back into the dog's bowl so she wouldn't catch hell. Turning the console television on low, he sat near his dead wife's ashes and stared at the screen, not seeing it, remembering instead the moment he had brought her home. The moment he'd cradled Michelle in his arms and carried her back across the threshold in Maine, placing the cremation urn in her favorite chair. Taking her out into the garden one last time, and inside her greenhouse that she loved so.

He remembered, and he did not sleep until the evening sky began to lighten.

2

There were voices murmuring throughout the house, figments of faraway voices—he could hear them whispering. One voice in particular lifted above the rest, distinguishing itself from the haunted chorus of sighs and moans.

"Gad'reel . . . Kas'deja . . . Ara'ziel . . . " he listened to it say, reading the names in that familiar voice without bottom or mercy.

" . . . Ver'rier . . . Fla'uros . . . Sem'yaza . . . " Booming in his head now, echoing down corridors of time.

" . . . Yom'yael . . . Del'ardo . . . Luc'ifer . . . " So terrible, so final and resounding.

The voice was Enoch's, as always. Enoch the Scribe, who went on their behalf to plead their case, but who came back only to cite the decree and to condemn them one by each—paradise denied.

"You few, you Watchers . . . once you were like stars in the sky—the eyes of the night, whose task it was simply to watch—*now are you sentenced for your degradations, for defiling yourselves in the blood and*

the flesh of unholy, unsanctioned unions. You once-shining sons of God . . . fallen away as snow falls into shadow . . . and so, will you remain bound here in the valleys of this world until final judgment, to be blotted out in consuming fire—turned to ash from within, spirit and form. Erased, so that you will never even have been. *And your progeny shall be called demons upon the earth . . . and this earth will become their prison, with no hope of transcendence for them or their charge . . . "*

Simon Julian jolted awake, inhaling the fetid aura of Shaw-Meredith House around him, and his first thought was that he had been crated up and buried alive somehow.

But it was just the ceiling of the room. He found himself floating, levitated all the way to the hewn beams, hovering there, his face pressed against them. When this realization came, down came *Del'ardo*—again—with a yell of surprise. He crashed to the floor in stark wonderment, limbs flailing with the sudden drop, feeling his leg twist to its breaking point when he landed. Julian reared up and screamed in rage, staggering, almost toppling back as the knee gave out before he regained his balance.

He had fallen asleep, real sleep, for the first time in so long, and this had been its result.

Once his eyelids had closed and he actually *slept*, he'd risen straight to the ceiling like some horizontal apparition. Then, the dreams of darkness had reached out, snatchy dreams of being manacled down in that jagged gulf while names of the damned were called off.

His recurrent nightmare, always coming home to him, if only every few centuries or so.

The pastor limped painfully and groped for a light-switch, panting.

Flipping it on, he took up the calamander wood box and held it, caressing the streaked patterns across its ornate lid. He set it upon a table, put his spectacles on and then opened it, lifting the scrap of cream-colored velvet fabric inside to examine the contents.

His mementoes—the sacrifices he demanded.

William Salt's severed forefinger was here, among other things: a human tongue; someone's gouged-out eyeball, its watery cobalt-blue iris fixed and staring . . . someone's rotting penis; several molars and a slashed-off woman's breast, pancake flat, rose-red nub of nipple still intact, as if it'd been pressed flowerlike in a scrapbook at one time.

A tiny, aborted human fetus, freeze-dried and perfectly preserved.

The old man's fingers grew longer as if to touch it but faltered. It had been a mistake, this. The fetus had been gotten rid of by an insane, scarlet woman many years ago. A woman who, as it turned out, wanted only to birth the spiritual entity of their union and not the actual physical hybrid-child they had conceived. Thus, she'd induced a self-abortion and ended the life of their offspring.

And thus, Simon had loosed his fury upon her and ended *her* that day—one of those rare *hands on* occasions, best not spoken of. Like the incident in the church basement.

But oh, how scarlet she had run for him.

The Reverend gazed a while longer on his macabre collection, enveloped in the decrepit grayness of the house. Shadows moved fervently along its thick walls, remnants of things long dead—anxious now, it seemed, anticipating a new visitor which might come into their fold. The specters levitated as Julian had, hungering at the prospect, rising to the beams to hang suspended there and leer, and to wait for company to arrive.

He replaced the velvet cloth and closed the hand-carved rectangular box, hearing a rustle outside in the night, like rain or sleet at the shuttered window. Except it wasn't rain. And it wasn't sleet.

It was the whispering black wings of the moths.

CHAPTER NINETEEN

I

THE FOLLOWING DAY *The Rock River Guardian* carried a story about the newest plague pit found near town, and how the grisly remains of twenty-four hapless souls had been pulled from the mass grave so far. There was no mention of Henry Putnam's inexplicable rebirth last night, of course, just a short paragraph regarding the family's tragic carbon monoxide deaths.

Tommy called Franklin's cell phone and they agreed to get together out at Blessing Acres orchard, after he wrapped up his schedule early for the day. Richard and Katie stopped off at the Nightlight Inn to shower and grab a change of clothes first. Richard hadn't wanted to do it at Deadmond's, hadn't wanted to hang around there for anything other than breakfast and morning coffee with George. So, after pulling on some oversized sweatshirts and clean blue jeans, they reclined on the neatly made beds and watched cartoons awhile, eating microwave popcorn from the motel's vending machine lounge.

He paid the room up for another night—tomorrow would be their last day here, and Richard sure as hell wasn't staying overnight in the peculiar Brazier Drive home again. Not after last evening, not after Glee and her dwelling's *weirdness*.

It was another nice afternoon, temperature-wise, but clouds were already on the increase, building to the west as Richard swung off the service road and into the apple orchard's visitor parking lot. The storm front George had spoken of was drawing closer, he reckoned.

They sat in the Blazer and waited alongside a few other vehicles in the unpaved gravel lot. At a quarter past two Tom Truitt's pickup truck pulled in, and Katie and Richard climbed out.

The three of them walked through the open gateway and on down a sloping hill, past the blue-lettered *Blessing Acres ~ since 1915* sign to a cluster of outbuildings. Seated back was a lime-colored farmhouse and its round barn, where a heavyset man of late middle age, with an affable face tucked under his Purdue Boilermakers cap, lingered and greeted the scant patrons, introducing himself as Zeke Blessing, owner and proprietor of the whole shooting match.

They tried the Candy Kitchen structure first, where they sampled little wedges of freshly cut fudge before wandering over to the Pie Barn to buy some hot pizza slices and old-fashioned glass bottles of Dr Pepper. There was plenty of apple-cinnamon cider flowing, and sheep and lamb blankets for sale—the ruins of an antique, steam-powered tractor sat near the doors of the great round barn looking as if John Deere himself might've once ridden it.

When they were done, Truitt and the Franklins took a stroll through the Petting Corral.

"What was your mother-in-law bawling you out about last night anyway?" asked Tom as Katelyn ran ahead over scattered straw, and Richard stiffened.

"You heard that?"

"I saw her come out when I was pulling away."

Richard kicked at the straw. "Eh, she's just the same bitch she always was, that's all," he said. "Hasn't changed much. You know?" Truitt nodded.

"Doesn't matter," Richard went on. "We're out of here tomorrow. *Sayonara* to her."

Tommy eyed him. "You gonna keep in touch this time?"

"Count on it. Definitely."

The goats and sheep drifted toward his daughter at once. She seemed to enjoy feeding them handfuls of cracked corn and alfalfa hay pellets from the coin-operated dispensers, but became quiet after she reached into their wire pens to touch them, to stroke their snouts through the gaps, and caress the creases at the top of their heads. Soon Katie was fidgeting and had retreated from the animal pens with a look of distress.

Richard held her by the hand as they headed out to walk the perimeter, surveying Blessing's 75-acre spread and the wide expanse of his crops: apple orchard on the east side of the farmstead, his pumpkin patch to the west, and row upon row of lush spruce and fir trees, with an open grazing plain that stretched off into the distance behind the round barn and house.

"I haven't been out here in years," said Truitt. "Aren't the owners part American Indian or something? Mixed-blood family?"

Richard squinted. "I think so, yeah. Place has gotten bigger since I was a kid."

They meandered up to where some horses were hitched to a hay-filled wagon, and a chestnut Shetland pony was saddled and tied onto a carrousel spoke for the children. Blessing met them, a vintage soda-pop bottle in one huge fist. Tommy grinned crookedly at the label: Prickly Pear Cactus Cooler.

"Zeke Blessing," said the burly farmer, "owner and proprietor of the whole darned shootin' match. Five dollars'll get the little lady a ride on Apple Butter here—she just goes round and round in a circle. Hayrides are eight-fifty but they take you all over. Banner day, ain't it? Rain a-comin' though."

Richard concurred, paying the man a five and telling him the pony ride for Katelyn would be fine.

The small copper-red pony twitched her ears and long mane about, eyes suddenly alert. Blessing held the Shetland's bridle down with his free hand, nodding for Richard to go. But when he moved to lift Katie up she hesitated, and backed away from her father, looking like she might cry.

"No, that's okay. I don't want to hurt her."

"You won't hurt her, sweetie," Richard said. "I promise. Come on, let me help you."

She raised a tiny hand to fend him off, her lip trembling. *"No,"* she repeated, low-voiced, and he saw tears welling. "She's sad, Daddy. They're all . . . so *sad.* Please . . . "

Richard felt a sudden wave of emotion, for her, or coming from her. He swallowed hard.

"Butter's never been the sad type," Zeke Blessing insisted. "I guarantee you can't hurt her by riding her, little lady. She loves giving rides."

Richard watched Kate closely, noting her reaction

to the big man's words. *Please,* his daughter's pearl-gray eyes begged, *don't make me.* Richard cleared his throat. He kept his gaze on hers, nodded that it was all right. She came then and he picked her up in both arms, feeling her quiver against him. He looked to Tommy, who looked sympathetically back.

"I can't," Katie whispered, and Richard wondered how long it would be before she figured out where most of her food came from. Before she became painfully aware of it, and became a vegetarian because of it.

"Um, I think we'll need a rain check. Sorry."

"No apologies, sir," said the farmer. He slipped Richard's five dollar bill back to him. "Your little lady could use a treat, by the looks of it. Might I suggest our Blue Moon ice cream? Finest around—over at the Pie Barn." He patted the pony's thick, muscular neck and drank his soda.

"Thanks. Sounds good."

They made their way back toward the outbuildings, leaving Blessing to trudge Apple Butter around on her rotating spoke. As he carried her in his arms, Katie breathed into Richard's ear: "Someone's *beating* them, Daddy. Kicking them. Someone's hurting the animals here."

"Who is, Katie?" Richard glanced from side to side in suspicion. "That man back there?"

She frowned. "Don't know. I don't think so."

Inside the Pie Barn again, Richard and Katie shared a Styrofoam dish of the Blue Moon while Tom opted for a large piece of Dutch apple pie. Katie only toyed at the ice cream, licking her spoon. Richard tried coaxing her into a debate whether the pale greenish-blue confection tasted more like vanilla, almonds, sweet marshmallow, or none of the above. In the end they couldn't make up their minds.

As the three were about to go, Tommy spotted a small makeshift structure due north on the big man's acreage, near the edge of the Christmas tree grove. They detoured over before leaving. It turned out to be another animal pen, covered with a dark protective tarpaulin and sitting all by itself, far from the Petting Corral. A young woman with a pair of scuffed wrangling gloves on and wearing faded jeans and a T-shirt hung close by. She carried a feed pail and shooed the farm cats away, sending them back toward the house. There was a silver ring in her pierced lower lip and a strained tiredness around her eyes, marring an otherwise pretty face from which her black hair had been tied back. She called herself Jodean and they learned she was Blessing's oldest daughter—they also learned from her what was in the enclosure.

Katie saw it first, a white snout poking out at ground level, black tip of nose wrinkling, sniffing the air. She inhaled sharply.

"Bison calf," said the gloved woman, setting her heavy pail down. "He's still pretty young."

Richard nodded. "I hear they're making a comeback. Been seeing a lot of them around lately."

Jodean smiled. "You haven't seen any like ours, mister. Ours is special."

Tom and Rich stared at her, then past her to the sheltered structure. They looked closer: *Miracle*, a hand-stenciled piece of plank declared above the pen's door. The snowy-white snout prodded at the wire, letting loose a snort.

"White buffalo," Jodean told them, and Richard's daughter inhaled again with surprise.

"They're magic," said Katie simply, looking to the smiling woman.

"That's right, sweetie. Some people believe they *are* magic."

Richard knelt in a crouch, trying to see inside the hay-strewn pen. "Albino?"

"No," answered the woman, shading her eyes, "not pure albino. But he's the first true, white American bison calf to be born in many years, far as I know. His momma died. We're keeping him separate, isolated from the other animals until we can find out what this disease is. He's a sick boy, our Miracle is."

"What's the matter with him?" Tommy said.

Jodean shrugged. "Nobody can tell us. Could be something congenital, or it might not. We can't be sure. Coming on fast, though. He's getting weaker every day. Doesn't want to eat." The young woman rested a gloved fist upon her hip. "Can't stand saying it, but I don't think our sick boy is long for this world."

Katie made a choked sound and inched forward. "Can I pet him, please?"

"I'm afraid not, sweetheart. We don't know what's ailing him yet. No one can touch him until we do."

"I really should pet him." Katie drew nearer to the enclosure, extending her hand out. Richard stood up quickly.

"Jodean says you can't, Katelyn. It might be dangerous. To you and to him."

"But . . ."

Richard moved to intercept her. "She said no, hon. It'll be okay."

278

"It won't, Daddy. Let me touch him. Just once, before the—" Katie stopped dead, looking at something behind her father. It was a field hand who had come into view, leaning against a shade tree on one of the hills. She glared, not blinking. "That's him," said Katie, eyes clouding over dark as she spoke. "He's the one."

Richard craned his neck to follow her stare, glancing over his shoulder and up the hill to the dark silhouette of the man in a cowboy hat and boots standing beneath the tree.

"He's hurting them," she murmured, and Richard saw the startled way Jodean Blessing regarded them all suddenly.

"What does she mean? Hurting who?"

Richard picked up Katie again. "Oh, she's just fussing," he lied. "Been fussing all day." He caught a glimpse of the weak-looking white calf inside the pen, its eyes runny, hidden from the bright light, saw it trying but unable to rise. Richard gritted his teeth at the sight. "Good luck, Jodean. Come on, Katie-Smatie."

Katie continued watching the field hand. "What should we do?"

"Not right now."

"But he's bad. Like the men at the church, Daddy."

Richard tensed. "We'll talk about it later, hon," he said low. "No scenes, okay?"

She blinked as he carried her. "Wait! I didn't pet the sick boy yet!"

"Katelyn, there's nothing I can do. Please, let's just go."

"Don't you believe me?" his daughter said, staring at him. Sadness echoed in her small voice. "You don't even believe me."

He walked with her in his arms, Tommy following them up toward the parking lot gateway. Katie had begun to cry, Truitt noticed.

Jodean raised a gloved hand to the little girl as they departed, and saw the girl wave back.

2

That same day, Glee decided she'd take a drive to clear her mind, but as she braked at the stoplight her mind was anything but clear.

Instead, she found herself half-remembering the way things used to be. It was simpler back then, fewer complications. And, of course, she had been the only one at the beginning. Glee studied the masculine gold ring on the finger of her right hand, its square stone and miniature intaglio portrait.

She had been his first. He had given the ring to *her*, of all the many he could have bestowed it upon. She recalled the moment—the way he took her, ravishing her so violently and so completely, despite her protests that she was already married to George.

Despite her exquisite screams.

That was thirty-five years ago; everything was different now. Once, he used to make passionate love to her all through the night, fucking her upon the silken bed Glee's hair created beneath them, leaving her with claw marks and with badly bruised thighs and her brain muddled in fog afterward, never quite knowing what had happened. He'd been handsome, magnetic. Not like now. Now he was just a lecherous old wretch—an *aberration*—rotting inside those church walls of his, and inside the walls of that

280

blighted house, lusting after anything with a bit of trim between its legs.

Glee looked up at the light, noticing the largish Cholke woman sitting opposite her in a Public Works Department truck, looking back at her, waiting on the same signal as she. Someone stood at the curb ready to cross: Meg from the coffee shop, wearing her hairnet, and toting that bulky camera around her neck everywhere she went.

Sluts, Glee thought abruptly, primping at her pinned-up coiffure, *all of them. He's lost his mind, cavorting with sluts.*

Yes, he'd truly been something. Once. But *now,* animalizing, befouling women like this. Young and old, no matter. Churchgoers or not. Good God, he even had a legless one . . .

Glee caught her own reflection in the side mirror, saw her mouth drawn with revulsion as the mental image of the disabled girl in a wheelchair bloomed behind her eyes. *Completely lost his mind.*

"Vile," she sneered aloud, and the sound of it startled her inside the enclosed car.

The stoplights changed over to green and off everybody went, Glee Deadmond and the Cholke woman in their vehicles, and shutterbug Meg Bilobran on foot. They each glanced at one another in passing, and then continued along their way.

3

The sour-sweet smell of the skunk was back, Rich noted. Tommy had been right—the Blazer still reeked of it.

Katie was sulking in the seat next to him, her lips an angry pout.

"Your face will stick," he warned her jokingly.

"It's not funny." She glared out the window as they drove, dried tears streaking her face. "You never believed in me. Not ever."

Richard cleared his throat. "That isn't true, Katelyn."

"Yes it is." Her tone was accusatory, filled with hurt. She straightened, wiping at her eyes, seeing something up ahead.

It was the bridge.

"Um, Katie? What did you mean before, he's bad like the men at the church?"

"I'll show you," said Katie in a hush, not listening, "both of you. Stop, please."

"What?"

"Please pull over, Daddy. There's something I want to show you."

"Katie—"

"Pull over and stop now! Right here!" The girl slammed her tiny fists on the dashboard. It wasn't a request: she demanded it of him. He gaped at his daughter in bewilderment. Truitt was following close behind them, a Springsteen ballad belting from his rusted-out truck. Richard blinked his taillights, flagging him over, and they both steered off the road.

It was early yet, but the shadows were already lengthening as they parked and got out. Tom appeared at a loss, to which Richard could only shrug. He reached for Katelyn's hand as they walked and she pulled away.

They were at the mouth of the Anasazi Bridge, and

it was blocked off—it had been that way, in fact, ever since the late 1970s. Ever since . . .

"Someone died here," Katie said, walking ahead, "someone you know." She glanced back into their unsettled faces. "This way."

They stepped onto the bridge, moving hesitantly around the orange metal BRIDGE CLOSED sign, which barred their way. About halfway out they stopped, hearing the Rock River as it rushed along below them. Katie touched the crumbling stone railing.

"Ollie Echoes," she began, and her father felt his skin chill. "You went to school with him, played baseball in the summer. Played checkers with him. He invited you to stay for dinnertime—dawn-fresh sweet corn, his parents called it. Because their corn was picked fresh every day at dawn."

Tommy and Richard looked on, speechless.

"This is where he died when he was thirteen. Ollie Echoes." Katie stared out at the water.

She was right. The name had been mispronounced, but otherwise she was right: *Ollie Echols.*

"The thing at Granna's house. It's him. There are others, but that one is him. He's been waiting for someone to come."

The thing *at Granna's house.* Richard teetered back on his heels. *Seee . . . how I've waited for you.* Oh, my Christ—

"Why did he drown himself?" Tommy asked her, as if it was the most natural question in the world to ask a child.

Katie took a deep breath. "He didn't," she said low. "He jumped in. To save his cat." She pointed to the

283

water, leaning forward slightly. "There. The policeman knew, only he wasn't the policeman then."

"What?" uttered the two grownups in concert.

Katie looked at them, and something flickered in her gaze. "Mr. Priewe knew. He threw the cat in."

They stared open-mouthed at her, shivers rippling through them, settling into their bones. The river sounded far away all of a sudden. *Told you,* Richard wanted to boast, *didn't I? Didn't I tell you?*

He cleared his throat. "Why would he do that, Katelyn?"

"Hates them. He caught Ollie's pet cat in a cage. Hated its crying, the way it hung around his yard crying. So he trapped it. Put bricks inside the cage, and threw it into the river. But Ollie Echoes saw."

"Fuck me," said Tommy under his breath, and Richard grabbed him by the arm in order to steady them both.

"What else, Katie?"

His daughter was frowning. "Ollie followed him, saw what he did. He jumped in. To save his cat. The water was freezing, chunks of ice floating in slush. His head hit one of them. He drowned."

Richard closed his eyes, trying to think. His mind reeled. He seemed to recall that officially, yes, Oliver Echols had drowned, but also that a broken neck had been one of the 'impact injuries' listed at the time of his death, from him hitting the water. Everyone had just assumed it was an accident. That is, until a rumor had gotten started around the Val.

"The policeman knew," Katie repeated, "only he wasn't the policeman then."

Richard's eyes flashed open. "Mr. Priewe saw this happen? He didn't try to help him?"

"No . . . he didn't help. Didn't do anything. He told people how Ollie Echoes was crazy. Taking drugs maybe. But he knew the truth. Always knew."

They exchanged glances; Truitt ran his fingers through his hair. "Son of a bitch," he said to Richard. "That son of a bitch. He watched him drown, and then he lied about it. Goddamned piece of *work*."

"The cage is there . . . still there," Katie informed them, pointing at the coursing water. "He's lost his way. Like Mommy used to tell us."

Let me in, that voice in the darkness came swimming back to Richard. *Oh please, let me come in.* "Katelyn, is Ollie here? Right now?"

The girl lowered her gaze to the stone bridge under her feet. "Yes."

"We didn't know," he said after a long pause, almost choking on the words. "Tell him I—tell him we're sorry. None of us knew. We were just kids."

Katie continued staring at the ground. Finally she looked up. "He knows," she said, voice trembly. "He was a kid, too."

Richard clenched his teeth, and started pulling his sweatshirt over his head.

"What are you doing?" Tommy said. "Where do you think you're going?"

"Into the river. To find a cage."

"The hell you are. You know how strong these currents move? And the silt?"

"Just let me do this, all right, Tom? I'm not helpless you know." He went on yanking his arms out of the sleeves until he felt Truitt's hand on his chest.

"Nobody said you were helpless, Rich. But I'll go down. Stick close to your daughter, why don't you?"

"Listen—" Richard began, irked.

His friend stared him squarely in the face. "Stay with her. I think she probably needs you."

Rich's shoulders slumped. Heaving a sigh, he pulled the sweatshirt back on. He watched then as Tommy got undressed, stripping down to his gray boxer briefs. Richard gripped him by the forearm and helped lower him over the edge, back a ways where the bridge's underside was nearest to the water. Tommy eased himself in, and immediately started to shiver. He asked Katie where it was again and the little girl pointed. Then, he took several deep breaths and looked up at them.

"Back before ya can miss me," Thomas said, held his breath, and plunged outward and beneath the rushing dark Rock River.

Richard and Katie stood together at the bridge rail. Feeling the seconds tick by and slip away, Richard chewed at the inner lining of his cheek. "You know I love you, right?" he told his only daughter after a half-minute had passed.

"Yes. I love you, too, Daddy."

Richard watched the surface, his fingers thrumming on the disintegrating rail, knocking flecks of masonry loose. He leaned back and glanced at his wristwatch, then leaned forward. Soon he was checking the watch again: one minute. And again: a minute thirty. Now panic wormed into him, knotting his insides. He shifted to his left, trying to think, hazarding another look just as a tremendous splash came and Truitt resurfaced ten yards out from where he'd gone under.

His friend was kicking toward the bridge, gasping,

stroking against unseen currents which tugged beneath the surface. Richard hunkered down as far as he could and extended his right arm. Tommy hesitated, wiping his eyes clear and squinting up.

"It's there, all right," he spluttered, breathing hard. "On the river bottom. Couldn't get to it, but it's there. Steel cage trap . . . bricks and small bones inside. Ribcage, looks like. She was right."

Richard fixed on Katie's face, smiling at her. "She's always right. Didn't I tell you? Get up here." He glanced down again, reaching, and slowly the smile slid from his lips. His eyes grew wider, as did Katie's beside him.

"Tom, give me your hand," said Richard calmly. "Now."

"What is it?" Tommy asked, registering their expressions. "What's wrong?"

"Let's go. Come on."

Truitt thrust his body vertical, lunging out of the chilly water and grabbing for Richard's arm. "Move your ass," Rich grunted, straining. He hauled him up hurriedly, dragging his dripping form onto the edge of the bridge.

"Shit," said Tommy, teeth clattering, "we double-parked or something?"

Richard gave a quick nod, tipping his glance over the side and back down. Tom followed the look and caught his breath. No one moved.

Below them, dying fish were on the rise—dozens, popping up white-bellied all around where Tommy had just been treading water, as if they'd followed him lazily to the surface. The three watched in amazement and then alarm as their numbers continued to grow,

287

the gulping fish washing up as far as they could see, until their lifeless multitude began literally to blanket the river.

4

William Salt unbuttoned his immaculate jacket, reaching shaky fingers inside it, and took hold of the Sauk war hatchet. He stared in disbelief at the theater marquee across the street, the troubling arrangement above its doors—

TKE HUR AND LE VE NOW

—and at the person in front of those boarded-up doors, snapping pictures and whirling with effortless grace.

The woman in a hairnet, armed with a big Canon 35MM camera.

Salt saw her fire off several rapid shots at the abandoned Lawrie Theater and the mural on its side wall, eye pressed to the viewfinder. He observed her sweeping and clicking randomly here and there, even aiming the long-focus lens in *his* direction once as she returned full circle back to the theater's Depression-era façade.

Gaze narrowed, his face hardening into dark, unforgiving stone, the Native American man checked both ways and crossed Brazier Drive, watching for anyone else as he strode swiftly. The area appeared deserted to him.

He slid the small ax out of his belt and held it low, flat against his leg as he approached. He felt the leather-wrapped haft grinding, wanting to crack under his fierce grip. When he got to the sidewalk, Salt first reached up and used the head of his weapon to rake the black letters off the stained canopy billboard, obliterating its loosely arranged message; the offending plastic pieces raining.

Meg Bilobran gasped, startled by his intrusion. She stared a moment, confused, something in the Indian's eyes causing her to back away a step. Then Salt lunged at her and seized the camera from her hands, yanking it toward him even as Meg spun to flee. A shriek for help escaped her, but the Canon's strap tightened around her throat and cut the cry short. Next instant she was being pulled through the side lot past the mural. Pulled through undergrowth behind the vacant movie house.

She fell and was dragged across the ground kicking and flailing, stark terror ripping at her, the strap choking off her air. Her eyes bulged and her face began bluing as Salt pushed through the tangled thicket and put his shoulder to the old wooden door at the back of Jack Lawrie's theater. He drove into it again, until it gave way, and he hauled Meg through the rear entrance.

Her hairnet hung in the undergrowth, torn loose by snatching brush.

Inside, Salt dragged the once-pretty woman up the curving stairs to the gloom of the upper balcony, throwing her into one of the back row's moldering seats. He stood behind her and broke the camera open, removing the film, ignoring her whimpering pleas. Grabbed the strap and twisted it viciously about Meg's neck, lashing it tight at the base of her skull.

He faced the garroted woman, unraveling her film as she bucked and kicked and slowly strangled, fighting to claw the camera strap free. Pigeons fluttered in panic to the safety of the collapsing dome above. The exposed roll of film dropped to the floor. And suddenly he was on her, teeth clenched in a grimace and his large hands encircling her throat, thumbs crushing her larynx. The Indian shook her, throttled her to make sure, and stepped back.

Meg Bilobran sat gurgling, bubbles dribbling from her lips. He watched the last traces of life as they ran out of her body like sand, her oxygen-starved brain convulsing. Seeing her this way in the musty shadows, Salt's own breath began coming in irregular hitches now.

He unbuckled his dress slacks before the woman's dimming gaze and let them drop. He violated her then, raped her open mouth as she slumped dying in the theater chair, arms dangling bonelessly at her sides. Her eyeballs might have rolled back once and looked up at him, some horrible diminishing awareness still there, but he couldn't be certain. Nor did it matter. He violated her as she died, and even after she had died.

She made the same wet sounds Aaban Darwish had made in the church's basement, it occurred to him . . . those same gagging sounds, as she passed from this world into the next.

When he was finished, William Salt drew his slacks up and buckled them, sliding the hatchet back into his belt. He kicked the unraveled film under the seats. Propping the woman up in the chair, he licked her once, twice, tasting the horror on the corneas of her wide-flung eyes. Moving behind her again, he took out

290

the Darwish boy's survival knife and slashed off her scalp, trying not to get any blood on himself.

Covering her stilled, defiled form with some filthy sheet plastic he found on the floor, he left her to the pigeons and the coppery-scented darkness, pulling the back door of the derelict Lawrie Theater shut in his retreat.

CHAPTER TWENTY

I

HAT THE HELL are you doing here?" came a voice from behind them, just as Tom was hiking his work boots on. They all turned together, and when Richard saw Chip Priewe standing at the mouth of the Anasazi Bridge by the metal A-frame sign, it felt as though ice-cold river water had suddenly seeped into his stomach, filling it.

"Answer me," said the police chief, smacking on Clorets gum. "This bridge is closed to the public. What are you doing here?"

"Why's that?" Tommy asked, shaking droplets from his hair. "Why is it closed?"

Priewe studied them. "Safety reasons. How did you get yourself all wet there, Thomas?" He chewed briskly, hand rested on the butt of his holstered service revolver at his hip.

"We saw the fish," Richard said, trying to think of a way out of this. "From the roadway. Dead fish, floating in the river. We're wondering what caused it. Any ideas?"

The uniformed chief peered over the side, taking in the spectacle. "Not a clue. But you people need to clear off here. Now. It's unsafe."

"Sure thing," said Richard, collecting his daughter. "Let's go, guys."

Truitt straightened, his clothes stuck to him. He followed Rich and Katie around the orange BRIDGE CLOSED sign, but then slowed his gait, lagging.

"Ollie Echols used to live next door to you, didn't he, Chief?" Tommy said, and Richard's heart sank straightaway into his bowels.

The police chief went rigid. "What did you say?"

"You heard me. Oliver Echols—you remember him, don't you?"

"Maybe everyone better hold it where they are." Priewe maneuvered in front of them. "All right, what's going on? What's this about the Echols boy?"

Tommy smirked. "What's going on? I'm thinkin' you're one fucked-up prick, that's what's going on. And I'm thinkin' I know what you *did*."

Priewe's face twitched. Reaching behind him, he cautiously withdrew his handcuffs.

"What? You're going to arrest somebody now? Give me a break."

"Turn around for me, Thomas."

"Whoa, hold up," Richard said. "Who's being charged with what here?"

"I think a night in the lock-up for trespassing might do everyone some good. But your little girl there, she'll have to—"

"No way." Richard's voice came out dry, and shaky. "No damn *way*. We haven't done anything."

The police chief fixed his gaze on Franklin. "Oh? What are *you* going to do? Call your father, the attorney?" Richard's eyebrows rose, and Priewe twirled the cuffs. "That's right, I did some homework."

He laughed and chomped his Clorets. "Mother deceased, but pop's a big-shot lawyer up in Minnesota. I know."

Richard bristled, standing his ground. "I don't need my father for this," he heard himself say. "All I need is a call to my agent's legal department in New York City. One call—that's it. So think real hard before you stick us behind bars for no good reason, Chief. Because these attorneys will want answers." Richard's tone had dropped to a stage whisper and Tom grinned slyly, water dripping from his tangled hair. "You better stop and think who the guilty party really *is* here, and whether you want it coming to light or not."

A flash of anger, more chewing. Tommy said: *"Prick-we."*

"Don't ever call me that again," Priewe advised, the debate over. "Turn around, both of you."

Katie had slipped past her father during this, and she reached a tiny hand out and touched the police officer's leg. He glanced down at her, curiosity lining his brow, and all hell let loose.

Time hung suspended, unmoving, then it exploded back to speed. Chip Priewe stiffened as if an electrical charge had been shot through him. He glared all around, eyes huge, head jerking in every direction as he swallowed his gum. He screamed out and staggered, breaking contact with the little girl. He'd gone stark white, they saw, the blood draining from his face, a look of dread replacing it. The handcuffs fell and another wrenching cry of dismay spilled from him. Richard and Tommy gaped.

"What is it?" uttered the chief shrilly, eyes shifting back and forth. "Who . . . *where did they go?"*

294

Priewe spun wildly, stopped dead. "Piss shit—no. They're *everywhere*. My God." Unsnapping his holster, he drew the weapon. Richard yanked Katie behind him by her shirt and kept her there, his pulse ratcheting up as the man continued to ramble. "Keep them away from me. *Getawaygetawayget—*"

He was nonsensical, grimacing like a lunatic, and just when Richard began to comprehend what was happening, his daughter started to speak.

"He'll kill his wife," Katie said. "Kill her. Hide her in the crawlspace until it's safe. Under the house."

Richard and Tommy stared, their mouths open, astonished beyond words. Katie's eyes were vacant, half-lidded. She looked away and went on in that toneless voice.

"Fold her in half. Inside a drum. He'll fold her in half. Fill it with cement until he can find someplace. Drop her in the river someplace—"

"What did she say?" Priewe was asking over the sound of the water.

"—the *cunt*," Katie finished huskily, and Richard went cold.

"What did she say?" rose Priewe's voice.

All at once it hit him: the police chief's rush of madness, their distant stares. Katie had touched his leg, allowing him to *see*. Allowing him a glimpse of something best left unperceived. Yes. *She touched him* . . .

"Cunt," repeated Katie, grimacing as well, and the sound of it coming from her innocent visage shook Richard to his core. He saw the chief whip around, searching in vain, and then the gun was swiveled slowly in their direction.

"It . . . it's *her*. Isn't it?"

Richard braced himself, shielding Katie behind his own body. His eyes darted to the vehicles, seeking any chance to make a desperate spring. Goddamn Tommy, putting them into this.

"Wh-where?" Priewe stammered at the girl, shuffling towards her. "Where did they go? What do they want?" His lips were stretched taut, quivering.

Tom moved up, arms spread wide, blocking the man's advancement. "What does *who* want? There's no one here, you crazy fuck! Look."

The chief's gaze focused, locking on Truitt's face. "You—*Thomas*—you make them *get away!* Keep them away."

"You're the one who's going away, Chip," said Tommy, "for what you did. Your badge disappears on this one."

The sickened smile was collapsing and he cocked his pistol, the muzzle leveled at Truitt's chest.

"Go ahead, pull it. Won't make any difference. You know why? Because you're going down. You'll do time at Marion State for Ollie Echols. You'll bleed out of your *ass* for Ollie Echols, Chip. Sure as you're standing there. *Finished.*"

Chief Priewe stumbled back as if stricken, the service revolver quaking in his hand. He accidentally upended the metal A-frame sign (despite the heavy sandbags slung across its leg crossbars to keep it in place) and the resulting crash was tremendous. He scrambled for his squad car, hunched in on himself, head still whipping about and his face aghast.

"Run, prick," Tommy called after him as the chief keyed his ignition over and sped away. "That's right.

Fucking douche." He kicked in disgust at the fallen handcuffs, turning. "Did you see that?"

Richard had Tommy by his shirtfront. "What is wrong with you?" he shouted. "We could've been killed! Katie could have—could've been . . . *right here.*" His arms were trembling. "Jesus Christ."

Truitt tore free, pushing him off. "Take it easy, dude. He's gone. It's over."

"Over? Are you kidding me?"

"Simmer down, all right? What's he gonna do? Nothing, that's what. It's over." Tommy looked to Katelyn, who was still gazing strangely, and shivering now. "Did she cause all that?"

Richard only shook his head. "What were you thinking . . . god*damn* it."

Tommy cleared his throat. "Well, tell you what *I'm* gonna do. As soon as I find Palm Clemency? I'm telling him about this, that's what. Everything. What happened to Ollie. The cage down there. See what he says, how he wants to handle it." He managed another smirk. "Priewe's dirty. Somebody needs to know."

Richard was no longer listening. Instead, he watched his daughter as her shivers grew, her eyes glimmering; Katie's teeth chattered.

"Don't worry," Tom said, seeing his friend's unease, "Palm is one of us. He named his own daughter Cimmeria, for fuck's sake. After *Conan the Conqueror's* homeland. And if we can't trust a black guy who digs Robert Howard like us, who the hell can we trust?" Tommy clapped him on the back and laughed. "Your agent's legal department—good one, man."

2

After supper, Zeke Blessing wedged his old alma mater Purdue Boilermakers cap down onto his head and marched off to the fields, a fresh soda pop in hand. He spied none of the barn cats dozing in their places on the hay bales, which struck him as unusual. But his daughter Jodean was back at the pen, he could see, performing the smudging ritual again, fanning sacred smoke into the animal's shelter and hoping against hope for . . . well, for a miracle out there.

Blessing walked along, extending a wave to the lean field hand, Shaw standing up on the hill as he went by.

The orchard and adjoining pumpkin farm didn't have many visitors on weekdays like today, especially here at the edges of town, but weekends would be getting busy now, with more and more family outings taking place amidst these scenic, rolling hills. It would stay that way through October and November, straight on until mid-December before tapering off at season's end.

He looked up as he trudged, following a line of geese in the sky as they made their way south in search of warmer climes and open water. Sometimes Blessing felt like doing the same, but there were too many things to be done with running the family business. Even during off-season. Still, he was already dreaming of retirement, of leaving the place to the next generation.

The Pick-Your-Own pumpkin patch came into view, and he frowned—every other crop row had at least two or three rotten pumpkins on the umbilical-like vines, shriveling on the ground. They appeared *frostbitten*, although overnight temperatures hadn't dipped anywhere near the freezing mark yet. This hadn't been here before, he realized.

Blessing was staring at the mottled orange shells dotting his field when shouts of concern rose up behind him, people calling his name, yelling for help. Dashing back across the open expanse, he puffed for the orchard groves on the far side. He pulled up short, stopping in his tracks.

"W—what is it? *What the—?*"

Several apples hung lifeless from the branches, black-red, some of them oozing their once-sweet juices in putrid syrupy drips. Blessing gaped, unable to take his eyes off them. Two of his hired hands, Gus and Ernesto, stood nearby, pointing up. A ladder lay tipped over at the base of one of the trees. Zeke edged forward, squinting overhead. He started and dropped his pop bottle.

A dark-skinned snake dangled from one of the tree limbs—it looked like there were others, too, but he couldn't tell for sure in the fading light. The one he *was* sure of however squirmed and twisted itself free. It managed to fall right out onto a basket of robust, brightly colored apples in front of him: Ginger Gold, and Honeycrisp, and Red Delicious . . .

Blessing tripped and toppled backward, losing his hat when his ass hit the ground hard. He scooted away, trying to get up. The cries of the hired hands were rising in volume, becoming heated. Accusatory. He caught words in broken Spanish with meanings he was vaguely aware of—*liar, cursed tongue* . . .

accountable—and all at once Ernesto removed the twin baling hooks hanging from his belt and buried their rusty steel points straight between Gus's shoulder blades. The real yelling began then as the hooks were drawn in opposite directions, and Blessing saw the fallen black snake uncoiling its loops from the basket to slither warily around his forfeit Boilermakers cap, writhing over the embroidered Purdue Pete mascot.

Lordy, thought Zeke Blessing, scrambling to his feet and running for the round barn as high screams filled the air. *Oh dear Lordy, the serpents are loose in the garden.*

3

Even with the heat cranked up in the Blazer, Katie still shivered. The little girl opened the glove compartment and removed her dead mother's winter scarf, smelling it before wrapping it absently around her neck. She stared out her window as Richard drove.

It was time to go. Get their shit gathered and go to the motel. Scatter the ashes and get out of this town. Enough.

There was a car parked in front of the Deadmond home, so Richard swung into the driveway alongside the house. He walked Katelyn up to the door and knocked twice before going in. George put Blondie into the backyard and came from the kitchen, stood beside him in the foyer.

"Jack Lawrie's here to see you," he told Richard, flooring him. "Lorraine, too."

"*What? Where?*" *Holy hell.*

George coughed. "Lorraine called asking for you,

said they needed to see you. Something important, son. They're outside. Didn't want to come in and wait, I guess."

Richard's gaze flicked to the front door in wonderment. George said: "Dark blue Buick out front."

"Okay. Um . . . okay. Thanks."

He saw Katie standing motionless by the television, the turquoise scarf wound about her. She had Michelle's urn cradled in two hands, her cheeks flushed. *What next?* Richard felt the headache as it began pulling at the back of his scalp. *Perfect.*

"George?"

"Yes?"

"Would you look after Katie? Make her some hot chocolate or something? I don't think she's feeling well."

"Of course, Rich."

"I'll be right back. Don't let her out of your sight, okay?"

"Sure."

Richard smiled weakly and went out the door again. He could see them now, the Lawries sitting in their blue sedan. Rubbing his face, he went down the steps and walked to the curb, his innards knotting.

You brought this on yourself, Richie boy.

Lorraine got out of the driver's side and hurried around the car toward him, her hair dark and wild. She wore a look of distress and he stutter-stepped, hesitating at the walkway.

"Richard, thank God . . . " she said, wobbling on her ankle-strap spike heels. Her warm hand touched his arm and he felt the tips of her long fingernails.

"Really nice to see you, Lorraine. What's up?"

(*"Sodomy."* It was all he could think, a random memory firing off and filling his brain, triggered by the touch. *"Sodomy,"* she had whispered both times he'd had sex with her, so softly he could barely hear it, reaching back and digging her nails into the flesh of his forearm as he held her small waist in the perfumed shadows and thrust into her from behind. She first moaned the word while climaxing, legs wrapped around his neck, his tongue flicking and swirling inside her musky wetness, explaining to him after the shuddering orgasms had finally ebbed that it was merely a purging of sorts. Her way of exorcising old demons from when she was molested and sodomized by a 'family friend' as a teen. Richard recalled being horrified at this, but Rainey, cigarette between her fingers, had insisted she loved sex, adored it in all its forms, especially anal sex—she just always made sure to utter the word at some point during the carnal act itself, if only to expunge herself of the blame and the shame of what had happened to her so long ago: *"Sodomy."*)

Lorraine Lawrie threw her arms around him and said, "Something's wrong with my Jackson. He won't go to the hospital, but he insisted on coming here. He's got something for you." Richard felt her breath on his neck. "Please, Richard, can you talk to him? Convince him to get checked? He'll listen to you, darling."

"Sure, but . . . I don't understand." Richard watched the Buick, perplexed. Lorraine released her embrace and moved to the automobile, rapping gently on the passenger-side window.

"Jack, sweetie? Richard is here. Like you wanted." Her voice rose. "Jack? Come on, open up." She tapped the glass again with her knuckle, and the window began powering down. Richard inhaled.

Lawrie looked bad. Like death warmed over, as the saying went. He wore BluBlocker aviators but his face appeared sunken in around them, falling back into itself. The teeth beneath his dry, cracked lips protruded because of this. He sat stiffly in the front seat and stared straight ahead with something resting on his lap.

"You're the one," said the ailing Navy man, garbled, guttural. Richard frowned.

Lorraine led him closer and he bent to peer into the car. When he glanced back, Lorraine nodded.

"Jack?" said Richard, unsure. "Admiral? It's Richie Franklin. You all right?"

"The one," Lawrie repeated; his words came slow and thick, like a drunk shooting up heroin might speak.

"What was that, sir?"

"Took it." He was thrusting something into Richard's hands. "Winked at me, the son of a bitch."

Richard looked down at what he'd been given. It was a Bible, the object the admiral had been holding in his lap—removed from its lectern not twenty-four hours prior when Lawrie had hugged himself and ran out of the church with it beneath his jacket. Leatherbound and tattered, really, *really* old. Rich lifted the worn cover and saw it was printed in a foreign language, glimpsed *D. Martin Luthers* on a crumbling inner page, *1670* below that. German. Over *three hundred years* worth of old. But why—

"*He took it!*" Lawrie crowed, convulsing violently, and Richard's heart leapt into his throat. "Made him

. . . made him chew off his own *tongue* . . . and he took it! *Make him give it baaack . . . "*

Richard stepped away. "Jesus, Rainey. How long has he been like this?"

"It started last night. Said he couldn't feel anything in his extremities, couldn't taste his food. His hearing is starting to go." Lorraine bit at her lip, her voice dropping as she cupped her mouth. "It's almost like he's not all there, Richard. Like he's losing his mind. His senses."

"Senseless," tittered the admiral, hands fiddling with one another upon his lap. He twitched, and his dry lips moved as if in silent prayer.

Richard's frown deepened. He was tired and his head hurt, and he could not comprehend any of this. Lorraine was touching his arm again.

"We were so sorry to hear about your wife, Richard. You must be devastated. This is just awful." Lawrie made a high-pitched noise in the car, and Rainey sighed. "I'm at my wits' end, what with Jack and everything. Plus our exchange student that we host hasn't come home since yesterday. All this insanity with the church. I don't know what to do. Oh God, Richard." Her hand crept up and caressed the side of his face. She was biting her lip once more—he tried to keep his gaze from wandering to her plunging neckline. "God, if we only had a little time, darling. Just to visit and to reminisce. We—"

"Lorraine!" Jack screamed. *"Quiche Lorraine!"* He flung open the passenger door and suddenly bolted from the sedan, scrambling off toward his closed-down theater. Richard stood frozen with shock, then he and Lorraine were after him, sprinting across Brazier

Drive. Halfway up the block they at last corralled the zigzagging man. He spun around wildly, sunglasses dangling on one ear. Richard saw his blank, idiotic stare—eyes turning milky white beneath their lids.

"Was it *huge*?" asked Lawrie. "*Did she tell you? How huge was* it?" Lorraine went pale.

"Admiral Jack?" said Richard, teeth clenched. "Can you see me, sir?" He passed a hand in front of his eyes.

"Blind," Lawrie said, and Richard felt his guts twist. "We're blind, all of us here . . . but not you."

After a few calming minutes they led him in the direction of the vehicle, Lorraine hooking his BluBlockers back in place over both ears. Her high heels clocked along the pavement as they walked him carefully. Richard heard a dog barking somewhere.

Once he was in the passenger seat, Lorraine buckled her husband up and shut the door. Her look of utter helplessness caused Rich to lean into the Buick a final time. "Jack, you listen to Rainey now. She's going to take you to get looked at. Listen to her. She knows what's best, Jack. Do you hear me?"

The stranger inside the car shook his head. "Every man's leavings." When Richard started to straighten, Admiral Lawrie's fingers closed viselike on him. "Get the bastard," he said remotely.

. . . *Is he talking about me?* wondered Richard, easing himself loose. Lorraine faced him, and again his eyes fought to avoid her tanned cleavage. She hugged him, kissed his cheek. He waited for it—some sort of pass, a stealthy grope maybe—but nothing more came.

"Thank you, Richard. Goodbye," she said, and hurried into the street.

She was crying as she got behind the wheel.

Richard crouched to retrieve the Bible he'd dropped in the grass, and glanced up: Lawrie was looking his way, as if staring right at him from the passenger seat. He saw himself reflected in the aviator lenses. "Admiral, sir? What's this book for exactly?"

"Get the bastard," croaked Jack. Then the power window rose and they were pulling away.

Richard watched the dark blue sedan vanish down Brazier Drive. He touched his cheek absently where Rainey's lips had been, not sure of anything that had just happened, or why. Tossing the tattered book into the Chevy without thinking, he turned toward the house and started up the porch steps. Blondie was still out back, he could hear, barking her head off.

The front door to the Deadmond home stood ajar.

***

A chill breeze stirred as night began to fall across the valley. Lights came on slowly throughout town, like sluggish fireflies coming to life. Other lights were going off, the day's business already done.

Mr. Lehman locked up his Candle & Quilt Shoppe for the evening, and strode with purpose across the street, whistling tunelessly. He entered the little Styx & Stonze Botanicals store, hoping to catch the owner Mrs. Van Meers still inside. She came out of a darkened back room, holding a half-eaten cupcake, and gave him a curious little smile.

That was when Mr. Lehman produced the small nickel-plated handgun he had bought for protection, called the old woman a blaspheming pagan bitch, aimed the .25 caliber and shot Lillian Van Meers point-blank in the center of her curiously smiling face.

CHAPTER TWENTY-ONE

I

SIMON JULIAN RECLINED naked in the arms of Jesus, surveying his chapel's sanctuary for the last time.

He had shed his clothes and folded them neatly, applied some eyedrops, and had ascended into the welcoming outstretched arms above him. The Reverend sprawled corpselike in the large Christ statue's embrace, blinking until his eyes cleared. His gaze fell upon the stained glass windows over the alcove.

Where next? he wondered, feet and hands dangling, head craned to one side. Hop ship for a life abroad, another continent—or remain close by? Explore this doleful heartland a bit longer.

Kansas, say: to the small town called Codell perhaps—ravaged by a tornado on May 20th of the year 1916 . . . and then again one year later on the same date: May 20th, 1917 . . . and again precisely one year after *that*: on May 20th of 1918—all three storms coming on like enraged beasts in the early evening hour.

So many places full of hopelessness and human grief. Places of maddening solitude exacting heavy tolls, where crops might be destroyed by massive grasshopper swarms blotting out the sun, descending to devour whole fields. Or destroyed by drought, or unrelenting rains wiping out thousands of acres. Farmers and their corn-fed wives and children succumbing, sinking to collective knees and praying blindly in the grip of these godless eclipses, or sun-baked dust, or the roiling floodwaters.

Ironic, that: how the great rampaging floods could never wipe away *his* kind completely, as was intended. How the spirits of those fallen ones that survived the deluge ended up wreaking the same havoc in ghostly form that they had always wreaked while in physical form. Exactly the same—farcical.

The Orient, he mused, eyelids fluttering. Yes. Distant, fragrant Asian provinces where the myriad atrocities perpetrated every single day against every sentient, living being would be enough to feed his hunger to its brim, where death . . . the harvesting of lives carried on ceaselessly, ever constant. Death *infinitum.*

He'd been before—the thirteenth century?—in some diminutive village port or other on the Yellow Sea, watching the harbor burn in the night. Literally. Rutting some diminutive princess or other while fiery debris from a passing comet's tail rained down like molten hellfire upon the water, igniting the ships' square sails: sailors, Chinese junks blazing away out in the illuminated harbor. And him, fucking his princess/whore, the agonized screams of the seared and dying a pleasurable accompaniment to their act. He remembered being truly content at that moment. Truly.

Julian closed his eyes and smiled, memories dancing over his vast consciousness.

He would find somewhere else to light, no worry. A new nesting ground in which to mingle, just as he'd found this place, and the comfort of its pits and bones. The bounty of female flesh to be had.

Glee had welcomed him deep into her—his maiden bride, so to speak. Not at first, though, but eventually. He had ended up staying.

Now it was on to a new place, to the next host and his newest bride-to-be. The surrogate should be young, he knew, his transition into it a smooth one if at all possible; the less complications the better. The old man sighed. On and on it would go like this, the sequences repeating themselves, until some dying star somewhere inevitably ate this dying planet on which he languished. Swallowed it up whole, with all its inconsequential inhabitants.

But not yet.

How fortunate for him that Glee had let it slip once in the throes of passion, or in the muddled euphoria after, rather, how her daughter's final wish was to be cremated and have her ashes brought home and scattered. *Here.* For it was precisely then, in that single moment of crystal clarity, that Julian had decided not to wait. Not to wait for Michelle Franklin's cancerous cells to take over and kill her, not to await her resulting death from the disease, but instead to hurry her arguable end along, knowing full well that the exceptional young child and she would make their way back home again. Procured, and brought directly here to become his own.

He was *Orchestrator*, after all. Yes. And the gifted little one would be his *instrument*.

Reverend Julian opened his pale eyes and glared

at the darkening stained glass windows. *You're not the only one who has sacrificed, you jealous, sanctimonious bastard,* he thought. *I've sacrificed just as you. More so . . .*

2

The living room was empty, the house still. No sound came from within—only Blondie's incessant barking outside. Eyebrows raised quizzically, Richard moved through the entranceway and across the foyer, doing a double-take.

The copper urn wasn't there.

He called out, heading for the kitchen, and got no answer. Richard stopped with his hand on the swinging door, smelling something hot. Something burning? Dread bloomed in the pit of his stomach and he pushed his way into the kitchen where an empty pan was sizzling on the stove, the liquid boiled out of it. He shoved the saucepan back and switched off the burner, wincing from the heat. Then he let the dog in, noticing the cocoa canister and two clean mugs sitting on the counter.

Blondie scrabbled across the tiles and through the swinging door to the living room, nose sniffing the air. Richard closed the back door and stood in the overwhelming silence for a moment. An icy sensation skittered up the small of his back. He hurried after her.

Groaning sounds came, and Richard saw George sprawled on the floor in the hallway, struggling to sit up. The German shepherd had found him immediately, was leaping frenzied at him.

Richard ran. "What happened?" He bent, and tried

to drag the old man to his feet. They teetered into the coat rack, sending it over loudly. Richard froze. "George, where's Katie?"

Deadmond groaned again, hand clasped to the side of his balding skull. There was blood at the temple. His other fist held something crumpled.

"You're bleeding. Where's Katie, George?" Richard looked around. "Kate?" He heard his own voice rising: his esophagus felt as if it had closed. "Katie-Smatie?"

"Gone," George muttered, disoriented, and Richard's heart seized coldly.

"What did you say?"

"Took her. Hit me with something. He—"

"Who took her? *What are you talking about?*" Richard had Deadmond by the upper arm and by one lapel, shook him. The brass key flopped out on its cord. "Who did? Where is she, George?"

The old man sobbed. "She's gone."

Richard jerked him halfway up, glaring into his face as Blondie whined and began to bark again. "Damn you, where is my daughter?" he said. "*Who* took her? What *happened*?"

"I couldn't see," George said, "couldn't see them." Richard let him sag down the wall and propped him there. He sprang toward the Cornish staircase but halted, indecision suffocating him, raw panic driving him outside and down the front porch steps instead.

Heart hammering in his chest, he tried to draw breath into his lungs and found he couldn't. His eyes swept back and forth for any sign of her. Anything. He searched wildly around the house, yelling her name, looked through all the bushes. Up and down the street. On the verge of screaming, Richard ran back inside.

He staggered, his legs almost giving out, then he dove at the telephone and upended the entire stand. He was untangling the mess when he remembered the cellular in his own pants pocket. As he dug it out, George spoke again.

"Don't tell anyone, Richard," he rasped, crawling. "He said not to tell anyone, or else . . . oh mother of *God*. What have I done?" His fist opened, releasing a scrap of yellow notepaper he was clutching. George pushed it away as though it were infectious.

Cell phone lowered, Richard walked over and slowly picked it up. There were two words scrawled in black Magic Marker across the unsigned note, two words only:

NO POLICE

Richard stared at the crinkled paper, his hands trembling, a strange taste in his mouth. He heard his pulse thrum in his ears, making his head pound, making him want to pass out. Heard the old man's mutterings in the hallway.

"Gone," George wept. "I'm sorry . . . so sorry. Dear God in heaven, my honey Kate is gone . . . " He shuddered wretchedly, reaching for the German shepherd's collar.

Richard fled the Deadmond home in blind, dark terror, the screen door banging shut behind him.

3

William Salt caressed the dead girl's hair between his fingers, holding it to his lips.

He kissed it tenderly; she had been his first.

In the murky light of the Nain Church's basement Salt listened for any motion coming from Reverend Julian above. Detecting none, he glanced down at his matted scalps.

One of them had been taken from witness Nate Bitters, the night librarian in Golitha Falls, Maine, where he had run the woman down in the road. This other of course from Meg Bilobran—fresh as fresh could be. The third, the one he cupped in both hands, it had belonged to *her* . . . his first love.

She'd had pigtails and her name was Hannah, and that's all he ever knew. She had been his girlfriend at the Catholic-run Indian boarding school in Wisconsin, when he was eleven and she merely eight. He recalled pushing the frail, small-boned girl on the swings. Kissed her under an ash tree once.

When he saw another boy swinging and laughing with her one wet afternoon, something inside him had come apart. And he killed eight-year-old Hannah.

Angry and hurt, Salt had lured her into the woods behind the old mission with little candy root beer barrels, and then he had strangled her. Unearthing a rusted tin can top while burying her, he'd used the jagged metal edge to cut away Hannah's scalp. Then, Salt had finished filling in the hole, covering her open eyes and mouth with dirt and leaves.

I saw where her tonsils were removed, he thought now, *at the back of her throat before the earth filled it up.*

The Native American man held the girl's scalp to his lips in the dimness of the storage room. Strange, the things one remembered. Yet he never knew her last name.

He had buried the scalp well away from her spindly body, under the ash tree where he'd kissed her. Years later some of the nuns finally found the murdered girl who had gone missing so long ago, but William Salt had been transferred to a government boarding school in Illinois by then.

Decades passed before Salt chanced going back, well after prison, and the Indian girl's hair had still been there—even if the school and Catholic mission hadn't—beneath the ash tree, under a fragment of black shale rock where he'd buried it. He had kept it close ever since; she had been his first.

And she was with him still, little Hannah. *Yes.*

Sometimes he sensed her at his back, watching. Could feel her dead gaze upon him. He would turn and see nothing, of course, or sometimes . . . sometimes he would catch a glimpse of a frail girl out of the corner of his eye. Waiting. Hungry. But nothing would be there.

Salt heard noises above him, movement coming from upstairs. He put the scalps back one by one into the dried-up paint can from which he'd removed them: the fat librarian's together with Meg Bilobran's, and lastly Hannah's.

He had wanted to add Aaban Darwish's to his collection, but it was not his to take. No matter. There would be others soon enough.

Another sound now, the doors to the church opening and closing. He picked up the lid he had pried off and covered the paint can again, replacing it among the array of cans on the shelves. Suddenly he felt her in the storeroom with him, his *Acheri*, the spirit of the small Indian girl named Hannah, gray-skinned, eyes staring, her mouth filled with dirt.

"Go away," whispered Salt to the shadows.

He turned, saw nothing in the gloom. There was never anything . . . but he knew she was there. Unseen, lingering close by him. The hungry girl. His murdered first love.

Pulling the chain on the dingy light bulb overhead, he climbed the basement steps to the church's main floor.

4

"Hello? Is anyone here?"

The words wafted through the sanctuary, fading to silence. Then: "Someone is indeed here. Come in," said Reverend Julian, "come in."

Two figures shuffled forward, one large, one small. Julian watched from behind his lectern, watched them as they hesitated.

"I . . . I brought her," came the voice, "like you wanted."

"Come closer, please."

Syd Cholke moved into the light, leading the little girl in front of her carefully, grasping her by both shoulders. "Here she is." Her voice wavered, belying her demeanor.

The girl wore a thick winter scarf, and clutched the urn to her chest. She appeared to be in a stupor. Julian frowned. "What have you done to her, my dear?"

"Nothing. I swear it. She was like this when I gra . . . when I found her." Sydney's gaze dropped to the floor.

William Salt entered.

"Prarsheen," the Reverend said, "take the child

315

and wait for me outside in the vehicle, will you? We'll be taking my car. You'll drive us to the house directly."

The Native American man nodded and crossed the chapel without a word, lifted the girl, carried her out in his arms. Sydney spoke faintly after he had gone. "Can I have her back? Please?"

Julian stared at the masculine-featured woman. "What?"

"I did what you wanted. I even left a warning against contacting the police. Isn't—"

A tremor skimmed along the church's inner walls. "I asked no such thing. I fear nothing from any police."

Sydney cleared her throat. "Where is she? You promised."

"Do you mean Alice?" A smile touched his wrinkled lips.

"Yes," said Sydney, "Alice. She's my heart's delight."

Julian stepped down from behind the lectern and Syd saw that he was completely nude, scaly-skinned. She blanched at the sight.

"Did you think you would win her back? Did you?" the old man singsonged, drifting near. He snorted. "Alice is mine. The child she carries is *mine*, and you"—Julian stabbed one bony finger at her, thinking: you are *unlit, dead inside* . . . but instead finished his sentence—"you deserve better."

Sydney's lower jaw quivered. "You promised."

"You deserve better, my dear," repeated Simon, drifting closer still. *Rut her,* echoed a voice within him, unbidden. *Rut the flesh.*

"Can I see her please? If I could just talk—"

"No. Alice doesn't want you anymore." He paused,

took a deep breath. His smile widened. "But *I* do. Come here, my pet. Come to me."

Cholke saw with mild shock that the naked pastor had an erection and she tensed, turning to leave. He had hold of her arm in a blink.

"P-please," she stammered, "I thought this was what you wanted. That if I brought the little girl here, you'd return my Alice."

"First things first."

"I . . . I'd like to go now."

"But aren't you flattered?"

"You're blocking the way."

"*Ach* . . . by all means."

"My arm—you're hurting it."

The Reverend tut-tutted her, and began to change before her eyes. To unfurl and grow, to augment, becoming something *more* indecent, limbs flexing unnaturally. He shuffled her around and led her into the heart of the sanctum, toward the pulpit, and the raised platform upon which he preached. Drew her down then, ignoring her objections, tugging her clothing from her as she was lowered.

"Open your soul for me, pet." His smile showed double rows of teeth.

"*No* . . . "

The Julian-Thing mounted her, enfolding the woman in its ancient, fire-blackened wretchedness, penetrating her. Sydney began to scream: sheer, bloodcurdling cries which eventually gave way to primal sounds, bestial grunts and moans as she widened her legs.

After, the screaming came again.

***

He ran through the streets, had no idea where he was going, just ran. He looked for her everywhere, anywhere, in every corner, each yard and driveway and inside every car that passed him. He stopped people on foot, asking if they had seen her, a six-year-old girl wearing a sweatshirt and jeans, with chestnut-colored hair and a turquoise scarf around her neck. His only daughter—Katie was her name.

They must have thought him a lunatic, the wild look in his eye, his hair blown from running helter-skelter, no rhyme or reason to his flight.

Nobody had seen her.

He stood in the middle of the street holding his side, breathless, put a hand to his chest and felt the tightness there. Making mewling sounds, he lurched off in the direction he'd come. Found his way back and jumped into the Blazer, reversed out and barreled down Brazier Drive.

Richard *was* a lunatic at that moment, scared shitless. Out of his mind with dark possibilities. He murmured her name as he drove, begging that nothing terrible—

Another sound, deep in his throat. "Where are you, Katie?" he said hoarsely to himself, "whereareyouwhereareyouwherethefuck*areyou* . . . " The initial burst of adrenaline he had experienced at the house was gone, and exhaustion started to replace it. He blinked over and over, his eyes stinging, glazed with panic. Fear tore him in ten different directions, and Richard thought he may rip apart at the seams any second.

Who—why—? his mind shrieked. *Money? No, no. This isn't happening. Who could have taken her? Lawrie? Don't be foolish.*

Priewe?

"Oh Christ," he moaned. But why? Why *no police*? It didn't make any sense. What was he missing?

Think, you stupid fuck. Before . . .

A wave of guilt overtook him, a feeling like he might vomit. He tried to focus but couldn't because of the throb at the back of his skull. *Have to find her. She could be hurt, and it's getting dark. Find her—nothing else matters.*

Gritting his teeth, he fumbled an Excedrin bottle out of the glove box and popped four of the white etched tablets into his twisted mouth, washing them down with some tepid bottled water from the console cup holder and gagging.

Unable to control his racing heart, or the horrible panic constricting his chest and threatening to seize him, he shifted madly in his seat and strangled the steering wheel with wringing hands. He went past the renovated Riding Club stables, saw a few lights on and a car parked there. And past the Gospel Book Store after that. Then Richard crossed Honey Run.

An idea came to him through the paralyzing dread.

***

The monster roared, spraying the mannish woman's insides with its frothy seed.

Sydney wailed in agony, felt the burning spread within her. The Reverend crumpled to the floor naked, spent. He kneeled before her wide-open legs as if in worship. Syd began to crawl away, sliding down the three-step riser painfully, dragging herself on elbows and knees under Christ's woeful gaze. Something trickled between her thighs and Sydney's inquisitive fingers came away with bright blood upon them. She sobbed as she clambered along on her belly.

Simon Julian was getting to his feet, limbs shaking. He reached and steadied himself on the lectern while the woman struggled to stand, mumbling incoherent words to herself. Pulling up the torn work overalls clinging to her, Sydney shrugged her exposed, heavy breasts back into them, feeling the sting of bite marks over her mauled flesh. She blundered toward the doors in a daze, groped for the silver handles. The old man saw her cringe when next he spoke.

"Fear me," Julian warned, "for I own you now."

Syd Cholke slipped out the doors, violated. Betrayed.

Empty handed.

The fire had faded to a dull warmth coursing through her body, filling her with a headiness, an eerie dimming of her thoughts. Still, she had been polluted here in this place, she could feel it . . . could feel the corrosions already beginning inside her. The *conceiving* of something.

She left Nain Church with her head lowered, her tear-stained face hidden as she withdrew, wondering what brand of fate awaited her beyond the church's threshold.

S

Richard opened the screen and rapped on Tom Truitt's front door. When it swung gently inward, he found himself wide-eyed.

Tommy was on the sofa bed in the living room with two young women.

He watched in sickening fascination as the naked girls, a blonde and a brunette, took turns sliding their eager mouths along the shaft of Truitt's erect cock, all up and down it, swallowing it in succession. Their heads bobbed. Tommy lay on his back at attention, a bottle of Usher's scotch within reach on the stained bedside table. He appeared to be watching the big-screen TV, but one of his hands toyed between the brunette's thighs.

Richard cleared his throat, and the petite blonde rolled startled from the mattress and looked up at him, doe-eyed, nipples accusing him pertly. He saw the tiny sweet pea bouquet tattooed just above her shaved genitals and felt his face flush. "Company, Tom," she said.

"Richie," slurred Truitt, "there you are. Get in here. Guess what?"

"Um, Katie's disappeared, Tom," Richard said shakily. "I need—"

"I found Palm and told him. Or he found *me*. Told him about Prick-we and Ollie Echols and about the bridge, for what it's worth. Never mentioned you. Don't know if it'll do any good or not, but I figured what the hell. Right, dude? Anyway, he had some news for me. Wait'll ya hear."

Richard moved inside. "Tommy, can we talk alone a minute?"

Truitt kept going. "You'll love this. Seems my Aunt Cassie got herself stung to death out at her place yesterday, stung to death by her own honeybees. Isn't that a scream? Allergic to bee stings her whole life and never knew it . . . or never cared, I guess."

Richard went silent; the curvy brunette stopped what she was doing.

Tommy touched the cross-nail pendant around his neck, and stretched for the bottle. "I had to identify the body. She didn't die straight away, they told me: she hung on for a while in the ICU, then she quit breathing. Just like that. Yep. She was an okay gal, ol' Cass was." He took a slug of the scotch, made a face, and glared at the label. "Phew, no wonder the House of Usher fell."

Richard stood very still. "I'm sorry about your aunt. Look—"

"Hey! Where are my manners. Want a drink, man? Quick fuck? This here is Tish." The blonde was sitting on the edge of the sofa bed, slender legs crossed. She waved. "And this one's Maria." Tommy slapped the dark-haired girl's bare ass and she raised up, smiling. She was large-breasted with cocoa skin, he saw, and plenty of curves to go around.

"Have to pay upfront, is all." Truitt drank. "Tish there can be your Michelle if you want but this one's mine. Maria is my Kyoko, and she's all mine. Right, babes?"

"Will you quit screwing around?" said Richard, desperate. "This is serious. I think something's happened."

All of a sudden the bottle of Usher's came hurtling at him, smashing against a nearby wall. Richard flinched in shock.

"If you don't want to join the fun, that's fine," Tommy said drunkenly, "but I'm in mourning here. So just show yourself out." He laughed. "Go ahead. Your bitch mother-in-law is probably waiting on ya. She can tell you some more about what a bad influence I am. *Convict piece of shit,* yeah, that's it. Better hop to."

322

"I don't know where else to go," Richard whispered. "I need your help."

"Get lost, Rich, will ya?" Truitt cut him off. "I'm busy." He yanked the petite blonde high onto the bed with him until she was straddling his face. Tish began to grind her shaved sex up and down on him, clutching the back of the sofa bed for balance and squealing with delight.

Richard ran a trembling hand through his hair, pulling on it. "Please. Katie is missing. Somebody took her. They've *kidnapped* . . . will you help me?"

Maria was back at work, taking Tom's fading erection into her mouth again and gobbling it deeply with skilled, even strokes while Tom grabbed two handfuls of the blonde's ass cheeks and enjoyed the meal being fed him, lost in his arranged threesome.

"Please . . . " He felt his throat catch. Backing out through the door, Richard turned and steadied himself on the jamb a moment before closing it quietly behind him.

***

Tish continued to grind and writhe, riding Tommy's face, riding the crest of her climax when it came and squealing. The dark-haired girl paused over him, on her hands and knees. "Come on, baby," she purred. "Let that shit go for your Maria. Come for me, baby." She returned to her hungry wet work.

Tommy sat up abruptly, tossing the blonde off onto the pillows beside him. He nudged Maria from his crotch with regret. Wiping his chin, and trying to shake away the cobwebs, he wished he had the scotch bottle back to rinse out his mouth.

"Did he just say Katie's missing?" Tommy Truitt spluttered. "Somebody fucking kidnapped her?"

6

The town had begun to darken.

Sunny Delia Aubel—SunnyDee to her most privileged of friends, and oldest of the Aubel clan's daughters at twenty-five—jolted her son with the 50,000 volt stun baton, and then hauled the boy outdoors. She carried a slim, dog-eared paperback with her as she stomped. *American Princess* announced the T-shirt she wore, gold letters sparkling against a red-white-and-blue heart. The boy made no sound as he was dragged through the leaves behind the guesthouse where they both stayed, mother and illegitimate son, and on down to a fenced corner of the Aubel Farms property.

"You will honor thy mother," she told him, coming to a halt, "and you will start speaking like other children do. Not *reading*, but *speaking*. Do you understand that?" When he didn't answer, she stuck the electric baton in his mouth and fired it.

She chained the convulsing boy to the doghouse near the fence, tightening a length of metal leash around his neck and cinching it in place with a padlock. Sunny informed her son there would be no dinner for him now, and that if he did not start to speak soon she would have to castrate him. Or worse. She left him in an unrecognizable heap beside the doghouse. The paperback book, a copy of Bradbury's *Fahrenheit 451*, assigned to him by her son's special needs teacher, got tossed into the lapping flames of one of the burn barrels still going as she passed by them.

The irony of this was lost on Miss Aubel, beyond her stunted grasp.

Shortly after, when a man named Peachock stepped out to his garden to fill his birdfeeders for the next morning, he was set upon by three hooded intruders waiting for him. They knocked him down and began kicking him viciously. He tried to call out but something jolted him with an electric crackle and incapacitated him, sealing his fate.

Mr. Peachock, a substitute teacher at the local center for autistic children, was then hacked to pieces with meat cleavers that the assailants held.

When they had finished, one of the intruders stooped and rummaged in the crimson grass, picking up a severed left foot. This figure, the lone female of the trio, paused long enough to throw the dead schoolteacher's foot into his backyard wishing well as the others retreated through an alleyway, the irony lost on her.

Hurrying to catch up, she skulked off with her companions as night continued its slow, velvety cascade over the Val.

The town began to darken, and the darkness was red.

***

When he brought the prostitutes back and dropped them at the derelict freight yards where he'd found them, Thomas watched from his truck as the two young women crossed the railroad tracks and handed their money—*his* money—over to the man waiting there. He continued watching until Maria and Tish had drifted along down the tracks, in search of new opportunities. Then he got out and started walking toward the nameless pimp.

He approached cautiously, keeping his hands in

plain view where the other could see them. The pimp recognized him when he got closer. They talked, and the man produced a vial and tapped a little white mound of powder out onto the back of Tommy's hand, which Truitt snorted up through a snip of beverage straw offered to him. He clenched his teeth when the blast of coke hit, feeling himself sober slightly, coldly. The pimp laughed.

After knocking words back and forth for a bit they nodded in agreement. Tom gave him all the cash from his chain wallet, unsnapped his Invicta wristwatch and gave him that as well. The two wandered back to a hidden vehicle where the man dug under his car seat briefly, pulling out a small bundle wrapped in oilcloth. Before handing it over, the pimp reminded Truitt that he was an ex-felon, and that this here was parole violation—big time. He asked if he knew what he was doing, and Tom said yes.

Double-checking his surroundings, Truitt made his way across the railroad tracks and thought about his Aunt Cassie. Unwinding the bundle and letting the oilcloth fall, he tucked something into his belt, climbed back inside his Dodge pickup, and drove away from the freight yard and the dwellers inhabiting it.

¶

Richard kept the gas pedal jammed down, gnawing at the tender lining of his cheek and tasting blood. He had to see George, see if any contact had been made. Had to find Glee—she might know something, where to look maybe, what to do. Blondie and her keen senses could aid in the search, too.

The four Excedrin were wreaking havoc: it felt like an acid spill in his guts, even as the headache started to abate a little.

Nain Trinity Lutheran was ahead on the left, a vehicle parked behind it. He made a quick decision and swung sharply into the Glassman Avenue lot, standing on the brake and leaping from the SUV. He tried the rear door of the church in vain—locked. Heading for the double doors on the far side, his eyes went to the other vehicle in the parking lot, the Land Rover Discovery sitting there.

The sodium lights were coming on overhead, and Richard squinted in the rapidly declining daylight. He stopped cold in his tracks.

Someone had traced *WASH ME* onto the Land Rover's mud-caked side. The words leapt out at him through the grime; he stared back, mouth open. A runaway nightmare thought broke loose and struck him and the sweat on his back turned to ice.

No good look at the driver or plates: just WASH ME, *for Christ's sake.*

Richard tried to move closer but his legs wouldn't work. He heard a sound and whirled toward it, ill-prepared for what he saw under the ravaged bur oak tree, the sight of the skeletal Sallow Man lingering suspiciously there on the church steps. Franklin reeled, not trusting his own vision even as the Sallow Man raised one tremulous arm and uttered something.

"Gaaa," he said. *"Kaaa—"*

Richard glanced at the Discovery, at the token written in mud. He swung back to the ghastly figure, to the pallid visage and hairless head, repellently ugly,

its yawning mouth trying to form syllables:
"Kaaaaaa—"

He rushed him then, madly, charged the Sallow
Man and launched into him at full force, driving him
backward, slamming his misshapen skull off the stone
steps. Richard began hitting him, pummeling the
chalk-skinned face beneath him as a hollow howling
noise rose into the air.

"Where is she?" he screamed, saliva flying from his
lips. "Where, you fuck son of a bitch? *Where is she?*"

His clenched fists connected again and again with
the man's gulping, stricken mask. He heard himself
screaming, heard the cell phone ringing in his pocket.
But he was gone. Lost in a reddened haze which
blotted everything else from the world.

8

It was Tommy who stopped him, Tommy driving along
Kennedy School Road with his cell phone to his ear
who spotted them entangled on the church steps and
swung his truck up Glassman Avenue. He dragged
Richard off, grappling him to the ground. When
Richard bellowed in rage and lunged at the ragged
man again, Tom wrestled to snap him out of it.

"Stop . . . do you want to kill him? I said stop!" He
shook his friend hard, shouting into his livid face.
"Stop it, Rich!"

Richard's eyes finally cleared, and he gaped from
Tommy to the form sprawling on the steps, back to
Tommy.

"Holy Christ, don't you know who he is?" said
Truitt shrilly.

"Sallow . . . M-Man," Richard said, out of breath. "He—*he's*—"

The gaunt man touched his own face, held bloodied hands up before him. His withered arm worked a handkerchief out to press against his mouth. He pulled a small meal planner notepad from his trench coat, and a pen, with which he began scratching.

"—he killed Michelle, Tom. *He abducted my daughter!*" Richard rolled to his knees, wheezing, and the Sallow Man blinked owlishly, his eyes huge beneath their hoods of flesh. Something terrible passed over his battered face and the pad fell from his fingers. He shook his too-large head in horror.

"Are you nuts?" came Tommy's reply. "This is Owen Croom. Don't you remember him?"

"No. *Who?*" Richard squeezed his eyes shut, forehead to the ground. "Look, no seeds . . . " he rasped, nearly laughing. "What did you say?"

"Owen Croom. He's been kicking around this town for years."

The injured Sallow Man had found his footing, wobbling on broomstick legs. He was shaking his swollen head from side to side. *"Gyyaaaa—"*

"Go home, Owen," said Truitt, and Richard began scrambling off the ground.

"No!" he yelped. "Grab the bastard, don't let him get away!"

The pale, wretchedly thin man bolted, limping in obvious pain and vanishing around the building. Tommy had to immobilize Richard again, snaring him by the legs.

"Goddamn it, Rich, he couldn't have done those

things. Something's wrong with him . . . he's real sick. He's always been sick."

"Bullshit. He was here last night in this church. I saw him."

"Okay," Tom said slowly, "but he's had cerebral palsy on one side of his body since birth. His left arm is almost useless because of it. And he has seizures." Richard lifted up in surprise, and Tom told him about Croom's seizures, how he was losing the ability to walk and eat on his own. The illness was what caused his face and head to appear like that, he explained: hydrocephalus it was called, water accumulating in the cavities of his brain that had to be drained off regularly, or else it would kill him.

"Jack Lawrie looks out for him, lets him stay in one of his rentals for free. I heard it's drafted into his will so he'll always be guaranteed a safe place to live, even after the admiral is gone."

Richard was stunned. He had no clue what Tom Truitt was talking about, had never heard any of this before. Or if he had, it must've fallen through the cracks of his mind, and slipped surreptitiously away. Gone, like so many other bits and pieces of his memory.

"The guy chewed off his own tongue once," Tommy added. "Hell, I think I even heard that his spine is damned near detached from his pelvis now."

"My *God*, I'm going to puke," groaned Richard, appalled by his three-way partaking friend's revelations. He twisted upright and slid his cellular out, checking it with trembly hands. "Someone was calling me," he said, "just a second ago. Who was it? Wait . . . oh Christ. Who called my phone?" He was yammering.

"That was me, Rich. Trying to reach you. Tell me what happened tonight."

"Well," Richard began, sitting on the ground like a child, "I came here looking for Katelyn, and then I saw the Sallow—I saw this guy Croom you're talking about. Whose Land Rover is that, Tom?"

"Don't know. Tell me what happened with Katie. Start from the beginning."

So he did. Her disappearance from the house (in a mere matter of minutes) while he dicked around outside playing *Cuckoo's Nest* with Lorraine and Jack Lawrie. The slip of paper with the warning about the police, and George Deadmond totally out of it and crawling across the hallway floor like an infant, seeing nothing of use, conveying the same. He told it all, the whole story.

"Where have you looked so far?"

Richard stared at the church. "I thought maybe it was Priewe. I have to . . . *find* her." He rose and sprang up the stone steps, jerking on the church's double doors with no success. "This . . . *whose fucking Land Rover is that?*"

"I don't know, dude," Tommy said. "Tell it to me again. Anything else you might've left out."

"There isn't anyth—" He stopped, eyes shifting down, and bent to pick up the meal planner notepad. His gaze sharpened. "The fuck is going on? What is this?" he said distantly.

Tom looked also. Between the lines on the green paper, Owen had written TAKE HER AND LEAVE **NOW** BEFORE THEY in shaky block letters, and then nothing below it. Their eyes met.

"Jesus, we gotta get him back here," Richard said,

holding Truitt's stare. "He knows something. And you let him go. They'll . . . I have to—"

"No," mumbled Tommy, "something's wrong. Very wrong with this."

Richard dialed and put the cell phone to his ear. "Busy signal at George and Glee's. Maybe someone— oh, for fuck's *sake*." Another groan escaped him. "I knocked the telephone off the hook when I was there. It must still be off. Unless . . . "

"Let's go, Rich." Tommy left his truck parked on Glassman Avenue. "You drive," he urged, heading for the Blazer. "I've been drinking."

"Yeah, no shit. Sorry to get you away from the *girls*."

Richard screeched out of the lot and drove aimlessly. "Where first?" he asked, white-knuckling the steering wheel with renewed eagerness. "Deadmond's, or to find this Croom guy?"

"Neither," said Tom, and Richard stared at him. "None of this feels right. The dead fish . . . Cass and her bees. That freak show at the church. Now Katie? No, something more is happening here, man. Something strange. Strange like I've never seen." Truitt's brow was creased, his thoughts straying. "Too many places to search, too much ground to cover, but there might be a way."

"I said where first, Thomas?"

When their eyes locked Richard saw a glimmer of fear for the first time in Tommy's pinched expression, maybe ever. His nose was running. "Someplace else." He left the words hanging.

"We can't go to the cops. So where then?"

"I know someone who can find your daughter.

Get her back to you. But there'll be a price to pay, Richie."

"What are you talking about?"

"We're heading out. We need to get away from town."

"The hell we are—"

"Listen to me. I know what I'm doing."

"I asked you *where*?" Richard's teeth were clenched.

Tommy took his time before answering. "Beulah the Witch. She's still alive."

"What?" He nearly let go of the wheel.

"Never died," Tommy said, almost whispered. "She faked her own death all those years ago, and she went into hiding. So people would leave her alone. But she can help find Katie. I know she can. She helped me once when—after my—" He cleared his throat, eyes darting away. "After Kyoko was raped and murdered."

Richard realized his mouth was bone dry. At some length he found his voice again. "You're saying she's an actual witch?"

Looking straight ahead, Tommy reiterated: "There'll be a price, though. There always is."

"Meaning?"

Tommy's stare had gone vacant. "Let's just go. We're heading out."

"Where am I going, Tom?" asked Richard warily.

"The Island," Truitt told him. "St. Angell Island."

PART THREE

NOW AND AT THE HOUR

Out of the somber night the poets come . . .
—Robert E. Howard

CHAPTER TWENTY-TWO

I

THERE ARE PARTS of Illinois known for their inspiration, places of important historical significance and remarkable beauty. Places to give one pause, just knowing they could exist in a flat, windswept floodplain state such as this. On the flipside of that coin, the dark side of it, there are also areas of desolation and blight-ridden anguish. Stark places where menace walked, natural and unnatural, where even nightbirds chose to hide and take to roost rather than sing their evening songs.

The Island was of the latter.

Angell Island was named after Clarissa St. Angell, first woman from the township of Blackwater Valley ever to graduate college and actually earn a degree. She had been born into poverty out on the remote island in the year 1860, and the poverty of the place had only increased since then. Along with the decay and disrepair.

A hodgepodge of shabby little houses and trailers, the 33-acre tract of land sat floating off shore in swampy muck out on the river. There was one passageway on and off, Riverreach Road, and when the downpours came and rising water engulfed that narrow access strip, the two hundred or so residents who called this place home would take to their fishing boats, or rely on volunteer firefighters to pull them out to safety. The flood-prone isle remained unincorporated—an obscure, rundown corner of Appalachia smack in the middle of the flowing currents.

Some looked at its advantages of having no taxes, no government intrusions, and saw their own ideal slice of heaven: a world unto itself. Others looked at it as just another trailer-trash shithole. An open scab upon the river's skin.

"Jesus," murmured Richard as he slowed the Blazer to a crawl, edging forward over Riverreach and onto the Island. There was trash everywhere, newspapers blowing, rubbish strewn in yards and littering the sides of the unpaved streets.

"The land that fucking time forgot," said Tommy.

"This can't be safe to live on. Why don't they clean it up?"

"No garbage service anymore. No repairs done. County won't claim responsibility, and neither will the Val. They're on their own out here, but they like it that way, I guess. The native islanders." Truitt shrugged. "Cops don't even bother patrolling it. They swing past and keep going."

"Great."

"Remember when we were kids, and those two Jehovah's Witnesses drowned in the flooding? Got caught ringin' doorbells out here and were just swept away by the rainwater." Tommy searched for a joke there, but thought better of it.

"I'm getting the feeling we're being watched," said Richard uneasily.

"Oh, we are. You can bet your ass."

Amid the leaning ramshackle homes stood one that looked different, with dried cornstalks and grapevine wreaths, and twisted grapevine symbols adorning its clapboards, not much more than a shack itself really, but with flagstones and an immaculate yard in front and no junk or torn trash bags anywhere to be seen. Tommy gestured. "That's where we're going. Furnace Street." Before Rich could question, he went on: "She needs cleanliness to do what she does. No clutter. No filth."

Richard parked on what passed for Furnace Street and shut the engine off. "Tell me about the business with Kyoko," he said.

Truitt's breathing deepened, slowed. "She took care of them for me. The ones who killed my fiancée. Never went near them, never touched them, but she took care of the bastards just the same. While I was inside at Marion so I'd have an alibi."

"The train tracks," Richard said low, and Tommy nodded. "And the price you paid?"

Tom looked him in the eye. "Knowing I'm responsible. Carrying it around every day."

Richard pulled his keys from the ignition.

"Plus, I had to have sex with her," Tommy confessed, and Richard dropped the keys, had to fish around the floor of the Blazer to find them; his hand brushed the German Bible as he straightened.

"*How's* that?"

"It's magic, supposedly. Sex is. And semen—she said it was magic she could use. Don't ask, man."

"Oh, this just keeps getting better and better." Richard popped two berry flavored Rolaids into his mouth.

"We need something of Katie's. Or something she touched, at least."

Richard considered it, then dug in the backseat and came up with his daughter's special activity book.

Tommy clicked his fingers. "The note. Do you still have it? The message about the police?"

"I left it at Deadmond's," said Richard, eyes closing. "Ran out in such a hurry, didn't think—I must've let go of it. Damn." After a long moment he opened his eyes and picked the Bible up off the floor, shoving it at Tom. "Here, take this. Maybe we'll . . . just take it."

They got out, and Richard dropped the locks with his remote. "Will our ride be up on blocks when we come back?"

"Nobody touches it," said Truitt, "not as long as we're *here*."

The two men walked up the flagstone path in the spreading dusk. "This is the craziest fucking thing I've ever heard of in my life," Richard muttered, stomach in turmoil, his nose wrinkling from the aroma of taint.

Before they could knock, the door to the little clapboard house creaked open. "Enter," a voice wafted out from the fire-lit shadows within, startling them both. "You and your friend, *eh*?"

They crossed the threshold into darkness.

2

Lamplight flickered, and something circled the room

in muted whispers, rising up the walls and into the high corners like bad dreams upon waking. The old man didn't notice—or paid no attention—but the little girl did.

Katie sat on a window seat and watched Reverend Julian limp about the cavernous parlor of Shaw-Meredith House with a tan travel valise, gathering last-minute oddments and ends.

The old man carried his secret carved box the same way the girl held the copper urn: jealously, guarded, as if she might never let go.

The shutters were open, and Julian saw the sun had set. It was dark beyond the tall arches of leaded glass. She had not spoken a word since her deliverance to him. He turned from his preparations.

"You'll be coming with me, child, do you understand? You are mine now, and I will be the only family you'll ever know from this moment on. Whatever you do, do *not* try to run away from me. Because although I will appear different to you in our future concerns together, it will always be me with you. *Always*." The girl said nothing. "Not to worry. You will learn what this means in time. All in good time, pet." Julian smiled.

"Adventure awaits," he said and winked.

Katie looked out the bay window and wondered where her father was, felt tears welling behind her eyes and fought to keep them there. She began humming softly, began to rock.

Julian picked up the telephone receiver and dialed Glee Deadmond's number. *"Ach,"* he breathed, and hung up from the busy signal.

The presence in the room clung together a bit

341

longer, spiraling out, a single rippling mass, then it splintered and flew apart. The spectral echoes crisscrossed, gibbering insanely to each other. Malevolent. The floor lamp blinked again, and an immense wrought-iron chandelier trembled high above Katie. She observed them in silence, her eyes roving to and fro.

Both Meredith sisters were there, poisoned. Poisonous. The hanged undertaker and his wife, as well. And the mad, tragic Shaws: souls broken, sickened; their pitted clown-white faces agape, feverish. Leering at her.

Others, too. Many.

They hovered in the air, reaching, drawn to the girl and her irresistible brightness. Wringing and wrenching so hungrily, ravenous for her. Coming closer—but how to do it? Through the glass? Electrocution? Or the great chandelier, yesss . . . falling . . . crushing limbs and that brittle skull.

Yessss . . . sss.

Lamplight flickered, and the torment trapped within the house's bones for so very long crept across its thick squared walls, draining energy from them. Contorting, the wraiths descended like spiders from the lofty ceiling, starving for light and for life, reaching out to claim her.

Julian went to retrieve his camel-hair coat from the hall closet, leaving the small child by herself briefly, alone and rocking on the window seat.

"Don't hurt me," whispered Katelyn to no one. "Please, don't *hurt* me."

3

Glee stared at the yellow scrap of paper in her hands, her purse over one arm, mouth a tight line. She looked at George slumping in his recliner, Blondie at rest but alert on the Oriental rug below, one forepaw curled under. Glee closed her fists into claws and mangled the notepaper.

"Think," she said again.

"I couldn't see," replied George, holding his head, "already told you. It's all a blank. I was nearly unconscious."

"You're lying. Don't lie to me."

George gazed at her in wonderment. "My God, why would . . ."

"I said *think*."

"I can't think anymore, Glee. *Please*. I'm . . . I don't know who it was." He leaned against the chair arm. "What are we going to do?"

"You silly, stupid—" Her words trailed off in mid-sentence as she threw the purse down. The expression she wore was grim, bewildered, her brow furrowing. She checked her watch and then fell silent.

"Why don't you love me, Glee? Did you ever?"

"*What?*"

"Have you ever loved me? Or was it all make-believe. Everything. Our whole lives together. Was it?"

Glee gritted her teeth. "You fool. You absurd, foolish old man. That's what you choose to say to me now? Really?"

George started to speak, and Glee told him to shut his mouth. She was trying to remember something.

She crouched and righted the phone stand, placing the receiver back in its cradle. What had Katie said to her, told her was so important? Last night, right here . . .

"It's him, isn't it, Glee?" George prodded. "Always him. That piss ant—"

"*You're* to blame for this," she said, the words coming in an angry rush. "Nobody but you, George. You, and that worthless son-in-law you think so highly of." She rose, her forehead creasing even deeper.

"—that piss ant church turnkey—"

"Will you be quiet? Will you?"

"—*him*. Controlling you, owning you. And you letting him."

Glee sucked breath into her lungs, where it became instant venom.

She glared icily. "If you don't shut up I'll cut the heart out of your chest." Moving away, she fought to concentrate. To remember what it was. She fixed her stare on George again when he made a pained sound behind her.

"Something to add?"

George shrank into his chair, out of the way of her wrath, and Glee cast her intense gaze about the room, searching, trying to connect the dots.

. . . last night, right here. A book. Something about reading a book to her.

Dots.

Glee started for the bookcase but turned back. There it was, on her computer hutch beside the keyboard, the thin edition Katie had brought to her. She looked down at the small flimsy book with its cracked spine and gold lettering—*From Wealth to Poverty* by Rev. Austin Potter—and suddenly recognized it as a turn-of-the-century collection of daily temperance sermons and personal anecdotes she had bought at a rummage sale once, written by some long-dead Methodist minister. Stories she used to read Brookie when she was a little girl growing up inside this house.

But what was the passage again? The page number and chapter? Katelyn had mentioned them, and now Glee couldn't recall.

"Chapter seven," she said to herself, thumbing through it, trying to think. Still connecting the—

Glee stared at the polka-dot hair ribbon marking the place, the one she'd used yesterday to tie the pretty bow into Katie's hair. Michelle Brooke's old dotted ribbon which Kate had left here for her to find. Chapter seven, page twenty-nine . . .

Lifting the worn book, her lashes began fluttering behind her crystal lenses as she read the paragraphs:

> *But there was one—a night blooming cereus—which was a particular favorite of Grace's, and which, even after she knew she had not long to live, she hoped she would be spared to see bloom. But when she perceived she was failing so rapidly—quietly, peacefully, sinking to rest—she said—*
>
> *"Mamma, darling, I have looked forward with a great deal of expectancy to the time when my cereus should bloom. I now know my hope in this respect will not be realized, but I want you, mother, when it opens out its pure white petals and its fragrance perfumes the midnight air to remember I shall be in*

345

heaven—among fairer flowers, with sweeter perfume; for they have not been cursed by sin. And while you mourn at my absence remember I am with Jesus—'Absent from the body, present with the Lord.'"

And now as the mother tended these flowers, and lovingly lingered near this special favorite, around which such tender memories lingered, the flood-gates of her soul were mercifully lifted up and she "eased her poor heart with tears."

Glee tottered as she finished, numbing lips pressed together. Behind her George stirred to life. "Everything revolves around *him*," he said. "All the girls in town—"

Glee stifled a gasp, letting the book fall onto her desk. She made her way unsteadily to where her husband sat, and held out her hand. "Give it to me please." When he was slow to respond, she waggled her fingers and said, "Put the key in my hand, George."

Caressing it first, George pulled the cord over his head and laid the long brass key on his wife's palm without protest. Glee went to the kitchen and inserted the skeleton key into the basement door's lock. Twisting it hard, she left it in the keyhole and opened the door, clicked on the stairway light and then descended into the sweetish, cloying reek rising to meet her. Nothing could be heard for a time.

Several minutes later she climbed the basement steps, groping up them, a look of dislocation about her. Leaving the door ajar, Glee moved to the kitchen counter and stood in silence a moment. Then she gently slid a large butcher blade from the maple knife block and carried it into the living room.

"How long now?" she asked, standing behind George's recliner, thumbing the back edge of the sharp knife.

When he spoke his voice quavered. "A few weeks maybe, since right after . . . since *she* . . . "

"You should have said something, George." Glee drifted past him, and retrieved her handbag. She dropped the butcher knife inside and slung the purse over one arm, taking out her car keys.

"Where are you going?"

"Use the icepack on your head," she said, "and rest awhile." She found Blondie's leash, and at its jangling the German shepherd walked unsurely up to Glee. The dog remained still as she was fastened up.

"Glee?"

Walking to the front door, she halted and turned back, the dog turning with her. "Rest there, George," was all she said. Glee left her husband slouched on the arm of his chair, deflated, more haggard looking than she'd ever seen him. She left with Blondie at her side and shut the door. But once outside she buckled, collapsing partway to the front porch. Tears came, of grief and of regret, scalding her eyes, spilling over. She sobbed once, only for a second, catching the alien sound in her throat even as she made it. She swatted at moths in the shadows.

Whining low, the leashed animal nudged Glee with her cold nose. Eventually Glee pulled herself up, still shaken, sniffling. Regaining some composure, she touched the heavy square ring on her finger, touched the empty, cushioned place where her absent breast should have been. Then she raised her head high and led Blondie down the porch steps.

CHAPTER TWENTY-THREE

I

AY YOUR NAME for me," the old woman said. "Speak it now."

Hesitation: "Richard Franklin."

She repeated his words, pronouncing them slowly—"Richard" came out as *Ricard.*

"Now say mine." Her tongue darted over shriveled lips that were barely there. "Say it."

A small red fox with half its tail gone was circling around his shins, he'd noticed, brushing against them. "Witch Beulah. But I'm not sure . . . " Richard swallowed. "Beulah the Witch."

The puckered mouth curved. "Why have you come this night? What would your pleasure be, *eh*? And why should I help you?"

"His little girl—" Truitt began.

"Let him speak it himself, Thomas." Her eyes glinted obsidian-black in the firelight. "Well?"

Richard spoke, going over it all again, telling her about Katie and raking fingers through his hair, telling her that he had nowhere else to go. She listened, allowing him to finish before beckoning them both.

They followed her through the dark, followed the

swish of her skirts across the bare wood floor; all the curtains were drawn and she had candles going, and a meager fire in the hearth. It was pretty much just a one-room shack, sparse on furnishings, with a narrow bed and an old *spinning wheel* tucked against the back wall—and a fox, of course.

The woman looked back and said, "Are you afraid? Hmm?" A husk of laughter floated after her.

She led them to a dining table in the corner, and Richard had fumbled his wallet out before Tommy could stop him.

"I can pay you. Whatever it—"

"Put that away, *Ricard* Franklin," Beulah ordered brusquely, eyeing him. "Where do you think you are? Some tourist witchcraft shop in Salem? You're not."

Richard's mouth closed, and he replaced the wallet. She was barefoot, short of stature, all of five feet tall at best, stooped slightly at the spine and leaning towards the plump side, with wiry hair that had turned to gray long ago. But when she scolded him he obeyed without thinking. The old lady reminded him of his grandmother, it dawned on him.

She told them to sit, so they sat.

Creeping to a wood-burning cookstove, she moved her stewpot away from the heat. A loaf of freshly baked bread was cooling there; its summery-buttery smell hung in the air like a warm invitation. "You have blood on your hands," she said, her back to them, and Richard started. He saw the Sallow Man's dried blood still on his knuckles and ducked his fist beneath the draw leaf table.

"It's been a bad night for you, *eh*?" said Beulah, drawing her crocheted shawl about her and turning.

"All right, let's see what you've brought us. So we can find your missing cricket." Richard had already laid Katelyn's coloring book upon the tabletop, but the witch stopped cold as her gaze came to rest on the leather-bound Bible that Tommy grasped.

"Where did you *get* that?"

Quickly, Richard said, "I gave it to him, on the off-chance it might . . . have something to do with all of this."

"Put it on the table, Thomas," the old woman breathed, hoarse, throaty. She sat down across from them and tugged her earlobe, astonished. "Push it nearer please." Truitt did, and Beulah used a metal carrot peeler to raise the cover an inch. She closed one eye and squinted inside the book, and Richard noticed the burn scars on her hands for the first time.

"Can it be so? Gahh!" She dropped the utensil. "I always knew. Always dreaded this coming to my doorstep." The curious fox sat close by, watching with keen oval pupils.

This won't be good. Richard smuggled another Rolaids into his mouth. *I'm sitting here with a long-forgotten witch from my long-forgotten childhood nightmares, and it will not be good.*

She cocked an eyebrow, studying them with probing stares. "You understand nothing of this, do you?"

"No," both men answered. "That's why we're here," Tommy hastened to add.

"Well then," she said, "let us see if—" Glancing aside distractedly, she snapped, "What are you looking at? Hmm? I'll take care of this, Pearl. *Shoo.*" At that, her little russet-red familiar went to the bed and hopped into it, turning in circles before curling up on the heavy patchwork quilt. *I'm dreaming . . . I must be,* Richard had time to think, and then Beulah reached one tentative hand out and placed her scarred palm on the Bible's cover.

It was only for an instant but they all felt it, felt the sudden *shift* in the room, as if everything had tipped just off-kilter. Flames leapt in the hearth and the braided candles hissed and shadows wavered across the walls, and the old woman recoiled, jerking away from the book as though she'd pressed her hand to the hot cookstove by mistake. That fast and it was done.

Far away in the woods overlooking town, Simon Julian paused at that moment with his camel-hair coat and turned to peer out one of Shaw-Meredith House's tall arched windows, frowning into the darkness, and gazing strangely to the west where distant lightning split the sky.

"As I suspected," Beulah said. She touched the child's coloring book next, caressed it, taking her time with this one. "Aah, my *pretty-witty*. My my." Once more a smile curved her puckered mouth. "This is all you have brought?" she asked, and they told her yes. She nodded, rising from the table and fetching a tin of spices with which she anointed herself and her surroundings. Then she retrieved twin broomsticks from where they stood beside a smoke-grained wall cupboard—handworked besoms with thick gnarled handles and sprigs of baby's breath and amaranthus tied on with blue and white bindings.

. . . And away we go, thought Richard dizzily when he saw them.

Holding her two garnished brooms out together,

the witch said, "Thomas, be so good as to prop these against the front door for me, will you? Handles crossed into an X." He stood and took one, but before he could grab the other he witnessed Beulah sliding her hands over it now, moving arthritic, spice-powdered fingers up and down the crooked shaft in a suggestive manner. She grinned toothlessly at him.

"Better than a man, *eh*, Thomas Truitt?" she rasped. "Lasts longer." She laughed until she began wheezing.

Tommy pulled a face and made for the door. "Funny."

"Bristles up, if you would," she clarified. He placed the broomsticks against the closed door and was halfway back when she spoke again: "Stay where you are!" Taking her seat at the dining table, Beulah told him, "Now remove the framed mirror from the wall right there—*very carefully,* please. That's the one."

In the half-light of the house, Tommy leaned over an antique hand-crank phonograph and took a small silvery mirror off the wall. He hesitated a moment, glancing into its clouded reflection.

"Ah-ah," Beulah said, "don't look too closely. No telling what you might see." The fire cast swaying shadows over the deep cracks in her face, the wrinkled skin. She passed her tongue tip over her lips. "Twist your mind inside out, the things you might see." Richard felt his scalp tingle. He stared into the old woman's onyx eyes and shuddered inwardly.

She instructed Truitt to stand with the speculum in both hands, the glass aimed out, toward the front door. To hold it and not to move or let go, no matter what happened.

353

"Behave and keep still for me, Thomas. I have business with your handsome friend here, *eh*?" She patted the back of Richard's hand, brushing his wedding band inadvertently. Her face darkened. *"Aah, no . . . "* She looked down, clearing her throat.

The woman opened both books on the draw leaf table before her, displaying their pages in the flickering light. She told Richard to lay his palms on each of them, and to concentrate on his daughter, his Katelyn Jane Franklin, to fill his every thought with her, as if that were not already true.

Reaching inside her faded blouse Beulah produced an egg-sized stone, a piece of rose quartz taken from the mucky riverbed, with a frosted outer crust and one of its cut sides polished into a pinkish clear window. When she pulled it out, Richard caught a glimpse of the same terrible scar tissue on the old woman's neck as her marked hands bore. She set the gazing oracle down in front of her.

"Are we ready, Thomas?" she said evenly, and he called over one shoulder that he was, his feet spread wide and the mirror outstretched in front of him. Nodding, she took a deep breath and touched the pages, completing the link on the tabletop: hand to book, book to hand . . . their arms creating the circle, closing it, the seer stone in the center between them.

"Away we go," Witch Beulah said, her eyes blazing full and wide into Richard's.

The air in the room intensified, and the firelight sizzled again. Then everything seemed to settle. The fox raised its head from the quilt to watch.

"Spirits of the air . . . breathe through me," intoned the woman, eyelids fluttering, "lights of the fire consume me." Her withered face took on a dreaming quality, thoughtful, bathed in the candlelight. Tommy could've sworn he felt something rush against him, like an unseen draft trying to push its way into the gloom-haunted house. He licked his lips.

"Infuse," said Beulah, perched in a half-awake state on her seat, *"infuse . . . me . . . "* Her body convulsed, the entire table rocked. "Rise, my lambs . . . my darlings," she grunted, an unnerving laugh coming out of her. A hush fell, and the witch cocked her head to one side, staring blankly. Her features had changed.

"Unborn . . . stillborn . . . ORCHESTRATOR OF ALL THINGS." Another spasm wracked her, and it sounded as if someone else was speaking their own guttural voice through her, forcing it slowly, gravelly: *"BEHOLD . . . OUR . . . FLESH."*

Like Michelle when she was hypnotized, Richard's mind jangled and he felt his guts roll, thoughts of Michael Sarrazin and pre-birth memories flooding his brain, disrupting the mental vision of his precious Katie. All at once Beulah pulled away with a jerk, causing Richard to jump. He saw her take up the carrot peeler and gouge her own palm open with it, almost cried out for her to stop. But he didn't, just sat gapemouthed as she ripped into the flesh of one hand with the peeler and snatched up her witch's stone, clasping it tight, the rivulets of blood intermingling with the frosted oracle, dripping in red splotches on the tabletop.

"*I see you,*" she said, cupping the rose quartz and gazing into its milky, blood-smeared window. *"Oh, I see you there."*

Tommy felt the push against him resume, had to

actually lean forward this time to neutralize the bizarre sensation. He felt the mirror's glass begin to give way and crack in his grasp and he sucked his breath in. "Um, something is happening," he said as loud as he dared.

Hearing his words the old woman emerged from her trance, at once becoming aware of the presence attempting to intrude. "Do not move, Thomas. Our veil must sustain us, conceal what we do here. The barrier will hold as long as necessary, *eh*?"

Locking eyes with Richard, Beulah told him: "I know where she is, *Ricard* Franklin. The little cricket . . . your pretty-witty girl. Her grandfather has possession of her, but"—she faltered, a grave sorrow twisting her face—"but his years are vast, his thirst for suffering and chaos vaster still."

"Her grandfather doesn't have her," Richard heard himself say, his mouth dry with fear, "that's wrong. She was kidnapped from there. What do you mean?"

"No," whispered the river witch carefully, shaking her head, rills of scarlet running, vanishing inside the sleeve of her blouse as she held the rock before her. "Listen to me." She leaned in close and Richard smelled the blood, felt his skull pound to the accelerating thrum of his own heartbeat as he strained to hear: "Her grandfather has her *now*."

She began to tell it then, the words bubbling like vomit from her lips, her black crystal eyes glittering in the glow of the candles.

2

Lorraine stood up and wiped between her legs, sniffing

the wadded bathroom tissue before letting it fall into the porcelain bowl. Liking the scent of herself at that moment, she slipped her fingertips inside the moist valley down there, daubing her silk behind each ear, slicking the gap of her cleavage with it. The sensor-flush toilet responded with a deafening whoosh as she moved away, slid her lace panties back up, and lowered her skirt.

At the sink Lorraine soaped and washed her hands, dried them off. Checking her gloss in the water-spotted mirror, touching the small mole near her mouth, she smoothed her skirt and then stepped cherry-lipped out of the hospital restroom into the brightly lit corridor.

She bought herself a coffee at one of the vending machines and headed back to her husband's ward. They had fast-tracked him and admitted him almost immediately, after a quick emergency room once-over, and had since begun the invariable barrage of tests: blood work, full X-rays, the whole bang shoot. It was a miracle Jack had gone along with any of it, she mused as she sipped her drink. Surely she owed Richard for that. If only he—

Lorraine turned the hallway corner, wondering what could have become of their young boarder Aaban, aware now of the men's stares following her, their gazes burning as she walked. Aware of the things they wanted to do to her taut, aging yet obliging body, the ways in which they ached to pleasure her and pleasure themselves using her. A few of the women, too.

She escaped into Jack's room, needing a cigarette, noticing the heaviness of the door as she pushed her way inside.

The room was dimmed, windowless, the overhead

fluorescents shut off. A wall light behind the bed was on and she could tell that Jack wasn't under the disarrayed sheets. Wondering if they had come and collected him again, she moved towards an illuminated switchplate and clattered into something in the dark. Someone's overcoat was hanging on the back of the door.

Lorraine flipped the lights on and screamed.

It wasn't an overcoat she saw but her husband on the back of the door, face pulled into a horrible grimace, dangling by his neck from a hook, from the belt he'd looped over his head and hanged himself with.

"Oh my God, no," Lorraine cried out, dropping her coffee. *"No, Jack!"* Calling for help, she grabbed his twitching form around the waist and tried to lift him off the door, without success. *"Nooo! Oh, no!"*

On her fourth desperate attempt Jackson came down, crashing to the shiny floor beside his panic-stricken wife. She yanked the belt away and blew air into his gulping, landed-fish mouth. He started to fight, pushing her off, blindly swinging his fists.

"Let me die," he said, wheezing, coughing. "Won't you let me die, whoever you are?"

Lorraine told him who she was: his wife, his Rainey. Jack's eyes stared up, unseeing. "I can't . . . I can barely hear you." His hands groped her. Milk-white membranes blinked, teeth bared themselves hideously. "Rainey?" he choked.

"Yes, sweetie," she said, wiping away tears, "it's me. I'm here."

His shrunken-in face twisted. The admiral lashed out, striking her, pulling her hair until she shrieked.

"Let me die, you whore. Goddamn you . . . *why?* Why, Lorraine?" He gasped, shuddering all over. *"What's happening to me?"*

Lorraine seized him, did her best to hold on, her cheek cut open, her nose bleeding from his flailing blows. "Shhh. You're going to be all right. I'll take care of you, I promise."

"Leave me alone, just let me die," Lawrie's voice rattled in his throat. "God please—let me die."

"No, Jack. No," said Lorraine, cradling him, rocking her husband in her arms. "I won't leave you. I'll never leave you." She kissed his ghostly pale brow, leaving her own tears and blood there. "You're going to get *well*. You have to. I won't let anything happen to you."

They wept together on the shiny white-tiled hospital room floor until someone came.

3

"Fallen away, they were called. 'Those Who Fell'. Not everyone knows this, or chooses to believe it."

Her familiar had come down from the bed and crouched near them, pricking up its white-tipped ears, flipping its short tail.

"The man himself is loathsome enough," Beulah went on, "but what lives and breathes inside—*worse*."

Richard was frowning. "Katie's with George? I don't understand you." He felt for his cell phone.

"Simon Julian, Julian Simon," said the old woman, "*he* is her true grandfather."

Richard glared at her. "You're mistaken. Is this a joke? Because it's not funny."

WILLIAM GORMAN

"Simon Julian, Julian Simon," she repeated, melodious. "It is him, and he has your child. His grandchild."

"I'm not sitting here and listening to riddles," Richard said, anger building.

"*No?* Gahh!" The river witch touched Katie's activity book with her fingertips, the blood-smeared piece of quartz still held aloft in her cut hand. "Your cricket . . . let me guess, *eh*? She can do things no one else can, see things no one can see. Such wondrous gifts, *Ricard* Franklin, abilities only dreamed of in dreams *within* dreams. Terrifying abilities that nobody else could possibly have. Yes, such a special cricket." Beulah smiled sadly. "Just like her mother was. The wife you lost—the wife they *took*."

"What did you say?"

The wind outside gusted, buffeting the night-darkened little house. The woman cleared her throat. "Wait. Stay put," she said, rising and dragging one of the chairs to the middle of the room. She offered it to Truitt, patting his shoulder and telling him to sit, and to keep holding the framed mirror that way. Then she returned to the table and sat back down across from Richard.

"*Who* took my wife?" he asked low, keeping his voice even. "Are we talking about the pastor from the church?"

"The same," Beulah said, caressing the open Bible's pages, turning them over.

"But—"

"Julian *is* your wife's biological father, your daughter's true grandfather." She paused. "Your wife, she was born a product of her mother's lusts. Your

360

little one—*her* power—ahh, hers comes as a stone comes skimming across the water, pitching forward, gathering momentum. But Simon Julian is the source. He is where it originates, your dead wife's power and purpose, and your cricket's as well. From the man himself, *eh*? This *thing* inside the man."

Richard found his voice. "It's not true. It can't be. Someone would have known."

"Listen to her," Tommy called out.

"Secrets, *Ricard* Franklin, we all have secrets," cooed the witch, and Richard swallowed thickly.

"You said they took Michelle. What did you mean?"

She was silent for a long moment. "Your wife was sacrificed. Run down. They killed her in order to draw you here. To ensure your return, so that you would bring the child with you to this place."

"Who killed her?"

"Lamentation, you see. He feeds on it. Physical, emotional distress—"

"Who killed her?" Richard's limbs trembled.

Touching, caressing of the pages. Then: "An American Indian man named Salt."

Richard reeled as though slapped, the breath stolen from his lungs. "The *Indian* . . . " He pictured the huge man with the ponytail and the immaculate suit, how he had gawked at their SUV that day; Truitt's jaw clenched somewhere in the shadowy room.

"If not him, another would have done so," spat Beulah. "Some other pawn. Julian sees himself as the great *Orchestrator*. Unrivaled. Absolute. Like pushing pieces around a chessboard this is to him, *eh*?" She rubbed a Bible page, turning her head, listening. "This Salt . . . dangerous, *vile* . . . but Simon manipulates

361

him, controls him with lies. Half-truths. Refers to him as his *Prarsheen* as if it were a badge of honor when in fact it is nothing more than insult: a mispronunciation of *Prairie du Chien* to be laughed at, since Salt's forerunners couldn't speak the name of their own Wisconsin village properly.

"Even the prized war ax he keeps close isn't genuine, just a replica from an old Johnson Smith catalog. Lies!"

"*What?* What does any of this—?"

"The Reverend is old, very old. But the *Watcher* within him is ancient. Deceiver, he is. Thief of souls . . . seeding the earth as he wanders its vastness. I shan't speak his real name—enough just to say that he has always been here. Since the world began." She turned the crumbling pages slowly, one after another, stroking them, and spying into the windowed oracle cupped in her bleeding palm. "Chaplain of Nazis now, is it? Aren't we clever."

The russet-red fox yawned smartly.

Richard gripped the edges of the tabletop and hung on, numb, lost. "Where is my daughter?"

"With Julian Simon and his Indian, his dupe."

"*Where?* What does he want? Why take her?"

"Because she is *of him*. Of his line. Hmm? Kindred heir. He wants her near to him, wants her magic to light his way, I'll wager. Keep him amused like a plaything amuses a bored, wayward boy on his sojourns."

"What danger is she in?"

"There's no telling. She shouldn't be harmed as long as she complies, does as she's told. But the *Orchestrator* will no doubt have other uses for—" The woman's mouth tightened. "—her *charms*." She continued on hurriedly. "Truth is, I've known of his being here for some time. Years now. He came for the sorrows of this valley, this plague-pit haven, came to bask in the despair we emanate here . . . our brokenness. The lasting impressions of it, *eh*? He seeks to pit us against one another, so that we destroy ourselves from within."

"You're talking like he's not even human." In his mind's eye Richard saw the resurrection of the dead infant and he bit down on his tongue.

"He *isn't!* Were you never in Sunday school? Julian is of the Fallen Race, one of the angels damned and hurtled to earth for mating with mortal women and contaminating mankind's genetics, siring children that grew into giants. In the Old Testament these ancients, and there are many, bestowed forbidden knowledge and sorcery upon their offspring: the cancerous hybrid rejects who were in turn hunted and burned so adamantly, driven into outer darkness. For thousands of years, before the Culling and after, the unnamed have roved and seeded the daughters of men in an agelong quest. Walking the earth, *spawning*, the exact way old Julie fathered your wife. Fathered her half-angel soul right out of the ether."

"Why doesn't someone just kill him then?"

The old woman scowled. "They have killed him. He only need wait . . . wait and migrate into another's form when able. To leave more human wreckage behind. Already the exodus has begun, beasts fleeing from this place directly because of *him*. Except the moths, that is. I've seen them. They come to escort away the forfeit dead—"

Beasts fleeing, Richard thought, her insane words all jumbling dreamlike together, and it made him think of the skunk on the highway that first day. Had it been fleeing also? Was that why it had run out so suddenly, in broad daylight, and died under his wheels? *Fleeing, trying to get away from here.*

Beulah went on, urgent to finish. "The Inundation couldn't destroy them. Terrible scourges and plagues failed to rid the world of them. So their spirits are allowed free rein, to wander and inhabit different hosts. Their purpose is singular, their strategy clear: the *Watcher's* goal is to hurt the offending deity by tainting and destroying its creations, spreading darkness. Oblivion.

"But condemned, earthbound spirits oftentimes have a tendency to break down the longer they are here. To degrade like matter, becoming incompatible with our physical plane. Becoming malignant entities. Demons, if you will. Spoiled meat . . . the ruination of lives."

"And I'm supposed to believe all this? Demons? *Fallen angels?*"

"You came to me. Do you think I lie? Do you, *eh*?" She tossed her head back. "It is *they* who lie, *Ricard* Franklin. Those Who Fell. They seek to corrupt, to lead us astray."

"From what?"

The river witch looked him in the eye. "From the divine knowledge of what we really are."

Richard glanced away, teeth gritting. He looked back. "You said other uses."

"Hmm?"

"Before . . . you mentioned other uses for Katelyn. I heard you."

She tried to conceal her dismay, caught off guard by him, but could not manage this. Her face visibly fell.

"What? What is it?" Richard's face crumpled as well. "You can't mean—"

"I'm afraid so," she said, and an icy coldness closed itself around Richard's heart and sank it like a rock down a frozen well. "Not right away, but ultimately . . . yes. When she comes into womanhood he will breed her like all the rest."

Richard's skin literally crawled, acidic bile rising. He thought of the girls, those pregnant girls at Nain Lutheran Church. The disabled one—the pretty blond with no legs and a plush-toy panda and with her belly bulging. He made a strangled sound deep in his throat as he leapt to his feet and knocked his chair backward.

"Sit down, *Ricard* Franklin!" Beulah ordered. "Your daughter's life depends upon you *listening to me now.*"

"No," he protested, choking. "I . . . that's not . . . "

The witch calmly said: "Sit back down or you'll lose her forever."

Richard appeared stunned, slack-jawed. "Say that again?"

"If you do not listen, you will lose your little cricket for good, and we'll never be able to find her."

He collapsed into the seat, his vision blurring. The fox flicked its tail. "W-what do we do? Please save her."

Beulah reached across the table and pressed her hand to his lips. "Shhh, *eh?*" She paused, then withdrew her fingertips from Richard's mouth and ran them over the pages one more time, her onyx irises sparkling. She stared into the egg-sized riverbed quartz, took a long steady breath, and at once began talking in random fragments. "So much death. So . . . *much*. Eye drops. My gold ring. Mustn't forget . . . " The spasms hit, contorting her face. *"Trapped inside this stinking body, this rotting cage of flesh and old bones far too long. TIME . . . TO . . . GO."*

She tore clear and came to herself at last, slamming the German Bible shut and shoving it away from her. "You will need this for the dark ahead," she said, "the dark work to come."

Richard gazed at old Beulah and heard Lawrie's final words to him rushing in his ears. *Get the bastard.* Good God. What in fucking hell had Admiral Jack run afoul of? How much of it was Glee involved in?

The witch called out and told Tommy to hang the speculum back on the wall, and to bring his chair and rejoin them. He did so, sparing a look into the silvery glass first and confirming that yes, the mirror had indeed cracked in its frame under the influences of some unknown . . . well, *some*thing. He drew up his chair and sat down beside his shaken friend.

Beulah recited obscure lore, telling them there were ways, certain ways of diminishing his hold in this world. Setting him alight, for instance; purging by fire. Or encasement entirely in silver somehow, some way— pure molten silver and its protective moon powers being the bane of such creatures' existence—and then dumping him to the bottom of the deepest ocean.

She tugged on her earlobe and lamented that short of these ideas, however, anything they tried would only stop the aging shell he now occupied and end with him *still* re-emerging in some other's stolen body, another place, another unwitting surrogate somewhere.

What they needed was a disruption of the flow of

events. Something unexpected, unleashed with brazenness and surprise which would give to them the upper hand, allow them to reclaim the girl, secure her and spirit her far away in the aftermath.

But they had to move fast.

Her hand meandered to Katie's book while she spoke, touching it again without realizing.

Richard grimaced at it all, chewing the inside lining of his cheek. He shifted nervously. "Tell me what to do."

The old woman sat and brushed the coloring book with her fingertips. Smiled, turned the page to one Katie and her mother had crayoned in together.

"Your wife—" Beulah said with a start, dropping the witch's stone to the table and placing her wounded hand on her chest. Her eyes grew wide. "I *remember* her now . . . she . . . brought me *flowers*." She looked at Richard in wonderment, marveling at this. "Brought flowers, and laid them in the field. The snowy field where my house used to be."

Richard blinked, the memory flooding back. *Yes.*

"I saw her," she continued slowly, "watched this lanky, beautiful *giant* of a girl laying flowers in my field. I watched from the wood that winter's day and—and you, *Ricard* Franklin. You were there holding her hand."

He turned glistened eyes away from the candlelight and nodded.

"And they *took* her," said the old woman, anger fluttering in her voice. "Then they took your cricket, too. Well—" She struck the tabletop with her fist, and Richard's stomach muscles tightened. "—now we get her back, *eh*? We get her back, and none will stand in our way. But we need something special to undo this. Something with much . . . how you say? Much rage. Yes, with much *zedon* to be had . . . to undo this."

She rose, and once more an unsettling husk of laughter escaped her, fitting somehow, in this decidedly odd little shack on Furnace Street. Rich and Tom exchanged glances.

Beulah gathered materials they would require, shuffling across the bare wood floor with her skirts swishing, bringing the tools together. Her mechanisms of necromancy: the colored candles needed, the etched stones and pieces of root; ground-up powders in little stoppered vials, a yew branch for casting the runes. An amber glass eyedropper bottle.

She made Richard put them all inside a burlap potato sack she found, along with the crumbling Bible, which she refrained from touching.

When she noticed his raised eyebrows, she told him firmly, "These enchantments are as old as your Bible itself, *Ricard* Franklin, when the Witch of Endor used them to summon up a dead prophet from the conjuring pits—Old Testament again, *eh*? Older, even, before Persia and Greece and ancient Rome these practices come. Hmm?

"Everything around us is alive, all powerful. Everything radiates with some kind of energy, and a true witch can harness that force and utilize it to her own end." Her eyes narrowed at him. "This is warfare, remember it."

Retrieving her spice tin, she sprinkled pinches of dust around the table before taking her seat. The old woman went over the details then, telling them precisely where to go and what they needed to do.

Repeating it, having them repeat it back to her. The high magic that must be performed—runic symbols to be scrawled in the dirt, names to call upon and the powers to invoke. Sepulchral rites, she introduced them to, going over strange words Richard would have to recite aloud, the language to be used, making sure Thomas memorized them as well, just in case. Plus the purification ritual to close shop with, and the dismissal for when all was said and done.

Finally, Beulah asked Richard to choose a spot, a place of seclusion where they might go unobserved, one with personal meaning to him preferably.

He could think of only one such place.

"But have a care," she warned. "The unnamed keeps minions, like this Salt. They will fight for him. Die for him. Stay alert at all times, and be bold. Yes, dark work indeed."

The old woman brought the bread loaf from her cookstove, and in the flickering glow of the melting candles they broke it apart and shared twists of the freshly baked bread. She called to Pearl, and the small spry fox bounced up into her arms where she fed it pieces of crust dipped in honey at the table. The sticky honey jar made Truitt think of his Aunt Cassie—his poor, bloated, bee-stung Aunt Cassie, lying dead and balloon-like on her gurney in the hospital morgue.

"Gahh!" uttered the witch, startling them. Pearl jumped down off her lap as she stepped from the chair and waggled her fingers. "Nearly forgot . . . mustn't forget!" She went to the smoke-grained wall cupboard again and returned with something else, a flat object wrapped in a dark fabric that looked very much to Richard like red buckram. She settled into her seat, and lifted a corner of the dull cloth to reveal briefly what was beneath: a piece of stained glass. Broken off, square in shape; sparkling glass with colored, climbing roses leaded onto it, a half dozen maybe, their barbed stems weaving curiously and creeping along its textured surface. Beulah covered the piece up, pushing it across to him.

"Here, give this to your special cricket if"—she glanced aside, then immediately returned her gaze—"*when* you get her back. This is for your Katie, *eh*? Tell her she may find use for it some fine day." Her eyes twinkled darkly.

Richard accepted the rose glass fragment, feeling of the stiff red fabric before placing it into the burlap sack with the other items. His brow became furrowed. "I'm sorry we gave you no peace," he said low, uncertain, "sorry you were harassed all those years. It was wrong . . ."

"Our consultation is over," she said. "We're done here. You must go."

Shaking his head in puzzlement, Richard stood up from the dining table with the bag. Tommy followed suit.

"Wait. There is something owed me first, *Ricard* Franklin."

"What do you want?" Richard asked uneasily.

The old woman tapped the coloring book, then snatched it up. "This will do." She reached and touched Richard's left hand next, rotating the wedding band there, and she pulled at it. He resisted, stiffening, and the witch glowered at him.

"Give it to me. It is the price I ask."

Reluctant at first, Richard slid the ring off his

finger and laid it in her scarred palm. He grabbed her hand as he did, not letting go, and traced the ugly burn scars up her wrist with his thumb.

"How did you get these?" he said. "Tell me."

Beulah locked obsidian-black eyes with his, pushing her sleeve back. "There was a fire in the schoolhouse where I used to teach the children, when I was young and filled with life. I tried—" Her voice wavered a touch. "I went back in, to try and save my schoolchildren."

"And did you?"

"No," said the river witch quietly. "Not all of them, no."

Richard caressed the scar tissue, holding her gaze. "What's your real name, Witch Beulah? Say it."

She tipped her head back, and the corners of her wrinkled old mouth turned up wryly. "My name is Valeska. It is the name my parents gave to me when the nurses took my cord and caul, *eh*?" She hesitated, remembering. "But my father . . . he always called me his Val. His sweet, bitter Val." She laughed.

Blackwater Val, Richard's mind echoed. *Once you're from the Val, son, you're always from the Val. Didn't you know that?*

He blinked the thought away.

"You can never return here," she was saying, rising from the table, "or speak of this to anyone. Tell *no one* what we've done tonight, *eh*?" The witch led them toward the door. "Do not come back to this house for any reason, no matter the outcome. Not ever, do you understand?"

"Yes." Silence. Only the crackling hearth, the wind in the trees.

"Kiss me," said the old woman, drawing close. "Put your lips to mine, *Ricard* Franklin. Do it now."

Richard stared at her in the firelight, shuddering inwardly again, recalling what Tommy had admitted earlier. He leaned nonetheless, lowering himself to her height. He felt one of her arms snake around his neck, pulling him against her as she rose up tiptoed on bare feet. Then her shriveled lips were touching his, that mouth closing over his mouth. He tasted her toothless gums and gagged. Squeezed his eyes shut. *And—*

Images swelled, momentary imprints ghosting behind the windows of his closed eyelids, branding his retinas. He saw moist ruby lips pouting, parting; bronze-velvet flesh warmed by the sun's rays, Michelle's flesh, her young thighs slick with summer sweat, images of her erect-nippled breasts rising and falling. Long-lost glimpses of her: his wife's snug silkiness enfolding him when he entered her, made love to her on some sandy beach in the late afternoon. Michelle's back arching, her long legs hiking up and bucking with each thrust. A sweet candylike scent overtook him, filling his nostrils with its intoxication—sand, the salty air, her musky honeysuckle sex. Richard felt a tongue slip into his mouth, teasing, touching his tongue, and he gasped as the skin tingled and crawled over his testicles. He began to grow hard.

"Let her fly," came a voice in his ear. *"When the time comes, you must let her fly . . . "*

The old woman had eased back. He opened his eyes and found himself staring into the depths of her black crystal irises again.

"Make an end of them," she said, "or we're doomed. The lot of us—doomed."

Then the river witch was clearing her broomsticks away, opening the front door and ushering Tom and Richard out with haste. Steering them along. Her final words drifted on the breeze:

"I'll assist you all that I can from here. Good luck."

The old woman and her fox stood in silhouette, watching their departure from the doorway.

"Luck?" Tommy remarked as they ran across the flagstones. "You know how lucky you are, man? How easy you got off? The things I had to do with her . . . let me tell you."

"Don't," said Richard, carrying the sack of arcane wonders and wiping a shaky hand over his mouth. "Don't you dare."

4

They had to climb the high, spiked wrought-iron fence because it was well beyond sundown now, and the graveyard's heavy front gates were locked from dusk to dawn. The two men moved through seeping shadows at the back of the cemetery, searching for the section of graves set apart from the rest. They walked up a slight rise to that place enshrouded by trees, the place they'd been instructed to go; the gloom and solemnity here seemed to have descended darker and deeper than anywhere else in the deserted cemetery.

Richard's flashlight illuminated the marble headstones as they treaded cautiously between their concentric array. There were menorahs, and Jewish stars upon them: clusters of grapes on some, or two lions with the Star of David poised above. Many bore engravings of trees with branches broken off, indicating life interrupted—the young dying too soon. Some of the grave markers had rocks and assorted sized pebbles on top of them, left behind by the living to keep down those buried here perhaps, to help them stay put. Richard swept the tops clean.

UNKNOWN BUT TO HIS HEBREW GOD read one of the tombstones. Another proclaimed THE MOST LOVING OF MOTHERS ~ HER WORTH WAS MORE PRECIOUS THAN JEWELS OR GOLD. They nearly tripped over a small, rough marker before the beam of light found it. BABY, it said simply, GIVEN AND TAKEN. Richard held his breath, the glove box flashlight quavering in his hand.

From the center of these rose a black granite memorial out of the earth, its chiseled epitaph designating it:

UNSTILLED RUN OUR TEARS
FOR THE SLAUGHTERED OF OUR PEOPLE
1933—1945

A bird lay dead in the grass, wings folded. Tiny wind chimes tinkled in a tree overhead. Richard's flashlight beam darted away. He crouched down with the burlap bag, a shiver going through him. This was it.

Richard mulled over what he'd been told out on St. Angell Island, trying to tighten his fogged brain around it all, the implications. He wondered how much George knew.

"This is the craziest—" he began, but stopped when

he felt Tommy grasp his shoulder. He exhaled, laying the flashlight on its side and taking the items from the sack, separating them in the dim light being cast.

The stained glass fragment wrapped in dark red buckram had already been removed, and tucked under the front seat of the Blazer.

Wind rustled the treetops, sighing through them, then dying. A damp chill had settled in. Shivering again, Richard rubbed his eyes. Tommy crouched beside him, neither speaking—not yet. He helped him arrange the evocation candles, placing the disintegrating Bible in the middle of the configuration. Tom moved away and left him to it. Left him to his dark work.

Richard struggled to light the candles and keep them lit. Ribbons of smoke rose as the braided wicks finally caught. He cupped the flames one by one, protecting them until they were stronger, his gaze lifting to the hulking shadow of Shaw-Meredith House in the woods above. A light was on up there.

. . . Came to bask in the despair we emanate here, the witch-woman had said, *our brokenness.*

He blinked, kneeling in dirt and staring up. His heart was beating double-time, his breath erratic. Could Katie actually be inside that house? With *them*? The old woman's words jarred him from thought.

This is warfare, remember it.

Clamping his jaw, Richard hunkered low and made the signs on the ground, scrawling powerful runes with the bit of yew branch, pushing the stones and pieces of root into the soil. He performed the magical spell as the witch had shown him, made the gestures in the air. Began scattering her botanical powders, the wormwood and the horehound. Richard's head whipped to one side, his eyes big.

"Did you hear that?"

Tommy seemed to notice nothing. "Keep going," he said. "Don't stop."

Richard drew the final forbidden symbol in the earth, anointing it with pulverized bone from a small vial. He flicked some into the candle flames, making them spit. Sprinkled the grayish bone powder over the Bible's leather cover. Then, he took out the amber glass eyedropper bottle, containing tears, and squeezed a few drops onto each of the graves. Human tears. On each adult grave.

Glancing about anxiously, Richard picked up his flashlight and surveyed the arrangement. Satisfied, he extinguished the beam. Truitt heard him begin the incantation amongst the mounds.

"Ani mechapeset otcha vedoreshet et sherotecha . . . "

As he'd memorized it, just as the witch had taught. Speaking deliberately, Tom mouthing the words with him. Ritually invoking the dead.

Summoning: *I seek you and demand your service . . .*

Tommy watched the candlelight go from orange to blue in the darkness, the wicks glowing brighter in their circle, giving off brilliance as the magic wove itself—as the wheel spun its threads. Shadows wavered, danced away and neared again. Richard continued to recite, a disembodied voice conjuring in the gloom. Opening the gateway for them, binding them with a promise of vengeance, imparting what need be done.

"Ya'aleh," he chanted at the end of it. *"Ya'aleh!"*

Richard worked the purifying rite upon himself,

the consummation of the spell. Ceremonial blessing of protection; an appeal for atonement. It was over.

Yet the word came out of him still. *"Ya'aleh."* Truitt's skin goosefleshed in the chilly night air.

Arise.

Richard slid the glass vials into the brown burlap sack and stood up with the flashlight. Everything else he left where it was. Then an eddy of self-disgust crashed over him like a black wave, staggering him, sending him back down on both knees. He saw the dead bird as he fell forward. "Help," he said, and looked at the memorial. "Forgive me . . . " Tommy went to him, bending, and Richard lurched up off the ground with a stifled cry.

"My God, something—"

"What is it?"

Richard stared wide-eyed. "I . . . I felt . . . " Gaping down at the graves, he rasped, *"Something moved."*

Tommy paused. "Okay. Get a grip on thyself, Rich," he said, jokingly, the way he used to when they were kids. "We gotta hurry."

Richard wasn't listening. He laid a hand on the grass, withdrew it quick. "Feel the ground. Feel it!" he told Tommy, an audible click in his windpipe. "Oh, my dear Christ."

"No," uttered Truitt, backing away. "Come on, let's get out. Remember what she said."

"What did we do?" Richard was trembling all over. He clung onto a headstone in nausea and horror and shined his flashlight at the alchemical markings and mystic symbols, at the candles burning atop the interred dead, a breeze trying to snuff out their flames now. "What did we do?" His helpless gaze fastened onto Tom's.

"I don't know, but it's out of our hands. We have to go."

As they retreated through the dark of Hebrew National Cemetery, Richard looked toward the Gothic mansion again. Stone-walled, impenetrable, brooding against a moonless overcast sky. "My daughter's up there, isn't she?"

Tommy said, "Let's get the hell outta here," and pulled him toward the spiked iron fence.

§

The storm trembled on the western edges of town, and the air had grown tangibly colder with its coming. Reesie Billups felt the chill and got up to close her bedroom window, crawling back beneath the covers where she stroked her swelling belly and felt the stirrings of her baby—unaware of the tubal cancer already taking vigorous hold deep within her—as her twin sister slumbered in pitch blackness across the room. Karl Kissick went looking for his missing Game Boy and found his kid brother, Carl, in possession of it—*yet again!*—only this time Karl-with-a-K fetched a steel hammer from his father's utility drawer and buried its claws deep into the back of Carl-with-a-C's skull, killing him stone-dead for taking what did not belong to him.

On Honey Run Road, neighbors were prowling the property of the late Cassandra Patrick this night. They carried gasoline cans with them, and bottles of liquid smoke, and they confirmed that the bees were still in the trees and bushes by the low, inert buzzing sounds rising from the shadows down near her backyard pond. These

378

concerned citizens couldn't see them but homed in on their lethargic droning which was steady and monotonous in the trees, like the aggravating hum of an electrical transformer. They fanned out stealthily and began spraying the liquid smoke, quelling the lowest bees into stupor before dousing the hydrangea bushes and locust trunks with the gasoline and setting them alight using sticks wrapped with gas-soaked rags. Hustling back up the slope as the flames rose higher, they listened to the sluggish bees as they began to buzz louder and burn in their writhing clusters and abandoned bird nests, imagined them screeching before they sizzled and popped. Somebody doused the standing box-hives alongside the house and lit them also. Then the neighbors ran, pausing at the roadway to watch the trees gleam a harsh orange-pink in the darkness, bees hissing as they took to the air on fire and cooked alive.

Out on Angell Island, the river witch Valeska gazed into her oracle and uttered *"Aah, no . . . "* hoarsely, shuffling to her front door and letting the russet-red fox named Pearl outside before sitting back down, gold wedding ring over her thumb, to caress the child's coloring book laid open on the tabletop in front of her.

The field hand named Shaw (last living descendant of village founder Augustus Shaw, truth to tell) made his way across the shadowy Blessing Acres grounds, feeling the cooling September wind on his pitted face. He brought a chain shank with him from the bunkhouse, and a doubled-up length of thick, greased mooring rope which he lashed against his gloved palm as he walked. The lean man in cowboy boots and matching hat disappeared inside the great round barn for his usual nightcap of release.

Registered nurse Lucy Dixon, taking the 'culling the herd' speech she'd witnessed the night before a bit too literally, forced her 91-year-old Alzheimer's-stricken grandfather down under his bathwater and kept his head there until the air bubbles at last ceased inside her clawfoot tub.

At that moment a man stood in a makeshift nursery somewhere, his hide crawling, staring into a crib at the infant who stared unblinkingly back into him—an unnatural single-mindedness there, not so much as a flutter in its watchful gaze—and when he could stand this macabre contest of wills no longer, the child's great-uncle plucked a pillow from the nearby daybed and held it over the baby's incessant stare, smothering it . . . ending little Henry Putnam's life for a second, decisive time.

Phil Jenrette cruised the freight yards seeking his own nightcap of release, visions of *Shasteen* and *Blaine*, and of *Tish* and *Justin* and *Ebony*, and of *Maria* causing him to salivate, erection straining at the zipper of his trousers, not aware that his long-suffering wife waited in her rocking chair for him to return home, cradling a jar of dense yellowish liquid for him in her lap this time as she rocked and wept: sulfuric acid her husband used for getting rid of anthills in the yard, chemicals capable of dissolving entire fire ant colonies neat as you please.

Meanwhile, the kid whose name nobody could ever remember went into the office of his amphetamine-addicted evening-shift supervisor and slit her throat with a long fillet knife as she hunkered over the circulation desk, terminating his secret affair with her, terminating his employ with her, opening the middle-aged woman up and spilling her—liver and lights and all—before starting off on his nighttime route. He choked and stalled and spluttered all over the sleeping village in his broken-down cargo van, leaving select glistening bits of her to be found as he delivered the morning edition stacks of *The Rock River Guardian* one last time, leaving her severed head inside her own curbside mailbox at her house, kissing its lips goodbye. Through his cracked windshield the kid observed something flash to the west as he drove, lightning crisscrossing the sky in the distance, but the darkness swallowed it back up with a low rumble.

Hearing the thunder reverberate, Julian summoned William Salt into his parlor and whispered, "If anything should happen, kill them. Gather the others. Kill them all, *Prarsheen*."—yet failed to notice the way the Indian man caressed the passive little girl's hair before exiting, a hidden desire in his deep-set eyes. Elsewhere still, also unnoticed, dusky shapes were gliding silently through the birches and oak trees of Shaw Woods, gaunt, ill-defined shapes, newly risen, gathering pace and cohesion, climbing along the ridge known to locals as Duck Blind Point, one of them—the revenant gripping an unclean Bible—fixing its dark sockets on Shaw-Meredith House above where a light shone in the arched windows.

But somebody *did* notice a female form moving through leaves and on down to a fenced corner where a boy remained chained. Her hooded zip-up was open, and she carried a meat cleaver in one hand and a 50,000 volt stun baton in the other. She slowed, creeping nearer like a panther on the scent, licking her lower lip . . . and suddenly someone spoke, causing her to jump. "What're you doing, SunnyDee?" the voice asked. She whirled at the other figure in the shadows, her heart shooting into her throat. It was Ditch Richards leaning on his pitchfork, lost in dark ruminations, a bloody bandage clinging to the side of his head where his ear used to be. "Don't call me that," Miss Aubel snapped, "only my friends can call me that."

Richards cleared his throat. "Asked what you were doing, I did." He paused, looking her up and down: *"SunnyDee."*

Her face twisted. "I told you not to call me that! You're nothing but a loser—an old drunk. You shot your own ear off. Everybody knows it. *And you don't get to call me SunnyDee!"*

The man spat on the ground. "Uh-huh . . . more like SunnyDee-licious, from what I hear. That's what all the married men in town say anyway." His gaze flicked to the boy, Miss Aubel's autistic son, fidgeting in the shadows by the doghouse, then back to her standing near the burn barrels, and to what she grasped tightly. "Get away from the boy there, bitch," he told her low, nodding. When she pulled her lips back and raised the dark-stained cleaver with a snarl, Ditch Richards ran her through dead center with the pitchfork he was leaning on, right in the middle of her *American Princess* heart T-shirt. She succumbed at his feet, mouth opening and closing, the fork's rusty tines buried in her chest, her eyes bulging in shock.

As Richards took out his pint bottle of Old Grand-Dad bourbon and drank from it, the chained boy opened his mouth and spoke for the first and only time in his life. "Go on, get on home now, Ollie," he said distantly, as though talking in his sleep. "The poets are coming." Then fell back into his unending abyss of silence.

And while the fires licked out of control at Honeycomb Haven, spreading from the upright wooden box-hives to Cassie Patrick's house and the outbuildings, the Gospel Book Store downtown blazed away itself like a beacon in the night—having been similarly torched—its hundreds of Bibles burning and melting, turning to holy ash inside the structure, before Glee Deadmond even had the chance to purchase a new one to replace her old.

CHAPTER TWENTY-FOUR

I

LISTEN, MY PRETTY-WITTY. *Listen to me now.*
Katie heard the voice enter her head, plain as day.
Felt it reaching from far off to connect with her mind
somehow. She stiffened involuntarily, her arms
tightening around the cremation urn. Was this a trick?

Your father will find you, it continued, invading
her thoughts, *but first you must trust me and listen,
eh? Close your eyes, cover them so that you cannot
see. They are coming. And your father will find you.*

There was a brief pause, a scanning of her
trepidations. *Who is this?* the young girl wondered,
eyes shifting.

*Your mother paid a kindness to me once. I am
repaying it to you. Do what I say, and do not look. No
matter what you hear, what you feel, do not look. Do
not see . . .*

I'm afraid, thought Katie, and the voice reached
into her head in response.

*Do not be afraid. You have your mother's gift. Let
it flow through you. Take hold of it, child. The power
lies within you . . . it is yours. It always has been, little
cricket.*

Little Katie-Smatie, it spoke. Then:

Cover your eyes now and trust me. Make her proud, eh?

It was gone like mist, pulling away—the psychic link dissipating. Gone.

Reverend Julian latched his tan valise shut. He frowned, searching the pockets of his camel-hair coat. The parlor lights flickered, and a sudden movement drew Katelyn's attention to the window behind her. She froze.

A blood-flecked crow had landed on the window's ledge out in the darkness, sat peering in through the leaded glass. It cawed mockingly at her. Katie shrank away at first, but she felt something strange . . . a faint vibration, coming from the copper urn. Purring, shivering through her, absorbing into her core. From her fingers down to her toes and everything in between, she felt it spread. Her thin chest tightened; her bones ached with it.

She held her breath, recognizing the bird for what it was: a grisly black-winged scavenger that blinded and killed its own nestlings in a crazed frenzy, nothing else—and she no longer feared it. Her eyes narrowed, irises going a smoky violet. Warm radiance had filled her, whether from the soft vibrating or not she couldn't tell.

Then something—the girl's glare, or something in the murky woodland beyond the lighted window maybe—caused the mocking crow to squawk in panic. Its gloss-black wings flared and it defecated and launched itself from the ledge. Mouth agape, it hit an ivy-covered tree in its rush and dashed the brains out of its sleek-shaped skull before tumbling dead into the brambles below.

Katie didn't see. She was already turning her gaze upon the others, the host of specters hanging greedily in the air, capering like schoolboys. Katie's eyes darkened to midnight this time. The hungry shades fell back without warning, drawing away from the girl in a madding swirl. They shrieked mutedly, howled in soundless confusion, clinging desperately onto the thick walls. And the haunters of Shaw-Meredith House bled straightaway into those squared blocks and out of her sight. A few remained at the ceiling, hanging like slashed bedsheets on a line, ruined mouths and sockets slashed wide in dread.

Hugging her mother's ashes to her, she saw the old man pass by with his trinket box and some eyedrops. Using one tiny hand she worked the winter scarf upwards around her neck until it covered her dark eyes like a blindfold. Then she sat cross-legged on the window seat, breathing slowly in and out, and waited for whatever was coming.

2

The Deadmond home was as quiet as the cemetery had been. It stood hushed, and very still: even the polished brass pendulum inside the longcase clock had stopped.

Richard called out for George and Blondie. There were no signs of either.

"Where the hell could they be?" The scrunched yellow note lay beside the recliner. Richard picked it up and stuffed it into his back pocket. He looked in George's study and viewed the pigsty of storage boxes and photo albums, papers piled all over the floor, the autographed baseball bat in its wall case.

The flowery scent was even stronger. Tommy and Richard went into the kitchen where it became overpowering. Both dog bowls were full, untouched. They halted and listened; the refrigerator whirred.

The checkerboard and pieces from Glee's upstairs sewing room were laid out on the kitchen table, two chairs slid back.

Franklin pictured Ollie Echols waiting to play a game—*clack-click*—waiting around year after interminable year for someone to show. He cringed, wondering if Oliver was nearby, and wondering how everything had turned so terribly bad so fast.

"Richie," said Tom, motioning.

The basement door was standing open, a corded skeleton key inserted into the lock.

Richard descended first, Truitt close behind. The light was already on. Halfway down a moan rose up to them, and a breathless gasp. They hurried. Concrete flooring extended before them at the bottom of the creaky plank steps, a washer and clothes dryer to the left, a chest freezer to the right. Beyond that, the furnace was visible in the shadows, and a cobwebbed water heater. It looked as if thin weeds had sprouted up through cracks in the concrete foundation. The heavy aroma knocked them back. More moaning came and they followed it, stumbling over an old screen door propped on its side, working themselves back to a nook under the stairs. And there they found George.

He lay sprawling on a section of earthen cellar floor tucked beneath the wooden stairs, on his side amidst climbing weeds. Richard leaned over his collapsed form to help him. "George, what happened? What are you doing dow—" He stopped, and he looked. Looked closely, staring in disbelief.

George struggled to breathe. "They're h-hers, Rich. See? Can you see them?"

Richard did . . . and he saw now that it was not weeds covering the dirt floor but gangly-looking plants, blooms of waxy cream-white petals on their stems. Immaculate heads drooping on the ends of woody, crooked stalks extending this way and that . . .

"Jesus," hissed Richard, awestruck. *"Cereus."*

"What?" Tommy said.

George was nodding. "Yes. Michelle's cereus." He tried to smile. One side of his mouth remained drawn downward despite the effort.

Richard sat him up, propped him against the wall. "What's wrong, George?" The old man grasped his trembling left arm tightly, as if trying to make it stop. Both eyes were vacant. Mouth downturned.

Stroke, thought Richard, *or a heart attack maybe.*

"I . . . I'm not myself . . . never mind, Glee."

Richard's palms were damp. "We need to get you out of here. I'm calling for an ambulance."

"No!" he stammered, catching his breath. "Don't— just leave me be. Pl-please." A shudder came, his head bumping the wall. He squeezed his eyes shut. "I want to stay right here."

"George, where's Blondie? Outside?"

"Glee took her. Went looking for Kate, I think. She knows about the flowers, son."

Richard and Truitt frowned, looking around them. An adjacent cellar room with no door and a hard-packed dirt floor gaped opposite them, and Richard saw the same eruption of life within: a sea of snowy pale ghosts floating, rank upon rank, stretching into darkness. Thick waves of fragrance surrounded the three men, a pungency of soil just beneath the vanilla sweetness.

George's bifocals were in the dirt so Richard brushed them off and put them in the old man's breast pocket.

Baffled, he asked him, "What *is* this? How, George?"

"Not mine. *Hers* . . . my Chelle did it," George said, fighting for air between sentence fragments. "Growing like this since her death, Rich. S-since the funeral. Filling the place. I've come . . . I come down here secretly, but now Glee knows about it. She knows." He chuckled weakly.

Not possible, no, Richard's mind gibbered.

These nocturnal plants peaked only once a year, twice at the most. *Ugly ducklings,* Michelle used to brag, *that opened into swans and took your breath away.* Night-blooming cereus encircled them, the same weedy hothouse flowers his wife used to grow, bursting into glorious life here in late September, in a lightless cellar yet. Spiny clusters of white all yawning together, and perfuming the air. Running riot down here where they should not be.

Thriving.

"I always knew," said George, eyes glazed, "always knew she wasn't my daughter. But I loved her just the same . . . loved her with all my heart. And n-now she's gone." His body stiffened, started slumping on its side. "Honey Kate . . . gone, too. Oh God—"

Richard held him up. "George, we're going right now to get Katie back. Tommy and I are."

Deadmond's slack-mouthed face responded. "You f-found her? Where is she, Richard? Is she all right?"

"We're going after her, George," said Richard, his throat tight. "It'll be okay. It's not your fault." Tom gave him an affirmative smile.

He let out a strangled sob. "*Thank God*. For you both." George's dimming gaze sought the white blossoms. "They don't wilt, don't ever die . . . do you see it?" Richard nodded, and his father-in-law went on. "They never close. She's here with us, my Chelle is. I pl-play checkers with her sometimes."

"Oh George, that's not—" He caught himself. "That's nice. That's nice, George."

"That's nice, George," the old man repeated, arm shaking. He was barely coherent, losing consciousness.

"I think you've had a heart attack, George. We need to move you."

George Deadmond fought to speak. "It's broken," he said. "My heart broke a long time ago . . . there's nothing left."

He drew in one long, labored breath and said quite clearly: "Banana pancakes for breakfast, Tom." Then he quit breathing and keeled over. Richard righted him, saying his name loudly. His eyes remained closed, the mouth sagged. Richard felt his wrist, checked him at the neck. Shook him. George fell again, head lolling. Didn't move.

"Oh no . . . " Richard clenched his teeth, staying crouched in that rising bed of night-blooming cereus. He massaged the old man's chest, watched his dulled face for something, anything. Nothing was there. Not any longer. He put a hand to his own mouth. "Ahh *shit*, Tom."

"What do we do?" said Truitt.

Richard shook his head. "Beats me. Nothing *to* do, I guess."

"Shouldn't we move him at least?"

"No. This is where he wanted to stay. Leave him." Taking a paint-splotched drop cloth from a shelf, Richard covered him with it. He squeezed George's outstretched arm, straightening to go, but then jerked away. In the partial darkness he saw the dead man's liver-spotted skin prickling, breaking into gooseflesh, as if his lifeless body were reacting to something unseen, some otherworldly peril beyond Richard's scope.

"Frittles," he murmured, and went cold all over.

"Rich?"

"Let's go," Richard replied low, so that none might overhear. He trailed Tommy up the stairs but paused at the top, eyes widening. Taped to the back of the cellar door was an envelope, like the others, a tiny *C* written on it. He wiped his palms on his pants, bit at his lip. Reached and yanked the envelope off the door and tore open its sealed flap, leaning back down into the light.

Inside the envelope were old papers folded neatly, messages scribbled on napkins, a jotted letter made out to Michelle herself from George—no, made out to *Chelle*. He blinked.

Of course. Chelle and I . . . *my C . . . my Chelle*. Richard's poor father-in-law, bound to this house, rattling around its rooms and in his grief leaving handwritten notes for his dead daughter all over the place, trying to keep her alive. If only in his own mind.

Among the folded papers he found Michelle's high

school report on Chief Black Hawk, the one Deadmond helped her with in younger times. Richard skimmed it, stopping to read a random passage. His arms fell to his sides and he let the pages drop from his fingers. They fluttered away, wafting down between the wooden plank steps, one of them coming to rest near the stilled cadaver's outstretched arm. Out of the basement the two men climbed, leaving George to the vanilla-scented shadows and nocturnal flowers below his house.

They used the second-floor restroom hurriedly, and then Richard removed the Sammy Sosa baseball bat from its glass case in George's study to take with them before closing the quiet Deadmond home up and retreating.

He would've grabbed a butcher knife to take along, as well, but it was missing from the maple knife block on the kitchen counter.

"THEY POISON THE HEART"

by Michelle Brooke Deadmond

(an excerpt)

Soon they tracked the hunted Sauk warrior northward to Prairie du Chien, Wisconsin, where finally he surrendered and was taken prisoner at Fort Crawford, thus becoming government property and a 'trophy' of war to be put on display.

Exhausted, and sick at heart, the 65-year-old Indian chief spoke in chains at the Prairie du Chien fort, standing shackled upon the original ceded lands of his great Sauk ancestors, his long resistance at an end now. The speech he gave that day told of lies and betrayal, of the deliberate, systematic extermination of his people. It would become Black Sparrow Hawk's

~~ Coda ~~

"I fought hard," he professed before his captors. "But your guns were well aimed. The bullets flew like birds in the air . . . my warriors fell around me." His discourse shifted to admonishment. "You know the cause of our making war. It is known to all white men. They ought to be ashamed of it." He went on to tell of a campaign of greed and broken trust, murder, and of those who had perpetuated it. He summed them up aptly: "The white men do not scalp the head. But they do worse—they poison the heart."

393

With the sun setting on him, the old warrior said his goodbyes.

"Farewell, my nation. Black Hawk tried to save you, and avenge your wrongs. He drank the blood of some of the whites. He has been taken prisoner, and his plans are stopped. He can do no more."

Chief Black Hawk was no angel. Far from it. Indeed, he once was known to stroke women's hair and comment on how fine for scalping it would be. But he showed dignity throughout his captivity until at last he did reconcile with his white enemies and was set free. Even so, Black Hawk never got over being vanquished and forever paid the price for it. What he alluded to in his surrender speech so long ago still resonates today.

He warned of evil, actual evil which pervades our world and poisons hearts. He cautioned not to lose yourself, I think, or let life steal who you are. That when fighting this evil not to let it take your humanity from you and turn your heart into darkness. To instead see it for what it is. And then to make your stand, even when all hope seems lost.

Each of us has a part to play—where we ultimately come to be depends on the choices we make, and upon those we choose not to.

After his death in 1838, Black Hawk's burial site was desecrated and his remains stolen. His fitful bones were moved from place to place over the next several years, ending up in an old historical museum. The building itself inexplicably caught fire and burned to the ground one night. It is believed Black Hawk's remains were consumed in the peculiar blaze, and no longer exist . . .

CHAPTER TWENTY-FIVE

I

THEY PARKED IN the cover of the trees and made their way across Jasper Park, out over its baseball diamond, through the foreboding shadows on the other side. There was scant light here, a few lampposts lining the bike path, some safety lights on at the red-brick shelters. Dark of the new moon, no illumination visible through the cloud cover in the sky, no pulse of stars.

On edge, Tommy and Richard milled about. The wooden bat hovered in Franklin's two-handed grip.

Tree frogs were croaking in the river birches overhanging the water—the exfoliating bark on the trees looked like peeling skin at this distance. Besides frogs, a chorus of crickets could be heard chirring in the dewy grass, their evensong waning, getting weaker with the cold. That sound alone was heartbreaking to Richard, signified the inescapable death of summer, an oncoming winter.

Tommy noticed the way his friend throttled the bat, the way he stared to the left, the right.

"Come on," Rich murmured under his breath. He looked at the hundred-year-old sugar maples above them, still majestic, standing sentinel like when they were boys. Richard remembered that feeling of how nothing bad could happen to them here, how safe . . . and *invincible* they always felt back then beneath their vigilant watch. The maple trees seemed to promise no harm would ever befall them, whispering it through their leaves on warm, velvet summer nights all those years ago. But he didn't have that feeling now.

Tommy no longer possessed a watch, so he asked the time. Squinting at his wrist in the dark, Richard said, "A little past midnight," then went silent, mouth tight. *Past midnight . . . September twenty-ninth.*

"Michelle's birthday," he thought aloud. "Today. This is it." Truitt didn't reply. "I smell wild onions growing somewhere," said Richard, "do you?"

"No. I don't smell anything."

Richard shifted his weight. "Huh."

Lightning flashed beyond the clouds and ochre light blossomed, illuminating the Rock River and its steep mossy banks. Thunder rolled echoingly. *"Come on."*

Truitt leaned close to him. "My Aunt Cass used to pray for me. Tells me for years and years, 'Do something with your life, Thomas. Make a difference.' She even said it when she gave me this cross. Well . . . I'm doing something, you pesky old broad. How do you like it?" He grunted. Laughed.

Richard cleared his throat. "Um, thanks for coming with me, Tom—"

All of a sudden the noises stopped—no crickets, no more frogs. No wind in the leaves. Silence. As if a switch had been thrown. Richard swiveled, blinking, and sucked in his breath.

From out of the darkened treeline, shapes emerged.

"Look."

They came like vapor, indistinct in the night gloom, passing through shadowy trees as though shadows themselves. There was something about their movement as they approached, an *otherness*, was all Richard could think . . . and he wondered if he'd gone completely mad as he watched, saucer-eyed.

Not alive. "Tom?"

"I see them."

One of the shapes was feminine, Richard sensed, the one that lingered toward the rear, stepping carefully. White-gray, obscured from view. They were bringing something with them—*something*—among their spectral ranks.

Dark-winged things flapped overhead and Richard and Tommy flinched away from the invisible wingbeats. When they straightened, their eyes went again to the figure inside that scattering of gauzy revenants. It looked semi-human. Humanlike, but not quite. Limping, jostled about. Shambling forward.

Lightning daggered the sky and Richard uttered: "Oh, my bleeding *Christ*."

It was Julian Simon, gibbering incoherently, drools of slaver hanging, his camel-hair clinging to him in gory shreds. The old man lumbered into what light there was and they saw how the body had been traumatized, face ruined.

You . . . you! thought Richard. *What in God's name?*

The pastor held a wood box in his torn hands, bearing it before him as he crossed the murky park in lurches, drawing nearer with his usurpers around him. The revenants came on, unspeaking. Their fleeting forms appeared emaciated; cheekbones jutting, clothes draped over creaking bones and grayish skin, their sockets deep and dark. Steam rose off them as they warmed from the insides out.

Seeing things out here, insisted that inner voice of Richard's. *Imagination playing tricks.* Yet a shudder invaded him, a twinge of primeval dread. He gulped cool air—it stopped in his throat when he got a clear look at Julian.

The Reverend's black tongue lolled, and a hank of his scalp with one ear attached had been ripped away, dangled by fleshy strings alongside his face like a grotesque Halloween mask blown loose. Nestled within the still-warm flap he saw the bat. It came crawling out of his raw, bloody scalp and made clicking sounds, then the damnable thing took to wing and flew off with its nighttime brethren.

"Flittermouse," declared Simon in a tittering voice, rheumy eyes roving in their red skull like caged beasts. He stumbled, dropping the dark-streaked calamander box he held and dumping its contents all over the ground. Richard caught a glimpse of the spilled offerings, saw what looked nightmarishly like a human fetus flip into the shadows. Someone's cobalt-blue eyeball skittered at his feet. His stomach constricted, gorge rising even as the raggedy pastor limped another two steps and pitched headlong into the dirt, limbs quaking.

Horrified, Richard heard himself say: "Jesus, *what*—where is Katie? *What's happened?*" Paralysis gripped him, and an awful thought chilled his soul, mixing shame with his fear and shrinking him.

They're mine now. I awakened them, raised them and bound them together, by the darkest of rites. They belong to me . . .

The legion of dead travelers halted. Stood unmoving, soiled and silent, smudged faces uplifted. Richard smelled damp earth, saw blue concentration camp ink tattooed onto some of their forearms; rope burns around one revenant's neck, the one that carried the leather-bound Bible. Julian was crawling across the ground, bringing his mutilations with him. Richard swallowed back rising terror and shook his head.

"No—"

Finally he spotted his daughter being shepherded forward, led by her small hand by the protective feminine shape he'd seen trailing the others. Katie Jane clutched her mother's urn to her. She appeared unharmed at first glance. She felt her way, Michelle's winter scarf covering her eyes, trusting the presence of the young Jewish woman to guide her, because she could not see for herself.

Thank you, Lord, Richard prayed, relief washing over him. *Oh, thankyouthankyou and all your everlasting Saints, for* that.

The female revenant was unclothed, and mournfully frail, her gaunt nakedness livid in the shadows: a crippled young mother who once—head shaven and body broken—had exhaled her final breath into the mouth of her asphyxiating infant as she cradled and rocked it and sang it to uttermost sleep. The stark sight of her slammed their hearts like the crush of a battering ram.

Along the bike path the lampposts buzzed and flickered.

Richard swore he heard the faintest lilt of a lullaby in the stillness, the most beautiful lullaby ever sung, surely, although the woman's lips did not move. She drifted near, brought Katie directly to him, reuniting daughter safely with father. Then she withdrew. Richard fell to his knees and snatched Katie in his arms, tugged her to him desperately, kissing her hair. He pulled down the scarf, searched her face, her eyes, asking over and over if she was all right.

"Yes, Daddy," said Katie, her breath coming in short hitches, squeezing him close with one arm. "I'm all right. She said you'd find me."

Richard bit back tears and kissed her round face, not comprehending. Only knowing that he had his daughter in his arms once more. That was enough. He stared up at the ashen deliverers, kneeling before the young naked woman and clutching Katie tightly to him. "Thank you," he whispered, "all of you. I . . . I don't know what else to say."

The figures stood mute, rooted, no movement among them, no cognizance—rictal mouths, hollow gazes, that was all. *Can they see me?* wondered Richard. When he could look on their wretchedness no longer, he turned away, before the sins of history could descend upon him. He hadn't anticipated this, no, had never expected anything like . . . like *this.*

"Richie," Tom said low, "the dismissal. Dismiss them, Rich."

He got to his feet, dazed, unsteady, grasping Katie's wrist and leaving the baseball bat on the ground. With his free hand Richard made motions in the air, tracing out the powerful symbols the witch-woman had shown him, charting the release which would come. He took a long breath and spoke the words in reverence. *"Alav hashalom ... "* Said it again, with greater effort: *"Alav hashalom."* The undoing of the magic had commenced.

May you rest in peace.

There was no response from the wasting revenants, just so many shadow-clad souls frozen in place. But they began to cloud over, to fade slowly from sight until they were insubstantial. Phantoms made of mist. Then those too were gone, given up the ghost, leaving only smoke and gloom.

Unsupported, the German print Bible fell to the earth as Simon Julian had done, skeletal finger marks visible, *seared* into its leather cover. Richard blinked in the dim light, blinked a second time.

The night sounds were returning, the crickets and frogs, the continual flow of the river nearby in the blackness, filling the night. Richard squeezed Katie's wrist to make sure she was there, that it wasn't all some dream.

All that remained was the Reverend, babbling senselessly, twisting his maimed body over the ground. "Well played," he warbled, "oh ... well played," and laughed.

Tommy said, "We have to finish him. Put an end to it."

"I know." *But, how does—?*

Richard drew Katelyn aside, thinking of what to say to her, thinking about the task at hand: the elimination of the horrid old pastor. The separation of his spirit from flesh—invisible silver threads and all that. Before he could speak, he noticed Tommy peering towards the woods, the color draining from his face. Tom pointed.

***

A pocket of underbrush rustled stealthily, and a little red fox with half a tail pushed its way unnoticed between the bushes and hunkered down in deep shadow to watch the goings-on with keen oval pupils, its chin resting on its forepaws.

2

"Something's out there."

"What is it?" Richard stared hard, scanning the copse of trees. "They're coming back?"

All he could see were massive tree trunks in the dark, in looming rows. Until lightning flashed, that is, and the trunks seemed to come alive and move, human shapes disengaging from the blackness, striding their way as thunder grumbled and shook the land.

"My ass, they are," said Tommy. "Looks like the Unwelcome Wagon found us."

"Fuck *me*."

Tommy blew out a breath. "Maybe later, after dinner and a show." One of his hands lingered at his belt.

There were a half dozen of them. One emerged from behind the red-brick shelters, the rest out of the treeline. Richard picked up George's prize bat and shot a glance at the Blazer, its front end visible where they'd left it, but it was too far to try and run. They backed away, scrutinizing Jasper Park and its shadows, the stand of aging timber surrounding them. Richard's head throbbed. He kept Katelyn shielded, blocking her off behind Tommy and himself.

"Ach," oozed the pastor through dirt and bile, "it's

good for you. Good for all the mongrels." He groped along. "The cattle cars await!" Facedown, he touched his Bible, feeling of its binding. "O, pray for these *mongrel* sinners."

The dark outlines advanced, moving farther into the light, and Richard's heart caught in his chest. One of the figures was that of a woman, a large dog next to her—

"Granna," Katie said remotely.

Glee Deadmond stopped walking, heeling Blondie at her side. Behind her came the bearded Dr. Mint and matronly church organist Mrs. Bluedorn from Nain Trinity Lutheran, and the Sallow Man . . . or Croom . . . *whoever* in hell he was, trench coat hanging on his scarecrow frame. Panic squeezed Richard's lungs.

Tommy eyed Croom. "Owen?"

Another form approached, someone Richard had never seen, a balloon of a man with a shovel on one shoulder. It made him think of the church service that crazy night, Glee's suggestion about marching guilty offenders out into the fields with lye and their own shovels. His mother-in-law's *Cornfield Solution*. This newcomer wore what appeared to be a Civil War uniform, his belly sagging out of it, one shirttail untucked and a gray cap on askew. He had a saber in a sheath at his belt.

"*Mikey?*" said Truitt, dumbfounded, and Rich recalled the cousin he'd spoken of, the Civil War reenactor. "Have you lost your mind? What the Christ *is* this?"

The Confederate soldier grunted, lifting his cap and adjusting it. "You shoulda joined up with us, Tommy, when you had the chance. Asswipe."

Richard thought: *Does he mean the reenactment group or The Glee Club?* He stifled a hysterical laugh, searching the park for the American Indian, Salt, desperate to spot him. To settle scores. He saw Chip Priewe coming into the light next, head rotating nervously, looking as though he might jump out of his skin. His pistol was in his hand.

Choking up on the baseball bat, dread in his guts, Richard steeled himself and got ready to swing. Before he could even breathe, however, his mother-in-law opened her mouth.

"Did you enjoy what you saw last night? In our bathroom?" came Glee's taunt, her purse over one arm; Blondie whimpered. "Your eyes crawling over my naked flesh . . . did you wish you could fuck me right then, Richard? Fuck me hard and good, the way you used to fuck my dead daughter? My beautiful Brookie?"

Richard's jaw fell. Appalled, he heard Tommy say grimly: "I don't want to punch your ticket for you, but I will, Mike. In a heartbeat." Truitt had reached into his waistband and was holding something low.

A sharp burning smell floated from across the river, something on fire somewhere in the night. Richard faltered backwards a step. He could hear distant sirens. At last he was able to speak. "Were you in on it, Glee? Did you have your own daughter murdered because of the Rev there? Just because that perverted fuck *said* so? How's the senate campaign?"

Glee cringed as if struck, cheek twitching. The others moved nearer in a wide semicircle. With nowhere else to retreat, Richard and Tom began drifting toward the old gallows tree, into the contorted shadows cast by it, keeping little Katie aligned behind them. The guy in the Civil War getup pushed forward, got too close, and Tommy feinted one direction and then dropped him with a short, wicked back-elbow jab to the throat. His cousin went down, losing his hat and shovel, stayed hunched there in gagging fits, fighting for air. Priewe jerked, gun hand jittery.

"Warned you," Tommy said.

Katie was murmuring, distress in her voice. "Daddy?"

"Everything's fine, hon," Richard told her, bat upraised. "Fuzzy-peachy." But a sick fear had enveloped him: they were being boxed in. As his panic deepened he felt his heart ramp out of control, the rhythm of it drumming inside his skull. He'd gone cold, gripped the wooden handle of the All-Star bat so tightly that both hands were numb, in fact. All the while backing steadily away, safeguarding Katie behind this physical barricade of theirs.

Too soon. I dismissed them too damn soon.

They came to an abrupt standstill under the tortured-looking Eastern cottonwood, pressed against it, nothing but the steep riverbank drop-off beyond that. Richard stumbled over the tree's thick roots. Swore, hefted the bat.

"Daddy," insisted Katelyn, pushing something upward at him. It was the urn: Michelle's ashes. "Daddy? Let her fly, Daddy . . . " He gaped at her.

Lightning flickered again, illuminating those assembled beneath the canopy of trees. Owen glared, his eyes like blisters in the fleshy hoods of his drooping face, watching everything. Dr. Mint withdrew a hypodermic syringe from his suit vest and popped the cap off the needle. Julian was trying to flip himself over, they could see, dribbling half-heard words into the grass. His raw fingers turned open the Bible's cover.

Rain had begun to patter down, and with it came a single, blood-speckled hawk feather wafting alone, spiraling slowly as it fell from the black tree branches above.

3

"Look out!" Richard shouted, too late, and William Salt descended like death.

Witnessing the hideous state of the Ghost Reverend, waiting as long as he dared for the others, Salt threw himself down upon them from his hiding place. He dove out of the gnarled tree and went for the strongest first, falling on Thomas Truitt, seeking to dispatch him quickly.

In his large fist he wielded the Sauk war hatchet, one of its two hawk feathers intact.

Tommy spun in shock as the bare-chested Salt slashed crossways twice with the small ax, forehanded and back. The blade caught flesh and Tommy cried out. Something went flying from his hand into the shadows. Then Salt was driving his prey to the ground, triumphant, rearing back with his razored hatchet high—

That's when Richard unfroze and lunged frantically, screaming and bringing the baseball bat in a vicious downward arc on the Indian's arm from behind. There was a dull snap, followed by an exclamation of pain. The tomahawk fell and he saw

Salt's right arm wrenched at an improbable angle, a nub of jagged white bone poking from it. Richard inhaled. Salt clutched his shattered forearm in disbelief, squeezing with his other hand as if trying to compress the broken bone back in.

Tommy was down, hurt in the dark and panting, an inflated Confederate soldier on all fours retching not far from him.

Tom, Richard wanted to call out, but his throat was locked.

The rest of the semicircle crowded in. The Sallow Man extended one arm and pointed at him through the taps of cold rain, his hydrocephalic head glistening. Dismay rose in Richard's chest at the sight. "Breeding time," said the malignity which was Simon Julian—the malignant tenant inside, rather—inch-worming himself closer.

Salt pivoted, bared to the waist, turning a murderous gaze on Richard. His muscled torso heaved, bleeding right arm dangling. He bent for the war ax and straightened with it in his left. Grimaced as he came . . . kept coming . . .

Blondie growled and strained against her leash, hackles raised, and suddenly she exploded forward, dragging Glee down and breaking away, leaping, sinking teeth into Salt's side. The huge Indian man grunted and reeled, his flesh ripping in the German shepherd's jaws.

He twisted loose somehow and cocked his weight back, pushing off and kicking with all his might. The savage punt connected with Blondie's ribcage and catapulted her, actually hurling the old dog against the massive tree trunk. Blondie flailed and let out a terrible shrieking squeal, bounced once, her body landing heavily on the knotty roots beneath the cottonwood. She continued to yelp in anguish.

"NO!" Katie wailed, and Richard thought simultaneously. He charged in and swung, teeth clamped, aiming for Salt's ponytailed skull this time. Salt deflected the blow by raising his shoulder and letting it take the brunt. The man snarled wildly even as Richard let the bat rebound back and then brought it downward, clubbing Salt's knee and feeling his arms vibrate with the satisfying crack.

"Bastard!" said Glee. She'd found her footing and stumbled at them, clawing one hand into her purse, seizing something, pulling it out. Steel glinted as Richard turned. Glee drew back the butcher knife she clutched—

God no, not this way. Not . . . this.

—and plunged it into William Salt's broad back, right to the handle. The American Indian bellowed in guttural surprise, his eyes flung wide, the air abandoning his lungs.

"You killing bastard," she muttered, and Salt wheeled on her, slamming his hatchet-filled fist across her face. Glee's head rocked back and she crumpled hard. Began to moan, began groping for her eyeglasses.

The spinning motion threw Salt off balance, his injured knee giving out. Richard stood flummoxed a moment. He came in again.

"Don't!" someone barked as Salt staggered, trying to reach back and pull out the knife stuck in him. "Stop moving or I'll shoot." It was Priewe, his revolver swinging this way and that. "Help the Reverend up."

Richard froze, his legs losing their strength. He hit the uneven ground and slid behind the cover of the tree's trunk, yanking Katie with him. But she leaned away, terror-stricken, pulling towards where Blondie lay on her side, paws thrashing feebly.

Crying, Katelyn knelt by the writhing dog. Richard huddled with her under the giant hanging tree. He touched the leash. Reached and touched Blondie's silver-peppered muzzle, brushing bits of leaves from her whiskers. She twitched. Her nose was warming, the eyes glazing. She'd voided her bowels and bladder in the rain.

Dying, a mental voice careened through his head, *just like Michelle did. No. Jesus, nonononoo.*

"No," said Richard, teeth gritted. Her tongue had fallen out of her mouth. He pushed it back in between her jaws. "*Ah.* Hell." It fell out again, and his hand came away trembling.

"Rich," Tommy spoke thickly in the near-darkness, "he got me. Fucker got me good, Richie . . . " Thunder rumbled in over his words. " . . . gonna *kill* that fuck, I am."

Hell. "Hang on, Tom." It was all he could think to say, but his voice wavered. He had no idea what to do. He risked a sidelong glance at them, eyes flicking from one to another. Mrs. Bluedorn had drawn a huge pair of metal sewing scissors out of her clothing, from between her rouged breasts, the bun in her hair tighter than the smile on her ratty-rouged face. She ran the blades along her fingertips, slipping thumb and digits through the rings. Richard stared, transfixed.

"Naughty boy," said the church organist, snipping air with the big scissors. "So naughty."

Katie shoved the cremation urn into Richard's arms with a final, forceful thrust.

"Let her fly," his daughter repeated. "Do it, Daddy." She was turning back to Blondie, her eyes stinging, her round face dirtied. She hugged the dog to her and lifted its head and rocked with it in her grasp.

Like a man in a fevered dream, unblinking, Richard shifted away with the urn and twisted off the lid. He half-straightened, looking for Prick-we and trying to keep his wits together, listening for whispery guidance from the sugar maples: "We won't leave you," he heard Katie sniffle through her tears, "will not leave you here."

All at once Glee began to shriek. Richard saw Simon on top of her, their hands grappling, thrashing—a tangle of limbs. The Reverend was *biting* her. Chewing on her face as Glee shrieked deep in her throat.

Hell, hell, hell . . .

His chest burned white-hot. Strength ebbing out of him, Richard rose on weary legs and flung the ashes into the air, loosing them in one enormous, smoky plume. Priewe got a bead on him, aiming with both hands. Then his dead wife's remains were raining down, and scattering, roiling back to earth around him. The semicircle hesitated, eyes in the air. Richard recapped the vessel and crouched. He might've sobbed.

Lying in the chill shadows, Tom brought his knee to his chest and kicked out sharply. Richard heard the sound of Confederate Mikey's jaw breaking like a cannon shot, watched Tom's cousin, who'd been struggling to stand, go facedown instead and vomit again. The police chief's gaze skipped away, aim disrupted.

"Stay down, asswipe," he heard Tommy say, saw him hoisting himself to a sitting position, shaggy-headed, pressing the gray soldier's cap to his neck. Saw blood in the dim light . . . *blood* . . . as an ice-cold wind keened through the park and shook its timber, ripping at the leaves.

Hearing his friend's rebellious voice, and feeling a sudden burst of adrenaline because of it, Richard seized that brief window of opportunity and surged forward, booting the cannibalistic pastor full in the side of his skull. The impact jolted him and Richard lost his footing. The copper urn rolled to the ground. Julian's head snapped violently and he groaned, releasing his lock on Glee. Richard caught sight of his lacerated scalp-and-ear tearing the rest of the way off and flying free as he slipped and fell in the mud, saw it sail like a fucking toupee through the veil of rain and settling human ash. His stomach lurched.

He scrambled out and wrested Glee away, dragging her closer. She'd lost one shoe, and her nose looked broken. Her tumbled hair was disarranged. Face bloody, moaning weakly.

William Salt sank to both knees, remained slouched there in the rainstorm, motionless, the butcher knife still in his back. Katie had begun to hum gently the way she and Michelle used to do together. The wind raged, rattling branches, churning the heavy gnarling tree above them and driving freezing rain into their slitted eyes.

Someone was screaming. Screaming to all hell and gone in the night.

CHAPTER TWENTY-SIX

I

THEY **SWUNG TO** witness Chip Priewe's demented features, to see him pointing with the pistol and backing away. Soon everyone was looking, gazes upturned. The high wind which buffeted the trees and tore across the shadowed ground had caught Michelle's cremains up, and up, keeping them aloft. Lifting and throwing them around with leaves and other bits of debris. Denying them respite—

Out of this blizzard of swirled grit and ash, uncannily, *shapes* were forming.

"The trees!" Priewe screamed, spittle flying from his mouth. His lunatic eyes shone moon-bright. "Oh, Christ. Hanging . . . in the trees. *Can't you fucking see them?"*

They did: apparitions in the night-dark limbs of the cottonwood. Something glimmering in the sleety rain. Thunder crashed and everyone jumped, lightning skittering throughout the clouds. The police chief howled.

Shadows were coming to life in the tree branches, undulating with an inner light. Changing particle and position, reconfiguring. But these weren't the bodies of the convicted and hanged, oh no. Priewe swayed on his feet, reciting desperate litanies as he watched. Richard saw them, too.

Madness! a warning went off, jarring him: That's what they call it. Full-blown, going around the bend. *Perfect.*

Dr. Mint suddenly hurtled forward with menace, the Sallow Man alongside of him, dragging his wasted leg to keep up. They came as one, closing the distance; Richard awoke with a gasp and fumbled in panic for the baseball bat. Owen made his move then, whipping a short length of electrical cord around the doctor's throat in a blink. He tightened it to the bone, kicked Mint's legs out from underneath him. His grayish-yellowy eyes met Richard's as he garroted the bearded man from behind, placing one knee into Minty's back and winding the cord up, wrenching it with his good arm. The medical examiner uttered a strangled screech and his mouth broadened hideously. Bones could be heard splintering. The hypodermic dropped from his clawing dead fingers within seconds. Richard exhaled through his teeth, saw his breath vaporize.

He could've broken me in two on those church steps, could have ended me with that one arm alone if he'd wanted. Wheee . . .

Truitt was feeling around through the wet grass. Owen bent near him, heard Tom muttering, "Help me find it, help—" but could see nothing in all that secretive darkness.

A noise rose from behind, whimpers carrying against the biting wind. "Daddy! *Daddeee!*" Richard moved to his daughter, saw Blondie convulsing on the ground and Katie trying to hold the German shepherd's body still. *"Please."* He lowered himself to help, his head swimming, and Croom was there. Shoulder to shoulder with him. Laying ghost-white hands next to Richard's, keeping the dog down. Rich stared in wonderment at this, at being so close to his bleached, misshapen visage.

He remained wary. Fearful even.

Katie placed her small left hand on Blondie's caved ribcage, splaying her fingers as wide as they'd go in the fur. They watched her face across from them as she frowned in concentration, her eyes changing hue. Richard pulled away slightly. Blinked to clear his vision.

Her pinky finger and the one next to it draped over two of Owen's withered fingers. Her humming grew.

Beneath the gallows tree Katelyn began drawing it, began *siphoning* the trauma out of the dying animal. Coaxing it into herself. Taking control of this raving, chaotic thing. Unfazed by the magnitude of her endeavor, the girl paused long enough for her eerie gaze to alight on her father's dripping face.

She's doing it, Richard thought, moving backward. *By God if she isn't . . . really doing it.*

Katie reached, extending her other arm out behind her, fingers stretching to touch the cottonwood's base. Seeking contact now, discharge: some substitute life form, another source of live energy whereby to be rid of its chaos. She stretched and let the raving thing flow through her as though she were a conduit.

Something rang out. A gunshot? Followed by more, together with the police chief's screams. "Too late," Priewe cried, driven over the brink at last, eyes rolling in his head. He stumbled and broke into a run, firing the pistol back at the spectral intruders as he fled. "Too late. Piss shit! *Piss—FUCK!*"

"Get down!" Richard hollered, startled into motion, shielding Katie in the confusion. Bullets whizzed by; one hit the great tree and ricocheted above them. Bark flew. *"Christ!"*

Then the police chief was away, vanishing into the opposite treeline, his gun dry-clicking as he went.

Richard stood up, his heart in his throat. He dug out the cell phone. "That's it," he said, glancing to Tom.

Tommy told him, *"Don't."* He'd tipped over, eyes staring skyward. Richard moved his gaze with him.

The motes convening among the branches resembled *people* in the rain. Some swanned gracefully. Others billowed, their tendrils coiling. All were descending as if from the heavens. Men, women—old and young. Coming down around them, rippling like static-charged fabric. They had begun to shimmer, giving off hints of what they once might've been as Richard watched, wholly mesmerized.

Woman-forms and man-forms touched to earth, emitting greens and whites and violets, their arms spreading, creating a circle of radiance. *Protecting us,* he realized. Glimmering like diamonds, come to keep the monsters sent against them at bay. Richard's breath plumed. He put his phone away and shivered, soaked to the bone. His eyes opened wider.

One of the apparitions was that of his departed wife. He recognized traces of her there . . . and yet *not* there.

Richard moaned as it hit home, reeling his mind with possibilities beyond the realm of anything he could hope to understand: *The ashes, they're—it's her.*

415

WILLIAM GORMAN

It's Michelle. *And she isn't alone. Others came . . . a host of dead others from the cremators. All those who burned and intermingled with her. I see a mangled young man killed in an industrial accident, and a woman who obviously died while pregnant; police investigator there in his dapper three-piece, the old fisherman with his oilskins still on, a teenage schoolgirl who was bullied into—Jesus, no—bullied into slitting her own wrists. I can see them. I* know *their stories. Mother of God.* He did sob then.

Mrs. Bluedorn fell back as smoky tendrils reached for her. Tommy's cousin lifted up from the vomit-sodden ground, incomprehension filling his eyes. They cringed away, their rain-streaked faces manic.

The wind came up around the figures, sang *through* them. A large dog barked once, sharp and lone and distinct.

Richard saw Katie taking her hand from the gnarled, distended tree trunk. No fanfare, no lightning, thunder. Just Blondie standing on her own with her ears flat, sniffing the air, restored—like little Joey Spencer—and Owen looking curiously at his pallid hand in the shadows, shaking his head.

And his only daughter beneath the tree, her mother's scarf around her neck, hair tangled and wet and her cheeks flushed in defiance.

"It's trapped," Katie said, "it can never get out. I trapped it." She'd balled her hands into tiny fists. Richard's heart swelled.

"Brookie," said Glee. She was on her haunches in the mud, hands over her bloody face, compelled by the spectacle. "I didn't know. Oh, my beautiful Brookie." She began to mewl hoarsely.

416

Richard drifted toward Michelle's iridescence. It was neither solid nor living. Couldn't be real, he knew . . . but it was her nonetheless. He could smell her, taste her on the rain. Katie moved nearer also, the rejuvenated dog trailing behind.

"Mom," Katie whispered, pearl-gray color flooding her irises. She placed a hand into the small of her father's back even as Richard strove to reach out and grasp his dead wife's misty arm.

Someone said: "Well, isn't this touching." It was Julian. His gristly body had raised itself, the entity within driving it. Hoisting it vertical. An exhalation issued forth and Richard rocked back on his heels.

"Fledermause," said Simon, red-skulled, hideous, his finger bones clicking. *"Jetzt kommen."* The bats came then. Dozens upon dozens. Came swooping out of the trees and the night at his call.

"No," Richard uttered.

The din of oncoming leathery wings thrummed, low at first, growing impossibly loud. It blotted out all else as the bats dived and darted, making for the ring of bright figures. *Aiming* for them, spinning and weaving, flying in, flying out. Opening gaps in them. They sought to dash apart these spirit remnants, it was apparent.

They had begun doing so.

Richard wailed. He swung the wood bat overhead blindly but connected with nothing. Finally he relented, ducking away from the bedeviled swarm, his voice rising and falling in despair. He covered Katie's head and pushed her lower. Everyone else had gone low, as well, trying to avoid the havoc above them. Bats filled the park, summoned here somehow, mayhem fueling their rush. The high-pitched clicks and wingbeats grew unbearable.

Salt remained still as stone, no sign of movement. Head bowed in the sleet. Glee's kitchen blade buried deep in him.

There were hundreds now—the nighttime brethren returned. They dipped and slashed, cutting through the curtain-like remnants, wheeling in midair and coming around to strike again, tearing the circle apart. Undoing them. Scatters of light danced, their motes extinguishing like dying fireflies. Richard reached for his wife, saw the luminous woman-face turn toward him, filaments of color draining out of her. But all was lost.

The guardians' static-charged fabric blew loosely in bereaved tatters, shredding. Fragments turned black and swirled away. Destroyed. It was done.

Julian's winged maelstrom dispersed in all directions and was gone as quickly as it'd come. Pieces of spirit fabric still skittered, continuing to lose their luster and to darken. Fluttering up into the heavy branches where they clung like trembling leaves—

Along with the large black moths already there.

The glacial winds had dropped, lashing rain changing over to spitting snow. Richard straightened and inhaled the last of Michelle's essence as it dissipated into nothingness. Then she was gone, too, and all that was left of this cruelty were the snowflakes kissing his face, the things perched darkly in the trees. He closed his eyes and swayed, breathing in and out. He heard Glee sobbing nearby.

"No more of *that*," Simon Julian tut-tutted. Richard opened his eyes and stared in horror.

The pastor hung suspended in the air before him,

four feet off the ground, as if caught up in invisible wires. Some deep-hidden, primal alarm registered within Richard and his innards convulsed. *We're going to die here,* he thought. His hands tightened around the bat's wooden grip.

Julian said, "Rise, my lambs . . . my darlings." His long fingers lightly danced as if conducting a symphony, and a chill licked its way up Richard's backbone. Mrs. Bluedorn and Tom's cousin were inching upright on either side, their bravado returning. Mikey drew his saber from its sheath.

Croom had reappeared at Richard's side. Julian saw him and ceased his motions.

"Chicken farmer," he said, floating obscenely. He extended his head at them, his neck elongating. "I'll deal with you soon enough. But first things first, mongrels. Inbred mongrel sinners.

"Bring me the girl, *Prarsheen.* Fetch her to me. I want my pet *now.*"

With that, and the terror that it struck, they saw William Salt struggling to rise.

2

"Too late, piss *shit* . . . " mumbled Priewe as he untwisted the wire coat hanger and straightened its length. His shaking hands poked the metal tip into the vent hole, rammed it down again and again, trying to breach the cannon's powder charge—airtight, compact, the gunpowder as fresh as the day it was last loaded—the charge he hoped was still there, like that retired history-buff Navy prick Jack Lawrie always claimed it was.

If need ever be.

The police chief discarded the pried-open hanger and brushed snow out of his hair. He slid a folded sheaf of typewriter paper from his back pocket and rolled it up as tight as he could for his touch-paper, stuffing one end all the way down into the vent hole at the back of the old Civil War cannon until it stopped. He took out a lighter and began flicking it.

"Chief?"

Priewe jumped, nearly screamed. It was Palm Clemency; the black man looked unwell, looked about to be sick all over himself.

"Where've you been?" his deputy chief asked, voice strained. "You haven't checked in, haven't answered the radio once. We've been calling all night. Your wife told us—"

"You," Priewe said. "Get away from me, you."

They stood in silence on the grass in front of Memorial Hall in the windblown flurries.

Palm cleared his throat. "Town's falling apart, Chief. I've never seen anything like this. People are missing. We got multiple arson calls . . . and killings. *Killings*, Chief. Lillian Van Meers was shot to death in her store tonight, and Phil Jenrette's wife threw acid in his face. Then burned his privates off with it. He might not survive. The little Putnam baby is dead. *Again.*" He swallowed to keep his uniform from ruination. "Kid's great-uncle suffocated him, while the great-aunt slept in the next room. Calls keep coming. We can't handle—do you even hear what I'm saying?"

Priewe flicked the lighter, trying *not* to hear him. He touched the flame to the makeshift fuse poking out. When it ignited he stepped in front of the cannon, stared into the barrel's bore and waited. He licked his lips.

"What the hell are you doing? Here, you shouldn't do that."

The twisted-up papers burned down, went out, their edges fizzling just outside the vent hole. Priewe hurried to relight it, but the fire wouldn't take. His lighter started to sputter. "Goddamn it. *Piss shit!*" Dropping the lighter, he drew his revolver and dumped the cylinder, started reloading it, pushing the brass shells in slowly, shakily. Until all six chambers were filled.

Palm watched. "Is it true, Chief?" he whispered. "What Tom Truitt said about . . . about Ollie Echols?"

He whipped the cylinder shut and swung the gun at Clemency. "I said get *away* from me, nigger," Priewe said, and his bewildered deputy chief obeyed.

Priewe pivoted and pointed the weapon towards the vent hole, towards the singed, curled paper smoldering at the rear of the cannon. Keeping himself in front of its gorge he placed his right foot up into the wheel spokes, to elevate the angle of his downward aim. He cocked the hammer and squeezed the trigger, sending sparks off the corroded green patina.

Did it again—this second bullet nicked the vent's rim and rang loudly.

Palm moved back. He touched his own holstered gun, shifting, not knowing what to do. His mouth opened to speak but nothing emerged. So he watched instead, flinching with each report, watched Chief Priewe cock his pistol and fire, cock it and fire. Watched him squeeze off a fifth shot, spraying sparks everywhere.

Priewe visibly slumped, hung his head. Laughed. "Too late." A shadow passed over his face. He stepped off the carriage wheel and staggered. "Too late," he gibbered. He turned toward Clemency, raised himself upright before the cannon's throat again, waited a beat and

—an ember came to life inside the vent hole, glowed, the makeshift fuse catching momentarily, flaring, which sent a lone spark leaping into the cold darkness of the firing chamber—

then he said: "The world will die a cesspool of regrets." Priewe lifted the service revolver with its remaining single round and pushed its muzzle hard under his own chin, his expression dead already, his lunatic smile widening. He cocked the hammer back even as Palm Clemency yelled a warning and started forward. Even as that lone spark hit paydirt and set off the two-and-a-half pound charge of black powder packed deep within, blasting a rusted, twelve-pound iron cannonball out the barrel and straight through the side of Chip Priewe's head in the all-engulfing explosion.

The whole sleeping town heard the huge, dormant Union beast as it awakened and recoiled one last roaring, deafening time.

CHAPTER TWENTY-SEVEN

I

SALT BRACED HIMSELF, centered his weight, and began to clamber to his feet. Slowly. First one, then the other. He looked toward the treeline as he did, saw the front end of the Chevy Blazer glinting there like silvery, lupine fangs, its chrome-plated steel grille guard catching light. A shudder wrenched through him. Still he rose, forcing himself erect, the war ax in his left hand.

The others were drawing closer.

Glee snatched at Katie fearfully, nestled her to her side. Croom glared into their faces. He bent, retrieved something near Dr. Mint's fingers: the hypodermic syringe. He held it before him, flicked the plastic tube like he was testing it. *"Gyaa . . . ?"* his disfigured mouth emitted, a bad-natured grin forming. He thumbed the needle's plunger, had placed one foot on the shovel handle. They wavered in uncertainty.

Julian had gone quiet, head back, maimed arms and legs dangling as he levitated higher. Eyeballs rolled to white. He appeared to be in a trancelike state, his mouth slack, the breath coming out rancid.

The river rushed by not ten yards away, oblivious.

Glee forced the heavy square ring off her finger and with difficulty let it drop. She lifted Katelyn and held her in both arms. The Sauk Indian stared at the girl, something desirous in his deep-set eyes. He began to shamble forward, step by sliding step. Coming for her with Glee Deadmond's souvenir in his back.

Right then, far off somewhere, a tremendous explosion rocked the night, shook the land beneath them like a distant bomb blast. Everyone flinched. The Reverend's eyeballs righted into place.

Their hearts seemed to flatten with the concussion, stop dead inside their chests for an instant. Air exited lungs. The lights near the red-brick shelters and along the bike path flickered and went out, came on again.

Tommy saw an opening and crawled for it, drew himself up and clipped the tomahawk out of Salt's grasp, hurling it away. He turned in surprise, saw his war ax flip end over end into the blackness as Tommy attached himself to his leg, grappling to pull him down.

"Kill him," Truitt shouted. Salt kicked at him, limping, finally tugging a darkened survival knife from his belt. Tom punched the man's damaged knee twice and Salt yowled in pain. He pivoted, lifting Aaban Darwish's serrated blade and preparing to stab and cut into pieces this hindrance impeding him.

Tommy looked up and said: *"Kill. Him."*

Richard was there. He swung for the fences, cracking the huge Indian's skull from behind. Salt wheeled around and snarled like a feral beast, his jaws gaped to sink gnashing teeth into flesh. Instead of backpedaling Richard lunged in, met him head-on, eyes blazing. The baseball bat sliced the air and bashed Salt's mouth open in a great gout of blood, sending the

Indian's upper plate flying. He swung again, slammed it backhanded into his torn-open side, heard ribs break like kindling. And there it was, for one fleeting second:

A dazed look of fear crossed Salt's face, raw panic flaring to life inside him. Richard was on him in a heartbeat.

Here it comes. End of the trail, chief. Get ready for it.

The whistling bat took his kneecap apart and Salt crumbled with a screech. His stunned gaze flashed to the Blazer as he went down, to the CPS grille guard sneering in the dappled shadows. Richard was already shifting, taking up the two-handed grip.

Get ready, bastard. Motherfucker. This one's for the dog—

George's prize bat descended, and the bones in Salt's face crunched.

—and this one's for my friend. And this one . . . oh, this one is for my wife, you murdering cocksucking piece of shit fuck, you. And this one. And this—

"You got him, Richie," said Tom, collapsing back. "Finish him. Finish the fucker." One hand groped in the snow-whitened grass.

Glee turned Katie away as the blows rained down, vengeance finding a home at last, each downward arc of the bat ending in a meaty crack and another spluttering grunt of pain. The Confederate looked ready to pounce and Blondie growled, baring her teeth—chalk-pale Croom hooked a thumb across his own throat and no one dared advance.

In stark desperation Salt tried to hurl the knife, but Franklin swatted his arm back with the bat, breaking the wrist, and the throw went awry. He clubbed him viciously then where shoulder met corded neck. The Indian pitched over sideways, doubling up on the ground. He let out an enraged, strangled cry.

Finally Richard spoke through his killing-haze, giving that inner voice vent. "This one's for my wife, goddamn you. My beautiful, sweet, *dying* wife." He brought the baseball bat down with everything he had on Salt's temple. Bone and wood splintered, and both men jerked from the impact. The bat snapped in two as Richard reeled and fell.

"Murderer," he panted. His arms were shaking. His head throbbed dully. "Piece of shit *fuck*."

William Salt lay on his side, mouth and eyes filled with blood. His cheekbones and skull were fractured, cranial fluid leaking; one eye socket in his face looked lower than the other. Ribs staved in, shoulder broken. Arms useless now. Yet he opened his ruined mouth, breath shuddering in and out. Managed to gargle thick syllables which became words.

"Your wife . . . she . . . died in the road. Died . . . squealing in the road . . . like a *bitch* . . . "

He smiled: a nightmare grimace of split, mashed lips and bloody gums. Richard stiffened and clenched his teeth. Got close to him.

"Prarsheen," said Richard tightly, "is *Prairie du Chien*. That's all it means. They're the same thing." He paused to let it sink in. "Playing you all along, prick, leading you by the nose. Feeding you lies. Bullshit. Same with the ax. It came from a goddamn *mail-order catalog*."

Richard watched his face change as the truth permeated, the smile faltering before dropping away completely, saw the blank, red-ravaged mask contort and darken, took delight in seeing it. "You dim-witted, gullible fuck," he jeered. "He sure got his money's worth out of you, didn't he, asshole? Sure saw you coming. Miles away." Richard leaned closer, malice glittering in his eyes. "Who's the bitch now?"

Salt roared and thrust his shattered body off the ground, making a last-ditch grab for him, but it was all he had. His knee gave way. Richard drew out of range and watched him topple, coming down hard on his back. There was a sickening *chuck* sound as he landed fully on Glee's butcher knife and drove it up through himself. Richard gaped. He saw the blade tip sprout from Salt's chest, watched him cough blood and convulse.

Bathed in red, shirtless, his mouth gulped for air. He'd begun to chant something grim and unintelligible.

And then *she* came for him.

2

Only Katie saw the pale little girl moving through falling snowflakes, walking between them, so that none touched her. She stared over Glee's shoulder at her.

William Salt, too, of course. *He* saw . . .

The spindly girl approached out of the shadows. Salt's eyes grew. She stopped and locked gazes with Katelyn for one brief moment before she knelt over the dying man on the ground. Katie saw the bloody crown where her scalp had once been as she lowered herself to him. Then the frail, gray-skinned girl cupped her dirt-filled wormy mouth over Salt's mouth, kissing it, sucking at it hungrily. His ponytailed head whipped from side to side but her small-boned arms clamped it viselike into place.

Rich watched him struggle and kick. Tremors wracked him, his barrel chest spasming, a terrible noise welling up out of him. Salt's bladder and bowels let go. After that, stillness. Life had fled.

The spindly little girl fled also. With her recompense.

"Put me down," Katie told her grandmother. Glee protested and Katie said it again, so Glee put her down.

"Ah. Drowse awhile, and dream of me," lamented Julian, hovering in the murk. "I will sustain you." He glanced from the ill-fated Indian's corpse to the others, his remaining proxies. "Ruby Lee. Michael, dear, are you entirely worthless? Must I become *hands on* yet again? Pull yourselves together. *Do* something."

Katie saw her father shoot alert and straight. The standoff held firm. No moves either way. She crouched and picked up the discarded gold ring with the amber-brown setting, her fist closing over it.

The surge Katie felt was titanic, the emptiness which followed immediate.

Julian's eyes had fastened on Glee. She noticed him leering, hanging unaided in midair, and she spat. The pastor flared his nostrils.

"How common you are. Common female American stock." His flesh-stripped head bobbed at the end of his long neck. "And to think once *you* were my maiden bride of choice."

Glee raised up, one shoe missing, her bitten face on display. "You are *vile*," she said, her hair a crazed nimbus around her, "and your dominion ends here tonight."

428

"Incorrect," Julian challenged, voice echoing. "Preposterous. Don't you know me, Babylon? Harlot?" He lifted his arms and spread them apart. "I am come, and I shall come again. Forever and always. Unto the end of all time."

Biting her lip, Katelyn stood. She clasped her hands together, fingers interlaced around the ring, feeling its dangerous pull. Her eyelids were squeezed shut, head bowed sweetly as if in prayer. She let the darkness course over her, all that aloneness, so vast and devoid of light. Riding in, swallowing her like black sand. Distantly she heard Julian continue:

"I am all that has ever been, or that is, or that ever will be." He came, floating nearer. Katie could visualize this behind her closed eyelids. He resembled a loathsome marionette in motion. "Constant as the stars," the old man recited.

Through tides of blackness Katie saw his image began to crinkle, to change and turn, the ancient thing inside him flexing grotesquely. The airless dark which engulfed her grew thicker, stronger. She gasped to breathe.

Something showed itself then as Julian's façade slipped, something charred and hell-born, festering within: a glimpse of the bestial presence beneath the human skin—a monstrosity was there. It writhed. *Black fibers ran throughout it.* Richard saw double rows of teeth and he tried to cry out. Nothing happened. A choking terror had blocked his throat, it seemed, frozen his blood and marrow. His stomach dropped at the awful unmasking.

But Katie sensed light somewhere in the profound emptiness; fire burning, cleaving that eternity of

429

darkness. She felt it getting brighter. Warming her and blistering her flesh, garlanding her.

"Don't you know?" said what remained of Simon Julian. "Yea, you *will* know me now."

Katie's eyes flashed open. "Hush," she hissed at him, irises morphing, her gaze golden. "Stop that."

The tattered Reverend shape halted short. "What did you say, child?" Curiosity pinched its brow.

Katie's head was buzzing: she tilted it to one side strangely and leaned forward, watching him. *Watcher.* She clenched the heavy ring in her tiny right fist and revelation lit her face. "You're afraid," she said, "aren't you?"

"What?"

"You burned once—you'll burn again." A grin touched Katie's lips. "Afraid. So alone."

The Julian-Thing stared. *"WHAT?"*

Katie snickered. "Don't come any closer."

"You cannot escape me," spoke the marionette clad in bloody strips of camel-hair cloth. Its ardent gaze lingered about her features. "Best to abandon all hopes. They only make things worse, in the end."

"Liar," she said. "You lie." Katie squeezed the gold ring tighter and glowered up at him. Her eyes had narrowed, the grin curving. "Try it and I'll—don't make me *burn* you. Because I can."

Glee circled nervously, witnessing her granddaughter's state. "Katie, don't touch that. Let go of it please. Do you hear? Katie-Smatie?"

"Oh, I'll do it," Katie went on, her small frame taut, her voice no longer quite her own. "*Orchestrator.* Fallen messiah. *Del'ardo.*" Her glare smoldered. "I'll do it. You'll burn . . . *mongrel* . . . "

"Katelyn!" Glee threw herself to slap the ring out of Katie's hand. "Leave it be!" She shook her head until her gaze cleared, became aware, then hurt and frightened. The girl's teeth started clattering as a bone-deep cold gripped her, and Glee knew it wasn't from the sudden temperature drop. She hugged Katie to her. "It's okay, little bit. You're all right."

The Julian-Thing stared adoringly at Katie, eyes half-lidded and oily. Filmy. "O child, you will be mine," it said, quivering with delight. "I have waited so very long for one such as you." A grin of its own was forming, vulturine in nature. "Amazing girl . . . my pet. *You are MINE.*"

The utter desolation of it let loose as the marionette's face began to split, the mouth yawning colossal and black.

***

Richard and Glee stood rooted, their brains overloading, no chance for the circuits to compute this or even react yet. Leftover thunder reverberated beyond the snow-spitting clouds.

The Julian-Thing floated forward. *"YOU WILL WEAR MY MARKS ALL OVER YOU,"* its voice thrummed, *"SO THAT NONE WILL EVER DOUBT TO WHOM YOU BELONG."* A yearning sound expelled from the chasm of mouth, a howl to wake the dead, like that of a lost soul. *"I WILL CALL YOU CLOSE AND YOU WILL REACH FOR ME . . . NO OTHER BUT ME, CHILD."*

It gathered momentum, the receptacle threatening to come apart, the unholy cargo inside seeking to burst free. Bone and gristle stretched to the breaking point, flesh hung in folds.

431

"BEHOLD ME."

Jasper Park vibrated with its foulsome passage.

"MINE."

Richard's foot bumped something and he felt it cling. He looked down. It was the tiny, aborted human fetus he'd seen earlier—perfectly preserved—come crawling back from the shadows and clasping at his shoe now, groping sluggishly like an embryo caked in ice. He screamed and gagged with fright, jerking, almost falling in the snow.

. . . My lambs . . . my darlings.

With an awful cry, he plunged after his only daughter. "Katie, run! *Run!*" But the mutating entity was upon them and he was swept full-force out of its path, flung aside like a sawdust rag doll. Glee likewise. For one millisecond Richard glimpsed something demonic against the sky above him, mottled-black appendages unfolding, wanting to rise toward the heavens, smelled a stench of burnt bodies and sulfur passing by. He landed with a gut-churning jolt. His teeth rattled, and a blinding light exploded in his head so that he saw stars. Nausea followed. Everything started to spin.

The Julian-Thing swooped in under the heavy spreading limbs of the cottonwood tree. Hovering poised above Katie, it reached down and clawed at her, pulled the cowering girl up by her hair until she shrieked. Blondie began barking and snapping rabidly at the charged air.

"Get away from her!" Richard screamed. He fought to stand, struggling upright through a mire of reek and paralysis: it felt like drowning in thick molasses, like trying to surface through stagnant dark waters.

He thought he heard a noise—*crack*—faint and muted somewhere within his fogbound mind. Tree bark went flying.

Crack-crack-crack it came again, in swift succession. Gunfire. Richard saw the horrid marionette creature jerking and hitching in the air, falling. *Falling . . . dear God, yes.* Crashing to earth in spasmodic ruin. It was old Julie once more, transformation denied, his age-corrupted organs pierced, body penetrated by bullets. One had gone clean through his throat.

Richard made it to his feet and ran, still nauseous, clumsy. Slow-witted, he scooped his daughter up around her waist and carried her off. Got clear of the decrepit man-shape on the ground before stumbling and nearly going down himself. He could feel Katie's deep shivers as he held her, realized he had to get her out of the elements quick.

"As you wish," Simon gurgled, causing Richard to turn back. "So be it, mongrels. I can always *resurrect* her later on. Look to me, my pet. *Look at me.*"

Julian had dragged himself, had managed to lift up on one elbow and twist around. Putting flayed fingertips to his flayed lips and kissing them, he said: "Do what you're told. *Looook . . .* "

Katie peeked out from under her father's arm. Richard saw the cadaverous pastor grinning, blood-pink saliva hanging in ropes, saw his stringy hand open as he drew in breath to blow that kiss oh so gently toward them. He murmured something, so that none could ever have her, have what belonged to him, and next instant

crack

came the shot which rocketed through Julian's peeled skull and exited his face, blasting out cheekbone and socket fragments and one eye with it. His body heaved and kicked, his hand dropping, and the deviant kiss died with him in the spattered snow beneath the gallows tree.

Richard blinked in shock. He turned to search the shadows, to try and focus.

Tommy lay on the ground, tightly gripping a .38 caliber snub-nose. His other hand kept the soldier's cap pressed against his neck. His chest was rising and falling, Richard saw, rising, falling, his breath vaporous.

Glee had regained her footing, brushing her hair from her wounded face. The others gawked in a stricken sort of astoundment. Blondie continued to bark.

Finally Tommy let the revolver slip from his fingers—the .38 Special he'd gotten from a freight yard pimp for petty cash and a dinged-up Invicta wristwatch—and he shut his eyes as he sank back flat.

Richard lifted Katie and staggered with her, watching the other two in suspicion, wary of any more danger. He lurched and weaved drunkenly. "Double T," he said in the near-darkness.

But once up close, he could see that Tom Truitt was no longer moving.

3

"You k-killed him," said the Confederate, speech impaired, his jaw unhinged. "You killed the Reverend." The saber fell from his grasp.

They milled around Julian's motionless form, the broken clay pot. Owen sidestepped them, let them proceed past like lost spirits.

Glee was staring hard at the church organist, Mrs. Bluedorn. Watching her. "What did he make you give?" she asked her.

Fear lanced through Richard as he stood over Tommy. Black moths flocked the trees arching above them. More than before—scores now, he noted. From where, he knew not.

He was looking down at the blood.

Tom's shirt was red with it. Blood in his hair, on his hands and waxen face.

Richard crouched, heart thudding. "Tommy. Wake up." He shook him, and one of his friend's eyes fluttered open. Then the other. Relief flooded his system.

"Did I get him?" Tommy said, semiconscious, and Richard chanced a smile.

"Absolutely."

Tommy made a snorting sound. "Feast on *that* . . . " He was breathing with difficulty, the wool hat stanching the flow where Salt's ax had bitten.

"Come on. We're getting out of here." Richard grimaced and tried to help him sit up, balancing Katie in the crook of one arm. "Whose gun is that?"

"Don't ask," said Tommy, collapsing back. "You better just—I'm not gonna make this one, dude."

"Malarkey. Let's move it."

"I don't think so." Truitt gestured at his legs. "They quit working on me."

Richard lifted him again, and inhaled sharply.

The ground underneath was crimson with blood

loss. Seeped through the back of Tom's shirt, expanding red and wet. Crimson in the snow.

"Caught one of Prick-we's slugs, I think," Tommy said. "Can't feel much."

Richard moistened his lips. "Getting you to the hospital. Right now. Katie, I have to put you down—"

"*No.* Don't, Rich."

They found one another's eyes, and in silence they listened to the voices around them.

"What did he make you give?" Glee repeated, hands on hips, and Mrs. Bluedorn looked at her. The church organist flicked her tongue to the back of her mouth, probing where she'd removed her own molars with a pair of pliers. She stroked her abdomen, felt life there. She started to speak but Tom's cousin was hunkering down and pulling her with him.

"Hurry," he said, crawling feebly over Julian's remnants. "We have to hurry."

Glee and Croom observed them with baffled frowns.

"Can't go back," Tommy was muttering. "Don't want to die, but I can't go back to prison. Not gonna make this one." He fingered his Aunt Cass's horseshoe-nail cross distractedly. "Remember what she said, Richie. Don't tell *anyone*." The Civil War cap slid away from his neck.

Got the artery. Sure as shit looks like it.

Richard swallowed. "Tom, this . . . "

"Don't want to die," said Tommy in a whisper-thin voice. He cleared his throat, his nose wrinkling. His voice grew stronger. "Look after your dad for me, Katie. H-he's a real pain sometimes. You know?" That crooked grin appeared, and the girl shivered. Then: "I *do* smell wild onions. You were right. What's that, hhnnn? What do you want now, you pesky old broad? Go away." He stopped talking, breath abruptly gone, his arms at his sides. A single tear rolled from the outer corner of his eye.

"No. Stay with me, Thomas. Don't you dare. *Hey.*"

Both eyes remained open, fixed. Snowflakes drifted into them. Richard gave his shoulder another shake. He felt the heaviness of him, felt the whole world begin to shrink and darken, guilt and sorrow crashing down like twin iron hammers. *"Hey!"* he yelled in Tommy's ear.

This isn't happening. Get up. Please, get up.

"Katie?" he implored dismally.

"Too much," Katie said, her cheek to her father's chest. "Too late." Richard let out a moan. His throat burned. All he could do was stare, and wonder how it had come to this: Here. *Now.* Bled out. *In this place.*

Mrs. Bluedorn and the Confederate were on all fours, and to Glee's and Croom's amazement were lapping at the blood and oozings from the pastor's flesh body. Licking it up like farm cats at spilt milk. Glee watched, stupefied.

"What the hell are—? Stop, get away from there. *My God.*"

Mrs. Bluedorn glanced up. "It will sustain us," she said, gore dripping off her chin. "Come. Feel. It's moving inside me."

"God . . . *my God.*"

Katie spotted the tiny fetus crawling across the snow. Blind. Lost. She blinked in wonder, and in blinking knew it for what it was: an aberration. Something that didn't belong here, not in this pitiful condition. She hooked herself over Richard's shoulder, hung onto him. "Hush . . . " she whispered to it, lifting an unsure forefinger. *"Sleep."* The sad little embryo became still, and seemed to shrivel like wilting flower petals in the cold, to fall apart, unwanted. Its tiny limbs, heart and lungs dissolved, collapsing into dust which then merely swirled away with the flurries.

Katie shivered against her father as she watched its passing; a light shone in her pale pearl-gray eyes.

The earth began to tremble and quake beneath their feet.

4

time to go, time to go, time to go, time to go, time to go, TIME TO GOOOO—

5

Thunder, that's all. Leftover thunder. Above the thick clouds, in the Illinois nighttime somewhere.

Richard straightened with Katie, taking the death tally littered around them.

Damn this town. This goddamned town.

Salt and Julian, reduced to two stinking heaps of carrion: good riddance. Minty the medical examiner, facedown, an extension cord cutting so deep into his neck that it had opened the flesh. And poor Tommy, the best friend he'd ever had—voice quieted, heartbeat stilled forever.

Richard gritted his teeth and held Katelyn tight. Tears stung his eyes.

Crickets dying amid the snowy grass, to boot.

438

Katie felt the immense anger and grief, felt it trickling through his bloodstream, the toxins eating at his insides; she took as much of it from him as she dared. Suddenly she stiffened against her father. "Get away from the edge," she said into his ear. She sensed something coming. Her eyes glittered.

"Moving," someone uttered, "he's *still alive.*"

Richard's hair bristled. His head snapped around to see Simon move, see him writhe, the long fingers clawing dirt. Clutching at it, closing into a fist.

Richard froze, dread icing his veins. Just a reflex, he told himself. Final throes of this miserable bastard laid out here. Yet he shifted his gaze, automatically seeking the .38. Or the sword. Or even the fucking shovel.

"Time . . . to . . . go," said whatever was inside Julian. The fist lifted and came down, striking the ground. Again. The old man expelled a last breath, one breath. It rattled from the hole in his throat instead of his grinning rictus.

But the reverberation of the fist beat continued. What Richard had mistaken for thunder sounded again, the tremors growing louder, shaking the park, radiating out in waves.

"We need to get away from the river," Katie urged. "Quick, Daddy."

The earth shuddered like something was coming alive in its depths, shifting and rolling beneath them. Richard bit down hard on his tongue and stood back. He tasted blood.

Plague pit, the thought erupted in his mind. Something's down there. *Yepper, this whole damned town is built right on top of them.*

439

The land seemed to pitch underfoot, sloping. Richard backed away, his pulse loud in his ears. Backed away with Katie. He turned to run just as the ground opened up, solid earth collapsing from under the fat-bellied soldier and church organist, the sinkhole swallowing them. They plunged screaming alongside Julian's slack, bullet-raked form.

Blondie bolted madly but doubled back around with warning barks, trying to herd everyone away. Her leash whipped behind her.

Off balance, Glee toppled backwards into the cave-in, arms flailing to stop herself. Croom teetered on the lip. The syringe fell. By sheer luck Richard somehow had ahold of his trench coat with his free hand, yanking him back. As he did, Richard peered over the edge and down.

But there were no dead things to see, no corpses below shrugging off their shrouds and knocking jagged shards of stone or bricks from their fleshless, champing jaws. Grasping at roots as they pulled themselves out. It wasn't a plague pit at all. No buried settlers had awakened, brought to life by Julian Bardulf Simon's hemorrhaging, fleeing evil.

What *was* there was bad enough.

Richard saw the three of them thrashing, coiling over each other like snakes in a pit as they sank deeper. Cousin Mikey shrieked, tearing at his upturned face while dirt clots tumbled into the hole. *Gouging at his own eyes.* Mrs. Bluedorn clawed against gravity's pull and the loose soil. She slid down finally and began to scream, curling in on herself. Next to her in the soggy earth sprawled Glee with the wind knocked out of her.

The two women were holding hands.

Jostled by movement, by bodies bumping one another in terror, Julian's lifeless husk twitched at the bottom. Mute features stared skyward, the expression almost sardonic in the falling snow. Richard saw his arm flop limply.

Beckoning, he couldn't help but think, *like fucking Ahab.*

Glee looked up, and Richard read the plea in the whites of her frenzied, marble eyes: *Help me.* He winced as if struck, felt his guts tighten because she was too far down, the crater already deepening. No way of getting to her.

Dirt fell into Glee's mouth and she gagged, choking for air. In a blink that look changed. *Take care of George,* it said this time, her silver-streaked brown hair fanned out in the mud, one shoe still on her foot. Richard tasted something biting and terrible fill his throat. He dropped farther back as another steady, slow-rolling grumble echoed.

"Granna!" said Katie.

Owen leaned over, reaching. The ground heaved and he was thrown sideways. Fissures had begun to open, splitting off from the main collapse. Richard hauled the gaunt man in desperation.

"Save yourselves!" rose Glee's shrill voice from the pit.

The sinkhole yawned larger, the earth around it cracking, hard-packed dirt crumbling and rolling in on top of the others. Croom was twisting to be free.

"Forget it!" Richard shouted. "There's no way!" Croom tore loose and lunged, scooping up something before whirling back, lips pressed together. Next instant they were running, their eyes huge . . .

scrambling for the sandy diamond as though devils were at their heels. Richard clutched Katie to him, cold panic squeezing his heart. He could barely breathe.

A rumbling followed them, came thundering from behind: Julian's power raging still, dark forces trying to take them all with him.

You son of a bitch—die. Die already.

Owen snatched the dog's leash where she waited turning in circles and barking. He ran on with her, dragging his bad leg which startlingly didn't feel so bad anymore, he realized.

An awful rushing noise filled their ears, swelling and carrying through the darkness. Impossibly loud— a clamor like nothing they'd ever experienced. Gaining on them. Below it, people were screaming.

. . . no . . .

Richard spun with a cry, half-expecting to see Julian again, or find the ground splitting itself apart and an open trench racing to catch them and swallow them alive, fully expecting to piss himself if either were so.

What he saw hit him like a shockwave and stopped him.

The gigantic overhang of riverbank gave way and caved under its own weight, the entire section of Jasper Park where they had just stood breaking off and crashing into Rock River before their eyes. The banks literally disappeared, tons of earth and stone plunging downward, river birches slipping from sight. The sound made by the massive slab of earth falling in was horrific, the watery explosion colossal. And with it the distant screams ended, lost in a thunderous roar. Richard flinched.

442

Gone—bodies, the sinkhole, all of it.

"Christ Jesus."

A small reddish shape shot out of the shadows like a fireball, an animal of some kind. It flew from its hiding place so fast he nearly missed it before it was across the baseball field and away.

Richard's vision swam. He blinked his eyes rapidly, refocusing them. Dim lights hovered in the darkness on the other side of the river. Black water mirrored the churning, soot-gray sky above . . . water that would drown without mercy, claiming the living and the dead alike, the currents sucking them down. Take them straight to the river bottom, it would, ramming them against the rocks like so much sunken wreckage.

The moth-ridden branches teemed. A thousand black wings quivered. All at once they took flight, spiraling over the water on blurry beats of gossamer. Richard dipped his gaze as the large moths dipped, following their silhouettes as they plumed out and then upward, up, and into the snowy night sky.

Black water. Nothing could survive it. All that suffocating dirt and chunks of rubble. Crashing down like that. *Nothing.* The silt would get into their clothing, Richard knew, weigh them down, drag them under to where black rushing torrents would sweep them downriver, possibly for miles. No one could survive. Not in this cold, in these rapid-moving waters.

"Glee . . . *shit.*"

Another tremor jolted them, and the centuries-old cottonwood tree—the only thing left out there—twisted and leaned, losing its foothold on the remainder of the crumbling bank. Slipping away. Richard felt something at his elbow. This time it was Owen tugging

443

at *him*, a clogged warning in his throat. Pulling him back from the decimated park area. Toward the waiting vehicle.

"Daddeee . . . " Katie fretted. Richard took heed and went.

They reached the Blazer, keeping watch through the blowing snow. Richard popped the locks and they climbed inside—Croom and Blondie into the backseat and Richard and Katelyn in front. They slammed the doors shut and then Richard was grinding the ignition, throwing her into reverse. They lurched out of their cover in high four-wheel drive, swinging backward onto the narrow entrance road and skidding for purchase.

Richard hit the wipers, shifted, and gunned it again, his grip iron-tight on the steering wheel.

The last thing they saw was the gnarled cottonwood contorting and twisting, coming down, its massive root system giving way. Limbs outstretched, the tortured old gallows tree clung for another second or two, resisting the inevitable, before finally it toppled end over end into the turbulent dark water below.

Then it, too, was gone. Like everything else.

6

Palm Clemency entered the Public Safety Building's station room. He stood near the desks in a daze, brain matter dotting his uniform, bits of skull fragment stuck in his wiry hair. His ears still rang. He glanced around.

He was alone in the station—everyone out on emergency calls, no doubt.

Whole town's falling apart.

The deputy chief moved unsteadily to the washroom where he cleaned himself off. He took a packet of Alka-Seltzer from the medicine chest, dissolved the tablets in a coffee cup with some tap water, and gulped them down fizzing. Shuffling out, he lingered by the desks again. An inundated answering machine flashed bright red at him. Beside it he noticed paper sticking out of the manual typewriter on the police chief's desk.

Chip Priewe, shunning modern technology whenever possible, used an old black Remington Noiseless typewriter and nothing else for filling out his reports.

Noiseless, hell, he thought. More racket than a blown muffler. *Mm-hmm.*

Curious, he moved closer and squinted to read what had been typed in the center of the clean white sheet:

FUCKING CUNTS

Palm straightened. He looked around the room. Rubbing his unshaven face, he sat down grimly in the police chief's chair.

He rolled the typing paper out of the carriage and ran it through the shredder. Then, he found a fresh sheet and worked it into the Remington. Still out-of-sorts, he clasped his hands a moment, massaged his temples, and then began to type:

I was responsible for
the death of Oliver

```
Echols in 1977, and I
can t live with it any
longer.
He went in after his
cat. Drag the river at
Anasazi  Bridge.   I m
tired. May God forgive
me.


                    Priewe
```

Mulling this over, Clemency rolled down and added three infamous lines. From behind him came the faintest noise as the keys clacked, a stirring of curtains at the window. He did not turn around.

```
all  fled all  done,  so
  lift me
on the pyre; the feast
  is over
and the lamps expire
```

He smiled to himself as he read the words back—the typed message thought to be the last thing Robert Howard ever wrote before killing himself in 1936—and he nodded, satisfied with Chip Priewe's 'official' suicide note. Sensing the presence at his back, a shiver ran through him. A voice came lightly: the long, breathless sigh of a young boy, it sounded like.

If Clemency was unnerved, he didn't show it.

"It'll be okay now, Ollie, mm-hmm," he whispered,

not looking. "You'll see." He shivered again nonetheless.

His body slumped in the chair with an overwhelming tiredness. He sat for a time, eyes closed. When he opened them again he could see clearer.

Palm took a deep breath and reached for the answering machine, which flashed on the desk to his right.

***

Meanwhile, as ghosts wept and powder-winged messengers soared, a russet-red fox with half a tail made its way home through the snow. It loped along, bouncing into a crooked hop every so often in the backyards and alleyways it slyly traversed, eventually scampering across Riverreach Road and back onto Angell Island to share what it knew.

***

Richard motored through town, through dark empty streets. The Blazer's heat was blasting but he couldn't get warm. His mind and body were exhausted. Teeth on edge as he drove and stared ahead out the frosted windshield at the headlight beams illuminating his way.

At some point Owen reached over the seat and placed something carefully in Katie's lap, the object he'd retrieved. Michelle's urn, its copper lid clamped on.

Katie put her arms around it and hugged it to her.

The girl's fitful shivers were subsiding. She had pulled her mother's scarf up over her mouth and nose, Richard saw.

For some reason he chose to travel down Brazier Drive, warily past the somber Deadmond home with its electric welcome lights glowing in the windows. Other than branches blown down everywhere from the windstorm, nothing looked disturbed. He did not stop. Katie noticed the house and started to sit up. But she hesitated, easing back into her seat.

"Oh," she said beneath the turquoise scarf; Richard's knuckles whitened.

He drove past his crumbling mural, and then on up to Nain Trinity Lutheran with its weather-scarred bur oak out front. The Land Rover was in the church parking lot. Tommy's pickup still sat in the street, white fluff accumulating and beginning to cover it now.

Richard's grip tightened on the steering wheel. His gaze became blurred and dropped away.

Soon they pulled into the Nightlight Inn near the bypass, and to Richard the cheerless L-shaped motel at that moment was about the most beautiful sight he'd ever seen.

He parked close to their door and shut the engine down. Sat with his head lowered, chin to his chest. He asked Katelyn for the tenth time if she was all right. After a long minute had passed they hurried inside, unscathed for the most part yet looking as if they had come through a war zone together, sneaking Blondie into the double room with them.

Richard deadbolted and chained the door, turned a light and the television on. Blondie jumped onto one of the beds and rested with her tongue hanging out. "Try to keep her quiet, hon," Richard said to Katie, scratching the dog's muzzle. Her tail wagged.

He then went into the bathroom and stared into the mirror at the stranger looking back. Clutched the sink fiercely to keep from sobbing, or throwing up, stifling an animal urge to scream aloud. Fending off the crushing loss he felt.

Loss for his wife. Loss for his friend. For George, also . . . and he could still feel the way his father-in-law's prize bat had shattered on the Indian's skull, thank you very much. And Glee . . .

God, what about Glee? She might be alive, and we left her. I left her. Oh dear Christ.

Something clicked in his throat, a gravelly sound attempting to surface and escape, but he wouldn't let it. No. Mustn't let it. For to do so might well mean lunacy, and the ultimate loss of *himself*, too.

I won't scream. I will not scream.

While Richard stared, numb and silent, and tried to keep the vacant-eyed stranger gaping back at him from screaming as well—tried not to think any thoughts at all, for that matter—his daughter glanced up at Owen from where she sat stroking the German shepherd and said, "Thank you."

Croom tensed, not expecting this. Hands trembling, lips a tight line, he patted down his trench coat, looked around the motel room. His gaze found Katie's pastel crayons sitting atop the mirrored vanity table. Stepping over to it, the sallow man pulled a magenta crayon from its box and scrawled two words in thick, block-stroke letters for the little girl to see on the mirror's glass.

THANK YOU

CHAPTER TWENTY-EIGHT

I

YOU NEED TO say goodbye," Katie said, and Richard pulled off the road. Cornfields surrounded them on both sides here at the outskirts of town. The first snow of the season was melting, drifts of white caught between the rows.

Reports were breaking over the radio about the previous night's horrors. A spate of deaths in and around Blackwater Valley, and missing townspeople. Structures burnt to the ground. Palm Clemency had had a lot of questions, but Richard never faltered.

Now it was time to leave.

After they'd showered and eaten a little, recovered somewhat, Richard had gone to the Deadmond place first thing, found the door unlocked. Found George under the drop cloth in the basement where he and Tom had left him.

Moving fast, Richard gathered up Blondie's things: some toys, bowls, her memory-foam bed, loose cans of pet food and a large bag of dry nuggets, pills prescribed by the veterinarian for her arthritis pain—although he suspected she wouldn't be needing these right away.

He gave the tomb-silent house a quick once-over,

and without thinking removed the empty display case from George's study wall, placing it in the closet behind some stacked boxes.

Richard carried the items out to their SUV where Katie sat with the dog, put them into the back where three leather bags had already been loaded. Taking out his phone he dialed Glee's cell number and left a message concerning George, did the same with Tommy's, just to cover bases. Richard shot a glance at Owen, and the thin fellow wearing a trench coat nodded and moved away from the Blazer's side, began drifting across the street.

Then he called 911, and waited.

After the paramedics had Deadmond's body aboard the ambulance and Richard had given his signed statement, he watched them pull away through a group of onlookers, lights strobing. No siren—silent running. He lingered on the front porch, checking his watch. Started down the steps . . .

And up the walkway Palm Sunday Clemency had come trudging. His uniform appeared slept in. "Heard the ambulance call. Been looking for you, Rich."

Here it is. Fuck me.

"Chip Priewe's dead," said Clemency, freezing Richard halfway down. Palm briefed him on the police chief's bizarre demise overnight, and the part the old disused cannon had played, even the confession left behind. Richard listened, stunned, frowning doubtfully.

There was mention of other casualties, individuals still unaccounted for. Like Meg Bilobran from the café, and the Lawries' student boarder.

"Can't find the damn medical examiner either,"

Clemency said, "and we're going to need him. Population's shrinking fast. So, what's the story here?"

Richard had told him of his arriving early only to discover George in the cellar, non-responsive and cold to the touch. Very much deceased. Of covering him and dialing 911, and of trying to reach Glee on her mobile phone but with no luck.

Palm shifted his weight. "Shit. I'm sorry to hear that." He shook his head. "Why was he in the cellar, I wonder?"

"Don't know. Paramedics said it looked like a heart attack to them."

Clemency shook his head, pausing a few seconds more. Then: "Have you seen Tom Truitt around, Rich?"

Fuck. "Uh . . . we were hanging out at Blessing Acres yesterday. Haven't heard from him today yet. Why?"

"His truck is parked up at the church. One of the pastor's secretaries let us inside to check the place out. It was deserted, but you know what?"

"What's that?"

"Found a live hand grenade sitting on the old boy's desk."

Richard looked up, startled. "A hand—did you say a *hand grenade*? Jesus, we were there just the other night, Palm. To watch The Glee Club service."

"So were a lot of other people. No sign of the Reverend anywhere so far, or that shadow of his."

"The Indian," muttered Richard.

Clemency pulled a face. "Sauk," he said, with apparent distaste.

"Huh." Richard's brain reeled. He looked at Katie,

eager to be beside her. Eager to be gone from here in the worst possible way. "Well—"

"Crazy weather, mm-hmm," the deputy chief had interrupted. He eyed the cold, sunless sky, scratched his chin. "Something funny happening out at Jasper Park, too."

Fuck, fuck, fuck. "Oh?"

"They had to cordon it off, I hear. Section of the park fell into the river. Near the bend. Just collapsed away and disappeared. It's not there anymore. What could've caused that? Mine shafts, Rich? Another plague pit sinkhole?"

Richard winced. *Yepper,* he'd almost blurted, *this whole damned town is built right on top of them.*

Tommy's words came to him. *Remember what she said, Richie. Don't tell anyone.* The river witch's after that: *This is warfare, remember it.*

"Could be," he said with a shrug. "You never know. Say . . . I better try finding Glee, Palm." He checked his watch. "Then we have to get on the road. We're heading back today. Did what I came to do, scattered my wife's ashes and . . . "

Lord, get me out of here.

"Where was that?" Clemency probed.

"Duck Blind Point," said Richard without a blink. "She always loved watching the birds up there." He smiled wanly.

Palm nodded, cleared his throat. "Listen, Rich, I was wondering if you could stick around for a bit. Help us search maybe? We're stretched pretty thin and we could use every—"

Richard was shaking his head. "Ordinarily I wouldn't hesitate, but my daughter needs to get home.

Her school starts up again soon, and it's important that she gets back to some sort of . . . of . . . normalcy." He paused. "School's psychologist advised it."

Palm craned around, looked toward the Chevrolet Blazer. His brow creased in suspicion.

"Going somewhere with Glee's dog?"

Richard flushed, felt heat rising into his cheeks. "She's our dog," he said carefully, "Michelle's dog. My wife wanted me to bring her back for Katie, to help her cope better with all of this. So that's what I'm doing." He waited a beat, two. "Already cleared it with George and Glee."

"Ah." Palm studied the girl in the vehicle, watched her place a tiny hand against the glass, saw her lips moving, the window fogging. Heavy-lidded, his eyes blinked. His frown had relaxed. "Pet therapy, right?"

"Something like that." Richard smiled. Taking out his wallet, he gave Clemency a card with their Golitha Falls address on it; cellular and home phone information, email addresses.

Clemency stared at it. He handed him one of his own in return.

"I better try finding Glee," Richard said again, and they shook hands. "If I don't see you, good luck with everything. Keep in touch, Palm. Take care, you and your family."

Clemency said, "None of this can actually be happening, can it?" His voice cracked. "Look, if there's something you can tell me . . . I mean, you're a smart guy. You know things. Any help you could offer? Come on, man, you grew up here."

"I don't live here anymore," said Richard, holding

his gaze. "I don't know the first thing about this place anymore, Palm. I realize that now. Sorry."

"All we have is guesswork to go on, Rich, at this point. How about it?"

Richard started away. "You've got my number, I have yours. We have to get on the road. No choice."

"Yeah, but I really wish someone—"

Feeling his old friend pushing, Richard had glanced over his shoulder, looked him up and down, and pushed back slightly: "Just what the hell kind of town are you people running?" he had said, seeing the expression of embarrassment that pinched Clemency's face.

The deputy chief wandered after him nevertheless, calling out on the front walkway.

"Somebody left an anonymous tip on the station's answering machine. About Julian. The message suggested that he might've been a Nazi at one time. A former Nazi chaplain, can you believe it? During the war. Cuckoo for Cocoa Puffs, right?"

Richard turned back. "Huh," he said. Shrugged. "You never know."

"Know what I think? I think that goddamned Shaw cursed this entire town when he did what he did all those years ago. The plague pits, and everything else." Palm stood with his thumbs hooked on his duty belt. "Lot of unanswered questions still, Rich. I really wish someone could tell me what happened around here last night."

"So do I," Richard had replied after a moment, and kept walking.

2

Goodbye—you need to say it. Here, take my hand . . .

Richard asked Owen to come back with them, stay in New England awhile. But the gaunt man refused.

They dropped him at his house—Admiral Jack's rental property Tommy had told him about. It was a small, hip-roofed bungalow, single story, the bricks and foundation long ago painted a fading daffodil yellow. Out front was a narrow veranda-style overhang supported by three brick columns, all yellow, and rattan chairs for sitting. The street itself wasn't far from midtown proper or the bell tower Lawrie owned.

Then something baffling had occurred: Katie leaned close and told her father they should leave Blondie here with Mr. Croom . . . that it was the right thing to do.

Astonished, he insisted this wasn't possible. Out of the question, he said, and shook his head. Where on earth had she gotten such an idea anyway? She didn't know, she told him. All she knew was she felt it, felt that it was right. Because they were both alone.

"Alone is bad," Katie said. "Isn't it?"

"Yes, but that—"

"Mommy used to say so," murmured Katie. She grew very still. "Today's her birthday." Richard swallowed. It seemed he only had an instant to decide what to do—the right thing to do—so he chose.

He explained Katie's suggestion to Owen, asked him what he thought. Initially he looked as taken aback as Richard had, but then he became resigned, pleased even. Before Richard brought the dog's things in, he asked him if he was up for it. If there were any concerns he had. Owen's eyes glistened, and he smiled at Katelyn standing in his doorway with the shepherd.

Blackout curtains covered the windows, to keep bright light from filtering through. A desktop computer, old as dirt, sat inside an open rolltop desk in the furnished living room. Richard pointed to it, asked if it worked. It indeed did. He got his online address from him and gave Croom one of his business cards, told him to email or have someone call if there was any kind of problem, if he needed financial help with her, or for anything else that came up. Trouble from Palm Clemency perhaps.

"There won't be any," Katie had said.

Richard exhaled. "Have the Admiral call me when you get a chance, can you?" he said. Cleared his throat. "Or his wife. Whichever."

He gave Blondie's black-and-tan coat one last patting. She sniffed around, and he handed over the leash. It was hard to stomach, leaving her behind again. Katie bent and whispered into the dog's ear. Then it was time to set out. Owen nodded farewell, raising his hand as they departed.

In the vehicle, Katie was silent. Fidgety.

"Are you mad at me?" she asked, and wrung her little hands in her lap.

"No. Of course not. It's just—" Richard hesitated. "Are you positive about doing this, hon?"

"They belong together now," was all she could offer as explanation.

Richard wasn't sure what she meant exactly, but he thought he had an idea.

3

"You need to say goodbye," Katie repeated. Richard cut the radio, left the Blazer idling in neutral.

"All right," he said. "Okay."

Katie reached out her hand. Richard took it. He felt the surge almost at once, like a low-watt thrum coursing through him. Rather than fight it, he let it enter. The hair on his arms began to rise as *her* gift became *his* . . .

He saw them, straight out the passenger-side window past Katie's head, lingering in the cornfield. Someone was there. Watching between dry yellow stalks. Psychically attuned to his daughter now, he saw.

It was George Deadmond, and Glee. *Christ.* Others moving. Tommy in his ragged *Swan Song* T-shirt, a woman wearing a bright bandana with him. Ollie Echols, too, carrying his calico cat. And a little girl with pigtails Richard didn't recognize. Their bodies were whole, no trauma here. No blood.

Then came Michelle . . . his beautiful Michelle, tall and perfect again, untwisted, her skin radiant. She smiled and Richard's heart skipped.

Our angel, he thought helplessly, *our shining morning star.* He felt his throat tighten.

But then he felt something at his back, on the other side of the road behind him. Something . . . *else.* Longing to be seen, willing him to look. Katie told him no, warned him not to. That he didn't want to see it. He turned anyway, unable to stop his gaze from being drawn. He recoiled in horror.

He saw Chip Priewe, what remained after the cannon blast had taken most of his head and upper body away. And William Salt, caked in dark red, limbs and visage shattered. He grinned through a fractured skull and Richard's insides went cold. Beside the Indian stood Julian, naked and grotesque, flies lighting, rot already set in, the exit wound from Tommy's bullet visible in his ripped-open face.

A swarthy boy was there as well, sockets vacant, staring. His olive flesh was mottled, lower jaw wrenched asunder and mouth like a chasm, his torso burst wide. In his arms he cradled something—worst of all, Richard realized, too late—something which wriggled and screamed silently.

It was tiny Henry Putnam in his zip-up footed sleeper.

Aghast, Richard's eyes flared at these sights. He was vaguely aware of Katie's touch.

"Can't cross over," he heard her say, "they can't cross, Daddy. We're safe."

The figures languished in their snow-scattered field, mutilated, demanding attention. Dear God. The *deadness* of them . . . of their very beings. Richard could feel it. He choked on it, shuddering, pulling loose from Katie.

. . . The baby howled as if for its stolen soul.

Richard tumbled out the driver's-side door, practically fell into the road with a cry of dismay. There he gagged. His stomach convulsed. He huddled against the Blazer, breathing slowly and deeply, his eyes streaming.

Katie crawled out after him, knelt. She reached but stopped short. "Daddy?"

He was gaping all around. The figures were gone, nothing but dried cornstalks, empty fields rippling at the town's lonesome edge. At the crossroads.

"Is this—" he began, looking at her, groping for the words, "is this what you see? All the time?" He sounded horrified.

"Yes. Mostly." She shifted away. "I'm sorry. I won't touch you anymore."

Richard grabbed her up, clutched her to him with a sob. "My baby," he said, eyes welling. "Oh, my baby. My sweet little girl." He pressed his lips to her warm rosy forehead.

Finally he grew quiet, straightened with Katie in his arms. Feeling her hand at rest on his shoulder, he placed his own hand over hers and squeezed it.

They came back into view: Tommy, and the others. The cornrows were opening, parting for them. One by one they began to slip between the stalks. Dropping back, disappearing. Children, then the adults. He saw Tommy grin crookedly as he turned and went . . . Michelle last, smiling her wedding-day smile. Her eyes shined at him as she followed and vanished from sight like the dawn mist.

Richard held his breath. Stared into the cornfield with an aching—wishing her back. He sensed movement in the opposite direction, though, craned his neck to glimpse what was still there. His teeth clenched.

Simon Julian leered from the other field. The pastor's hate-filled face was livid, virtually lipless, a grinning death-head. Richard saw his arms lengthen, twisting clawlike as if to reach across the road and strangle them both, father and daughter, for bringing them to this.

Behind Salt, Mrs. Bluedorn scowled, caressing her river-bloated abdomen; Minty with his gashed throat; an unfamiliar woman who sported a red-white-and-blue heart in the middle of her blood-soaked top.

One of the Confederate dead lumbered among them.

They seethed with fathomless turmoil, regurgitated it, their murderous intent apparent. Richard watched the shades loom where they were, none of them attempting to verge the road, their eyes hollow, mouths baying yet no sound issuing forth.

What fresh hell? his writerly mind clucked.

"They can't cross over," repeated Katie, "no matter what they do. Can't cross the gulf." She spoke low into her father's ear. "They're trapped."

Priewe gestured toward the girl, pointed at her, beckoning Richard to come nearer and bring her along, wringing his hands together. Richard tasted bile rise.

Burn, you motherfuckers, he thought blackly. *Fucking burn, until there's nothing left. You'll never get close to her. I'll make sure of that.* Never. *So burn. Fuck you all, and burn. Every last one.*

Richard carried his daughter and buckled her into the passenger seat. Shut her door. Then he slid behind the wheel. Sat for a minute, listening to the engine idle.

Connection broken, he saw nothing now. But he felt their presence fouling the air, detected a hint of skeletal chill reaching for him from out of the deserted rows, prickling his skin into frittles. Richard closed his door.

He put the Chevy into gear and drove on, away from the stalks of corn swaying in unharvested vigil.

461

I am weary now of the word and vow
Of the winds and the winter weather;
I'll reel through a few more years somehow,
Then I'll quit them altogether.

—Robert Ervin Howard, *Surrender*

EPILOGUE

THE COLD HANGS on, and on. Sinks in deeper. Lost within it, forsaken, the duped and the defiled wander the streets of the Val in a haze. Wondering what's happened.

One of them, Syd Cholke, enters her Regan Street apartment and drops onto the sofa. Slumps alone in the dark. Much later she hears the front door open and close, hears footsteps enter sheepishly. Then delicate, auburn-haired Alice Granberg sits down. No words are spoken between them. After a time Sydney goes to her and kneels and places her ear against the small hill of Alice's belly, feels the baby roll lazily there. Soon both are dozing in this position, an empty birdcage on the end table nearby.

Mrs. Wintermute shrieks inside her narrow prison below ground, breath hitching in and out. She begs and she wails . . . screaming, screaming . . . and eventually becomes quiet at long last. Meg Bilobran sits propped in her theater balcony seat, draped in sheet plastic, eyes flung wide and staring, as if waiting for the main feature to begin.

In the weeks to come, somebody will discover poor Meg Bilobran. But not Mrs. Wintermute.

One day, while walking with his young son through the reconfigured municipal park along the river bend, Palm Clemency will pause as the boy spots something shiny in the dirt and crouches to find a man's gold ring there, which he decides to pocket and keep for his very own.

And when she gets her chance, Mrs. Chip Priewe vacates her nothing little town with a suitcase full of US savings bonds and light summer clothing, and never again steps foot in the state of Illinois.

Owen Croom, however, remains in the daffodil-yellow house with the German shepherd entrusted to him. He grows stronger and healthier with the passage of time, the symptoms of his cerebral palsy and hydrocephalus receding, much to his physician's confoundment. The man and the dog look after one another for many more years, until Blondie passes away naturally—free of pain—in her sleep one night.

With tears of incredible sorrow he buries her in the scant fields near the condemned bell tower. He plants asters and larkspur there and watches from the belfry opening, high above the tallest trees, as the purple flowers bloom and thrive each summer. Vigilantly he sets about tending the area, always watching over it, making sure the special place where she lies is well cared for.

Owen watches, and sets about his work, and dies.

***

Before getting out on the highway, the man with the small girl stops at Blessing Acres again—at the girl's behest. The proprietor's oldest daughter, a woman named Jodean, comes to the padlocked gates and informs them the apple orchard is closed due to recent unforeseen events. She tells the man she cannot allow him inside, not for what he speaks of.

He tries to procure their entry, offering the young American Indian woman money. But when the little girl pleads and in pleading calls her JoJo, the nickname her long-deceased mother always called her as a child, it convinces the young woman.

She opens the gates and lets them inside.

The girl makes straight for a covered animal pen with a hand-stenciled piece of plank above its door: *Miracle*. She bends down at the enclosure, begins to hum. Before she even reaches through the wire she has located it. A corresponding pain in the back of her head alerts her. She brushes the head of the wasting bison calf, supports it, zeroing in on the malignant region she senses, the aggressively spreading brain tumor which is killing it. Which *will* kill it very soon unless . . .

She massages the back of its skull, concentrates on the chaos radiating there like some kind of clock ticking down toward something. The girl's cold hands warm as she cradles the stricken animal. Hums. Feels the disease relent finally and *give way*, feels the baby white bison lick her jacket weakly. Then she rises and moves off, keeping her arms at her sides.

Her father turns and follows, wonders if he is doing the right thing or not. He will worry about much in the weeks and months ahead. Worry about Julian's re-emergence, for example. Once back home and settled in, and already fighting the blots in his memory, he will stop every so often for no apparent reason and press his ear to the ground to listen, as if something might be burrowing underneath him.

He will worry also about the inevitable phone call from his friend Palm Clemency when it comes. And come it will. For now, though, he is content in this moment. Until a dark thought takes shape.

She's flying, he thinks as they walk. *I'm letting her fly.*

The little girl changes direction, begins making her way up toward a shade tree on one of the hills. Her father keeps pace at a careful distance. He watches her as she draws closer, reaches out—

And touches the man in a cowboy hat and boots standing beneath the tree there.

Startled, the field hand looks down at her, at this six-year-old child tightly grasping his gloved fingers and humming to herself. An eyepatch covers one socket, and from the other a watery cobalt-blue iris stares out of the pitted face at her. It blinks curiously. He pulls his hand away but she hangs on, refuses to release him until it is done.

Until she's rid of it.

Finally the little girl lets go and stands motionless. She squints one eye shut against sunlight, which breaks at last through the easing cloud cover, and she smiles up at him the way children do.

Her father feigns apologies and leads her away. The girl turns back, waves goodbye to the man on the hill. He lifts his gloved hand in return. Frowns then, his eyelid twitching as he feels something is terribly wrong. But he shrugs the feeling off. Leans against the tree once more.

All comes into balance. The clock hands have reset—a new countdown begun.

The father thanks Jodean at the exit, gives the

American Indian woman a card and tells her to please keep in touch, that his daughter would love to hear from her.

Driving away now, he wonders what they'll find. Will they find cereus blooming perhaps, filling the sad little greenhouse and all of the ceramic pots? Clustering below their outdoor deck, below the house itself, sprouting up between cracks in the mahogany floorboards and linoleum kitchen tiles?

They make their way east. Toward home, toward the empty Dutch Colonial awaiting them . . . without her in their lives.

Their angel, their shining morning star.

THE END?

If you enjoyed this book, I'm sure you'll also like the following Crystal Lake titles:

Devourer of Souls by Kevin Lucia—In Kevin Lucia's latest installment of his growing Clifton Heights mythos, Sheriff Chris Baker and Father Ward meet for a Saturday morning breakfast at The Skylark Dinner to once again commiserate over the weird and terrifying secrets surrounding their town.

Tales from The Lake Vol.2—Beneath this lake you'll find nothing but mystery and suspense, horror and dread. Not to mention death and misery—tales to share around the campfire or living room floor from the likes of Ramsey Campbell, Jack Ketchum, and Edward Lee.

Pretty Little Dead Girls: A Novel of Murder and Whimsy by Mercedes M. Yardley—Bryony Adams is destined to be murdered, but fortunately Fate has terrible marksmanship. In order to survive, she must run as far and as fast as she can. After arriving in Seattle, Bryony befriends a tortured musician, a market fish-thrower, and a starry-eyed hero who is secretly a serial killer bent on fulfilling Bryony's dark destiny.

Wind Chill by Patrick Rutigliano—What if you were held captive by your own family? Emma Rawlins has spent the last year a prisoner. The months following her mother's death dragged her father into a paranoid spiral of conspiracy theories and doomsday premonitions. But there is a force far colder than the freezing drifts. Ancient, ravenous, it knows no mercy. And it's already had a taste . . .

Flowers in a Dumpster by Mark Allan Gunnells—The world is full of beauty and mystery. In these 17 tales, Gunnells will take you on a journey through landscapes of light and darkness, rapture and agony, hope and fear. Let Gunnells guide you through these landscapes where magnificence and decay co-exist side by side. Come pick a bouquet from these Flowers in a Dumpster.

Tribulations by Richard Thomas—In the third short story collection by Richard Thomas, *Tribulations*, these stories cover a wide range of dark fiction—from fantasy, science fiction and horror, to magical realism, neo-noir, and transgressive fiction. The common thread that weaves these tragic tales together is suffering and sorrow, and the ways we emerge from such heartbreak stronger, more appreciative of what we have left—a spark of hope enough to guide us though the valley of death.

The Dark at the End of the Tunnel by Taylor Grant— Offered for the first time in a collected format, this selection features ten gripping and darkly imaginative stories by Taylor Grant, a Bram Stoker Award ® nominated author and rising star in the suspense and horror genres. Grant exposes the terrors that hide beneath the surface of our ordinary world, behind people's masks of normalcy, and lurking in the shadows at the farthest reaches of the universe.

If you ever thought of becoming an author, I'd also like to recommend these non-fiction titles:

Horror 101: The Way Forward—a comprehensive overview of the Horror fiction genre and career opportunities available to established and aspiring authors, including Jack Ketchum, Graham Masterton, Edward Lee, Lisa Morton, Ellen Datlow, Ramsey Campbell, and many more.

Horror 201: The Silver Scream Vol.1 and *Vol.2*—A must read for anyone interested in the horror film industry. Includes interviews and essays by Wes Craven, John Carpenter, George A. Romero, Mick Garris, and dozens more. Now available in paperback, as well.

Modern Mythmakers: 35 interviews with Horror and Science Fiction Writers and Filmmakers by Michael McCarty—Ever wanted to hang out with legends like Ray Bradbury, Richard Matheson, and Dean Koontz? *Modern Mythmakers* is your chance to hear fun anecdotes and career advice from authors and filmmakers like Forrest J. Ackerman, Ray Bradbury, Ramsey Campbell, John Carpenter, Dan Curtis, Elvira, Neil Gaiman, Mick Garris, Laurell K. Hamilton, Jack Ketchum, Dean Koontz, Graham Masterton, Richard Matheson, John Russo, William F. Nolan, John Saul, Peter Straub, and many more.

Writers On Writing: An Author's Guide—Your favorite authors share their secrets in the ultimate guide to becoming and being and author. *Writers On Writing* is an ongoing eBook series with original 'On Writing' essays by writing professionals. A new edition will be launched every few months, featuring four or five essays per edition, so be sure to check out the webpage regularly for updates.

Or check out other Crystal Lake Publishing books for your Dark Fiction, Horror, Suspense, and Thriller needs.

About The Author

William Gorman grew up listening to ghost stories and dark fantastical yarns from his grandfather—a magician and former 'mentalist' during the last great, fading days of vaudeville—told to him in porch shadows on warm Illinois summer eves. His first book, a collection of local myths and legends titled *Ghost Whispers*, was published in 2005 and spawned the popular Haunted Rockford tours and cemetery walks now operating in his hometown.

In his spare time he hangs around with German shepherds and listens to classic rock & roll, and enjoys rereading the old-school maestros of supernatural fiction he grew up on whenever he can. He now lives in Ohio, where he is at work on his next novel and a new collection of ghostly tales.

Website: http://williamgorman.weebly.com/

Connect with Crystal Lake Publishing

Website (be sure to sign up for our newsletter):
www.crystallakepub.com

Facebook:
www.facebook.com/Crystallakepublishing

Twitter:
https://twitter.com/crystallakepub

With unmatched success since 2012, Crystal Lake Publishing has quickly become one of the world's leading indie publishers of Mystery, Thriller, and Suspense books with a Dark Fiction edge.

Crystal Lake Publishing puts integrity, honor, and respect at the forefront of our operations.

We strive for each book and outreach program that's launched to not only entertain and touch or comment on issues that affect our readers, but also to strengthen and support the Dark Fiction field and its authors.

Not only do we publish authors who are destined to be legends in the field (and as hardworking as us), but we also look for men and women who care about their readers and fellow human beings. We only publish the very best Dark Fiction and look forward to launching many new careers.

We strive to know each and every one of our readers, while building personal relationships with our authors, reviewers, bloggers, pod-casters, bookstores and libraries.

Crystal Lake Publishing is and will always be a beacon of what passion and dedication, combined with overwhelming teamwork and respect, can accomplish: unique fiction you can't find anywhere else.

We do not just publish books, we present you worlds within your world, doors within your mind, from talented authors who sacrifice so much for a moment of your time.

This is what we believe in. What we stand for. This will be our legacy.

Welcome to Crystal Lake Publishing.

We hope you enjoyed this title. If so, we'd be grateful if you could leave a review on your blog or any of the other websites and outlets open to book reviews. Reviews are like gold to writers and publishers, since word-of-mouth is and will always be the best way to market a great book. And remember to keep an eye out for more of our books.

THANK YOU FOR PURCHASING THIS BOOK

CPSIA information can be obtained at www.ICGtesting.com
Printed in the USA
BVOW06s0311080716

454858BV00022B/38/P